HONOR in the DUST

KAREN STOKES

GREEN ALTAR BOOKS
Columbia, South Carolina

HONOR IN THE DUST

Published by Green Altar Books, an Imprint of
Shotwell Publishing, LLC
P.O. Box 2592
Columbia, South Carolina 29202

This is a work of fiction. Any similarity with real persons or events is purely coincidental. Persons, events, and locations are either the product of the author's imagination, or used fictitiously.

2nd Edition

Kati Barnett, Editor.
Cover image by Sherri Scott.

ISBN-13: 978-1947660120
ISBN-10: 1947660128

To the Memory of My Brother
(1955-2014)

HONOR IN THE DUST

O Lord my God, if I have done this:
If there is iniquity in my hands,
If I have repaid evil to him who was at peace with me,
Or have plundered my enemy without cause,
Let the enemy pursue me and overtake me;
Yes, let him trample my life to the earth,
And lay my honor in the dust.

Psalm 7:3-5
NKJV

CHAPTER ONE

South Carolina Midlands, April 1865

DRESSED IN THE SHABBY REMNANTS of a Confederate uniform, a lone soldier walked down a country lane that was little more than two wagon wheel ruts in the grass. He was carrying no possessions except a blanket roll on his back and some odds and ends in a tattered canvas haversack. The gloomy, thickly overcast sky made it impossible to tell time by the sun, but the young man guessed that it was close to two o'clock. He had eaten nothing all day, and his stomach was so empty that it ached and writhed as if trying to consume itself in the absence of any contents.

Rounding a bend, he found himself on a better road that looked familiar. Within a few minutes, the barking of a dog told him he was near a homestead of some sort. After about a hundred more steps, a large, somewhat run-down looking farmhouse came into view. From what he could see from the road, it was like many other farms and plantations he had observed along his journey home. Those which had been visited by the destroying army of the enemy, even places like this one where a dwelling still existed on the property, had a barren, desolated appearance.

The young man approached the house slowly. A black and white spaniel, having scented and seen him first, was barking and straining on the rope that tethered him to a post under a tree. The soldier was about to speak soothingly to the frantic animal when he happened to look toward the house and caught sight of someone's face in a window. A moment later, a middle-aged white woman opened the front door and stepped out to the porch. As he came closer, he saw that she was something past middle-age and wearing a dress which had long since seen better days. Her scanty hair was faded to whiteness and her face, like her figure, was thin and angular. She looked him over with her pale blue eyes unsmilingly, with obvious fear as she shushed the barking dog.

"I'm a Confederate soldier, ma'am," he said, removing a battered slouch hat with so many holes in it that it looked as though it might have been used for target practice. "I have had very little food in two or three days. I wonder if you might spare a little."

His pleasant voice, plainly that of a fellow South Carolinian, eased her fearfulness, and she nodded and went back inside. After a while, the soldier could hear a low murmur of female voices behind the door, and then it opened again. A much younger woman stepped out this time, wiping her hands on a soiled apron. Her face was attractive but careworn, and she looked tired and apprehensive. Damp strands of blonde hair which had escaped the confines of a bonnet hung down in small festoons at her temples, and her sleeves were wet at the cuffs and just above. Obviously she had been interrupted in the middle of some onerous chore.

"My aunt is preparing some food you may take with you," she said, rather nervously.

"Thank you. I am very grateful."

The soldier found himself staring at the young woman's face, and abruptly dropped his eyes so as not to give offense. His polite, deferential manner reassured her, and she visibly relaxed. The other woman reappeared with a small but substantial meal wrapped in a handkerchief. She walked down the front steps and handed it to the stranger.

"May I ask your name?" the lady inquired.

The younger woman betrayed a momentary look of impatience and annoyance at the question. She seemed anxious for the soldier to be on his way.

The soldier looked down at the warm food he held, briefly closing his eyes as he savored the smell of it, and answered, "My name is John Hutchinson."

The two women exchanged a look of astonishment.

"Are you kin to the Hutchinsons of Belle Ville?" the older one asked him.

"I am one of the Hutchinsons of Belle Ville," he replied.

"John Hutchinson!" the younger woman said wonderingly.

"Do you know me?"

As he asked this question, he looked around him with an expression of surprise and dawning recognition. Before they could answer he asked, "Is this the DuBose place?"

"It is," said the young woman.

"It looks very familiar to me now, though it does look different. Nearly every place I've seen looks different. I didn't quite have my bearings, but now I know I'm close to home. I'm sure I have met you ladies before, but please pardon me for not recognizing you."

The younger woman spoke up again.

"That's quite all right, Mr. Hutchinson. We didn't know you, either. I am Emma DuBose, and this is my aunt, Mrs. Screven. I don't think you have met her before, as she has lived here only a year or so, but she knew your mother and father."

"Emma DuBose," he echoed musingly. "It seems I can only remember you as a child. You are so changed, I didn't know you. I suppose I am much changed, too."

"Perhaps it's the beard," she suggested politely, trying not to show her dismay at his appearance. She remembered him as a very handsome young man.

"I'm sure it's more than that," he muttered, half-smiling, glancing down at his filthy, ragged clothes.

"You're famished, Mr. Hutchinson," Emma said feelingly. "Please come inside and eat your food."

"I wouldn't think of entering your house in such a state, Miss DuBose. Perhaps I ought to be on my way."

"Sit out here on the porch and eat!" insisted Mrs. Screven. "It's about to rain, and you don't want to be walking home in a downpour."

The wind had been picking up, and rumblings of thunder had been heard for the last few minutes. The skies were growing so dark and threatening that it was plain he would not get far along the road before Mrs. Screven's predicted deluge would break over his head, so he decided to accept her invitation. They made him comfortable in an old wooden chair, and Emma disappeared into the house. Mrs. Screven took a seat beside their guest and watched with interest as he broke into his parcel of food. The young man devoured a sizeable chunk of cornbread in one bite and then ravenously tore into a piece of ham. After these first two inhalations, he slowed down and tried to eat in a more restrained, civilized way, suddenly cognizant that he was in the presence of a lady.

"Forgive us if we seemed unfriendly, Mr. Hutchinson," she apologized, "but it was not so long ago that we heard reports of Yankee soldiers disguising themselves in Confederate uniforms."

"I quite understand, Mrs. Screven."

"Oh, how thoughtless I am! I should have brought you something to drink. Would you like some water?" she asked.

He nodded, chewing on another piece of ham. Mrs. Screven went inside. Not long after she left, the air which he had inhaled, along with the food eaten much too fast, suddenly escaped in a deep, brief belch that he tried to muffle. He was sitting in front of a window and cast an embarrassed look inside the house. The ladies were out of sight, and he hoped that he was out of their hearing.

Mrs. Screven soon returned with a tumbler of clean, sweet well water for him. He drank it down in four or five great swigs. As he sighed a long sigh of satisfaction for a full, or nearly full, stomach, she went out into the yard and untied the dog. The animal bounded up to the house ahead of her and sat down near the soldier, clearly interested in the smell of the food.

Lightning flashed in the sky, followed by rattling peals of thunder, and the rain was soon coming down steadily.

"I'm glad to be under your roof," the young man remarked, picking up crumbs of cornbread from the cloth and tossing them to the dog. "I've walked through a thunder shower or two like this lately, and it isn't pleasant."

"You're just getting home from the war, then," said Mrs. Screven.

"That's right."

"Let me get you something else to eat."

"What you have been kind enough to give me is plenty, Mrs. Screven. I don't wish to impose upon your hospitality."

"Nonsense! A man who hasn't eaten in days needs more than that."

"Really, I ought not to eat much more now. I am not accustomed to large meals."

He was convincing, so she relented. Curious about him, Mrs. Screven was about to ask him about his family and his military service when Emma opened the front door and stepped out with a small cup of coffee—a rather scarce commodity in the household.

The young man's face beamed with gratitude as he accepted the drink.

"Coffee!" he exclaimed.

He closed his eyes and sipped it with a groan of satisfaction.

"Real coffee! I have died and gone to heaven."

"Has it been so long since you tasted coffee?" Emma asked, smiling only faintly at his humorous enjoyment, while Mrs. Screven covered a broad grin of amusement and laughed a little through her nose.

"Must be—months now," he replied between sips that he was relishing like ambrosia.

"I'm afraid we haven't much left, but I thought it might help to revive you. You said you had not eaten in several days, and I presume you've been traveling on foot at least that long."

"I've been traveling south for about two weeks, much of the way on foot, yes."

"May we offer you some more food?"

"I was just telling Mrs. Screven, I ought not to eat more right now. Oh, but thank you for this," he said, finishing off the last few drops of his drink.

They all gazed out at the rain, and Mrs. Screven stated with certainty that it was not a passing shower, but a storm that would last into the night.

"You must stay the night here with us, Mr. Hutchinson," she said.

Her niece agreed.

"If you insist," he said. "I shall be happy to sleep out here on the porch, if you will provide me with a blanket or two."

"I wouldn't dream of letting you spend the night out here. It will surely be quite chilly tonight."

"But Mrs. Screven—" he began to protest.

"We can provide you with some clean clothes, Mr. Hutchinson," she went on emphatically.

"Perhaps I could just wash these," he suggested.

Both women looked over his attire doubtfully.

"I don't know that they would stand a good washing," said Mrs. Screven. "Allow us to provide you with some better ones, Mr. Hutchinson. And—let me see—there's a large wooden tub of rain water by the barn. You could bathe yourself in it and change your clothes in the barn."

"I shall sleep in the barn, then," he said, and after that refused to yield to any further arguments.

"Believe me," he assured the ladies, "simply sleeping under a roof with four walls around me will be a luxury I have seldom enjoyed lately."

As Emma went back into the house to get the clothes, Mrs. Screven looked their guest over thoughtfully, casting a critical eye on his beard in particular.

"I imagine you might like to shave," she said. "But I'm afraid we can't accommodate you in that."

He touched his overgrown facial hair with some embarrassment.

"Perhaps I could just trim my beard," he suggested.

"I'll fetch you some scissors."

She jumped up and returned in a few moments, followed by Emma, who was holding a small heap of clothing and a bar of homemade soap. Mrs. Screven handed him a pair of scissors and a piece of oilcloth to keep the rain off. Murmuring his thanks, he accepted these things from the ladies, covered them with the oilcloth, picked up his haversack, and hurried off through the rain to the barn.

"Come and join us for supper!" Mrs. Screven called after him.

"I will!" he called back.

The barn was the smallest one he had ever heard given the name, part of it crudely and newly constructed. Two sides were the remnants of an older structure. The rest were made of assorted pieces of lumber, some of them charred, which might have been salvaged from a number of other outbuildings. There was a small trickle of rain coming in through a hole in the roof in one corner, but otherwise it was dry and comfortably warm. The only other occupants of the place seemed to be a cow and a mule, neither of whom seemed the least disturbed by his presence.

John found a likely place to make his bed and put down his bundle there. Nearby, in a corner, there was an old dressing table. It was broken, warped, and partly burnt, and mostly obscured by barrels, boards, and a few implements. He spied a movement in that corner and stepped closer to investigate, but the movement, he immediately realized, had been his own reflection in what was left of the table's mirror. He came closer, stared into his own eyes in a piece of clouded looking glass not much bigger than his hand, and frowned with dismay.

Taking off his perforated hat to see his full face, he thought he looked like some uncouth backwoodsman of the farthest frontier. His long, light brown hair was slick, greasy, and dirty, while his darker beard was wooly, matted, and unkempt. He was covered with dust and grime, and his ragged collar, once white, was disgustingly stained with sweat and dirt. He looked down at his hands. They were rough and raw, and black dirt lined all his nails. The rest of his body was just as filthy, and his clothes were little more than rags. Now that he saw himself, he was sure he had not imagined a certain veiled revulsion on the part of the ladies. It was no wonder, he thought; he looked like a wild man, and no doubt smelled like one.

John leaned in and took a closer look at his beard. A few tiny particles of cornbread were lodged in it and in his mustache. He uttered a mild oath as he brushed out the crumbs with his fingers. It was embarrassing to think that he had been seen by ladies in such a condition! He took out the scissors first and chopped off a few inches of his beard, trimmed his mustache, and then tried to cut an inch or two of length from his hair, but soon decided he was making too much of a mess of it and gave up.

He peeled off most of his old clothes and looked through the ones Miss DuBose had provided. The shirt and pants looked a little large for him, but he had no problem with that—better that they were not too small. She had also been thoughtful enough to include a towel. He picked it up with the soap and went outside. The rain had slackened a little, and he was glad to find the wooden tub on the side of the barn facing away from the house so that he had some privacy. He washed his face and hair first and then his upper body. Finally, casting several wary looks around, he lowered himself into the tub, pulled off the remaining rags, and finished his bathing quickly. As he rose out of the water, he loosely wrapped his old rags around his waist and kept them on until he was back in the barn where he dried off and put on the clean, dry clothes. He slipped on a pair of warm socks the young lady had provided, but waited to put on his old shoes, which were damp, muddy, and on the verge of disintegration. He wiped them off carefully so that they would at least look a little more presentable.

Facing the mirror again, John saw what he thought was a much improved version of the wild man who had gazed back at him before. He took up the scissors again and finished neatening up his now clean mustache and beard. Out of his haversack he pulled a toothbrush and an old hair comb, cleaned his teeth, and despite the many broken teeth of the comb, made it fulfill its purpose. He grimaced a little with pain when the comb touched a still tender spot on his skull. His hair was uneven on that side where doctors had cut away some of it to clean and treat an injury.

In another corner of the barn he found a little hay, not enough for a mattress, but enough for a pillow, which he covered with a soft handkerchief he found in the pocket of his borrowed shirt. He sat down and began cleaning his nails with a little knife he had with him, and before long, he began feeling drowsy in spite of the coffee he had consumed.

John put his head down on his makeshift pillow and closed his eyes. As he grew sleepier, he reflected on the blessings of the day–good food, a roof over his head, cleanliness, and the kindness of the household. The most pleasant image in his head, though, was that of the young lady.

"Emma," he breathed out, savoring the name aloud.

A pretty name, he thought, and then began to marvel at how different she looked from the Emma DuBose he remembered. The girl he recalled had been a rather plain, skinny little creature. She was certainly not so now. Her face was attractive and sweet, and he was sure he could call her beautiful, if she would only smile and brighten a little.

John imagined her face again and tried to put a more pleasing expression on it, but suddenly felt ashamed of himself when he remembered what little cause this young woman had for happiness. He knew that she had lost one of her brothers early in the war, and afterward her mother and father. Who knows how many other relatives and friends, she might have lost, and perhaps even a sweetheart or fiancé. Besides all this, what was left of her family, which had once been reasonably well-to-do, had apparently been reduced to poverty. Like so many other bereaved women of South Carolina, Miss DuBose had few reasons for smiles.

No longer tormented by gnawing hunger, John was already dozing off as he reflected on these things, and in his last waking thoughts, wondered where her eldest brother Theodore was. He was so tired, though, that before he could picture the young man clearly in his mind as he remembered him, he was sound asleep.

Emma paused at a window of the dining room and watched their guest hurrying through the rain toward the barn.

"I wonder if all our soldiers look like ragmen now," she remarked pityingly.

"The ones I have seen and heard of do," said her aunt. "But thank God another one of them has returned to us! I'm going to make Mr. Hutchinson a very nice supper. Do we have any more of the ham?"

"There's very little left, and what's left isn't very good, but I'm sure we can prepare an acceptable meal without it."

"I'll use what's left for seasoning, then."

Though it was a little too early to begin cooking for the evening, Mrs. Screven went on out to the kitchen, a smaller frame building connected to the house by a breezeway, to begin making her plans and some preliminary preparations for a meal.

The interruption of Mr. Hutchinson's arrival had sidetracked Emma and caused her to lose her momentum for the day. She had been working hard at the washing until the early afternoon, stopping only briefly for a bite of lunch, and then going on to other chores. Without interruption, she might have worked on as steadily until nightfall, but now all her energy seemed to dissipate, and she fell into an armchair feeling exhausted and distracted.

Never an idle person, Emma had always helped around the house, worked in her own flower and vegetable gardens, and had always kept her mind occupied with reading or study. Before the war, however, she had never been compelled to work from dawn to dusk for the sake of mere survival.

There were so many things to be done, she felt it was wrong to sit and rest a while, but she let herself rest anyway as her thoughts inevitably went back to the great event of the day–the return of John Hutchinson.

Emma had not seen him in many years; even before the war, she had seen little of him. Their paths never seemed to cross much, though their fathers had been very close friends. It seemed that she was always away from home for some reason when John was at his family's plantation, Belle Ville, and whenever she was home, he was usually away. When she left the female college at Barhamville during the war and came back to her father's house, where she lived now, John had already gone off to war in Virginia. She had never seen him in a uniform until today, if the rags he wore could be called that.

How strange it was to see the fine young gentleman she remembered in such a changed condition! It saddened her to think of him as he appeared now, especially since her most vivid memory of John Hutchinson was such a striking contrast. Many bittersweet memories came back to her as her thoughts returned to a day five years in the past.

In May of 1860, Emma had just celebrated her fifteenth

birthday. A party in her honor, and the anticipation of an exciting upcoming trip had enlivened an otherwise dull, rainy week at home. As one of her birthday gifts, her mother had insisted on the extravagance of an expensive new dress. Emma had chosen a lovely one of plaid silk with a full hoop skirt. The latest fashion in fabric and cut, it was adorned with a white lace collar and whitework embroidery "engageants," or flounces, which peeped out from the wide cuffs of long, flared sleeves. It was a rather sophisticated look for a fifteen year old girl.

Alone in her room, she stood before a dressing mirror and admired her striking, fashionable attire. Though the dress was beautiful and made her feel grown up, Emma could not compare herself favorably with the elegant, shapely ladies in the fashion plates of her magazines. She knew she was still too thin and girlish. Even so, she was very proud of her lovely dress, which she could hardly wait to display to her friends and cousins the following week on the family's trip to a tournament in the town of Pineville.

Emma's family always made a yearly trek to the South Carolina Lowcountry to Dr. DuBose's native parish of St. Stephen, where many families of that name still lived. Arriving there late on a Thursday, they spent the night at a cousin's house. Emma rose early the next day in anticipation of a day of great fun and enjoyment.

The annual tournament, also called a tilt or ring joust, was an updated version of a medieval joust in which the contestants tilted their lances at a suspended ring rather than at each other. The festivities began around ten in the morning at the race course on the outskirts of the village. On that particular day there was a chill in the air during the early hours, but it was tempered by a warm sun in a cloudless sky. Closer to noon the temperature was of a perfect coolness, comfortable for the crowds of warmly dressed spectators, and refreshing for the more active participants in the tournament.

Emma and a first cousin of her own age named Anne were close friends. The two girls kept some distance between themselves and their families as they walked arm in arm exchanging excited whispers with smiles and giggles while looking around with wide-eyed curiosity and excitement. Anne was in raptures over her cousin's new dress, and as Emma smiled with pleasure at her compliments, she observed that only the older girls were as fashionably attired and coiffed as she was. Her hair was carefully parted in the middle and gathered in a back knot at the nape of her neck, but was mostly obscured by a new wide-brimmed straw hat. Adorned with bright silk ribbons, it shaded her face in the sunlight.

"Why don't you hold your hat a while?" asked Anne. "You have such beautiful golden hair, you ought to show it."

"Mama will scold me if I don't wear it now."

Anne, who also wore a straw hat, nodded in understanding. Her mother had the same concern for her complexion.

"Oh, well," she said, "we may remove our hats when we take our seats."

As their families stopped to talk with some acquaintances, the two girls paused to take in the lively scene around them. Most of those attending the tournament hailed from Charleston and Columbia, but there were many persons from other parts of the Lowcountry and the state present also. Crowds of well-dressed, cheerful people were already taking their seats in the grandstands, which were shaded by huge canopies of red and white striped cloth. A section with the best view was reserved for ladies. The poles holding up the canopy were encircled with vines of ivy and flowers, and on top, colorful flags and pennants fluttered and flapped in the mild breezes. A few of the pennants bore sayings such as "Gallant Knights" and "Love of Ladies." Across from the grandstands, there was a sizeable crowd of spectators who preferred to watch the tilt seated in their carriages or standing. The lilting music of a band, sheltered in a pavilion, filled the air.

Out in the field, opposite the seats of the judges who occupied their own stand, three small, shiny metal rings were suspended about nine feet above the ground from the projecting wooden arms of three tall poles. The poles and cross-pieces, adorned with spiraling garlands and flowers, were placed roughly equidistant from each other on a course about a hundred and twenty yards in length.

"Oh, this is delightful!" gushed Anne, squeezing Emma's arm with almost painful enthusiasm. "Such pageantry and color! And such fine weather!"

Emma agreed wholeheartedly.

"Everyone in the family has so been looking forward to today," Anne went on. "Even Grandmama! She loves to watch the riders and admires them so much. I remember last year, when she sat beside me and said so proudly to everyone, the glory of young men is their strength."

"That is in the Bible," Emma informed her cousin.

"Is it?"

"Oh yes, in the book of Proverbs."

"Well, it is very true, isn't it?" Anne remarked.

The Dubose families found seats in the stands with a superb view of all the proceedings, but Emma and Anne sat apart from them with the ladies.A short distance from the crowds of spectators, the riders and horses were assembling near a wooded area where they would wait to take their turns in the tournament. At the blast of a trumpet, they rode up to the stands and presented themselves to the crowds, lowering their lances and saluting the ladies. The master of ceremonies, known as the Knight Marshall, addressed them and made a speech exhorting them to do deeds of daring worthy of the "fair gathering of womanhood looking on."

Emma had her own decided notions concerning chivalry informed by recent reading, and so, with a head full of *Ivanhoe* and other heroic tales of Sir Walter Scott, she scrutinized the knights to find those which best fit her ideal. As far as historical accuracy was concerned, she found some of the costumes of the riders disappointing, while others were magnificent. Their clothing was fancifully reminiscent of several periods of English costume. Most in costume were dressed in attire and accouterments of a medieval vintage, including full suits of armor. Some knights evoked cavaliers of Cromwell's day, while others wore clothing more suggestive of Elizabethan times. Quite a few of the young men simply wore their militia uniforms, to which they had added some flourish such as a colorful sash or a plume.

They all made a more or less dashing appearance in their costumes, but Emma quickly singled out a favorite when all the knights dismounted to listen to a ceremonial speech from one of the judges. One young man, in her eyes, stood out from among the rest. He was tall, though not the tallest, and his costume was not the most flamboyant, but he cut a striking figure in a tunic of cornflower blue worn over ordinary clothes and cavalry boots. The tunic hung from broad shoulders and tapered to a waist of perfect proportion, where it was loosely girded by a golden sash. A fanciful scabbard and sword, no doubt something manufactured for such occasions, hung at his side. His light brown hair was somewhat long and flowing, perhaps as a real knight of bygone times might have worn it, and his face was very handsome, as far as she could tell from a distance. Captivated by his appearance, Emma watched this particular cavalier whenever possible throughout the progress of the tilt.

When it was time for the contest to begin in earnest, the knights, in number thirty, walked past the stands, leading their horses. Many of these steeds had their own costumes of a sort; some were decorated with ribbons and plumes, and a few were draped with caparisons of richly colored silks. The handsome cavalier Emma had picked out as her champion led a beautiful white stallion dappled with spots and patches of gray, his tail quaintly braided and adorned with real flowers. When her favorite happened to pass near Emma, she was surprised to recognize him as one of her neighbors, John Hutchinson. He was no longer a teenage boy as she had seen him last, but a young man of twenty, or perhaps twenty-one, she guessed.

The knights, now on horseback, turned their mounts with not quite martial precision and filed off to the edge of the track where they fanned out and waited their turn at the tilt. A trumpet sounded again, and a herald announced the first contestant's name and title, Gabriel DuBose, the "Knight of Berkeley," who happened to be Anne's oldest brother.

"Charge, Sir Knight!" cried the herald.

Anne quivered and squealed with excitement as her brother entered the lists and made his first pass at the rings at a full gallop, then groaned and wilted with disappointment when the tip of his lance just missed the last one. The next three paladins, the "Knight of Malta," the "Knight Templar," and "Saladin," also missed one or two of the rings on their first attempt.

The sheer speed of the horses was thrilling. Emma's heart seemed to beat at the same pace as their hooves rhythmically pounded the ground. The riders held the wooden lances just above the right shoulder, some slightly leaning their heads and upper bodies to the right, their eyes fixed intently on the miniscule target. When they were successful, the ring would give a clink as it came in contact with the tip of the lance, sliding quickly down the shaft to collide with a leather guard protecting the rider's hand. The horses kicked up dirt and grass as they were pulled up from a full gallop after passing the last pole, tossing their heads and slowing to a trot.

A dozen or so more knights followed with varying degrees of success. Finally, Emma's favorite was next. The trumpet blew, and John Hutchinson came forward to be announced as the "Knight of Carolina."

On his first pass, he caught all the rings, but failed to carry them off. They slipped off his lance and fell to the ground, and a young black man beautifully dressed as a Moor picked them up to return them to their places for the next contestant. Emma breathed a deep sigh as she watched the Knight of Carolina barely miss the mark. He had come so close, she was sure that he would be successful on his next try. Like all the young men in the tournament that day, he was an expert rider, but to Emma he seemed to be one of the best. It took very skillful horsemanship and steady, precise marksmanship to take the ring (only about an inch and a quarter in diameter), while riding at full, breakneck speed.

Emma's admiration knew no bounds when on his second pass, the Knight of Carolina took all three rings on the tip of his lance with apparent effortlessness. As the day progressed, all the knights took seven passes at the rings. Emma's favorite carried off the prize four times out of seven. At the conclusion of the contest, the judges pronounced him the winner. She felt a flush of pride and infatuation as she watched John Hutchinson come forward and dismount from his horse to receive the victor's prize, a pair of silver spurs. He accepted them with a deep bow, and then held them up above his head for the admiration of the crowd.

"Choose now the Queen of Love and Beauty!" one of the judges directed him.

The victorious knight bowed his head solemnly, returned to his saddle, and urged his horse to cross a small distance to the ladies' grandstand, where he paused and gazed over all the female faces. Emma, seated toward the front of the stand, at last had a clear and closer view of him. His clean shaven face was slightly bronzed by the sun, and his hair was carelessly tousled from the day's riding. In keeping with the pomp and splendor of the day, he maintained ceremoniousness in his manner, but a smile played over his lips when he lowered his lance and pointed it at the young lady of his choosing.

"I select the fair lady Mason!" he declared loudly for all to hear.

All eyes turned to Miss Elizabeth Mason, who was the most beautiful young woman Emma had ever seen. Inclining her head slightly in acknowledgment and blushing with a beaming smile, she gracefully made her way out of the seats and walked over to a group of judges who were standing in the field facing the stands. The Knight of Carolina had dismounted and was standing with them, along with the Moor, who was holding a wreath in each hand for the ceremony of crowning.

The Knight and his Queen of Love and Beauty faced each other with a bow and a curtsey. The young man took a chaplet of white rosebuds and placed it on her head, very careful not to disorder her hair, which was parted into two smooth, glossy brown folds that perfectly framed the milky oval of her lovely face. Emma thought the white flowers made Miss Mason look like a bride, and felt a little pang in her heart. The Knight kneeled before his Queen, and she in turn crowned him with a wreath of laurels.

Two other knights were then singled out for acclaim. The principal judge announced the names of the two contestants who had been chosen, one for the best riding, the other for the best costume. Anne's brother, the Knight of Berkeley, won the latter honor for that day. Looking something like Sir Walter Raleigh in sumptuous silks and velvets, he made a dramatic bow and a flourish with his feathered cap as his name was spoken, eliciting laughter and applause from the audience. These two young knights then shyly chose their maids of honor and from their hands received their prizes.

After the awards ceremonies, the riders dispersed and mingled with the spectators, most of whom left their seats in the stands to mill about and socialize. Many friends and family members were invited to a light meal at the home of Emma's uncle Mr. Benjamin DuBose.

As the crowds began to gradually disperse, a number of the young men, still in high spirits, were challenging each other to impromptu races on the field of honor. Some people gathered to watch their antics, and Emma led her cousin Anne to the edge of the field because she saw that the Knight of Carolina was among them.

He conversed with his fellow participants, smiling and laughing frequently, showing strong white teeth, and tossing his chin in the air in a way that reminded Emma of a spirited horse. She guessed correctly that horseflesh was the main topic of conversation among these young gentlemen. Some of the knights were making short trial runs on their horses, and she noted how the others assessed the movements and performance of each mount and rider, plainly expressing in their faces and gestures amusement, disapproval, or acclaim.

Emma's cavalier watched a short race or two, then held a conversation with another knight who was holding the reins of a large, high-strung, mettlesome white stallion. A challenge of some sort passed between the two, and the Knight of Carolina mounted this horse. The animal bucked a little with him, registering displeasure with the unfamiliar rider, who quickly prodded him into a canter with his new silver spurs. The horse tossed his head defiantly and snorted as he moved, and after making a turn at the end of the field, broke into a faster run, apparently at his own discretion. The stallion was heading straight for the small crowd of spectators and fought the reins when his rider tried to turn him in a different direction. The crowd drew back, and the horse veered, slowing to a canter again and moving in a line parallel to them rather than into them. Then suddenly, the animal veered again and came to a stop as swiftly as it was possible to do from this speed, sending the rider flying over his lowered head to the ground. The Knight of Carolina tumbled violently into a small group of young ladies all scattering to avoid him, and one of his arms was flung straight into the skirts of Emma, whose knees he collapsed, sending her to the ground with him.

Immediately he was on his feet tending to her.

"I beg your pardon, miss!" he gasped hoarsely, just getting the breath back into his lungs. "I hope I haven't injured you."

As he came out of a momentary daze and focused his eyes on Emma, he recognized her as the daughter of Dr. DuBose. Thoroughly stunned, Emma could not answer for a moment, but tried to raise herself from complete prostration to a more dignified sitting position. The knight assisted her by taking her hands in his own briefly and giving her a gentle pull.

She took a deep breath and said, "I don't think I am injured. I hope you aren't hurt."

His look of anxiety and shame gave way to relief.

"I could never forgive myself if I harmed a young lady in any way," he said, "though I am sure I have caused you enough distress by making such a spectacle of us both."

Still recovering from her initial shock, and at the same time so arrested by the young man's nearness and attention, Emma did not even hear the cries and utterances of concern coming from Anne and others around her. Her cousin had been leaning over her, but stepped back when she heard Emma say she was not injured.

"May I help you up, Miss DuBose?" he asked, offering his arm.

Emma meekly slipped her hand above his elbow, her eyes widening a little in amazement at the power she could feel in his upper arm, which was like a band of steel.

The young man took his leave with another apology and a bow, briefly holding one of her little gloved hands between both of his. Emma wondered, if she had been a little older or prettier, if he might have kissed that hand.

The owner of the willful horse, one of the other knights, rushed over and took the animal's reins to lead him away while Anne and some older ladies fussed over Emma, offering comfort, brushing off her clothes, and assuring themselves that she was all right. The unfortunate rider meanwhile, the cause of all this consternation, had been stopped and forced to submit to a tongue-lashing from an elderly matron, who was wagging a bony forefinger at him.

"You young gentlemen ought not to be riding unruly horses near crowds of women and children," the lady reproved him indignantly, pointing to Emma when she said the word *children*.

"Oh, oh! She is calling me a child!" she thought, mortified. This bit of slander cancelled out all the pleasure and gratification she had felt when her Knight had referred to her as a *young lady*.

The young man apologized yet again, begged all the ladies in his hearing to forgive him for his disgrace, and backed off with several obsequious bows, this time suppressing a smile.

Emma watched him walk away and rejoin his companions.

Restraining themselves until they were out of the ladies' hearing, they led the Knight of Carolina off to a far corner of the field where she could see that much merciless hilarity and taunting was going on at his expense, on account of his unchivalrous and humiliating tumble. She imagined some wag among them must surely be making a joke about sweeping a young lady off her feet, and blushed to the roots of her hair at the thought of it.

She returned to a spot on the lowest level of the stands and sat there with a strange, pensive look.

"Emma, dear," said Anne, rushing up to her. "Are you sure you are well?"

She nodded slightly.

"I am fine...just...embarrassed."

But Emma really felt more sadness than embarrassment, having quickly come back to sober reality after allowing her girlish heart to thrill over a young man to whom she meant nothing. She reproached herself for such foolishness and tried not to think of him anymore.

She never saw John Hutchinson again until after the war.

CHAPTER TWO

MRS. SCREVEN CALLED TO EMMA from the dining room, and the young woman was abruptly roused from her memories. She came back to the present moment with the image of John Hutchinson as she had seen him five years ago, quickly fading in her mind's eye.

"My knight," she murmured, picturing him as he was now—a drab, ragged veteran—with a rueful smile.

Mrs. Screven walked into the parlor, wondering why Emma had not come to her or answered.

"Dear, you look so tired," she observed sympathetically. "Why don't you go upstairs and rest a while before we eat?"

"I think I shall do that," Emma responded, slowly rising to her feet.

"I'll take care of the cooking. Shall I call you in time to clean up and change your clothes?"

"Why should I change my clothes?" she asked listlessly.

"Well...we have a guest."

"All my dresses are equally sorry now, except for my black one. I suppose I should put that one on."

She always wore her mourning garb now to go out in public,

though such excursions were very infrequent. In other circumstances, she would have been wearing it every day, but she had to wear other clothes for her daily work. She was trying to preserve her mourning dress, the only good one she had left.

Emma went upstairs and lay down on her bed, closing her eyes and drowsing for about an hour or so. Still feeling weary, restless and useless, she got up from the bed, took off her apron, and inspected herself in a long mirror. She decided that a good scrubbing would do as much good as a change of clothes. Before she put on her black dress, she washed her face, neck, and arms at the washstand, then unbound her long hair, combed it, and gathered and bound it neatly at the back in a snood.

A stack of books was on her bedside table, and she thought she might read a while, but changed her mind when she remembered her aunt working away in the kitchen, and went back downstairs to help her.

When John woke up in the barn, it was dusk, and a darker one than usual with the continuing rain. His stomach had emptied and was growling for its promised evening meal. He felt around for the oilcloth, threw it over his shoulders, and left the barn to run over to the house.

He arrived at the door in his plain, somewhat oversize, but clean clothes, and the ladies invited him into the dining room and sat him down in a comfortable chair. His hair had been partially soaked again by the rain and clung to his forehead in places like seaweed on a wet rock, but otherwise he looked refreshed and reasonably presentable. As Emma served his plate she noticed that his dark green eyes seemed less hollow now; they looked brighter, and were fringed with black lashes which before, like the rest of him, had borne a layer of dust.

John was privately taking his own notice of the young

woman as she moved about the table. Earlier he thought he had detected, beneath her ill-fitting clothes and the apron that had covered her from neck to ankles, a rather splendid figure, and seeing her now in a decent, well-tailored dress, that suspicion was confirmed.

There was no meat on the table that night, but cornbread, sweet potatoes, and a few vegetables well-seasoned with the fat of ham satisfied his hunger just the same. After one generous helping the ladies offered him more, and more he could have eaten, but out of consideration refused, insisting that he was satisfied. He looked around the dining room and observed that it was plain and bare except for the table and chairs, some striped paper on the wall, and thin yellow curtains pulled back from a window. A wall against which a china cabinet or cupboard must have stood was empty, but what had once been there had left a subtle remembrance of itself in a large rectangular shape where the wallpaper was brighter.

Mrs. Screven had kept up most of the conversation during the meal, imparting news about friends and neighbors in the area they all knew or had known, and allowing John to eat while he listened and occasionally ventured a comment or question. They had seated him at the head of the table, with Emma at his right and her aunt on his left. Most of his glances were directed to his left, since Mrs. Screven was doing most of the talking. The few times Emma spoke during the meal, usually in response to a question by her aunt, John studied her, noticing the beauty of her hair and the blush of sunburn on her cheeks and the tip of her nose, and he was again struck by how rarely she smiled.

Fearing the worst, he hesitated to ask the young woman about her family, but there was no way to avoid it. Emma's father, Dr. Samuel DuBose, had been his one of his own father's closest friends, and John had attended the Military College in Charleston with her brother.

"Where is your brother Theodore, Miss DuBose?" he asked her softly.

When Emma did not answer immediately, Mrs. Screven did so for her.

"Theo died in February, Mr. Hutchinson. When he was sent home, it was thought he would recover from his wounds, but alas, they proved to be mortal."

"I am very sorry to hear it," he said compassionately.

Both ladies were silent for a few moments, and he sensed that it was best not to say more on the subject for now.

"Allow us to offer our condolences to you, Mr. Hutchinson, for your father's recent passing," Emma said quietly.

"Thank you."

"How is your brother Elias?" Mrs. Screven asked him.

"The last I heard of him, he was well. I am hoping he has returned to Belle Ville by now, or that he will soon."

Mrs. Screven asked John about his military service, but he volunteered only the sketchiest details of his career in the Confederate Army. After briefly describing his months in South Carolina in the Charleston Light Dragoons, followed by his commission as an officer of cavalry in a regiment serving in the army of General Lee, he finished by summing up the rest of his nearly three and a half years of service in Virginia and elsewhere in only a few brief sentences.

Both ladies noticed his reluctance to talk about the war, but Mrs. Screven was curious to know if John had ever been wounded and questioned him about that.

"I was wounded three times," he replied in a matter-of-fact way. "I was shot through both legs, in the thigh, both times, but fortunately they were flesh wounds, and there was no injury to the bone or arteries. I received the third wound on my last day in battle in Virginia, not long before Lee's surrender. My horse was shot out from under me. I went down, stunned by the fall, I suppose, and as the enemy infantry were charging, my skull was introduced to the butt of a Yankee rifle."

"Thank God you were not killed!" the older lady exclaimed. "How easily they might have shot you!"

"Or bayoneted me," John mused. "I've sometimes wondered why that soldier didn't, but he gave me such a blow, I suppose he thought he had done his work."

"God preserved you!" said Mrs. Screven, throwing up her hands in a gesture of praise and thankfulness.

"That may be," he responded thoughtfully. "I must say I was praying mighty hard as my horse went down."

"I have no doubt your prayers were answered, Mr. Hutchinson. How did you pray, if one may ask?"

As John searched his memory, he happened to glance at Emma, and noticed that her eyes were fixed on him very intently as both ladies waited to hear what he would say.

"I don't remember exactly," he finally replied. "I think I said, Lord, let me live."

"And so you did!" Mrs. Screven rejoiced. "I shall offer thanks for your life in my prayers tonight."

"So shall I," Emma added.

He thanked the ladies and began eating again to finish the last few morsels of food on his plate. Mrs. Screven waited until he was finished to ask John what happened to him after his brush with death.

"The Yankees took me prisoner and put me in one of their hospitals. When I regained consciousness, I didn't even know my name for a while, but everything soon came back to me. Most everything, I should say. I still feel that some pieces of memory have not yet come back, unless they were knocked out of my head forever. When I was sufficiently recovered, after many weeks, I was paroled. This was just at the time of the surrender."

"I am so glad you have returned to us, Mr. Hutchinson!" Mrs. Screven burst out feelingly, and then asked in a respectful tone, "Shall we call you Captain Hutchinson?"

"Unless you prefer to call me John," he suggested amiably.

"Oh, that is very friendly of you! Perhaps I shall. I knew your mother very well, you know. I held you once when you were a baby."

Hearing this, John cut his eyes toward Emma as if piqued and joked, "And Miss DuBose said we had never met!"

His jest caused Mrs. Screven to break into merry peals of laughter, and even elicited a real smile from Emma.

"Ah, she is beautiful," he thought, basking in that smile.

"It's so good to laugh again," Mrs. Screven sighed. "Sad as the circumstances are, I am relieved the war is over. Aren't you, Captain Hutchinson?"

"I suppose. I've seen horrors I never wish to see again, but..."

He paused, and the two women looked at him expectantly for what was to follow. Their expressions grew serious, reflecting his own now.

"I've walked through miles and miles of country that is little more than a burnt out wasteland," he resumed reluctantly. "A good part of what I have seen of this state seems to be in ruins. As for the relief many feel, I think it must be like that of a wounded man who has been in great pain and receives morphine to ease it. When the morphine wears off, a worse pain may follow."

This was all too vague and philosophical for Mrs. Screven;

she shook her head and sighed heavily; but Emma seemed to understand him, and her look of somberness returned.

"I beg your pardon, ladies. Please forgive my gloominess. You have made things so comfortable and pleasant for me tonight, I ought not to–"

Mrs. Screven suddenly interrupted him with a gesture, begged his pardon, and jumped up from her chair to fetch a dessert she had almost forgotten.

John continued his apology to Emma when they were left alone at the table.

"I'm afraid I have forgotten some of my manners," he said. "I've been too long out of the company of ladies."

"Your manners are entirely acceptable, Captain Hutchinson," she answered, with a polite but definite dismissal of his concern. "You are not the first to tell us such things."

John nodded and, having come to the conclusion that Miss DuBose was a sensible young woman and not overly delicate or fearful, he decided he could be frank with her. He leaned toward her with an earnest, intent look.

"Miss DuBose," he said, "as I've been making my way through the state, I've seen and heard of some very disturbing things going on. I must tell you, it concerns me very much that you ladies are living in this place alone, without protection. Is there no one here except the two of you?"

She shook her head in answer, her expression again mirroring his.

"Only the two of us," she said, "but we have some protection. Our neighbor Mr. Drawdy has been helping us. He is usually here each day for several hours."

"Jeb Drawdy? He has a small farm, doesn't he? Why isn't he working his own land?"

"He's trying to work some of ours and his, poor man. He respected my father so much and felt so obligated to him for all the medical care his family received from him with so little compensation, he says he must help us, and won't let us refuse him. I've been working in the fields with Mr. Drawdy, and even my aunt helps out in the vegetable gardens, though she is not accustomed to such work."

"Has there been any lawlessness around here?" asked John.

"A few incidents...," Emma answered somewhat evasively, adding, "We have a pistol."

"Do you know how to use it?"

"I do."

"Do you plan to stay here?"

"For now, yes."

John leaned back in his chair and crossed his arms, thinking.

"I should like to do what I can to help you and your aunt, Miss DuBose," he said. "With your permission, we can try and figure something out, but I suppose I shall have to find out how things are at Belle Ville first."

She studied him with a grateful but quizzical look, and was about to thank him when Mrs. Screven came back into the dining room carrying a tray. She laid out three saucers which each held a small pastry topped with apple jam.

"Well, that was the last of our flour and sugar," she remarked, taking her seat, "but I don't think there could have been a better way to use it. I have so been longing for something sweet! Your return, Captain Hutchinson, has given us cause to celebrate."

John took a few bites of the delicious dessert and complimented her on her cooking, and thanked both the ladies again for the fine meal.

"I confess I did do most of the cooking tonight," said Mrs.

Screven, "but Emma raised the vegetables on our table. She has a gift with green things, just like her grandmother. Why, that lady could make a dead stick grow by merely poking it in the ground!"

Emma smiled a little at her aunt's penchant for exaggeration, and John was glad to see her do that again, however faintly. When they finished their desserts, Mrs. Screven suggested that they retire to the parlor. Not looking forward to a long, dreary night alone in a barn, John was easily persuaded to join the ladies. He accompanied them carrying the oil lamp which had illuminated their supper table, and they sat down in that room.

As he seated himself on the sofa he noticed that its upholstery had several large patches of another fabric sewn into it. He also saw that the wooden frameworks of the other pieces of furniture were crudely repaired in various places, and that the whole parlor, like the dining room, was unusually empty of decoration.

Emma took her usual chair beside a small bookcase. John glanced over the titles, noting some rather weighty works of history, philosophy and theology, mixed in with a few novels and volumes of poetry, as well as books on gardening and cookery. A well-worn copy of *The Southern Gardener and Receipt Book* rested on top of the case, along with a Bible and an Episcopal prayer book.

"We usually read a little while in the evenings, if we're not too tired," said Mrs. Screven. "I should say, Emma reads. I like to have her read aloud to me while I sew. On Sundays, of course, we read the Scriptures. Reverend Shubrick has been so ill, we are compelled to conduct our own religious services of sorts on the Sabbath. Emma, won't you read for us tonight?"

Emma looked doubtful and reluctant about the suggestion, but John encouraged the idea, pulling out a volume on the history of England and leafing through it.

"I should like to hear you read, Miss DuBose," he said. "I see you have some very interesting books."

"Heavens, not the scholarly stuff!" Mrs. Screven protested humorously, noticing his choice of literature. "I don't care for that, and sometimes I don't understand it. That's Emma's private reading. She was always reading books out of her father's library. We have just finished one of Mr. Simms' novels. Weren't we going to begin another of his this evening, dear?"

"I thought we had agreed to begin 'A Tale of Two Cities' tonight, aunt."

"Oh, yes! I like Mr. Dickens very much. Well, then by all means, let's read that if you are willing."

As Emma began to read the book, John's mind wandered almost immediately. He had never been a great reader of novels and found it hard to concentrate on the opening passages, taking more enjoyment in the sound of the young woman's soft, pleasing voice than the words she was speaking. After a while his eyes drifted dreamily to her face, which he viewed in profile, and he found himself following the curves of her lips as they moved in speech. They were delicate, expressive, shapely lips, as pink and smooth and rounded as the petals of a rose, and rendered even more attractive by a slight overbite that gave her face a somewhat girlish appearance. Suddenly, imagining that Mrs. Screven's eyes had turned on him, perhaps disapprovingly, he immediately looked away and gazed up toward the ceiling. He forced himself to listen with more attention, but soon found himself growing dreamy again. Emma's gentle, fluent recitation began to remind him of another voice, another woman…

He saw himself as a boy at home, in a finely furnished drawing room lit by a fireplace and oil lamps. He saw his mother, a beautiful, dark-haired woman who was seated in an armchair near him, reading the same book to the family, just as Emma was reading now. He could also picture his father in another chair smoking a pipe, his grandmother at her sewing, his older sister Isabella lounging on a sofa, and his younger brother Elias and little sister Lise, seated on the floor listening. How long ago it all was, he was thinking–and then realized that it was not really not so long ago, and yet it seemed like another world now.

John had closed his eyes while he was remembering these things and others. Miss Dubose paused in her reading and he opened them. She was looking at him.

"I wasn't asleep," he said apologetically.

"Perhaps I have read too long," she suggested.

He shook his head, "No."

"I think we're all very tired. Please pardon me, but I don't think I can read anymore this evening."

Mrs. Screven expressed her disappointment, but could not persuade Emma to continue. She closed the book and marked her place with a ribbon.

While they had been sitting in the parlor, the storm outside had been renewing itself. The rain was coming down heavily again, and deep rumblings of thunder had recommenced. Mrs. Screven began to insist that John spend the night in the house. He refused at first, but finally gave in considering the less desirable alternative of the barn, and a slog in the dark through heavy rains and lightning to get to it. He had noticed a daybed in the corner of the room and agreed to sleep there.

"I'll find you a pillow and some covers," said Mrs. Screven, getting to her feet.

Emma put away her book and left her chair to follow her aunt.

"Good night, Captain Hutchinson," she said to him, pausing

momentarily in the doorway.

"Good night, Miss DuBose."

Long after midnight, after sleeping soundly for several hours, John came to a half-awake consciousness and a vague awareness that the rain had stopped. As he shifted to a more comfortable position on the daybed, he heard an unexpected sound and realized that an earlier occurrence of it was probably what had roused him from a deep sleep. Someone was talking inside the house, and he naturally wondered what was going on at this hour of the night with some concern. The voice grew louder, and he recognized that it belonged to Miss Dubose. He heard only her voice, however, and no other, which seemed to be coming from upstairs. He sat up and listened.

Her tone grew shrill and urgent. Then he heard a strangled scream. Throwing off his covers, he felt his way through the dark unfamiliar room to the foot of the stairs and rushed up to the second floor.

John saw a dim figure in white in the hallway and quickly realized that it was Miss DuBose. She was standing outside the open door of her bedroom in a nightgown and bare feet. Her hair was gathered in two long braids.

"Miss Dubose! What is wrong? What's happened?"

She let her head fall forward strangely and peered at him, blinking as if just awakened.

"Theo!" she quavered feebly. "Theo?"

While she was speaking, Mrs. Screven opened the door of her room and, tying up the sash of a robe, hurried out.

"Oh, dear," she moaned. "She has had the dream again."

"Are you all right, Miss Dubose?" he asked.

In the lamplight that flooded into the hall from her aunt's

room, Emma could see John more clearly now. She nodded drowsily in answer to his question.

"I beg your pardon for the intrusion," he said, "but I heard you cry out."

"Thank you, but I'm all right. It was a nightmare, nothing more."

"I have those myself."

Waking fully, Emma realized that she was standing before the young man in her night clothes. She quickly drew her arms up across her chest.

"I'll go downstairs now," he said, seeing her embarrassment. "Will you be all right?"

"Yes, I'm fine now. Good night."

Mrs. Screven put an arm around her niece and escorted her back into her room. Downstairs, John was in darkness again, and made his way back to his bed, one of his shins experiencing an unhappy encounter with a piece of furniture before he made it there. He picked up his covers from the floor and lay down, but before he could close his eyes again, he noticed a light from the direction of the stairs. It drew closer and brighter, and Mrs. Screven soon appeared holding a candle.

"Forgive me, but I wished to come down and fetch my sewing. It was so upsetting to hear her cries, I don't think I shall be going back to sleep soon. Emma wished me to tell you that she is sorry to have disturbed you."

"It's quite all right," he said, sitting up. "Please, tell her to think nothing of it."

Mrs. Screven nodded and stepped into the room to get her sewing basket. As she picked it up and turned back toward the stairway, John stopped her with a question.

"Does she have this bad dream often?"

"Not very often. Only once in a while, and only once before did I find her out of her bed as tonight, as though walking in sleep! Did she call you Theo?"

"Yes."

"Those are his clothes."

"Is the dream about him?"

"I don't know. She won't tell me what it's about. Well, goodnight, Captain Hutchinson, I'm sure you must wish to get back to your sleep."

"Good night."

John woke up in a room filled with the soft sunlight of early morning. As he slowly stretched and got to his feet, he heard footsteps on the stairs, and Mrs. Screven appeared again in the same spot where he had seen her the night before, now dressed for the day.

"Good morning!" she said. "Would you like some coffee?"

"Good morning, Mrs. Screven. I must refuse to take the last of your coffee, but thank you for the offer."

"The last of the coffee is no great loss to us. We prefer tea. Let me make you some. I'll have some with you."

"Thank you!"

He joined Mrs. Screven at the dining room table when she brought in two cups of coffee on a small tray.

"Did you sleep well?" she asked. "I mean, after you were disturbed."

"Fine, thank you. Is Miss DuBose unwell?"

"She isn't up yet. She usually rises before I do, but I suppose last night's disturbance kept her up a while, so I imagine she will sleep a little later this morning."

After she had answered him, Mrs. Screven fell to thinking,

and looked more and more pensive and absorbed as she slowly sipped her coffee.

"Emma," she murmured sadly, staring abstractedly at some point across the room.

Sensing that Mrs. Screven's mind was full of a subject that interested him, he waited, hoping to hear more about the young woman.

"I beg your pardon, Captain Hutchinson," she finally said, turning her attention back to him. "It always upsets me so when my niece has these nightmares. I hardly slept last night."

"Miss DuBose has suffered so many bereavements these past few years, I'm not surprised her dreams are troubled," he said.

"Oh, if you only knew, Captain Hutchinson!" she lamented. "There was never a more dutiful, devoted girl in the world. When her mother sickened and became an invalid, Emma had just finished her last term at the Barhamville academy and promptly came home to take care of her. The family still had servants to do the cooking and the cleaning at that time, but Emma never rested. She nursed her mother, and then my poor brother, all the while working for the Soldiers' Aid Society in any spare moment. She was always sewing and knitting for our soldiers, and growing things in her garden to help them and her family and neighbors, giving everything for the cause, even the carpet from her room!"

Mrs. Screven paused, sighed, and then went on, "Before her father fell ill he used to tend to the wounded soldiers coming in on the trains. Emma begged to assist him as a nurse, but he considered such work improper for an unmarried girl. After he died, Emma and I would go down to the depot to take the wounded men baskets of provisions. One day they took a soldier off the train who had grown too ill to travel. Emma talked with him and held his hand as he was dying. You should have seen the way that boy looked at her, Captain Hutchinson. It was enough to break one's heart."

Disturbed by the memory, Mrs. Screven paused again to compose herself.

"When Emma was old enough to marry," she continued, "she refused several young men who addressed her. The last to try was a cousin from Georgia, but that was when her mother fell ill. I think Emma liked him the best, but she refused him, too. He was a very kind young gentleman, and a rich rice planter, although I don't suppose he is rich anymore. We haven't even heard yet whether he is still alive. He was an officer..."

Her voice trailed off, her thoughts temporarily diverted to their Georgia cousin, and possibly projections of what might have been, but after a while Mrs. Screven came out of her private reveries and resumed, "And then it was such a blow when Emma's brothers were killed–oh, my dear nephews!–such fine young men! And if all that were not enough to crush one's spirit, we heard of the surrender. My niece was so shocked by the news, I thought she might expire before my eyes. She told me that it was as though the very ground had been removed from under her feet. Then, the very next day, we received news of another death in the family, Emma's beloved cousin Gabriel, who died in the hands of the enemy."

"Were they–sweethearts?" John asked, after some hesitation.

"Oh, no," said Mrs. Screven decisively. "But he was as dear to her as a brother."

"So she has really lost three brothers."

"Yes, you might say that. I don't know how Emma has borne up and come through all these things, except that she clings to her faith. But sometimes, Captain Hutchinson, I think the grief becomes too overwhelming for her. Yesterday was particularly difficult for her. It was Theo's birthday, you see, and I could tell that she was thinking of him a good deal, and probably about the day he died not so long ago. It was the day the Yankees came here and ruined the place. Oh, what a terrible time that was–the worst of my life! I cannot bear to think of it."

"I'm sure these past few years have been very hard for you, too," John suggested, noticing tears brimming in the corners of her eyes.

"Yes, that is true, but I am much older, and have lived most of my life, and most of it very happily with my dear departed husband. He was a clergyman, and the most loving soul that ever was. Emma, however, has not had that opportunity. She is only nineteen, but she has seen enough sorrows for a lifetime or more."

Mrs. Screven stopped, and they both sat silently for a while as she sniffed back her tears. John had been very much interested in learning more about Miss DuBose, and was glad that he had, but the narration of so many sad and unfortunate events and circumstances left him not knowing what to say, and even a little depressed. Seeing his heavy expression, Mrs. Screven apologized.

"I ought not to have unburdened myself on you, Captain Hutchinson," she said regretfully.

"Oh, no, don't think that," he protested politely.

His kindness soothed her, but the next moment, she was fretting with a different kind of remorse.

"Oh dear," she said. "Perhaps I ought not to have told you all these things. Emma might not have wished it."

"I'm sure there was no harm in it," he reassured her. "If you wish, sometime I will tell you my troubles."

John managed a smile when he said this, and she smiled half-heartedly at him in return. Mrs. Screven suddenly remembered a question she had been meaning to ask him.

"Did you marry during the war, Captain Hutchinson?"

The brief answer she received was, "No."

They heard footsteps on the stairs, and their heads turned toward the doorway as Emma walked in. There was momentary embarrassment on her face when her eyes met John's, but when no mention was made of the events of the night, it quickly passed. Mrs. Screven fetched her the last few drops of coffee in the house, and the three shared a light breakfast of hominy.

While they ate, John stole a few glances at Emma, who was very quiet. Considering her in light of all that Mrs. Screven had just told him, he wondered that a mere girl could carry the heavy, terrible weight of all those sorrows and adversities on her shoulders, yet she did. As a soldier who had endured four years of war, he had become somewhat calloused to suffering, but as he contemplated the young woman across the table from him, he felt his heart begin to warm and soften with a deepening compassion for her.

John asked about the condition of the farm. Both women sighed in discouragement before Emma spoke up to answer him.

"Perhaps it might be better if I showed you how things are," she suggested

"Yes, Captain Hutchinson," Mrs. Screven agreed. "We shall be glad for you to take a look at the place and give us your opinion."

They went outside and found a bright, cheerful sun just topping the trees. Its white, blinding disc was framed by three banks of steel gray, feathery clouds, two of which slanted diagonally over a horizontal layer of cloud, so that the whole resembled a parted curtain over a stage, just above which the sun presented itself. The sun soon disappeared behind one of the curtains, but its brilliance soon broke though again. Emma shaded her eyes, and in the full sunlight, as she was speaking to John, she noticed the luster of his honey brown hair, which had dried into loose wavy locks streaked with gold.

The lowing of a cow could be heard from the barn.

"Oh, dear," said Mrs. Screven, "I clean forgot about milking Dolly this morning! I should have done it before breakfast."

She headed for the barn, leaving John and Emma to make the survey by themselves. He looked over the present condition of the DuBose farm with a sickened feeling. Before the war it had been a well-maintained, pretty little place, bustling with life. He remembered that Emma's mother had kept a few specimens of a fancy, colorful breed of chickens that were never slaughtered for their meat, but allowed to strut about the yards merely to be admired for their beauty, like peacocks.

It was strange now to see a farmyard so lifeless and still. Where outbuildings had once stood–the smokehouse, stable, corn crib, barns, sheds, and other structures–there were only blackened heaps of rubble on the ground. Some ugly weeds had sprung up amid the ashes and charred remains, thriving on destruction like scavengers on carrion. As far as he could see from where he stood now, except for the dwelling house and its attached kitchen, the small, hastily rebuilt barn where he had bathed himself the day before was the only substantial building left on the place.

John remarked to Miss DuBose that it must have been terrible for her and her aunt to witness all this destruction.

"I don't wish to speak of it," she abruptly replied, frowning.

Having spoken more curtly than she intended, she begged his pardon, and John replied in the same apologetic tone, "I suppose it's something one would not wish to remember."

Emma showed him her vegetable gardens, which were looking a little battered by the night's storm, but still full of promise. Plantings of pole beans, cucumbers, tomatoes, and squash had just that week begun showing themselves above the ground as tender seedlings, while her other kitchen crops of beets, carrots, lettuce, and onions, which had been sown in late winter, were well along. John complimented her on the fine looking plants.

A scarecrow, which consisted of a sheet of tin suspended from a pole by wires, moved and creaked in the gentle breezes, flashing brightly whenever the sun broke through the clouds. They walked a fair distance out to an area which looked out on an expanse of open fields, most of which were bare. Several acres where crops of wheat and oats had been planted late in the previous year were only ruined fields of scorched and ploughed up stubble now. Emma pointed out a field where corn had been planted more recently, then showed John a few acres which were to yield a cotton crop. His heart sank when he saw how little land was under cultivation.

"It isn't much, I know," said Emma, seeing his dismayed expression. "But it's all we'll be able to do this year."

"Have you planted the cotton seed yet?"

"Mr. Drawdy and I got it in the ground this week. I suppose it was a little late to plant, but at least it's done. His wife has been ill, and two days ago she became so sick he couldn't leave her side. I'm afraid Mrs. Drawdy is dying."

John looked out over the fields.

"Miss DuBose," he said sadly, "this much land won't yield more than three or four bales for you."

"I know...but it's all we can do. We have no other way to raise cash, and even a few bales are better than nothing. Isn't that so?"

"Yes, that's true," he conceded.

"This place never was very profitable for my father," she lamented. "He was a very good physician, but not much of a planter, I'm afraid."

"What happened to your servants?" John asked, glancing off toward a grove of oak trees, where a few brick cabins stood empty and quiet.

"Our two best men went off to the war with my brothers. One of them stayed with a cousin of ours in the army. We don't know what became of the other. Some ran off to follow the Yankees this winter, and then an outbreak of typhoid took almost all remaining, though we did our best to help them. My aunt also came down with it while nursing them, but thankfully she recovered. Just last month, our cook, who was very old, passed away, too."

John thought about Belle Ville, and, wondering how things were there, he began to feel anxious to return.

"Miss DuBose, I think I should go on home, but before I do, I wonder if is there anything I can do to help you ladies today? I should be happy to be of some service to you."

"If there were some pressing need, I should be glad for you to help us, but... perhaps you are not aware that it is the Sabbath."

"Is it? No, I didn't know what day it was. In that case, I'll get my belongings from the barn and be on my way."

They walked to the barn, and Emma waited outside while he retrieved his haversack. He soon emerged with Mrs. Screven, carrying a bucket of milk for her. They returned to the house, where John said his goodbyes and thanked the ladies again for their kindness and hospitality.

CHAPTER THREE

THE HOUSE AT BELLE VILLE was still standing. From the road, John could see the large white two-story structure in the distance at the end of a long avenue of cedar trees. One of the finest dwellings in the parish, it had a stately, classical facade, with a two-tiered portico overarched by a pediment and supported by four Tuscan columns on each level. Several live oaks, gigantic in size, flanked the house on either side, shading the spacious lawn. The place was a sight for sore eyes, yet John's first impression was that the fine old mansion looked rather forlorn. It appeared somewhat weathered and unkempt, the multiple tendrils of viny weeds having crept several yards up some of the walls and columns. The magnolias, cedars, and camellia bushes that dotted the yards were overgrown, and the landscaped gardens which spread out on both sides and to the rear of the house, looked badly in need of tending.

"She is changed for the worse," he thought, "but at least she is not destroyed."

The plantation was quiet and seemed deserted. John looked far off in the direction of the servants' quarters. Had they all left the place, he wondered, or were they at church? As he walked closer to the house, he could faintly hear the sound of singing voices from the chapel about a half a mile away, and realized that at least some souls had remained.

He had almost reached the end of the avenue of cedar trees before anyone in the house caught sight of him. Uncle Israel, the butler, opened the front door and moved down the steps as quickly as his unsteady old legs would allow. The old man seemed to have aged a decade in the two years since John had seen him last; he looked frailer and thinner, and his hair, grayish before, had turned completely white.

"I said, that's Massa John. I knowed it was you," Israel greeted him, meeting him at the foot of the steps.

John had not known what kind of reception to expect from those who had once been called his father's "people," but this one at least seemed glad to see him. They clasped each other's hands, and the old man slipped his arm around John's sleeve and held on to him as they ascended the steps leading up to the portico.

"Did you receive my letter?" he asked Israel.

"Oh, yes, we been 'specting you for days now."

"Has there been any word from Elias?"

They had just entered the house, and in answer to this question Israel pointed to an unopened letter on a table in the entrance hall. John immediately took it up and read it. It was from his cousin Tom Townsend, a surgeon in the Confederate Army, and was written from Bentonville, North Carolina. Elias, John's younger brother, was one of Dr. Townsend's patients, and the letter related the news that they would both be returning to South Carolina as soon as Elias was well enough to travel.

"Good news?" Israel inquired.

"Elias is coming home."

"That's good!"

Tom's letter had taken nearly two weeks to reach Belle Ville, and did not hazard any guesses as to when they might depart. A postscript caught John's particular attention, but he folded the paper and tucked in his pocket to look at again later.

He stepped into one of the front rooms of the house, a large drawing room that looked unchanged at first, until he noticed the absence of certain furnishings, and the damage done to others, namely, a number of family portraits on the walls. Every one of them had been punctured and slashed to some degree. High on the wall in a place of honor, even the portrait of his great-grandfather, Colonel Thomas Hutchinson, a handsome, bewigged man dressed in a uniform from the Revolutionary War, had been cut up across the lower portion of the painting.

Israel informed John that Yankee soldiers had gone at the paintings with their bayonets.

"When were they here?" he asked grimly.

"Back in February, 'twas."

The old butler told him how a "bunch of bluecoats" had come to Belle Ville. They had just begun to rob and ransack the house when one of their scouts rode up and reported to the commander that some rebel cavalry were approaching. Israel said he didn't know whether the Yankees were running away or going out to fight the Confederates, but that they "left in a hurry." The soldiers in the yard had set fire to most of the outbuildings, but did not have time to complete their work, and the field hands had been able to put out the flames before too much damage was done. The soldiers did manage to take off most of the horses, however, and they had not left one dog alive on the place.

"'Cept for old Bonaparte," Israel added. "He was out huntin' with a boy when them Yankees was here."

"What of Reuben?" asked John. "Have you heard from him?"

Reuben had been his body servant during the war. John had

often wondered what became of the young man after he was wounded and taken prisoner.

"Reuben done come home last week," Israel told him.

"I'm glad to hear it."

John almost asked Israel about his son Joseph, but knew that the old man would be reluctant to speak of him. Joseph had disappeared during the second year of the war, and was thought to have headed for the coast, to an area under enemy control.

Answering a series of inquiries about Mr. Childress, the overseer, and others at Belle Ville, the butler followed John upstairs. He went into his old bedroom and opened a wardrobe that held his clothes and old militia uniforms and equipment. There he found a gun belt, a revolver and ammunition. He took out the pistol and inspected it.

"Any other arms in the house?" he asked Israel, who was standing in the doorway watching him.

Israel remembered that there were some hunting rifles hidden away in a closet under the stairway.

"Good, we'll leave them there for now."

The old man looked at John with a curious and concerned look, and then glanced at the revolver he was holding.

"I don't plan to use this unless I have to," John explained. "But I'm assuming there isn't much law around here right now, and I mean to protect this place."

Israel nodded in understanding.

"I'll sleep in Father's room from now on and keep this with me," he added, eyeing the bullet chambers he had just filled.

As John was holstering the gun, he happened to catch a glimpse of himself in the long mirror attached to the door of the wardrobe. He paused and studied his poorly chopped beard and hair in disgust.

"How's your barbering, Israel?" he asked.

After a hot bath, a luxury he had not enjoyed for over a year, John took out some of his old civilian clothes and tried them on. He had become a little thinner, but not so much that his clothes did not still fit. Israel had shaved him and cut his hair nicely. When he faced the mirror, he thought he looked well, but much older. The slight downward slant of his brows and eyes had become a little more pronounced, giving a suggestion of sadness to his expression, and though it disappeared when he smiled, it seemed to him that there was nothing youthful about his face anymore–nothing left of the boy in it.

When he was alone, he took out the letter from his cousin Tom and read over it again. The doctor was vague about Elias's condition, but John was grateful to know that his brother was at least still alive. The letter looked hastily written, and the postscript which he had noted earlier was nearly illegible. It was something about John's father, the words "Your father" being the only ones clear at first. He finally deciphered the scrawl to read: "Your father, on our last meeting, asked me to remind you about the <u>place</u>."

John was reminded of a conversation with his father on his last visit home when Mr. Hutchinson, fearing an invasion into the interior of the state, had told his son where he would hide the family's valuables if that seemed imminent.

He went into his father's bedroom, the centerpiece of which was a large, antique canopy bed with a finely-carved headboard that extended halfway up the wall. He remembered that his father had shown him how the house had been constructed in such a way that one room of the lower floor projected several feet below this second floor room and had its attic space adjacent to it, creating a small chamber behind the wall where the bed was situated. There was no entrance to that chamber. Mr. Hutchinson's idea was to cut out the wall behind the headboard, create a secret access hidden by the bed, and use the little attic as a hiding place.

John pushed the heavy bed away from the wall and could see the rectangular opening which had been cut into it and closed up with a thin board. He pried at the corners of the panel, pulled it out, and looked into the shadowy hiding place. His eyes dilated, not only from the darkness of the attic space, but at the sight of what it contained. It was full of boxes, chests, and parcels tied in paper wrappings. Further back, he could see the silhouettes of frames and silverware. There was a sheet of paper near the opening. He picked it up and saw that it was a list of the hidden items, including jewelry, important papers, and money.

"What kind of money?" John wondered with a sinking heart. "Confederate?"

He lit a candle and put his head inside the space, holding up the light to look around. The gilt of the frames and the polished surfaces of the silver reflected the light of the flame with multiplied glints of yellow and chrome. A large painting was propped in front of him, a second portrait of his great-grandfather Thomas Hutchinson created by a renowned artist of the time, and he was glad to see that it was unharmed. He opened a few boxes. The first was full of photographs and miniature portraits of family members. The second held Confederate securities, now worthless, and railroad bonds, also of doubtful value. Another box contained his mother's jewelry. He also saw one marked with the name "Reuben." It was full of money Reuben had amassed by hiring himself out, and John remembered that he had given it to his father for safekeeping while he was away in Virginia. He reached for the box and took hold of it, hearing the clinking of coins inside. He was planning to pass it on to its owner, but then thought better of the idea, reasoning that it was probably safer to leave it where it was for now. John lifted the lid of one of the larger chests and found that it contained the money–not paper, but gold. A little note placed on top was marked with the sum of six thousand dollars.

"God bless you, Father!" he cried, letting out a deep exhalation of relief.

His hands were a little shaky with excitement as he closed the chest.

"Thank God!" he murmured, and backed out of the little treasure chamber.

After John replaced the wooden panel and put the bed back into its usual spot, he leaned against one of the massive bedposts feeling stunned and breathless. He had feared the worst; all the way home through South Carolina, seeing all the destruction, he had been dreading what he might find at home. Now he could hardly believe how fortunate he was. Yet even for him, and for Belle Ville, things were extremely precarious.

John decided to take a look at the condition of the plantation and went outside. He walked far enough to view hundreds of acres of the cultivated areas from a distance. A white mist was dissipating over the land as the sun burned through the scattering morning clouds. The familiar fields, expansive and neatly furrowed, looked as they always had this time of year. Their sandy soil was ready to give way to the first tender green of the cotton plants, which would be coming up any day now, and by late summer, the land would be a sea of white bolls ready for the harvest.

Covered with the snow of southern summers, John recited in his mind, recalling a line from a Carolina poet.

This brief inspection reassured him, but he knew he needed to talk with Mr. Childress to find out more about the condition of the place. As he walked in the direction of the overseer's house, he began thinking of the money and other valuables his father had preserved for him, and feeling very thankful again for those things, and for Belle Ville itself, which seemed largely undisturbed, though he had seen enough indications of neglect, and many signs of the destruction that had been attempted. Comparing himself to many people he had encountered lately, he considered himself very fortunate indeed. The war had reduced almost everyone in the state, whether they had been burned out or not, to some degree of poverty. In many cases, it was an extreme degree—utter destitution—and he remembered in particular, with a stab of pity, a poor little family he had encountered only a few days ago on his journey home.

John had met them on a cold afternoon a few days before he reached the DuBose place. As he was passing by what had once been a small farm, he saw a young woman standing near the road at the edge of a woods. She was holding a bundled infant, and two small girls leaned into her skirts as if seeking their mother's protection. Both were clinging to bundles of sticks which they had obviously been gathering for fuel. Though wearing pieces of old blanket as shawls, all three were shivering in the cold breezes. John stopped, doffed his hat, and inclined his head toward the young woman politely. This courtesy emboldened her to approach him and ask if he could give them any food.

"Is this your place?" he asked, gazing at the charred ruins of a house, the only parts of which still standing were two blackened brick chimneys.

"It was," she said. "I've been waiting for my husband to come home, but I haven't heard from him in weeks. If he doesn't come back soon, we'll have to move on to my cousin's house in Amelia, if it's still there. Have you seen the village? Were the houses on Jamison Street burned?"

"I don't know. I'm sorry, but I haven't passed by that way."

"I don't see how we can stay here much longer," the woman fretted. "I've been ill for a while, and the neighbors helped us all they could, but they can't do for us anymore. They can barely feed themselves."

While they spoke John rummaged in his haversack and finally pulled out a few morsels of food. All he had to offer her was some hardtack and a few slivers of dried beef. It was the last of his rations. She took it and divided it three ways, giving somewhat larger portions to her daughters, who put down their little bundles of sticks and began devouring the food immediately.

"I would give them more," she explained in a distressed tone, "but I must nurse my baby."

The young woman had auburn hair and a sprinkling of pale freckles on her face. Though pretty, she was thin and haggard-looking. She wrapped her food into a fold of her rough shawl and asked him his name.

"Thank you, Mr. Hutchinson," she said gratefully. "We weren't sure where our next meal was coming from. I am Mrs. McColl."

"Is there any water around here, Mrs. McColl?"

"There's a big creek back in the woods. The Yankees poisoned our well, so we've been taking all our water from it."

"Any fish in it?"

"Usually."

"If you'll permit me to stay the night here, I'll see if I can catch some supper. Are you in need of firewood?"

"Yes!"

"I'll cut some for you if you have an axe."

Mrs. McColl shook her head sadly.

"We have nothing," she replied.

"No matter. I should be able to find enough wood for cooking. I'll gather as much as I can."

At the edge of the woods John found enough dry sticks and broken branches to make a small fire for a meal. Along with what the little girls had already collected, they managed to come up with a good supply of kindling. He followed Mrs. McColl along a path through the woods, and they soon came to a clearing where an old, decaying log cabin stood. Because of its secluded location, the soldiers who had burned the McColl farm had overlooked it. She told John it had been the original homestead of the place; a hired hand had been living in it for years, but in January he had suddenly taken ill and died.

"It is a poor place, I know," she added, "but without it we might have perished."

John left the pile of wood near the doorstep for the little girls to take inside and went back into the woods to look for more fuel. Mrs. McColl stayed behind to eat her food. His clothes and person were so filthy he was ashamed to ask for a night's shelter even in this humble, ramshackle abode, but the cold breezes promised to turn into cutting, icy winds after dark, and the thought of passing another such night outside was more than he could bear.

Deeper in the woods, he found a dead, dry, fallen tree and snapped off many branches. Its trunk was small enough to pick up and break into pieces against a sturdy standing tree. He unrolled the blanket he wore on his back and used it to carry the load of wood back to the cabin. He had heard the sound of running waters and walked back in that direction until he came in sight of a broad creek shouldered by a low bluff.

John walked over to its bank and looked around. Under a spreading shade tree there was a terraced area with a well-worn spot–a kind of natural seat, no doubt someone's favored fishing perch. He gave a little whistle of jubilation when he happened to spot a cane pole half-hidden in some weeds nearby. It was just what he had been hoping for. The pole even had a line attached to it, though when he pulled it out he saw no hook. The young man lowered his haversack to the ground and crouched over it, pulling out a small pouch of miscellaneous items, among which was a rusty fishing hook.

After he prepared his pole, he looked around for a likely spot to find bait. In a sunny spot he found a big rock which protruded slightly from the bank and overturned it. Sure enough, several fat earthworms squirmed in the damp, loamy soil the rock had hidden, and he captured them before they could escape.

About two hours later, as the sun was going down, he returned to the farm with about a half dozen fish of respectable size in his blanket, along with some wild strawberries he had found in a patch at the edge of the woods. Mrs. McColl cooked the fish over a fire, the largest and warmest the family had enjoyed for many weeks.

The cabin was a small dwelling of only two rooms. There was little in the way of comforts except for a few crude pieces of furniture, some cooking utensils and dishes, and a large family Bible, the only possession Mrs. McColl had been able to save from her farm house at the time of its destruction.

After the meal the young woman secluded herself in the bedroom to nurse her baby, and John entertained the other children by whittling doll figures from two pieces of pine wood, using a pocket knife he had happened across one day by the side of the road. The toys he fashioned were little more than stumps with straight stick arms and vaguely human heads, but the little girls were delighted with them. When they showed them to their mother, she made crude clothes for the dolls with some scraps of cloth, and painted eyes and smiles on them with a quill pen and a few drops of some homemade gall ink which had been left in an old writing table.

That night, John slept on the floor next to the dying fire, while the young woman and her children kept each other warm in a bed in the other room. The next morning, they breakfasted on fish again, and he left the rest with them for another modest meal. Anxious to be on his way, he departed early. Except for a few berries he carried with him, that breakfast was the last food he enjoyed until two days later, when he met Miss DuBose and her aunt.

As John walked past the fields of Belle Ville toward Mr. Childress's house, he wondered, as he had several times in the past few days, what had become of Mrs. McColl and her children. Had her husband returned? He had done what he could to help them, but being little more than a ragged pauper himself at the time, it had not been much. The thought of this helpless, starving family weighed on his mind and conscience so much that he decided he would have to take a wagon to her cabin very soon to offer some assistance.

After John's father lost his overseer to the army, he had great difficulty filling the position. Many of the men whom Mr. Hutchinson might have hired to manage Belle Ville were away at war. The first overseer he engaged turned out to be an immoral man, and a drunkard, and the next one, an incompetent. When the planter finally found Mr. Childress, he considered himself very fortunate.

Ralph Childress was an educated man who had once owned a sizeable plantation in the upstate, but some family financial difficulties had forced him to part with his property and work for others. Enlisting early in 1861, he had been severely wounded in one of the first battles of the war. His right arm had been amputated, and he had returned home to find that his young wife had died in childbirth, along with his newborn daughter. His old job had been taken by another man, so he set out to find work in the parish country, and soon found a place at Belle Ville. Mr. Childress was only partially disabled in the loss of his arm; he was otherwise able-bodied, and, as Mr. Hutchinson found to his relief, experienced, competent, and reliable.

In late January of 1865, Mr. Childress was struck down with the same influenza that had made his employer ill, his case turning more serious with pneumonia. When the Yankees came to Belle Ville in February and barged into his house, the old servant woman taking care of the overseer told them he had smallpox, and the soldiers fled his presence as if fired upon.

At the time John returned to the plantation, Mr. Childress was almost fully recovered, though still convalescing a little.

An aged servant named Maum Betty greeted John at the door and let him in. He found Mr. Childress sitting in a chair by the fireplace, wrapped in light blankets. The morning was chilly, but no fire had been lit since the day promised to turn off warmer.

Mr. Childress made a movement to rise as John came in, but was checked with a gesture. He put out his left hand, and John grasped it briefly in both of his.

"I'm sorry to hear you've been ill, Mr. Childress," he said, "but I understand you're doing much better now."

"Yes, much better, thank you. I'm able to be up and about most of the day now, but I rest as much as I can on Sundays. I'm feeling much stronger now."

John thought he looked well; his face had a healthy color, and his speech and movements were energetic. He was a tall, large-boned, broad-shouldered man, so powerfully built that the subtraction of an arm hardly seemed a diminution of his physical presence, and he seemed no worse in that respect in spite of his illness, except to appear a little less stout. Though his stature was imposing, his deep voice was low and soft, and his broad, square face, with its snub nose and mild blue eyes, had a pleasant and reassuring aspect. The same age as John, he kept his curly, sandy hair cut short and his beard of slightly darker hue neatly trimmed.

John sat down in a chair opposite him; he hesitated to speak, not knowing where to begin with his inquiries about Belle Ville. Mr. Childress waited expectantly, until he realized that he was the one who ought to be doing the talking. He began to give John a report of the conditions on the place which, though difficult, were not as dire as he had feared.

"Two years ago your father began planting less cotton in favor of other crops, to help the cause. We'll have an even smaller crop of cotton this year than usual, but with it being so scarce, it will sell very high."

"I'm glad to hear that," said John.

"I've struck an agreement with the freedmen," Mr. Childress went on to explain. "They're to receive a share of the crops and some provisions for a while. I hope that's satisfactory to you, Mr. Hutchinson."

"I'm sure you know best about that."

"Frankly, no one seems to know what's best to do right now, but all your workers seem to be willing to stay put, possibly until they see how things shake out. There's really not much else they can do."

"You'll stay on, won't you?" asked John, suddenly seized with dread at the thought of running Belle Ville alone.

"I'd like to, sir, for a while at least. I have a brother in

Laurensville who asked me to come help him in his store a while back, but your father was very good to me, and I couldn't just abandon Belle Ville after his death. I managed two other plantations before the war. I'm sure you'll find my testimonial letters among your father's papers."

"My father valued you—that's all the recommendation I need. By all means, Mr. Childress, stay as long as you wish. You're certainly needed here."

"Thank you, Mr. Hutchinson. I'll stay as long as you need me."

John asked him if he had encountered many problems with the freedmen.

"Not so much here at Belle Ville, though I know we are faring better than some. Colonel Heatly told me that some of his people are much changed. He said that they don't show themselves as friendly as they used to, and one or two have been insolent, even threatening. Apparently they've heard so many rumors and tales, they don't know where they stand or what they ought to do. When the colonel came back from the war he found that many of them were under the impression that the government had given them his land."

"Who told them such things?" asked John.

"The Yankee soldiers, I believe," said Mr. Childress. "Colonel Heatly told the freedmen that his plantation was still his own and that no one would stay on it but those who would work. One of his hands happened to talk with Yankee officers who confirmed what the colonel said. This man told the others, and since then Colonel Heatly says they have been working less grudgingly. Recently, some of his workers who left for a while came back to his place. The Yankees were giving them rations for a while, but ordered them to return to their homes. Every planter and farmer I have talked to has a different story, just as every place and person is different."

John shrugged.

"I suppose all this shouldn't surprise me," he said. "They are free now, after all."

"When I spoke with the freedmen here as a group, I fully acknowledged that fact to them, Captain Hutchinson. I told them they were free to do as they pleased, but offered them the proposition that I have already mentioned to you. They have taken Saturdays fully for themselves, but I think they understand that it is in their own best interest to make a good crop. They know the planters need them, and that if we don't work together, whether we like it or not, we shall all starve together. Even so, some still believe they will be given our lands."

"Who knows but it may come!" John speculated, wide-eyed.

"We are certainly at the mercy of our new masters now. God knows what will become of us! Their foot is on our neck, and everyone is bewildered. Many of your father's friends, other planters and farmers, have come here over the last few weeks looking for advice and guidance. Some of them didn't even know he had passed away. They all asked for you, too."

"They are mistaken if they think I have my father's wisdom," John replied somberly.

"Solomon himself wouldn't have the wisdom to deal with such ruin and disorder!" Mr. Childress complained, throwing up his one arm in a gesture of frustration.

"Still," John went on, thinking of the many worse fates that could have befallen his land and his family, "I'm grateful that our people conducted themselves so honorably during the war when they might have done otherwise."

"That's true," Mr. Childress agreed. "They planted the crops and saved the place from fire. Things could have been much worse."

"If you will have them assemble this afternoon, I should like to speak with them and thank them myself."

"I'll do that, sir."

On his way back to the house, John caught sight of a tall, strongly-built young black man walking alone. Though he was no longer wearing the beard he had sported during the war, John immediately recognized Reuben. They greeted each other with a handshake.

"Glad to see you made it back in one piece, Cap'n," Reuben said with his easy smile. "We thought maybe you was dead for a spell there."

"I came pretty close, I suppose."

Reuben bent his head, looking a little contrite.

"I tried to find you Cap'n, but, nobody seemed to know if you was dead or alive, then, after a while, I find out you been captured."

"I'm glad to see that you were not captured, Reuben, nor wounded. By the way, I have that box you left with my father for safe keeping."

Reuben brightened at the mention of his money.

"Will you keep it for me a while longer? They's been some stealing and such going on round these parts. I think it'd be safer with you right now."

John nodded and looked over Reuben's shoulder, noting broken fences, partially burnt outbuildings, and other signs of dilapidation all around the place.

"You're going to stay on, aren't you Reuben?" he asked.

The young man grew serious and looked away.

"I don't know sir," he muttered.

"It's up to you now, but there will be plenty of carpentry work for you at Belle Ville, and all around here for that matter."

"Nobody's got no money to pay me, Cap'n," he complained.

"You'll find it's like that all over the state. But you'll be all right, Reuben. You stay on here, and I'll pay you a fair wage."

"I don't want no Confederate money. It ain't worth nothing now."

"I won't pay you in Confederate money," John promised — but in a strangely muted, constrained tone of voice, startled and displeased by what amounted to a demand from a former servant.

"I'll think on it," said Reuben.

They parted, and John continued on his way, walking out to the family cemetery, where five generations of Hutchinsons slept in the ground. A marble obelisk rose above the grave of Colonel Thomas Hutchinson, a hero of the Revolution, as befitted a man of his rank and accomplishments. The rest of the plots were marked with more modest headstones, and the most recent one, that of his father, bore only a wooden cross as yet. Someone had neatly carved his name and dates into the wood:

Abel Hutchinson, 1801-1865

A marble angel mourned above the resting place of John's mother, sitting atop a gravestone inscribed with her name and an endearment, "*Isabella Glover Hutchinson, Beloved Wife*," along with a verse from the book of Ezekiel: "*Behold, I take away from thee the desire of thine eyes*." Her plot was flanked by two diminutive stones marking the graves of two children who had died as infants. Next to one of these was the headstone of Elise, John's younger sister, a frail little girl who had died at the age of twelve. Its inscription read: "*Fairest, sweetest, daughter & sister. Blessed are the pure in heart, for they shall see God."*

John did not linger long here. The sight of his family's graves, especially that of his father, who had been dead less than three months, became overwhelming, and he had to turn his back and leave them.

Just before dark that evening, seeking solitude, John went out to the upper portico. The early night air was only mildly cool, and there was no breeze. Lighting a cigar he had found in his room, he sat down in a rocking chair and put his feet up on the rail. He had never craved tobacco, having smoked fine cigars chiefly because they were considered something delectable and desirable by his fashionable friends in Charleston rather than for any particular taste for them. After a few puffs on this one, which had an unpleasant flavor, he wondered why he had bothered to light it in the first place. He put it out on the heel of his shoe and tossed it away. A glass of wine would have been a preferable companion, he reflected, but his father had been a teetotaler, and there was no such thing to be found in the house.

The twilight sky was hazy, cloudless, and monotone; except for a dim, fading glow in the west, colorless as white moonstone, the rest of it was a dome of deepening gray, and just as empty as he felt inside. Matters of sheer physical survival having been settled for the moment, John's thoughts had turned inward, to memories of the war, the shock of defeat and failure, and the ruin to which he had returned. They were thoughts that made him so sick at heart that he could not keep them in his mind for long–and yet they were there, as real and vast and undeniable as the darkening skies over his head and in his eyes.

In all his life, he had never felt more lonely and desolate than he did that evening. The house, without his family, especially his father, seemed lifeless and bleak. On a larger scale, all that he had been fighting for–four long years–was lost. The world of his fathers was gone. His country and his state were ruined and subjugated, and would, sooner or later, he feared, be made to drink a cup even more bitter than that of military defeat.

What made these things so painful for him was not so much the horrors he had seen during the war, or the kinsmen and friends he had lost, though these were terrible enough, but the fact that it had all been for nothing. So much struggle, death, deprivation, and suffering–all for naught!

The only consolation he had now was the consciousness that he had done his duty; he had done his best and all he could, and would have gladly sacrificed his life, many times over if possible, to have seen a different outcome.

But what was he to do now?

John thought about the agreement Mr. Childress had struck with the freedmen, and wondered how long those arrangements would last. The field hands who had stayed on might soon begin showing signs of restlessness and discontent, just as those of Colonel Heatly had. The workers could leave Belle Ville, one by one, a few at a time, or all at once–leave him high and dry, with hundreds of acres of land without hands to work it. Then what?

It was John's natural and normal disposition to be hopeful and cheerful, but in the face of such disheartening possibilities, he could sense despair trying to taking hold in him. He felt it creeping into his veins like a slow poison, and suddenly rose from his chair and went inside the house as if to flee from it. He knew that if he was to survive he could not dwell on such deadly memories and thoughts. Perhaps in the future there would be time and strength for such reflections, but not now, not yet. He told himself he had to make the best of his situation as it was, and that he ought to feel nothing but gratitude that he was better off than most others, at least for the present.

John went back to his father's old room and sat down in a comfortable chair to take off his boots. Trying to think of pleasant things, he reminded himself that his brother Elias and cousin Tom would be home soon. He wondered how Tom's sister Laura was doing and decided he should call on her tomorrow to find out.

Then he remembered Miss Emma DuBose.

CHAPTER FOUR

THE NEXT MORNING, enjoying the luxuries of comfort and home, John lay in his bed and thought about the day ahead of him. He remembered that his first obligation was to pay a visit to his cousin Laura in the village. After that, he thought he might ride over to the DuBose farm.

As the memories of Miss DuBose grew clearer and more vivid in his mind, he was motivated to get out of bed and go into his old room to find something presentable to wear. There he opened the wardrobe and contemplated all the clothes it held, most neatly folded on shelves, except for a few coats which hung from hooks on the inside of the door. Despite the scarcities of the war, his father had managed to preserve much of his old apparel. Among the possibilities were several handsome, expensive suits of light, earthy colors, and beautiful silk vests, some of them striped or embroidered, but they all struck him as inappropriate attire for someone in mourning. After a little more deliberation, he pulled out a dark suit and a plain pearl grey vest to put on.

The sight of his old civilian clothes, and part of an old militia uniform, drew his mind to the past. Each of them called up particular memories, and while John dressed, he studied them again, thinking of the times he had worn each of them.

The finest suit he owned had been made for him in Paris during a grand tour of Europe made possible by the generosity of a wealthy relation. A few months after his graduation from the Military College in Charleston, John had gone to work for his uncle, Mr. John Hutchinson the elder, the owner of a Charleston cotton exporting establishment. The following year, this same wealthy gentleman financed a trip for John and his cousin and best friend Preston Townsend. Both young men had inclinations toward a mercantile career, and their uncle considered that it would be educational and profitable for them to see England and the continent and at the same time acquaint themselves with the commercial houses there with whom Hutchinson & Company did business. Provided with letters of introduction which they did not fail to present to the appropriate persons, John and his cousin did in fact make useful contacts. They learned a great deal about the international cotton trade, while at the same time enjoying themselves as tourists for seven months seeing the usual popular attractions.

When John returned to Charleston, he resumed his job at Hutchinson & Company as a lowly assistant to the shipping clerk, but it quickly became apparent that he was suited for higher responsibilities, and within a matter of weeks he had passed on his sampling bag and marking pot and ink to a new assistant, and was moved up into the position of clerk. Among other duties, he kept the shipment and order books, and before long, he was handling some of the correspondence. Mr. Gordon, a partner in the firm, declared that no clerk could write a better business letter than young Mr. Hutchinson, and that when John acquired a mastery of particulars known only to more experienced and knowledgeable hands, he would turn the responsibility over to him in its entirety. John's fluency in French also proved very useful to the company, which carried on an extensive business with France and other countries on the continent. John's grandmother, a lady of Huguenot descent, had taught him to speak French since infancy, and what he forgot after her death was refreshed when he took courses in the language in college.

John's father wanted him to learn about business, but only insofar as it would be useful to the young man when he took on the responsibilities of a planter. Consequently Mr. Abel Hutchinson was very displeased when his son informed him one day that he intended to make Hutchinson & Company his occupation and Charleston his home. Knowing John well, Mr. Hutchinson suspected that his decision had as much to do with his predilection for the entertainments and social life of the city as his professional ambitions. It was true that John preferred lively Charleston to his comparatively quiet parish in the middle part of the state, but it was also true that at that time in his life, he had no wish to take on the heavy responsibility of a large plantation and all the souls and burdens attached to it. Someday, he knew he probably would have to take it on, but as long as his father was healthy and strong, he preferred to remain on his present course in life.

In Charleston, John lived at his uncle's mansion on Tradd Street. The old businessman, a widower, had fathered three children, all of whom had died young, and he had since then diverted all his paternal impulses to his nieces and nephews, especially his favorite and namesake, John. The elder Mr. John Hutchinson provided gifts and extra money to the young man and made sure that he was as well dressed and equipped as any Charleston-born blue blood, and sometimes allowed his nephew to entertain friends at his fine home. John had many friends, and even some of them who were from far wealthier families envied his good fortune in possessing the proverbial rich and indulgent uncle.

During his first few months in Charleston, John was asked to serve as a second in a duel. He declined, but not long afterward, came close himself to drawing pistols with another young man over a rumored insult, an incident that sent his pious father into paroxysms of exasperation and near despair. Though John was not overly proud or hot tempered, it was expected that a gentleman should defend his honor and reputation, and he was prepared to do that. Fortunately, friends acting as go-betweens ironed out the matter to the mutual satisfaction of both parties, and it passed off as a misunderstanding, with no harm done.

A few of John's closer friends were members of the Charleston Light Dragoons, a mounted volunteer militia company composed of elite young men mostly from the Charleston area. One of them invited John to join. Though attracted by the glamour of a cavalry unit, he hesitated at first, but when he was assured that a strict military discipline was not enforced in this gentlemanly group, he submitted his application and was promptly accepted. The duties of the Dragoons were not onerous, and they were much admired by the crowds, especially the young ladies, who watched them on parade and in their functions at ceremonial events. John considered it an honor to become a part of this prestigious militia organization and to serve beside young men from the finest families of the state, and even his father (a great believer in civic service) was proud of his affiliation, and provided him with a good horse and the money for his uniforms and equipment.

On the day of his first muster as a Dragoon, Mr. Hutchinson and his younger son Elias visited Charleston to congratulate John and admire him in action. The following morning, standing near the courthouse, they watched him ride past with the rest of his company on their way out of the city. The Dragoons had been called upon by the governor of the state to ensure that two convicted murderers were executed in Walterboro, a village some fifty miles away. These two white men had hunted down a runaway slave with dogs and killed the man, and for their brutality, had been sentenced to death. Because one of them was from a well-to-do family, it was feared that his friends or relations might try to effect his escape, and so an armed guard was deemed necessary. Honored to be of service to the governor, the Dragoons carried out their mission with appropriate vigilance and solemnity. The criminals were transported to Walterboro on a journey without incident, and after witnessing the hanging, the young militia men returned to Charleston.

A few months after John joined the Charleston Light Dragoons, there was another important development in his life. He fell in love.

John first saw her in church, on a fine, balmy morning in the very early spring of 1860, while he was attending the wedding of a relative in in Beaufort, South Carolina. His first cousin Caroline Porter was marrying Peter Johnstone, a young naval officer. During the ceremony, John noticed a young woman with lovely brown hair seated in a pew a few rows away from him. Her profile was striking, and when she happened to turn around for a moment, he saw her face in full. From this one brief glimpse, he experienced a kind of shock to his senses, and sat in his pew preoccupied with this feeling throughout the wedding. When he was able to observe her at much closer range during the breakfast that followed, he thought she was the most beautiful and graceful creature he had ever seen.

After the meal was over, he was standing with Miss Emily Parker, another female cousin, and his sixteen year-old brother Elias, who had noticed John's awestricken look and followed his eyes to the source of it. Miss Parker also noticed John's entrancement and asked him if he would like to be introduced to the young lady.

"That is Miss Elizabeth Mason, a very dear friend of mine, and a cousin of the groom," she said with a confidential smile.

Suppressing mirth at his brother's expression, and sensing that he would now be ignored for the rest of the day, Elias left John and Miss Parker to seek out more congenial and interesting company.

"Would you be so kind as to introduce me to your friend now?" John asked his cousin.

She took his arm and guided him in the desired direction. They waited politely as Miss Mason concluded a conversation with another wedding guest. John was standing close enough to touch her, and breathed in her perfume. She was so beautiful that his heart began to beat with crazed, irregular throbs of varying intensity, and when the young woman finished her conversation and turned to him and Miss Parker, it was all he could do to produce a smile without a nervous twitch.

"I should like for you to meet my cousin," said Miss Parker. "Miss Mason, permit me to introduce Mr. Hutchinson."

The young lady smiled and inclined her head.

"It's a great pleasure," John said with a bow.

"This was such a lovely wedding," Miss Mason remarked. "The bride, your cousin, was simply exquisite, and I thought Peter looked extremely handsome in his dress uniform."

Knowing that her friend had a predilection for military men, Miss Parker piped up to inform her that John was a member of the Charleston Light Dragoons.

"How splendid!" she responded, looking pleased. "I saw them on parade last year, and admired them very much. I must have glimpsed you then, Mr. Hutchinson."

"I am sorry you did not, Miss Mason," he said. "I have only

been with the Dragoons a few months, and was not in the city at the time you mention."

"My cousin," Miss Parker explained, "was in Europe the greater part of last year. His father is Mr. Abel Hutchinson of Belle Ville in St. Thaddeus Parish."

The mention of that parish drew a look of special interest from Miss Mason.

"Do you live near the village of Amelia?" she asked him. "I have a dear friend who resides there, a Miss Susan Heatly."

"Belle Ville is only about ten miles from Amelia, and I do know Miss Heatly. She is a good friend of my sister Isabella."

"I believe I have heard Susan speak of a Miss Isabella Hutchinson. She married Mr. Edmund Stewart a few years ago. Is this the same lady?"

"The very same," said John.

"Then I have met your sister here today. An elegant lady."

"We call her Belle," said Miss Parker. "Very fittingly, I think."

Miss Mason graciously agreed.

After more conversation (but much too little as far as John was concerned), several wedding guests came up to speak with Miss Mason, and he was forced to share her company. Finally, he had to give her up altogether as her mother took possession of her and drew her off to talk with other relatives.

"That went well," Miss Parker remarked as she walked away on John's arm.

"You think so?" he asked tensely.

"Of course! You made a good impression. I can tell she admires you."

Later, as the morning wore on, John stood alone, and inconspicuously, he hoped, watching Miss Mason from afar. After a while, his cousin George Taylor came up to speak with him with Elias in tow, and immediately noticed something oddly serious about him.

"What's the matter?" he asked John.

"Lovesick!" Elias gleefully whispered in George's ear.

John overheard his brother and gave the boy such a look that he backed off and left them without another word, this time laughing out loud once he had reached a safe distance.

Mr. George Washington Taylor, Esquire, who practiced law in Charleston with his brother Albert, was about five years older than John, and matched him very closely in height and build. He had glossy, luxuriant, dark brown hair and an equally handsome beard that was always carefully tended and groomed.

"Looks as though Elias may be in need of some protection," the young lawyer observed humorously, speaking with a strong, distinct Charleston accent. "Tell him I will act as his solicitor if he wants one."

There was no answer from John. George looked across the room at the young lady he was watching and smiled more broadly.

"So, John Hutchinson is now numbered among Miss Mason's admirers," he said. "It's a long list, you know."

"I am not surprised. Do you know her?"

"Only slightly. Her father is a client of our firm."

"Are you on the list?" John asked, turning to eye George briefly.

"No-ho!" he laughed. "I never mix business with pleasure. But I do think Miss Mason is very beautiful."

"She is certainly that."

They both gazed at the young lady in silence, and after a while John asked his cousin, in a somewhat bantering tone, "Keeping your head buried in law books and legal documents as usual, George?"

"Have to. Very busy these days with several important cases."

"You're a single-minded man."

"It's my curse," George chuckled softly.

John tore his eyes away from Miss Mason again for a few moments to study his earnest, diligent cousin with unconcealed amusement.

"You know, George," he said, "I predict that you will present a very interesting spectacle when you fall in love. I think it will be rather like watching a big, sturdy building tumbling down in an earthquake."

"You're an interesting spectacle yourself," George replied a little testily, bristling, and making a move to turn away. "I shall leave you to your contemplations."

"There now, cousin," John said soothingly, giving him a conciliatory pat on the back, "I was only jesting."

Mollified, George remained, and the two young men began conversing about politics, a subject hardly less touchy than love. When the wedding festivities were over, John traveled back to Charleston by steamboat with George and his older brother. Albert was anxious to get back to his wife and newborn son, and was thinking of them as he stood on the deck with his brother and cousin. All three men were quiet as they looked out over the choppy coastal seas.

John had his own preoccupation as he watched the hypnotic movements of the waters. More and more possessed by Miss Mason, he was picturing her again in his mind, and wondering if there was perhaps something prophetic in the fact that they had met at a wedding. He liked to think that there might be.

The following week in Charleston, Miss Parker arranged to

bring John along on a friendly visit to the Mason household, and soon afterwards, a courtship began. It was interrupted for a matter of months when Miss Mason went abroad to Europe with her family during the summer, but when she returned to Charleston in October, he pursued her more ardently than ever. In December, after obtaining permission from her father to do so, John asked Miss Mason to marry him, but the young lady put off giving him a definite answer, protesting that she wished to know him better before making such a decision.

In February of the following year, when John danced with Miss Mason at the Saint Cecilia Society ball, he was still waiting for her answer. Less than three months later, the war began, and the Charleston Light Dragoons were called into service in the coastal defenses.

Mr. William Mason, a wealthy Charleston merchant, had been in declining health for several months at the time John proposed to his daughter. Though the finest physicians had been called in on his case, his condition slowly and gradually grew worse. In the spring of 1861 he became gravely ill, and his wife and daughter tended to him day and night.

Elizabeth and her father were very close; he confided in her as he did in no one else; and early in his illness, he broached a subject with her that they had never talked about before–religion– and after their unusual conversation, the young woman observed this formerly proud, irreligious, and self-sufficient man begin to undergo a transformation. Eventually, he surprised most of his family and everyone who knew him by sending for a clergyman.

The minister Mr. Mason chose was highly regarded in the city and throughout the state for his piety and learning. He came to the house frequently, talking and praying with the sick man, and

Elizabeth formed a friendship with the minister, who often talked with her and her mother after his visits with Mr. Mason. He was relatively young, being thirty-five years of age, and a childless widower. Though Mr. Mason's physical condition steadily worsened, his spirit grew more humble and serene, and at the end, his peaceful death made a deep impression on his daughter.

During the last phases of her father's illness, John began to notice a change in Elizabeth. She became distant, preoccupied, and indifferent to many things they had formerly enjoyed together. Such pleasures as the theater, the races, and social gatherings no longer seemed to interest her, but, thinking that she was only grieving for her dying parent, John paid little attention to the change in her temperament. Just after the war began, he asked her once more to marry him. Again, still unsure than ever of their suitability for each other, Elizabeth asked for more time, and once more, John was disappointed and bewildered. He was certain that she loved him; she had accepted his attentions over those of other suitors from richer, grander families–so why did she hesitate? With no idea that her affections were turning toward a young minister, John finally attributed Elizabeth's continued resistance and indecision to an understandable preoccupation with her father.

After Mr. Mason passed away in late August, John knew that Elizabeth could not consider matrimony until a period of mourning had been observed. He waited patiently for two months, during which time, busy with military duties, he saw little of her. Then one afternoon, handsomely attired in his best uniform, he came to her house, and happening to find her alone, asked her if she would now give her promise to marry and set a date for their wedding on some appropriate day in the future. This time Miss Mason gave him a definite answer. It was no.

Asking his forgiveness, but saying nothing more, Elizabeth

turned and walked away from him, and the next thing he knew, he was blinking his eyes against the bright sunlight outdoors. Somehow, his legs had carried him out of the Mason house and on to the sidewalk, and were taking him toward Tradd Street. When he reached his uncle's house, his mind still reeling in stunned disbelief, he leaned against the tall brick wall that surrounded it feeling physically ill. He opened the gate and walked unsteadily up to the door. Caesar the butler spoke to him; John did not even hear him. He went upstairs to his room and fell on his bed. His own servant Joseph came in, concerned, and asked if he had need of anything.

"Yes," John answered in a dull tone, not looking up, "bring me something to drink."

Knowing what he meant, Joseph frowned.

John spent the next several days drinking heavily. His uncle was out of town at the time, and knew nothing of it, but an elderly cousin who called at the house one afternoon learned about John's dissipation from the servants and passed on the information to his father, who wrote him scathing letters. He made himself so ill with wine and liquor that it took another several days for him to recover. He finally emerged from his bodily malaise feeling only a little less sick at heart, not having had much success at drowning his troubles in drink.

The pain of rejection began to inspire some ungentlemanly resentment toward Miss Mason, and one night, sullen, brooding, and unable to sleep, John sat down at a writing table and tried to tally up a list of her bad qualities, though he soon found that he could put little to paper. Still, he told himself, the young lady was too reserved, too remote; she lacked warmth, and possessed little in the way of a sense of humor. These were very grave faults, he decided over several glasses of wine, with a mind muddled by them. He then recalled an unpleasant conversation with her in which she had reproached him for neglecting church services. It was true (and he had to admit it to himself) that he had grown careless of religious observances since taking up residence in Charleston. Bent on enjoying his new independence and a measure of autonomy, he had for quite a while scarcely given religion a thought outside Sunday services, but he bristled now with newfound indignation over her reproach, and decided that Miss Elizabeth Mason had become far too religious since her father's illness. Most likely, she would not have been a good match for him; he would never have been able to please her, heathen that he was.

Eventually, thinking more clearly, but also nursing wounded pride, John came to the conclusion that this break with Miss Mason might have been for the best. Perhaps he had merely been infatuated with her, and had not really loved her after all. She was so beautiful, it was possible. He began to believe it probable as time wore on, and his pain diminished, slowly but steadily.

In November 1861, the Dragoons were stationed in an area near the coast about sixty miles from Charleston to watch for the possible approach of the enemy inland and to guard an important railroad. John was still suffering because of Miss Mason, but managed to find enough distractions to keep her off his mind most of the time.

His friends and comrades were always eager to relieve the boredom and monotony of camp life with any luxuries they could provide for themselves, enjoying the diversions of card playing, and horse races they held among themselves and other cavalry companies in the area. There was betting on both these pastimes. John usually won and lost roughly equal amounts with his wagers, until one embarrassing and considerable loss came his way, and he was forced to apply to his uncle to pay off his debt. The elder Mr. John Hutchinson expressed his profound disapproval, but gave his nephew the money anyway, along with a stern warning, and reported John's vices to his father.

One afternoon at the Dragoon camp, Joseph was sitting under a tree studying his Bible and jotting notes in the margins. Like some of the other servants who had been born and raised at Belle Ville, he had been taught to read for this very purpose, and, along with one or two others, he had also learned to write. As he was meditating over a passage in Romans, a soldier walked up to him, called his name, and handed him two letters addressed to "John Hutchinson, Jr." Joseph went to look for John, and was not surprised to find him in one of his favorite spots in the company of about a half dozen of his friends. It was an unusually warm day, and under the shade of a large spreading live oak tree, they had set up a card table, and were lounging around it in camp chairs, while a servant with a wine bottle on a tray moved about and refilled their glasses. They talked and laughed freely as they studied their cards, tossed out their wagers, smoked cigars and cheroots, and sipped a fine champagne.

A new, very young recruit watching the card game was commenting on what he regarded as the rather lax military discipline of the group. Though he granted that the Dragoons carried out their picket duties and maintained their horses and arms well, the young man said he was surprised by the amount of time they spent at leisure.

"What, would you have us in drills half the day?" an older Dragoon protested, adding, a little haughtily, "Surely you don't think that gentlemen require the same rigor of discipline as private soldiers."

"But–after all," the young man objected somewhat awkwardly, "aren't we to hold ourselves in readiness?"

Suddenly absorbed by an interesting development in their

card game, the players let his question go unanswered. While John was contemplating his hand, Joseph approached. He stopped and looked on the scene of gambling and drinking for a few moments before he spoke, his handsome black face plainly displaying his disapproval. One of the Dragoons noticed this and found it amusing.

"Your man does not approve of us," he said to John facetiously.

John looked up and acknowledged Joseph's presence with a nod, and then replied indifferently, "Joseph does not approve of anyone except for the good Lord, and perhaps my father."

"That company is far above us, indeed!" another gentleman laughed.

After the general mirth died away, John asked Joseph what he wanted. He was handed the letters, one of which was enclosed in an envelope bordered in black. On both John recognized the handwriting of his aunt, Mrs. Catherine Townsend. She had recently been widowed with the death of his uncle, so the sight of the mourning stationery did not alarm him at first, but she usually only wrote to him when she had some news of his cousin Preston, and he was anxious to know what this might be.

"Excuse me, gentlemen," he said, rising.

John was slightly inebriated as he walked back to his tent, followed by Joseph, but he quickly sobered as he began to read the contents of the first letter, which bore an earlier postmark than the other. It was a short note stating that his cousin Press had been seriously wounded in battle and taken to a hospital in Richmond, Virginia. John looked at the date of the note again; it was over a week old and must have been delayed somehow in its delivery. He wondered why his uncle John had not contacted him about this matter, but then remembered that Mr. Hutchinson was out of town on business. A weakness in his knees prompted him to sit down on his cot as he opened the second letter, the one bordered in black. After scanning a line or two, John let the paper fall to his feet, covering his face with both hands. Joseph looked on with sympathy, surmising that John's cousin had been killed. The letter reported that the wound his cousin had received was a mortal one.

John fell back on the bed, overwhelmed with grief. Preston Townsend, his first cousin, his best friend, and a man as close to him as a brother, was dead. He could hardly believe such terrible news. After a few minutes he asked Joseph to read the rest of the letter to him.

The young man picked up the piece of paper and read aloud slowly, sometimes finding the elegant but shaky handwriting a little difficult to decipher. Mrs. Townsend wrote that her stepson Preston had been shot down on the field of battle leading his men. As soon as the family received a telegram bringing the sorrowful news, she had traveled to Richmond to nurse him herself in an army hospital. A ball had entered his pelvic area and lodged there, causing an agony which even morphine could not alleviate. Press lingered for a week with no hope of recovery, and his stepmother was thankful when he was finally released from his terrible sufferings. She had prayed with him several times during his lucid moments, and felt now that she could be at peace concerning the safety of his soul.

Joseph paused in his reading and looked over at John. His face was turned away.

"That's enough," he said, and asked to be left alone.

That night, John was unable to sleep. Anguished and oppressed with a feeling of shame, he was thinking of Press and numerous other friends and relatives who had gone to Virginia, where the real fighting was. Men were dying in Virginia, he reflected. While he enjoyed relative ease and safety, men were dying in that place.

Why—he asked himself—why wasn't he there?

The Dragoons had enlisted for a period of three months in state service, and in late November, that time came to an end. The day before they were to be mustered out, John presented himself to his commanding officer and tendered his resignation. He had obtained a commission as a lieutenant in a South Carolina cavalry company from his home district that would soon be on its way to Virginia.

John's proud and generous uncle insisted that he should have a new uniform even finer than the one he had worn in the Dragoons, and outfitted him in one, along with the best equipment and accouterments. As John's horse had developed a persistent lameness in one leg, his uncle purchased an expensive thoroughbred for his use in the cavalry. The owner of this horse had called him Bellerophon under the mistaken notion that this was the name of the steed of the great Alexander, and was mystified at John's amusement when he expounded at length on the animal's martial namesake. Bellerophon was a magnificent sorrel, and John was very proud of him, but the animal's rather grandiose name was soon shortened to Billy.

The new regiment John had joined was traveling to Virginia by railroad from his parish, and he went back to Belle Ville for a few days to see his father and brother before he had to leave. He returned there dressed in civilian clothes, bringing one of his old uniforms and other clothing and belongings back with him to store at home.

The first person John met in the house was Uncle Israel, who was coming down the stairs with a look full of excitement and jubilation. His happiness spilled over in his greeting to John, whose shoulders he shook as he laughed and sighed, "Thank the Lord, thank the Lord."

"What is it, Israel?" he asked, smiling at the normally impassive butler. "What are you so happy about?"

Israel announced that his son Joseph was going to be a preacher, that he had been "called to preach the gospel."

"Ah-h..."

John cast an obviously gloomy look upstairs, but congratulated Israel.

"I suppose that means he is leaving my service. Tell Joseph I shall miss him. He will be difficult to replace."

"Oh, yes, sir! I'll tell him!"

Israel continued on his way, and John lingered at the foot of the stairs a little while mulling over this unexpected development. He was not so irked about losing his manservant, though he did regret that to some degree, but knowing his father as he did, John was sure that Mr. Hutchinson was at this very moment contemplating a comparison between his own eldest son and Israel's, and finding the former lacking. For the past few years, having failed to live up to the lofty standard of character and conduct that Mr. Hutchinson expected in his children, John had received little else but disapproval from his father.

"He's envying old Israel now!" he thought grudgingly.

A moment later he heard the voice of his brother Elias from the hallway, where Israel was sharing the good news with him.

"Well," John said to himself, "there's Father's consolation. At least Elias is not a disappointment to him."

His younger brother walked up to him and now, as always, greeted him with a tilt of the head and a half-serious, half-joking look that inquired, "Well, have you forsaken your wickedness yet?" But at least his censure was mixed with good humor and a natural admiration for an older brother. The two were happy to see each other, and expressed their mutual affection with an exchange of droll, disparaging remarks and sounding claps on the back.

Elias had a slimmer physique than his brother, but at seventeen, was nearly as tall as John. His smooth, delicate face had always had an almost feminine beauty, and becoming acutely aware of this fact in his early teen years, Elias had kept his dark brown hair very short except for a thick shock that fell over one of his finely-formed, slanting brows, for the purpose of creating a distracting asymmetry. Lately he had grown something of a mustache, and was attempting to add a goatee to it. Like his father, Elias was devout, and had recently made the decision to prepare for a career in the ministry. He had just come home from his studies with Rev. Shubrick, the Episcopal priest who lived in the nearby village of Amelia.

Elias put his arm around his brother's broad shoulders as they walked up the stairs together and began a conversation John had hoped to avoid while at home, knowing it must inevitably end in arguments and hard feelings.

"You must help me convince Father to let me join the army," the boy was saying energetically. "I think it's grand that you're going to Virginia. I wish to go, too."

He was a passionate young man, and the fervor of patriotism sweeping over the state had taken hold of him powerfully. The indignation he felt over the war which had been brought against his country burned as hotly in him as his religious zeal.

"You're only seventeen," John reminded him.

"I shall be eighteen soon."

"Soon? In five months!"

"Five months...the war might be over by then," Elias

muttered slowly, as if thinking aloud.

"You should thank God if it is," his brother replied, with a touch of anger that surprised and abashed the boy a little.

"Yes, you're right, John," he said. "But I want to help make sure that it is over soon, and that we're victorious. I wish to do my part."

"You know Father's not going to allow it yet. He told me a while back that he's planning to send you to the theological seminary in Camden."

"Oh, you know I'm too young for that," Elias responded gleefully. "Besides, I hear that the school is going to have to shut down soon. All the students are joining the army!"

"Well then, you can continue to study with Reverend Shubrick, or go to college in Charleston. That's what he'll say."

In this matter, John found himself in agreement with his father, not much relishing the idea of his young brother going off to war.

They found their father at the top of the stairs; Mr. Hutchinson had just emerged from his room, where he had been talking with Israel.

"John!" he cried happily, and made an unusual demonstration of affection by putting his arm around his eldest son's shoulder for a few moments.

He was a tall, handsome man of sixty with a stooped but still sturdy physique. His hair, which was very thin on the top, revealing a shiny pink scalp, was a mixture of oyster white and a few remaining strands and streaks of its former hue of light brown.

Mr. Hutchinson was overflowing in his enthusiasm about Joseph, and very pleased to have the chance to see John before he had to leave for Virginia.

"Israel just told us the news," Elias remarked, glad to see

that his father was in a good mood.

"I am so pleased! The Methodists are going to license him to preach, and I am not surprised, for I know him to be an honest and upright young man, and sincere in his faith."

"Joseph will make a fine preacher," John agreed.

"I don't know why Israel was so timid about passing on his son's request to me. As if I could refuse the old fellow anything! Come, let's go downstairs and talk. I wish to know all about your new regiment, John."

Later in the afternoon, after a long conversation with his father, John went looking for Elias and found him in the library. His brother was sitting in a large armchair with a book, his long legs draped over one side, and one hand hanging down to the floor, his fingers fiddling with a strip of leather that served as a bookmark. John smiled and tried to imagine Elias as he might be in a few years, as an adult, and a clergyman too dignified and serious to sprawl and lounge in a chair this way.

"What are you reading?" he asked, though not particularly interested.

"Robertson's sermons," Elias replied, smiling and throwing up his free hand in a flourishing welcome.

"Are they dull?"

"No, they're very good."

"Can you tear yourself away? I haven't seen you in a while, and I thought you might like to make good on your last threat. Or have you forgotten everything Mr. Siegling taught us?"

John was referring to one of their favorite tutors, a German gentleman who was a great believer in physical fitness and who had instructed them in wrestling and other sports. For several years now Elias had been trying to best his brother in various tests of strength, and in his most recent attempt, thought he had come close to at least matching him, and had promised to prevail on their next contest.

"You'll soon be losing that smug grin, brother," he said laughingly, swinging out of the chair.

A friendly wrestling match ensued, but as usual John proved himself the stronger. Mr. Hutchinson heard the sound of scuffling, grunts, and laughter coming from his library, and looked in. By this time the two brothers had gone to the floor, and John had Elias pinned down on the carpet, though he refused to yield, and was still struggling. As their father watched, he saw them as little boys again, and for a moment, despite his patriotism, he fervently wished that they were still boys. He left the room before they noticed his presence and walked upstairs again. The door of John's room was standing open, and his new uniform was laid out on his bed. Mr. Hutchinson went in to take a closer look at it, running his fingers across the dark gray wool of one sleeve.

Feeling a pang of compunction as he thought of John, he wondered as his mind's eye looked back over the years, if he had been too harsh and domineering with his sons, especially his eldest. The fear of losing John had softened his heart, and he was viewing him in a much different light than before, realizing that, though the young man had disappointed and grieved him many times, he never done anything truly dishonorable. Mr. Hutchinson, having been raised to be always mindful of duty, had lived his life accordingly—as a vestryman of his church, a commissioner of free schools, a member of various learned and benevolent societies, and a state legislator of several terms—and it was difficult for him to understand how his son John, a young man raised with the same strict discipline and religious instruction, and provided with a good education and many good examples, might wish to live only for his pleasures, with little or no thought of his duties to others, or to God.

But perhaps all that was passing away, Mr. Hutchinson

thought hopefully, and childish things would now be put aside. Wasn't this uniform of service a proof of his manhood and worth? Gazing down at the gray suit, he suddenly felt very proud of John, and had no doubt that he would prove to be a fine officer. He only wished that he could be at ease concerning his son's spiritual welfare.

Mr. Hutchinson heard footsteps on the stairs, and John soon appeared in the doorway. He was surprised to find his father in his room.

"I was just admiring your uniform," Mr. Hutchinson explained.

"It's a very fine one," said John, walking in, his face a little flushed from his exertions with Elias. "I shall be proud to wear it."

A spasm of fatherly love mixed with sorrow and fear suddenly caused Mr. Hutchinson to embrace his son. This was an occurrence so rare and singular that John could not restrain his emotion, and, burying his head in his father's shoulder, uttered words which had not been on his lips for many years.

"I love you, Father."

"My son," he said tearfully, "I love you dearly. Come back to me."

When they released each other, Mr. Hutchinson kept his hands on the young man's shoulders, gripping them tightly.

"Take care of yourself, John," he admonished. "Don't seek for foolish glory, but be brave, as I know you are, and do your part manfully."

"I will, Father."

"Do you have everything you need?"

"Well...you did deprive me of Joseph."

"Oh, yes! You will have need of a manservant. What about Reuben? He is strong and dependable, and quite the marksman. I hate to lose a skilled carpenter, but I suppose we can do without him for a while."

"Thank you, Father."

"So it's settled then. Reuben will accompany you. Mind you write to me often, and do not neglect–"

John knew that he was about to be advised on religious duties, but, seeing his son blink down a look of displeasure, Mr. Hutchinson stopped and hastily remarked instead, "I know you will do what is right."

With this, John saw that his father was trying to show himself more trusting and loving.

"I shall write as often as possible," he promised, smiling faintly.

Mr. Hutchinson grew tearful again at the thought of his oldest son going off to war. He was already anxious enough for his youngest, and knew he would be unable to keep Elias from doing the same before long. He embraced John again and held him tightly.

"We must trust in God," he said, uttering the words as much for his own encouragement as for his son's. "We are in his hands."

On John's last full day at home, a Sunday, he went to church with his father and Elias. The Episcopal chapel in Amelia was situated on the main street at the top of a low hill, and was relatively new, having been constructed only about a dozen years before the war. In a region where the Episcopalians were vastly outnumbered by Baptists, Methodists, Lutherans, and Presbyterians, Mr. Hutchinson and a few other planters of that denomination, including his dear friend Dr. DuBose, had helped to establish the chapel just a few months before the death of John's mother. John remembered climbing up to the top of the scaffolding on the steeple as it was being built to survey the countryside. With boyish imaginativeness, as he looked off toward the southeast, where the low coastal plains gave way to the beginnings of the gently rolling landscape of the midlands, he sometimes fancied that he could see faraway Charleston.

The little stone building was overflowing with men in uniform the day that Sunday, the population of the village having temporarily swelled with troops that were bound for Virginia the next morning. Normally the church had ample room for the few families who were regular attendants, but many of them had foregone that day's services in order to make room for the soldiers. Mr. Hutchinson offered to share his pew with as many young men as could crowd into it.

Towards the end of what seemed to John an exceedingly long service, he began to experience a strange uneasiness he had never felt before—like a premonition of disaster—but afterward, amid all the excitement and preparations for his departure, he soon forgot about that feeling.

The next morning at the depot, the time drawing near for John to board the train, Mr. Hutchinson was serious and calm as they said their goodbyes. There were no tears. His grave look was mirrored by John, in whose mind the idea of going into battle, and therefore, possibly to his death, was just beginning to take hold as a sobering reality.

Elias held on to his brother's arm, full of pride and boyish excitement, and while John and his father talked, he watched all the movements of the soldiers and officers as they boarded or prepared to board the train. After a while, one of the soldiers close by caught his particular attention. A fresh-faced young man in a new Confederate uniform was walking toward the train surrounded by a group of ladies who all seemed to be trying to talk to him at once. He was little more than a boy, and Elias, who guessed him to be no more than eighteen, eyed him enviously.

The women, obviously doting relations, were fussing over the young man so much that he began to look embarrassed as they came closer to the crowds of other soldiers. Several of the ladies approached an officer, an older man with the rank of sergeant, and beseeched him to take care of the boy, their "dear one," as Elias overheard one high-pitched voice saying

The sergeant, a swarthy man with a forbidding, almost villainous looking countenance, stood stiffly with his arms crossed over a broad chest. As he listened impassively to the ladies, his eyes traveled from female face to female face, briefly assessing each one, and at last to that of the young man in their midst. The women were so lavish of entreaties on the boy's behalf and instructions for his care, that the sergeant had little opportunity to make any answer. He seemed to be waiting for them to finish, but they went on too long, obviously trying his patience. Finally, interrupting them, he bellowed out an order in a clipped, commanding tone, and as a result the young soldier promptly fell in line with a group of privates making ready to board the train in an orderly fashion. The sergeant bowed to the suddenly speechless ladies, said something to them in a low voice that Elias could not hear, and then turned on his heel to follow his men, who were now filing on to the train.

The ladies called out final farewells and blessings, fluttered their handkerchiefs, and smiled at their darling through tears. As the rough-mannered sergeant disappeared into the passageway of the car, Elias saw him put a hand on the shoulder of the "dear one" and give it a few gentle pats.

Mr. Hutchinson meanwhile was giving his eldest son more advice and encouragement, mostly repetitions of things he had already said, and John in turn kept reassuring him that all would be well. He attempted a smile, and could not help but feel proud of his son, so handsome and resplendent in his cavalry uniform. But a moment later, he looked so desolate and bereaved that John felt sorry for him. The young man struck a cheerful, careless tone, filling his father's ears with more details about the trip to Virginia and his regiment because he could see that Mr. Hutchinson merely wanted to look upon him a little longer.

When there could be no more delays, he embraced John a last time.

"I shall pray for you, my son," he whispered in his ear. "Day and night."

"So shall I," said Elias, squeezing his arm.

"Then no harm shall come to me," said John, and left his father and brother with a kiss.

CHAPTER FIVE

AS USUAL, EMMA WAS UP before sunrise, and after breakfast she promptly went to work in her vegetable gardens. During the past week they had been neglected in favor of the cotton planting, and were badly in need of weeding. Normally they were as carefully and diligently tended as a delicate infant child for they meant food, which had been ever in scarcer supply since the last year of the war.

The late winter crops she had planted had been trampled and all but destroyed by the Yankee soldiers who had raided the DuBose place and burned down most of the farm buildings in February. Emma had managed to salvage and replant a few vegetables–some English peas, carrots, onions, and sweet potatoes–but the result was only a meager showing for all the hard work she had put into her large winter garden. She was most distressed by the loss of the sweet potatoes, a needed staple food she had hoped to replenish for another year; last year's crop, stored in the potato cellar, was almost gone now. Fortunately, in the previous autumn, she and her aunt had gathered a harvest of apples and pecans from two small orchards on the place. The pecans had survived intact in storage, and some of the apples that were stored for a number of weeks were dried or made into preserves.

From her own stores of seeds and from seeds and seedlings acquired from friends and neighbors, Emma had the makings of a much better spring garden. Like all farmers and gardeners, she had been very busy in April, planting pole beans, cucumbers, eggplants, tomatoes, and squash. She had prepared the earth herself, as a few surviving chickens on the farm trotted and clucked about her feet, pecking at the grubs and worms that were turned up. Later, before the first tender shoots of the seedlings appeared above the ground, the poultry were fenced out.

Prior to the war, Emma had gardened for pleasure alone, and had spent much of her energies on flowers and other ornamental plants. She had also taken pleasure in the cultivation of a kitchen garden of her own, with no help from the servants, but gardening for food was an absolute necessity now, and she surprised herself with the amount of gardening, farming, and washing she could do outside, in addition to the cooking, cleaning, and mending which went on inside the house and kitchen. She worked from before dawn until after dusk; survival demanded it, and in a strange way she was grateful for the necessity of constant toil. It kept her from dwelling on her sorrows too much, and at night in her bed, in solitude, after her prayers, the temptation of bitterness and despair hardly had time to creep into her mind before she was asleep from sheer physical exhaustion. Except for those times when bad dreams troubled her, she slept the sound sleep that such fatigue usually brings, and when she woke each morning, her thoughts were immediately set on the necessary chores and activities of the new day.

Little weeds had spouted all over the garden, and as she began digging and pulling them up, she thought of John Hutchinson, and wondered how he had found his own fields and gardens at Belle Ville. She had heard that his plantation had not suffered as severely as many others in the area, but did not really know if this was true, and so had not told him, not wishing to give him any false hope.

In the middle of the morning, Emma paused a few minutes to stretch her aching back and take a drink of water before she went back to weeding in the garden, but she was soon interrupted. Within a few moments, she heard a horse approaching. She looked up and, shading her eyes in the sun, saw a man on horseback near the house. From where she stood she viewed him in profile, and could see that he was a well-dressed, gentlemanly looking man. Feeling apprehensive as she always did at the sight of strangers, she approached him warily. When the gentleman turned and looked at her, she recognized John Hutchinson.

He was clean-shaven now, and by way of greeting smiled and removed his civilian hat, a much finer hat than the one he had worn before. Today he looked like the John Hutchinson she remembered from her girlhood. He was older, of course, but still a young man, and except for a certain air of maturity and authority, and a few lines that were more deeply etched in his face, Emma saw little change in him. He wore a dark charcoal gray coat with a black band of mourning tied around one sleeve above the elbow.

"Good morning, Miss DuBose," he said, dismounting.

"Good morning."

Her gloves were dirty from the weeding, and she hid them behind her back.

"I've brought you and your aunt a few gifts to repay your hospitality. I hope you will accept them."

John was opening a saddle bag as he said this, and drew out three small parcels neatly tied together.

"Tea, sugar, and flour," he announced, holding them up with a slight bow.

"Wherever did you get tea?" she marveled.

"Oh, I did a little horse trading," he answered cryptically, with a humorous grin. "Though I'm afraid I wasn't able to find much tea. It is only a small amount"

"Any amount is welcome. How kind of you. Thank you, Captain Hutchinson," she said gratefully.

"I forgot to bring the clothes you lent me, but I'll get them back to you. The flour is a bit heavy. Let me take it inside for you."

When they reached the steps of the porch Mrs. Screven was just opening the door to go outside.

"Good morning, Captain Hutchinson!" she said, taken by surprise by the change in him. "Well, I must say, you have certainly improved your appearance with the disposal of that beard!"

"I must admit, I was glad to be rid of it," he laughed.

Admiring him, Mrs. Screven first noticed the gentle cleft in the middle of his chin. She thought it very becoming, as she suddenly realized that his whole face was an exceptionally handsome one. She also thought John's coloring more pleasing minus the beard, with his light brown hair, now neatly trimmed, and his clear green eyes.

"Captain Hutchinson has brought us a gift of flour and sugar, and tea," Emma told her.

"How gracious of you!"

Mrs. Screven took his hand and briefly pressed it as she thanked him. They walked into the parlor, where he placed the packages on a table. When John turned around, he noticed that Emma had disappeared, but she was soon back in the room with clean gloveless hands, and sat down with him and her aunt.

"How did you find things at Belle Ville?" she asked him.

"Not too bad, considering. The hands have stayed on, and the cotton has been planted. My overseer, Mr. Childress, was very ill for a while, but seem to have managed the place well in spite of that."

"How fortunate for you," Mrs. Screven remarked.

"Yes, I am very fortunate, indeed. The house is still standing, and most everything else is intact."

"Any news of your brother?" Emma asked.

"Yes! There was a letter waiting for me about him. My cousin Dr. Townsend is with Elias at a hospital in North Carolina, and will bring him home when he's well enough to travel."

"I'm so glad he's alive!" said Emma. "How badly was he hurt?"

"He was wounded, but Tom really didn't make it clear how seriously. I'm very anxious to see him."

"We received bad news yesterday after you left, Captain Hutchinson," said Mrs. Screven sadly. "Poor Mr. Drawdy's wife passed away."

"I'm sorry to hear it."

"We also had some very good news this morning," she added, brightening. "A neighbor brought us a letter from the village from Emma's uncle in Greenville, Mr. Theodore DuBose. He is coming to stay with us a while. An old friend who is traveling to Charleston is bringing Mr. DuBose here in his carriage."

"That must be a great comfort to you both."

Emma noticed a look of relief in John's face when he said this. She remembered the concern he had expressed for their safety and was touched. He offered her some help with the farming.

"I talked with one of my men about working for you, Miss DuBose. Amos said he would be willing to do that for a while, and live here in one of the cabins with his wife, who could also be of use to you. He's a good man, and very reliable. He was my brother's servant in the army for a while, until Matthew took his place."

"But we have no way to pay them wages," Emma objected.

"I could pay them," said John, quickly adding, "My father would have wished it."

"That is too kind, but we couldn't ask you to do that."

"Well, perhaps in few months, when the time comes for the picking, you might consider using his services."

"I'm sure you need him at your own place. I think we'll be able to manage."

"Well, I for one certainly don't fancy picking cotton," Mrs. Screven sniffed, raising her eyebrows very high as she contemplated such an unpleasant prospect.

"Mr. Drawdy and I will do it," said Emma. "And by that time, his son should be able to help us."

She explained to John that young Henry Drawdy was recovering from some minor wounds and would soon be fit for farm work. John knew that Emma worked in her gardens, that she had helped to prepare and plant the corn and the cotton, and that she toiled at washing and other household drudgery, but the idea of a young lady working like a field hand picking cotton was too much for him, and he recoiled at the idea that she would even contemplate it. Though he kept his objections unspoken, Emma could sense his disapproval.

"How long will your uncle stay with you?" he asked.

"A few weeks, or perhaps much longer. It is indefinite," Mrs. Screven answered, though the question had been directed to Emma. "We expect him tomorrow or the next day."

"Perhaps you would allow me to pay a visit after he arrives. I should like to meet him."

"Of course! Come and have supper with us Thursday evening. We shall be very pleased to have you as a guest again."

After leaving the DuBose farm, John rode into the village to visit his cousin Laura Townsend. On his way home from there, he met a wagon on the road and recognized as one of its passengers Mrs. McColl, the lady who had given him shelter in her cabin a few days before. He spoke to her, and the driver, an elderly man in ragged clothes, brought his mule to a stop. Mrs. McColl did not recognize John at first; well dressed and beardless now, he had to explain who he was.

"Are you on your way to Amelia?" he asked her.

"Yes, I have nowhere else to go at present. Mr. Hutchinson, this is my neighbor Mr. Malone."

John tipped his hat to the man.

"Mr. Malone was on his way to the village and offered us a ride."

She was holding her baby, and nodded toward the back of the wagon, where her two little girls were asleep on some canvas and straw.

"If you don't find your cousin there," said John, "you come to my place, and I'll see if I can be of some assistance to you. Ask for Belle Ville. Everyone knows where it is. You passed the road to it not long ago."

Mrs. McColl thanked him, but before John rode on, she informed in a low voice that she had received news of her husband. Glancing back at her girls again, she whispered, "He is dead–killed at Bentonville."

John rode home, and in the late afternoon, the wagon carrying the young widow and her children rumbled down the drive at Belle Ville and pulled up in front of the house. John happened to be standing on the lower portico talking with Mr. Childress as they drove up, and quickly explained to him who she was. They both walked out to meet her.

"My cousin's house was burned, Mr. Hutchinson," said the young woman. "She is living with an elderly lady in the village, helping her out, but there's no room for us there, nor is there enough food. I have other family in Laurens District, but it so far away, I shall have to write to them to see if they can take us in."

Mr. Childress, who had been studying the young woman and her little ones sympathetically, perked up at the mention of his home district in the upstate. John remembered his manners and introduced Mrs. McColl and her neighbor to him.

"I'm ashamed to throw myself upon your charity, Mr. Hutchinson," she went on, after acknowledging Mr. Childress, "but I don't know what else to do for now."

"Don't worry about that, Mrs. McColl," he said. "You are welcome to stay here until you find a better situation for yourself and your family."

She thanked him, blinking back tears, and John held out his hands to her to help her down from the wagon. Mr. Malone, who was holding the baby, passed him on to his mother while John lifted the little girls out.

A little while later, while the McColls and their neighbor were enjoying the first good meal they had eaten in many weeks, Mr. Childress begged a word with John about the young lady. As long as she was at Belle Ville, he said, the only proper arrangement was for her to have a place of her own, and he offered his house to the widow and her children.

"It's very generous of you, Mr. Childress," said John. "If you insist on giving up your house to them, it's all right with me. You can stay here while Mrs. McColl is with us."

"Oh, no, sir, I wouldn't impose upon you in such a way. The old overseer's house is still standing and I can take that. Your father was going to have it torn down years ago, but never got around to it, as it wasn't a matter of much importance."

"Is it livable?"

"Tolerable enough for me."

"Mrs. McColl will feel badly to put you out of your house."

"Oh, it is nothing, sir, really. I don't have many belongings. I'll move them out right now so that she and her family can take the place by tonight."

Though John was sure that he would have offered to do the same for any woman in her predicament, something in Mr. Childress's look and tone gave him the idea that he was quite taken with the young woman. He agreed to all the arrangements.

After Mr. Childress moved his few belongings out of his house and moved in Mrs. McColl and her children, John walked over to the place to see her. He offered her his condolences again on her husband, but the young widow did not show much emotion as she spoke of him. She had wept many bitter tears while her children slept, but was determined not to give way to her grief in their presence. She insisted that she did not wish to be idle, and that she must repay his charity by working for him. The young woman looked so weak and starved, he was hard pressed to think of something that she would be able to do. He told her to rest for a few days.

Mrs. McColl did take some time to rest and recuperate, but two days later, early in the morning, she came to John at his house to ask what work she could take on.

"I'm a very good seamstress," she informed him.

"You can help with the sewing and mending, then," he said. "Ask Mr. Childress what's needed."

"I was thinking I might also have a garden and work it," she suggested. "That would be useful, wouldn't it? There's a large plot behind the house someone has used before."

John gave his permission for the garden, and Mr. Childress was prompt to supply Mrs. McColl with the seeds and tools she required. Though she was planting somewhat late in the spring, the overseer assured her it was not too late by any means.

The low wooden fence that surrounded the house Mrs. McColl occupied had caught sparks from the February fires and had to be repaired. Later that morning, John set about replacing the parts which had burned away. While he was working, Mr. Childress walked up and offered his help. With his one arm, he held pieces of wood in place as John cut and nailed them. John knew his carpentry skills were not impressive, and could see that Mr. Childress was harboring much the same opinion, though he tried not to show it.

"I'm sure Reuben could do a much better job at this," he said.

Mr. Childress dismissed the idea, but lied so poorly that both men wound up laughing over it.

Mrs. McColl was nearby in the yard. She had just begun to prepare the ground, and looked up when she heard Mr. Childress addressing John as Captain Hutchinson.

"Is it Captain Hutchinson?" she asked.

"People seem to insist upon calling me that, but I don't mind Mr. Hutchinson," he replied.

"I'm sure you earned your rank. My husband was made a captain just before—"

Mrs. McColl stopped and turned her eyes down to the ground. The two men looked at each other awkwardly. Neither could produce any appropriately delicate response to the young widow's remark, until John thought to ask her what regiment her husband had served in.

"Mr. McColl was in the 21st, in General Hagood's brigade,"

she said.

They nodded with sympathetic acknowledgment and turned their attention back to their work. After a while, Mr. Childress noticed that the young woman was having difficulty breaking up the soil with the hoe. He knew that the ground was not very hard, and surmised that she lacked the strength.

"I don't think Mrs. McColl is up to such work yet," he whispered to John, who watched the young woman for a few moments and agreed with him.

"I'll do it," said John. "I'm nearly finished here."

Mrs. McColl had not been working long, but had already paused to rest. John walked over to her and spoke to her, and she hung her head as if ashamed.

"I haven't quite got my strength back yet," she explained. "I'm sorry to be so useless."

"Don't you worry about it, Mrs. McColl," he said. "You can help with the planting. That will be easier work. In the meantime, you must rest and take care of yourself."

She nodded, still shamefaced, and turned and slowly plodded back to the house. John soon finished his repairs on the fence and began to work the garden plot, but by mid-afternoon he was forced to stop when a terrific thunderstorm broke. The heavens had been darkening for several hours, and they crackled and flashed a while before the rain came down. John made it back to his house just as the downpour began–a blowing, hard-driving rain in which it would have been impossible to work outside. He went upstairs to his room and tried to nap, but the loud clatter of the rain, along with frequent thunderclaps and other tremendous rumblings and booming of the skies kept him awake.

He had always disliked rain, especially this kind. Though it watered the earth and was a giver of life, there was also something destructive and corrosive about it that depressed him, and made him feel his isolation. Though he was not much affected with loneliness when he was occupied with work, or at night, when fatigue quickly relieved him of any such trouble, he felt it acutely now. He thought about Miss DuBose, and wondered what she was doing at her house. Working, no doubt. But were her thoughts possibly drifting in his direction, as his were to hers?

Emma's uncle, though a decade older than her late father, looked very much like him. A recent widower with only one living child of his own, he was a tall, lean, clean-shaven man with hair as white as a cotton boll. John thought the way his long white mane flowed down to his shoulders from the bald, round dome of his head, somewhat in the style of Ben Franklin, made him look a little like a gentleman from an earlier era. His clothes, though not old-fashioned, were certainly out of fashion, and threadbare. His manners were somewhat blunt but gentlemanly, and at least on first impression, the old man and the young man decided that they liked each other. Mr. DuBose had been told of John's offering of help to the ladies and his expressions of concern for their welfare, so the captain was already in his good graces before they met.

Mr. DuBose claimed to be a little hard of hearing, but neither John nor Emma had to raise their voices when speaking to him. His deafness was only evident sometimes where his sister Mrs. Screven was concerned. At times he would seem to miss something she said or asked in order to change the subject, obviously to put an end to some line of chatter that he apparently found tiresome.

He had arrived at his niece's house late on the previous evening, and had spent most of Thursday resting up from his long journey. Mrs. Screven was eager to know what Mr. DuBose might be able to tell them of friends and family in Greenville, she and her late husband having lived in that neighborhood for many years. At supper she plied her brother for all the news, questioning him endlessly about this cousin or that acquaintance.

"Adele!" he finally protested. "I'm sure we are neglecting and wearying our guest with all this talk of persons he does not know. Besides, so much of it is bad news, I am quite weary of it myself."

He turned to John and quickly changed the subject. Mr. DuBose was a retired lawyer, and had never been a planter, but he had, like his brother, an interest in agricultural science, and asked John what he thought about their prospects for the farm. Though John tried to frame his answers in the most diplomatic and optimistic way he could without dishonesty, Mr. DuBose could see that he was really not very optimistic.

"Well," sighed the old gentleman, "I'm the one who advised Emma to try to plant some cotton if possible. I was thinking if they, that is, we, could just sustain ourselves on this place for a while, to tide us past these difficult times, perhaps things might improve, or at the least, we could get by long enough to find ourselves better situations. I'm not so worried about myself, of course, being old and not long for this world, I'm sure, but I am concerned for these ladies God has put into my care. You have seen though, Captain Hutchinson that the two of them have done at least fairly well so far without me."

"Nonsense," Mrs. Screven contradicted him. "Whatever would we have done without the help you have given us?"

She explained to John that her brother had generously provided them with money for many necessities after the death of Dr. DuBose.

"He has done without many things for our sake, I am sure," she added, looking at him both reprovingly and affectionately.

Continuing with his agricultural theme, Mr. DuBose complimented Emma on her gardens. He had apparently conducted a thorough examination of all the vegetable crops, and commented favorably on them all in detail.

"You have a gift for growing things, like my mother," he said to her approvingly. "Green things always thrive under your care."

"I was telling Captain Hutchinson that very thing," Mrs. Screven chimed in, as Emma blushed a little at all the praise being heaped on her.

Throughout the evening, Mr. DuBose made every attempt to steer the conversation away from all sad or serious subjects, though it was not an easy feat to find pleasant things to talk about. Emma's smiles were still infrequent, and he seemed to be trying to cheer his beautiful niece (who was, as John understood from Mrs. Screven, Mr. DuBose's favorite among all his nieces and nephews–his pet and his darling).

The old gentleman talked about happier times, the days of her childhood, and a particularly happy summer Emma had spent with her uncle and his wife in the mountains of North Carolina.

"Remember how you collected specimens of the mountain plants and flowers?" he reminisced.

"Yes, I remember. I believe I still have the little book I made to press them in," said Emma.

"She was quite the little scientist," he laughed, winking at John. "And only ten years old!"

"Scientist, indeed," Emma scoffed. "I thought they were pretty."

"Ah, it was more than that! You pestered me to find out their Latin names and such."

Mr. DuBose continued these reminiscences for a while, until

Mrs. Screven decided that he had gone on long enough, and managed to wrest the conversation out of his control. She began to talk about the delicious tea they were enjoying with the meal.

"I understand we have you to thank for that, Captain Hutchinson," Mr. DuBose interrupted.

"Merely a token of thanks for the kindness and hospitality of these ladies," John replied graciously.

A back and forth contest between Mrs. Screven and her brother for the direction of the conversation continued, and gradually became more overt and even a little contentious at times. At one point, the lady grew exasperated at a claim of deafness he made after interrupting her once again.

"You may be hard of hearing, Theodore, but unless you have also gone blind, you can certainly see that my lips are moving!" she complained.

Amused, John gave Emma a smile he thought the older people did not see. She was also amused, and was suppressing a smile, though it showed in her eyes, and as the two shared this private bit of humor, Mr. DuBose glimpsed their exchange out of the corner of his eye. A moment later, when he glanced at John, he also noticed something very telling in the way the young man's gaze lingered on his niece after she looked away.

"So," he thought, "we have a lover."

After a full moon rose that night, John started his ride back to Belle Ville. His time with the DuBose family had been enjoyable, though he realized that most of its pleasantness was mere facade, an interlude of artificial cheerfulness and sociality mostly manufactured by Mr. DuBose, and made possible only by temporarily ignoring a great many painful, crushing realities.

Yet in spite of the artificiality, there had been one very real charm and pleasure for him that evening—the company of Miss DuBose, who seemed to be the only bright spot in his life at the moment. She had interested him from the first time he saw her, but he was beginning to feel more than mere interest. As he rode along, he pondered the possibility that the young lady might be thinking of him in the same way, but could come up with no evidence of it. As yet, no such feelings on her part were apparent, and though he sensed that Emma liked him, he was afraid that there might not be any room for him in her grieving heart.

At that moment, Emma had just blown out the candle on her bedside table and was putting her head down on her pillow. She found herself thinking about John Hutchinson, but soon an urgent voice of caution inside was warning her to put a stop to it.

"Don't, don't!" warned the voice. "Whatever you love, you lose."

Blotting out his image, she turned her thoughts to prayer, and comforted herself by closing her eyes and moving her lips in silent recitation until she fell asleep.

The next morning, Emma woke up much earlier than usual, and lay in her bed for while in the darkness, thinking. John Hutchinson came into her mind again, but she would not let herself dwell on that subject. She thought instead about another young man, one who had wished to marry her some three years past, in the second year of the war. She tried to imagine what her life might have been like if she had married him. Would he have returned to her after the war, or would she have been left a widow, perhaps with a fatherless child to raise? Thoughts of this suitor led to memories of Emma's mother, who had fallen ill that same year.

Her troubles began the day she received the news that her younger son Richard had been killed in battle. Mrs. DuBose collapsed, and had to be carried to her bed. Dr. BuBose diagnosed the severe bodily weakness she suffered afterward as a nervous disorder, and her family anxiously attended and watched her for several days. One morning, Emma had trouble waking her mother, and when she did slowly return to consciousness, there was something vague and disconnected about her. Her husband sadly surmised that his wife had suffered a partial stroke in her sleep. There was little he could do for her as a physician.

From that day on, Mrs. DuBose was never the same. Though she recovered some of her strength, and attended to a few of her household duties as before, she grew more and more moody and irritable. She talked much less, and sometimes trailed off into a strange self-absorption in the middle of a sentence. There were hours and days, however, when Mrs. DuBose seemed sensible, calm, and much like her old self.

On one of these more lucid days, she talked with her daughter about Lieutenant Gilbert Habersham, a second cousin from Georgia who, during a recent visit, had fallen in love with Emma. She had just turned seventeen, and the young officer had written to Dr. DuBose seeking his permission to ask for her hand in marriage. Her father had given his consent on the condition of his daughter's willingness.

"You ought to accept the lieutenant," Mrs. DuBose urged her daughter. "He is a good man, and seems to love you very much. Don't you like him, Emma?"

"I am fond of him," she said, "but–"

"Then you ought to marry him," her mother said decisively. "I wish you to."

"Mama!"

"It will help me so much to know that you have someone like him to love you and take care of you. Marry him, Emma."

"And go and live in Savannah with people I hardly know?"

she objected. "No, I shall stay here and take care of you, and help Papa."

"But if you married Gilbert, I'm sure he would agree to let you live here with us while he is away at war."

"Oh, Mama, I don't know if I love him. I don't know. Perhaps I am too young."

"I was just your age when I married your father. He was older, of course, but we did very well."

"I know..."

"Mr. Habersham is handsome–and very rich," her mother reminded her.

"Yes, that is true," Emma admitted, "but I don't know..."

"Good heavens! He is a good and decent Christian man, and that is all you need know! I shall have your father speak to you about this matter."

Her mother's tone of voice troubled Emma; she had never been so querulous and demanding with her before.

"Papa won't force me to marry anyone," she said quietly.

"Perhaps he can persuade you. You sacrifice too much for our sake."

"Mama, I sacrifice nothing."

"I don't know about that. I think, but for us, you would let yourself love this young man."

"I don't really know him well enough to love him!"

"Oh, Emma, for my sake, please consider him," said Mrs. DuBose, shifting to a plaintive tone. Will you please think on it, for me?"

Emma promised that she would.

The next day, the family received a note from an officer reporting that Theo had been seriously wounded. Mrs. DuBose came upon her husband weeping over the letter. He assured his wife that the wound was not mortal, and that their son would recover, but the strain of the worry took a toll on her in her fragile condition, and before long she became confined to her bed. Emma wrote to Lieutenant Habersham and gently and courteously declined his proposal, explaining that her mother had grown so ill that she could not consider such a serious step at the present time. The young man continued to correspond with her, courting her through his letters, but after a year passed with no results, he finally gave up. Emma did not see him again, and after another six months, she learned that he had become engaged to a young lady in Savannah.

Her brother Theodore had recovered from his wound in a hospital in Richmond, and after a furlough at home, went back into the army. Despite his recovery, however, Mrs. DuBose did not improve. Gradually, she began to lose her grasp on reality. The only blessing in her condition was that she seemed to be freed from the torment of her grief and anxiety for her sons; she talked of the youngest as though he were still alive. She grew weaker every day, and then one evening at dusk, was finally released from all her earthly troubles. Not long after she passed away, Dr. DuBose fell ill and died. His widowed sister Mrs. Screven came to live with Emma.

CHAPTER SIX

DURING THE LAST FEW REMAINING DAYS of April, and throughout the month of May, Captain John Hutchinson was a regular visitor to the DuBose place. He was seen there at least weekly, and usually more often. Normally he tried to find an excuse for each call other than mere sociality, and any lengthy visits were reserved for Sundays, the only day for any leisure. On one occasion John asked to confer privately with Mr. DuBose to get his thoughts on some matters concerning his father's estate, and afterward stayed on for supper, and then for several hours more in the evening.

Sometimes, after a trip into the village, he would bring back letters to Emma or her aunt from friends there, but these occasions were rare. He made as few trips to Amelia (or what was left of it) as possible; the village was now garrisoned by United States troops, black and white, and he had no desire for contact with any of them.

After asking permission to go hunting in the woods on the DuBose property, John made a few visits to the farm for that reason. He was told that Sentry, the black and white spaniel belonging to the DuBose family, was an excellent hunter, and took him along. This animal was the last of Dr. Dubose's prized hunting dogs, the only one to escape the destruction of the farm. Sentry had hidden in the woods, where he stayed for weeks before cautiously venturing to return to his home, lean, hungry, and dirty, with one of his ears mangled and scarred, probably from an attack by another dog or some wild animal. Sentry had always preferred the company of males, and seemed particularly fond of John, who must have reminded him of his former masters, Emma's brothers.

Happiest when hunting, the dog bayed joyously when he saw that it was time to go into the woods and fields, though any hunting on this plantation was no longer for pleasure but for necessity, and he somehow seemed to understand this. Back in his old element, he was a careful tracker and assistant; he made few mistakes, and always obeyed John's commands.

The first of these hunting expeditions yielded an unexpected reward. One afternoon, John came across a sow and her piglets rooting about deep in the woods. She had either wandered from a farm or plantation, or had been sent out into the woods to be preserved from Yankee depredations. Either way, he reckoned finders keepers. He hurried to the barn and came back with a canvas bag and some rope to capture the animal, and found that she was much easier to catch than he had anticipated. Not the fattest sow he had ever seen, and probably unused to finding her own food, she was perhaps famished. The obstinate creature would not be led by the rope, so he had to wrestle her into the bag and carry her back to the farm. The sow squealed loudly and struggled all the way, but all her eight little children miraculously trotted along behind, grunting and fretting as they followed the sound of their mother's voice.

Emma and her aunt and uncle heard the racket outside the house and rushed out the door to find Captain Hutchinson toting a bag toward a sty Mr. DuBose had recently rebuilt, leading a fussing, trotting procession of little piglets like the Pied Piper. When the three recovered from their laughter, John explained his good fortune, which was really theirs, since he insisted on their keeping the animals.

That day was the first time John had actually heard Emma laugh, and the sound was very pleasant to his ears. Since her uncle's arrival, he thought she seemed more serene. Her constant look of sadness had subsided, and he was glad for it, but she was now so calm and self-possessed, he found it hard to guess what she might be thinking. As far as he could detect, the young lady still showed no signs of being in love.

Jeb Drawdy, the farmer who had been helping Emma and her aunt, resumed his usual work at the DuBose farm just a few days after his wife was buried. He had gone back to work at his own place the day after the funeral, grieving silently for the dead, but forced to work for the sake of the living. His son Henry had returned home that day, and after a visit to his mother's grave, joined his father in the fields.

Though nearly everything else at the Drawdy farm had been destroyed, the house had survived. The Federal soldiers had finished their work quickly in Mr. Drawdy's case. While they burned his fields and outbuildings he pleaded for his house, for the sake of his sick wife who was inside. An officer ordered the dwelling spared, and the main body of soldiers rode off. As a parting gesture, one straggler tossed a burning brand into the parlor through an open window, but Mr. Drawdy had been able to put out the flames in that room before any serious damage was done.

A kind-hearted but singularly ugly man, his deeply creased face was an etching of unpleasant angles, and his teeth were stained brown from the longtime use of chewing tobacco. He had served in the Confederate Army for two and a half years, returning home when he was wounded, blinded in one eye. Three of his sons had also served; the eldest had died at Cedar Creek in Virginia, and another, Nathaniel, as far as the family knew, was still a prisoner of war in the North in Illinois. Against his father's wishes, Nat had lied about his age to join the army. The youngest boy Henry had a fine, strong physique, and a face which mercifully bore more resemblance to his late mother than his father, and he and his father relieved Emma from much of her toils in the fields, insisting that she must only tend to her kitchen garden and other less strenuous chores.

In May, Emma was busy in her gardens, helped sometimes by her aunt and uncle. The cotton and corn were showing promise, and Mr. DuBose hired a man from the village to construct a few needed outbuildings for the farm, spending much of his time alternately supervising and assisting him.

During one of his numerous visits in the month of May, John enjoyed the rare privilege of a private conversation with Emma. One sunny Sunday afternoon, as he approached the DuBose house on horseback, he saw a carriage driving away, and from a distance he recognized Mrs. Shubrick, the rector's wife, and a young man who must have been her youngest son. They headed off in the opposite direction without seeing him.

"How old would Alfred be now?" John wondered.

He decided that he must be about nineteen or twenty—just Emma's age. He recalled the rector's son as a bright, handsome boy, and experienced an unexpected stirring of jealousy.

The DuBose family received him politely that day but, he fancied, a little less warmly than usual. As John handed Emma a letter he had picked up for her in the village the day before, she glanced at the envelope with a frown, and seemed preoccupied afterwards. Mr. DuBose looked a little unwell, as did Mrs. Screven. She was repining, almost tearfully, Mr. Shubrick's bad health and the long dearth of church services everyone in the parish had endured for so long because of it.

"Was that Alfred with Mrs. Shubrick?" John asked her, when she finally seemed finished with her lament.

"Yes, it was. I must say, he is looking well. Such a pleasant young man. He is engaged to Miss Mary Lovell, you know."

"No, I didn't," said John, concealing his relief.

Mrs. Screven began complaining of a headache after the Shubricks left. She apologized to John, excused herself, and went upstairs to rest, leaving him alone with Emma and Mr. DuBose, who had begun looking drowsy in his armchair.

John reluctantly decided that he should make his visit a brief one today. The family had already entertained guests, and he thought his company might be too much of an imposition on their day of rest.

"Well, I must be on my way now," he said apologetically.

"Won't you stay a little while?" Emma asked.

John could not tell whether her request was merely one of politeness. He wanted to think that it was something more, but nevertheless decided that he should go.

"You'll pardon us, Captain Hutchinson," said Mr. DuBose. "My sister and I are a bit out of sorts. I for one slept quite badly last night, so I am a poor host today."

"Quite all right," said John.

Emma followed him to the door and out to the porch to see him off. John paused on the steps and asked her if she was feeling out of sorts today, too.

"No, I am well," she replied.

"You seemed a bit dismayed when I gave you your letter."

"It's from a cousin who is also a dear friend. Her mother has been very ill lately, and I thought it might contain bad news."

"But it might contain good news," he said encouragingly.

Emma was still holding the letter. Taking his tacit suggestion, she opened it and read a few lines, then looked at him and smiled.

"You were right. It does. Clelia writes that her mother is much better now."

"Then I'm happy to have brought you good tidings."

John watched her fold up the letter and replace it in its diminutive cover to finish later. During the pause, he began to wish he had not said he was leaving, now that–for the first time–he had Emma to himself. She broke the brief silence, asking him if he had received any news of his brother, and with that, their conversation resumed and continued to flow for nearly half an hour. While they talked, Emma leaned against a post looking down at him. John remained in place on the steps, his back pressed against the stair rail, not daring to move–even though his legs began to ache–fearful that he might break the spell that made her linger.

He thought Emma would finally break it when she realized how long she had been keeping him in conversation and apologized.

"You said you must be going, Captain Hutchinson. I'm afraid I have detained you too long."

"You don't detain me against my will," he said, smiling. "I didn't wish to impose on your uncle, but if you don't mind my company I am happy to stay a while."

With that they left the steps to sit down on the porch. As John took his chair, he glanced through the window and saw, with the feeling that it was almost too good to be true, Mr. DuBose sound asleep in the parlor.The old man's arms were crossed over his stomach, his chin nearly touching his chest, and the spectacles he wore for reading had slipped down to the tip of his nose.

Emma asked John's advice on some farm matters. When that subject was exhausted, their conversation somehow turned to the day's other visitors. John told Emma about a conversation he had with the rector's wife when he chanced to meet her the day before in Amelia.

"She overheard me when I collected your letter, and asked about you and your family. She said she felt she had neglected you and your aunt, and meant to call on you very soon."

"We were very glad to see her today," said Emma. "We've missed the family so much. They were away for quite a while, you know, for the sake of Mr. Shubrick's health."

"Mrs. Shubrick spoke very highly of you, and mentioned your work in the Soldiers' Aid Society. She told me you were her most tireless laborer."

"She is too kind," Emma responded modestly. "All the ladies in the Society worked very hard to clothe and feed our soldiers."

"And I'm sure they were very grateful for it," said John. "I remember the kindness of many ladies in Virginia."

This remark prompted Emma to ask John about his experiences in the army there, and though he usually tried to avoid the subject, he was willing to talk about it in order to remain in her company a little longer. He described a number of notable battles in which he had participated, and she was surprised that he had seen so many that were now famous names of the war.

"You're wondering how I survived?" he laughed. "So did I, Miss DuBose. I had so many close calls I was really quite surprised to find myself alive at the end."

"Your father told us that you were in some of those battles, but did not mention them all," said Emma, adding hesitantly, "I do remember that he said you were too reckless on one occasion."

"Oh, no! I was never reckless with my men."

"With yourself, then. Mr. Hutchinson showed my father the letter your commander sent when you were wounded. The colonel praised you very highly for your gallantry, but your father feared that you had acted recklessly under the circumstances he described."

"No, no," John said dismissively. "He couldn't know all the circumstances merely from a brief account in a letter. What we did helped to turn the tide of a battle, and the wound I received wasn't really serious. That wasn't recklessness."

There was a glow of admiration in Emma's eyes as she listened to John talk about his military service. He wanted to think that it was something more than patriotism which inspired that look, but could not tell for certain. He found he was not able to fathom those serene, beautiful blue eyes.

"Your father was so proud of you," she remarked after a pause.

"Was he?" said John, deeply moved to hear this from her, but trying not to show it.

"Oh, yes," she assured him. "You made him very proud."

They heard a voice from inside the house. Mr. DuBose had stirred from his nap and was asking for Emma. He could see her through the window.

A little while later, as John rode home, he thought about his conversation with Miss DuBose, saw her face, and gazed into her eyes again, remembering that he had not seen what he had been looking for there. Contemplating her beauty, intelligence, and goodness, he could not help but feel a growing attraction, but he wondered again, with some discouragement, if she would ever feel anything for him beyond friendship.

In the afternoons, while her baby slept in a basket at her feet, and her two little girls played in the yard under her supervision, Mrs. McColl liked to sit out on the porch and do her sewing there. Mr. Childress got into the habit of stopping by to speak with her when his work was done most days. He never went inside the house or even set foot on the porch, but stood in the yard talking with her respectfully and attentively during his brief visits. Her young daughters had been afraid of his deformity at first, but when they became accustomed to him, they would let him talk and play with them a little while each time he called. He brought them little treats and presents when he could, and eventually, the children became so fond of him that they began to greet him with hugs and kisses.

Early one afternoon, Mr. Childress was on his way home to clean up and change clothes. A cow had wandered into a swampy area of the plantation and mired herself there, and he had spent the last hour helping some of the hands recover the animal. He had wiped and dried his face with a rag, but the rest of him was thoroughly wet or covered in mud. As he was walking past his old house, he saw Mrs. McColl working in her kitchen garden.

She had stopped to rest after an hour's weeding, and was leaning against the fence, staring off at some indefinite point with a sad, preoccupied look. Mr. Childress guessed she must be thinking of her husband, and for that reason, and his untidy appearance, he hesitated to intrude on her. He kept walking, but when Mrs. McColl saw him and raised her hand in acknowledgment, he changed his mind and made a turn in her direction.

As he approached the garden he admired the neat rows and beds of healthy young plants, a sight almost as pleasing to his farmer's heart as the young woman's pretty face.

"Mr. Childress!" she said, inspecting him up and down.

"You look as though you have been toiling in the brick pits of Goshen."

He laughed and explained about the wayward cow.

"They can be such stupid creatures," she remarked.

"Indeed they can," he agreed. "Your garden is looking well, Mrs. McColl."

"Do you think so? I am doing my best with it."

"I don't think anyone could do better."

A flush came into her cheeks at his compliment, and she lowered her head to hide her face under her the brim of her bonnet for a moment.

"When I had a place of my own, my wife used to keep a nice garden for us."

Mrs. McColl looked up at him and asked, "You lost her during the war?"

He nodded slowly. During a silence, both lapsed into private thoughts of bereavement, but Mr. Childress soon spoke up to change the subject.

"Did you say that you are from Laurens District?" he asked her.

"Yes, my family has a farm just outside of Laurensville," she replied.

"Is that so? I have some people there."

"I know some folks with your name."

"Then I'm sure we have some mutual acquaintances," said Mr. Childress. "My father has a farm near Dorrohville. I was born and raised there."

"That's not so far from Laurensville."

He asked her what her name had been before she married.

"Goodwin," she told him.

"Well now, I knew a Seth Goodwin. Is he your kin?"

"That must be my cousin Seth. He went out to Mississippi a few years before the war."

"Yes, Seth did that. It must be the same person. How did he fare?"

"He was doing well for a while. He was a very good farmer. But when his little wife died out there, it was very hard on him. He took to drink, and was standing on the very crumbling verge of a drunkard's grave before he changed his ways."

"Poor Seth! That's a pity. I don't drink myself."

Mrs. McColl nodded in solemn approval and felt moved to quote from the Scriptures.

"Wine is a mocker, strong drink is raging, and whoever is deceived thereby is not wise," she recited.

"That's the truth, Mrs. McColl," the overseer replied in hearty agreement. "Are you a Baptist?"

"I am."

"So am I."

The widow's two little girls suddenly came bursting out of the back door of the house and, tripping over each other, tumbled down the steps to the ground. Their mother made a movement toward them in alarm, but when she saw that they were laughing, merely sighed in exasperation and relief. Mr. Childress smiled and shook his head.

"Well, I must be on my way," he said, looking down at his muddy lower half.

One afternoon, a friend passing through the area brought John a letter from his cousin Tom Townsend, who was with Elias and Matthew, announcing their imminent arrival at Belle Ville. John decided that a large couch in the drawing room would do for a daybed, and moved it into the library, which had always been his brother's favorite room. During his convalescence, he thought Elias might prefer its surroundings to a bedroom. It was a spacious, sunny, handsome room, and its large window looked out on a garden. The library had been left largely undisturbed by the raiders, and the shelves were as full of books and pamphlets as they had been before the war. Their father's theological works, his books of Greek and Roman history and poetry, as well as his collection of agricultural journals and treatises, seemed to be intact.

On the day Dr. Townsend and the others were expected back, John watched anxiously for the wagon that would be carrying Elias. He sat by a window in the drawing room and wrote a few letters, glancing out each time he thought he might have heard the sound of an approaching vehicle. After two hours passed, he sat out on the portico a while, and then came back inside and went into the library to make sure everything was ready for Elias there. Still waiting, he sat down in a chair that faced a wall full of bookcases.

Growing reminiscent, John thought of how often he had seen his father in this room, seated by the fire or the window, meditating over religious passages, or perusing writings on scientific farming only a planter could find interesting. In addition to the classics, Mr. Hutchinson had compelled his sons to read quite a few books of both sorts in their youth. He had also sent both boys out into the fields to observe the way that crops, especially cotton, were cultivated and harvested, and year after year, even required them to roll up their sleeves and learn the work firsthand, and help with the ginning of the cotton, the care of the livestock, and other tasks. Taking part in all this, John and Elias had gained an understanding of all the operations which produced food, clothing, shelter, and implements, and which made Belle Ville virtually a self-sufficient little world in itself. In his younger days, Mr. Hutchinson had not been above working on the lands himself in order to assess and improve them, and John smiled to think of him with the dirt of the fields under his fingernails.

Looking in to ask a question, Israel interrupted his thoughts.

"Dr. Townsend and Matthew should be here with Elias soon," John answered.

A few moments later, as he walked outside to look for them again, he finally heard the rumblings and creaking of wagon wheels in the distance.

Elias was reclining in the back of the open wagon, the upper part of his body shielded by a piece of tent cloth. As they slowly approached the drive leading to the house, Dr. Townsend, who was seated beside Matthew, the driver, announced to him that they were home, and Elias moved out from under the covering and changed his position to see the familiar trees along the road. It was a sunny day, and the light flashed hypnotically in his eyes through the overhanging branches and leaves as he looked up at them. He sat up when the wagon turned into the cedar-lined avenue, and the next sight which met his eyes was his home.

John had gone back inside for a moment to tell Israel that the wagon had arrived. Elias saw them emerge from the house together and walk down the steps to greet him.

Matthew jumped down, opened the back of the wagon, and, holding a crutch for him, helped the young man slide off to his feet.

Though John had made great effort to keep his emotions in check, he was already weeping before he got a good look at his brother. When he did see Elias clearly, he was shocked by the change in him. Dressed in a torn, dark blue uniform, he was very thin, and looked as frail and decrepit as an old man, his jaws stubbled with the beginnings of a beard. John clasped him in his arms, wracked with deep sobs. Elias began weeping, too, and leaned against his older brother heavily, so much so that John felt he might collapse if he let go of him.

"John, I'm so glad, I'm so glad," he was murmuring in a choked voice.

John's throat was so constricted with emotion he was unable to speak. When he regained control of himself he placed a kiss in his brother's hair and dropped one arm to release him from his embrace. The other arm he kept around his waist to hold him up. Israel came to his other side to help him in the same way.

"Mas' Lias," he said gently, putting an arm around him. "You glad to be home, I know. We gone take good care of you."

"Thank you, Israel. It is good to be home."

Elias leaned heavily on the two men as they walked him to the steps. Israel found he was too unsteady to support him on the climb up, and yielded his place to Matthew, a much younger man, who handed him the crutch to carry. They took Elias into the library and placed him on the daybed John had prepared for him.

He reclined there with a sigh, exhausted from the long trip. Israel made him comfortable with some pillows and light quilts, observing his young charge with alarm, though he did not show it. The old man hardly recognized this haggard, emaciated creature as Elias Hutchinson.

John had barely acknowledged his cousin Tom as yet, but as soon as Elias was situated in the library, he turned his attention to the doctor and was surprised to see that he also looked ill and weak. After a brief embrace, John drew up a chair and sat Tom down in it. His face, which bore a strong family resemblance to John, with the same dimpled chin, was pale and drawn, and there were dark circles under his eyes.

"You don't look well, cousin," John said anxiously.

"I'm not well. I've been feeling worse each day," the doctor said in a weak and wheezing voice.

"Perhaps we should get you into bed, too."

"No, not here. I'd prefer to go home. My sister can take care of me. You need to take care of Elias."

"I'll have Matthew drive you home."

"Thank you. I've already asked him to do that."

"If you have need of anything–"

"I'll let you know," said the doctor.

Tom raised himself up from the chair unsteadily and made a sign for John to follow him out of the room, saying goodbye to Elias before he walked out. They left the young man in Israel's care.

The butler tried to place a light coverlet over his legs, but Elias refused it. He sat up with a sudden burst of nervous energy and began to tear at the buttons of the coat he was wearing with trembling hands.

"I wish to change clothes immediately," he said vehemently, with a look of revulsion. "Bring me some of my old clothes, Israel, and get these god d–"

He stopped abruptly when he saw the startled look on the old man's face. Israel had scarcely ever heard a curse word from the lips of Elias, and certainly never the one he had almost uttered.

"Get these damned Yankee rags off me!" he snapped, almost panting with anger.

Israel was already prepared with some clothes he had brought downstairs earlier. He stepped over to a chair in the corner of the room and brought back a clean shirt and a pair of pants.

John and the doctor paused to talk on the portico where Matthew, patient and quiet as usual, had been waiting for a few minutes.

"I'll be there directly," the doctor told him, and he returned to the wagon.

John was looking at his cousin apprehensively.

"What do you think, Tom?" he asked.

"Elias...looks badly, I know. He is very ill, and I've done everything I could to help him, but now that he's home with you, I believe he might rally."

A sob of relief rose up in John, and he momentarily covered his face. He had been fearing the worst.

"How badly was he hurt?" he asked the doctor.

"Some shell fragments hit him in the lower leg, gouging out a little bone and flesh. The wound did not appear serious at first, and was thought to be superficial, so he received little attention except to have it wrapped. When I found him a few days later, his leg was swollen and inflamed. He was already enfeebled by a bout of dysentery before getting wounded, and was so weak, I didn't wish to risk an amputation, so I drained the wound and washed it with a solution of hydrochloric acid. I also removed a shell fragment near the bone. The wound closed, and seems to be healing as far as I can tell, but Elias is still very, very weak. I don't know exactly what is wrong with him, but a man's body either overcomes such a thing or succumbs to it. We must help him overcome it."

"I shall do everything possible to help him, Tom."

"Feed him well. Neither of us has had a decent meal in weeks, though the farmer whose house we used as a hospital tried to provide whatever he could. You must see that Elias gets lots of vegetables, and wheat bread, not cornbread. Milk, if he can tolerate it, meat broths, tea, and perhaps a little wine, if you can get some. I shall try to find some brandy for him. He is in considerable pain sometimes, though he doesn't like to show it. I've given him an anodyne, and I'll leave something to help him sleep for the next few nights. He seems comfortable where he is. I wouldn't move him upstairs unless he insists. I'll come back to see him when I'm feeling well enough."

After this speech Tom stopped to catch his breath, and John nodded gratefully. The doctor took a small bundle of sleeping powders from his bag and handed it to him.

"Israel is a good nurse. Give these to him and tell him what I said about the food."

"I will."

John embraced his cousin, and could feel him trembling a little.

"Thank you, Tom," he said. "Thank you for all you have done for Elias. God knows what might have happened to him if he had not been in your care."

The doctor started out the door, but paused momentarily and turned back to John with an apologetic look.

"I'm sorry about the Yankee uniform," he said. "It was all I could find for him. The Yankees used the same house as a hospital, and left behind a few things. Elias didn't realize what he was wearing until we were well on our way home, and he wasn't very happy about it."

"I imagine so," John muttered.

When Dr. Townsend was gone, he returned to the library. Opening the door, he could hear Elias and Israel talking in lowered voices, and as soon as he came in Israel left the room to get some water Elias had requested. John took a seat in a chair opposite the daybed and smiled at his brother, trying to show only his joy at his return and not betray his anxiety for him. He noted the change of clothing but said nothing about it.

"I thought you might prefer this room," he told Elias.

"Yes, I think I do. It's pleasant in here."

As Elias looked around, John could see that he took some comfort in the familiar surroundings.

"The last time you and I were together in this room, we had

a wrestling match," Elias reminisced. "Do you remember?"

"I remember. You almost bested me that time."

The younger brother smiled weakly at this falsehood.

"I'm afraid I couldn't contend against your little finger as I am now, John."

"You'll get stronger, brother. We'll make sure of that."

Elias lowered his head and stared down at the floor. He suddenly seemed to be withdrawing into himself, as if no one else were there. After an awkward silence, John tried to revive the conversation by recalling their last meeting during the war.

"The last time I saw you, we were in Richmond, weren't we?" he asked.

"No," Elias corrected him, "it was Charlottesville."

"Ah, yes. I remember now. It was a Sunday, and you dragged me to into not just one, but two church services that day, I recall."

Elias made no response to this other than a frown. From his daybed, he looked out the window in the direction of the family cemetery, but could only see the very top of the oak tree there beyond the intervening hedges and other trees.

"I should like to see Father's grave," he said quietly. "How empty this house must seem without him."

"It does, indeed."

John could see his brother's eyes and head beginning to droop in exhaustion.

"I'll take you there when you feeling better," he said. "You've had a long journey, and I think you should rest today."

"Yes, I am tired."

Israel brought in a decanter of water and a glass, and after taking a few sips, Elias yawned and settled down under his light covers.

"This couch is a comfortable bed," he remarked, closing his eyes.

"If you prefer a bed, we can always bring one down for you. Are you hungry?"

"A little, but I'd like to rest before I eat."

Elias gave another yawn, and wiped away the moisture that it brought to his eyes.

"Rest then," said John.

Elias fell asleep quickly, and John rose and went to the door of the library, which was slightly ajar. He saw Israel in the hallway and beckoned to him with a gesture.

"He's asleep right now," John told him.

"That's good."

Following the doctor's orders, John repeated Tom's instructions about Elias's food and care. Israel, who had a low opinion of physicians in general, lifted his chin and rolled his eyes upward as he listened.

"I don't need no doctor to tell me all that," he sniffed.

"I know, Israel," John said in an assuaging tone, "but Dr. Tom asked me to pass on these things to you, and also these powders."

He handed the little package of sleeping powders to the butler.

"I done told Sibby to make some chicken broth for his supper."

"Thank you, Israel."

John went back into the library and resumed his seat opposite his sleeping brother. In repose, at that moment, Elias looked deathly, and John experienced the same feeling of shock he had felt on seeing him for the first time that day. He watched his brother with a troubled air, sickened at heart to see how frail, how like a skeleton he was. He had felt all his bones when he embraced him earlier. The sleeper stirred and sighed, and as he shifted position his breathing became more audible in faint, intermittent snoring. John remembered what Tom had said–that Elias had a chance, that he might rally–and he determined he must operate on that hope.

Watching Elias sleep, John began to drowse, and an hour or two went by in quiet rest for both of them. Later, a low sound woke him. As he opened his eyes, he realized that Elias had spoken, though still asleep. John sat up and studied him. Elias sighed and mumbled incoherently. The muscles of his face moved in little spasms, and his fingers gently clenched and unclenched a few times. Was he dreaming, John wondered, or was his body experiencing some pain or discomfort in unconsciousness?

Just before nightfall, Elias woke. John lit a few lamps, and Israel brought in some broth, bread, and weak tea. The old servant looked on with satisfaction as the patient ate, but frowned with displeasure when he pushed the food away only half consumed.

"Won't you eat more?" John urged him.

"Not tonight," he sighed. "I'm sorry, Israel, that's all I can eat now."

Israel took away the remains of his meal, and John pulled his chair closer to Elias's bed.

"I hope the journey wasn't too rough on you," he said, taking his brother's hand. "I suppose a wagon was preferable to a carriage. At least you could recline and rest on the way."

"That old wagon was all we could get, but it wasn't bad, and I did rest," Elias assured him.

Elias pressed John's hand, leaned closer, and studied him in the lamp light.

"Let me look at you, brother," he said. "You look well. When did you get back?"

"In April, and when I came home, I found Tom's letter about you waiting for me. It was the best news I had received in a long time."

"And what have you been doing with yourself, John?"

"Oh, I keep myself busy one way or another. A good many of the fences and outbuildings need repair or replacement, and I've mainly been working on those tasks. I should say, I've been helping Mr. Childress and Reuben with them. My carpentry skills are not greatly admired, but I think they are improving."

Elias asked if there was any word of their sister Isabella.

"She and the family are still in Anderson. Edmund has relatives there, you know. I wrote to her that you were coming home, and she begged me to send you love from her and the family. They would come and see us, but the baby is ill right now."

"My little namesake?" Elias asked. "I haven't even seen him yet."

The news about the baby seemed to depress him, and he closed his eyes and let his head fall back on his pillow wearily.

The conversation soon turned to practical matters of immediate importance, the most practical and important of all being survival. John told Elias about his correspondence with Mr. Simmons, their late father's lawyer, and the status of the estate. They then discussed the freedmen and the farming of the land, but Elias showed only a vague interest in all these matters, and had no advice to offer.

"I'm sorry, John," he sighed feebly. "I don't think I can be of much help to you here. I'm quite useless."

John assumed a confident, encouraging air.

"We're going to get you well again, Elias," he said.

The invalid opened his eyes and stared up at the ceiling, then closed them again.

"Tom and Israel will work their wonders on you," John added, trying to sound as cheerful as possible.

"They are both good doctors, aren't they?" Elias responded listlessly. A moment later, he looked at his brother with a discernable glimmer of interest in his eyes. He gestured for his glass of water, and after taking a sip, asked about their cousin Laura.

"She's fine," John told him, "and very anxious to see you."

"I don't wish her to see me like this," he said with sudden agitation. "She isn't planning to call tomorrow, is she?"

"I don't think so, not with Tom being so ill."

"Don't let her come here, John, please."

"As you wish. I'll go and see them in a day or two, and I'll explain to her that you're not ready to receive visitors."

"Yes, tell her that."

Elias finished his water and handed the glass to John. He looked preoccupied and hesitant to speak. His brother guessed what was on his mind.

"Laura had her nineteenth birthday last month, you know," John remarked casually. "She told me that her friends somehow came into possession of some calico and made a new dress for her."

"That was good of them. Have you seen her often since you came back?"

"I called on her when I first returned, to see if she had need of anything, and I have seen her a few times since then. She's as pretty as ever."

"Married?" Elias queried faintly.

"No, not married, nor even engaged as far as I know."

CHAPTER SEVEN

TWO DAYS AFTER ELIAS'S RETURN, John rode into Amelia to see his cousin Dr. Townsend. From a window, Laura saw her cousin riding up, and rushed out to greet him. She was Tom's half-sister, the daughter of his father's second wife, and except for her dark hair, did not look like the doctor at all. Her looks strongly favored those of her mother, who had passed away in the third year of the war. Slim and somewhat tall, she had dark brown, almost black hair, and large, fine brown eyes.

"How is Elias?" she asked breathlessly, taking hold of John's sleeve. "I so wish to see him."

"He's resting, Laura. He's very weak, you know."

"Has he spoken of me?"

"He has. We have talked of you, but he's not receiving any visitors right now. He doesn't wish to see anyone until he feels a little stronger."

"Not even me?" her doe eyes seemed to ask, and she looked so hurt and disappointed that John felt sorry for her. He removed some food he had brought from his saddlebag and gave it to Laura. She thanked him, and he asked about her brother.

"Tom is very ill. He has diagnosed himself with a mild case of pneumonia."

"May I see him?"

"I believe he's awake now. I'm sure he would be glad to see you."

They went into the house, and after Laura set down her packages on a table, she showed John into a bedroom on the first floor. Tom had just begun dozing again when they entered, and started slightly as he woke.

"Sorry to disturb you, dear," Laura said to him gently. "I thought you were still awake. John is here to see you."

"That's all right," he wheezed. "How is Elias, John?"

"There's been little change in him as far as I can tell."

Tom wearily sat up in the bed as his sister placed some pillows behind him for support.

"I wish I could take care of him, but I'm quite the invalid myself right now."

Laura picked up a tray which had held her brother's dinner and left the room with it.

"Is there anything I can do for you?" John asked him.

"Laura's made a list of a few things we need."

"I'll get it from her."

John glanced behind him to make sure that Laura was not returning.

"I believe I upset her just now," he said in a low voice, turning back to Tom.

He coughed and asked, "She asked about Elias?"

"I had to tell her that he's not receiving any visitors. It's what he wished me to say, particularly to Laura. He doesn't want to see her. I should say, he doesn't want her to see him."

"I'm sure Laura was very disappointed. Elias all but proposed to her, you know."

"Did he? He didn't tell me."

"Elias wrote to her to tell her his feelings just before he was wounded. My sister showed me the letter, and read part of it to me. Laura wrote back favorably, but she never heard from him again."

"If Elias could see her, perhaps it would help him," John suggested.

"I wouldn't force the matter, not yet," Tom cautioned.

John wanted to do anything and everything he could to help his brother, but he could see that the doctor was right, and dropped the idea of an immediate reunion.

"Poor girl," he said sadly. "She must be miserable. The way Elias was writing to me about her in his last letters, I knew he loved her, but I never heard more of it."

"Laura was hoping that he would come home on furlough so that they could get married."

Tom made a heavy wheezing sound as he breathed, and leaned heavily on the pillows, his head thrown back, as though the effort of sitting up had exhausted him. He looked so terrible that John began to feel as anxious for him as he did for Elias, and the doctor noticed the concern he momentarily betrayed.

"I'll be all right, John," he reassured his cousin. "I'm just worn out. I didn't take care of myself as I should have, and now I am paying the price. Rest will be the best medicine for me."

"I'll go now and let you rest, then," said John, pressing his hand.

Tom sighed and looked at him with a strangely preoccupied, mournful expression. He looked as though he had something to say, and opened his mouth, but instantly closed it again and looked away.

"Is there something else, Tom?" John asked uneasily.

"No," he answered. "Forgive me, but I am feeling very feeble."

John removed a few of the pillows so that the doctor could recline again. On his way out he met Laura in the parlor. She handed him a little folded piece of paper.

"For Elias," she said. "Will you give it to him?"

"Of course, Laura."

"It's just to let him know that I am thinking of him and praying for him, and would very much like to see him if he will allow me."

She had another piece of paper that she also gave John. It was the list of needed items that Tom had mentioned earlier.

"Our cupboard is nearly bare again," she said.

Though she seemed reluctant to ask for more charity, even from a close relative, she added, "I didn't write it down, but I was just thinking, if you could spare a hen or two, it would be nice to have eggs for Tom. All our poultry was stolen when the village was burned."

"Certainly. I'll send them to you tomorrow."

"Thank you, John," she said, taking his hand. "You've been so good to take care of me."

"We must both take good care of our brothers now," he told Laura, trying to encourage her, and himself.

On Sundays, Emma worked as little as possible. There were a few small indispensable chores to be done, of course, but for the most part it was a day of rest and reflection, as it had always been in her family.

A fine, sunny afternoon drew her to her favorite place outside. A small ornamental garden had once graced the eastern grounds of the house, and remnants of it still existed. Some of the garden had escaped damage, but even here, neglect, necessitated by the need to expend all energies on sheer survival, had led to a reversion to weeds and wildness. Emma did not really mind this condition of things, though; she liked its quaint, romantic, forgotten look.

There was a small area circumscribed by rows of boxwood shrubs and a low stone wall on two sides, and when she secluded herself in this shady corner, she could almost imagine that she was in her garden of old, before much of it had been ruined or destroyed. Here, part of a sandy pathway bordered by bricks survived, along which, in former days, varieties of flowers had bloomed lushly beginning at this time of year. Only a few were in bloom now.

An iron bench too heavy to carry off remained in this spot, and Emma sat down in it with a book. She had been reading for about an hour when she was joined by her aunt and uncle. She rose to give up the settee to them.

"Oh, but where will you sit, dear?" Mrs. Screven protested.

"I'll fetch a quilt and sit on the ground under the tree."

Within a few minutes she returned to the garden with an old coverlet and spread it out on a grassy spot in the shade of a water oak. Emma opened her book again, and within a few minutes, another visitor arrived. John had decided to pay the DuBose family a call, with no good excuse except that it was a mild, beautiful spring day. He was not surprised to find them outside enjoying the fine weather.

"How kind of you to come and see us today, Captain Hutchinson," said Mrs. Screven, looking apologetic. "It's very awkward that we have no other seat to offer you here in the garden."

"Perhaps Miss DuBose will allow me to share her spot under the tree," he suggested very casually, though his heart throbbed once or twice with pure fear.

"Certainly," Emma responded politely, folding out more of the quilt to make room for him.

John sat down beside her at the very edge of the cloth; this left only a space of inches between himself and Emma, or at least between him and the perimeter of her outspread skirt.

At first, the conversation flowed among all the parties, but after a while, Mr. DuBose and Mrs. Screven became absorbed in a more private chat about a relative, and John took the opportunity to speak with Emma.

"What are you reading?" he asked. "It seems that every time I see you at leisure there is a book in your hands."

She showed him the book, a history of the French Protestants, written in French.

"I believe I read that in college," he recalled, then hesitated. "No, I am thinking of another book, about Charles the twelfth. It must have been that one of my tutors made me read the Huguenot history."

"What did you think of it?"

"Honestly, I don't remember much about it. I'm afraid I wasn't much of a scholar."

But after saying this John surprised her by taking the book from her, reading aloud a passage in French with a faultless accent, and then accurately translating it into English. Emma looked impressed as he handed the book back to her.

"You read that very well," she said.

"My grandmother insisted on our learning and speaking French from infancy," he explained. "She was raised that way, I suppose. After she passed away, I seldom used the language until I studied it again at college."

"You traveled abroad, did you not?" Emma asked. "I always wished to do that."

"I spent some months in Europe. Speaking French was very helpful there, of course."

"Did you visit Paris?'

"Oh, yes."

"How did you like it?"

He commented favorably on the beauty of the city, but when she asked about its citizens, he was less complimentary, and immediately suffered some embarrassment, remembering that, like his grandmother, the DuBose family was of French Huguenot extraction.

"I beg your pardon," he said, smiling apologetically.

"That's quite all right, Captain Hutchinson," she responded, not offended, but amused.

Emma closed her book and set it aside. She glanced at her aunt and uncle, who were still talking between themselves, and then turned her attention back to John. His mention of the military college he had attended had stirred her curiosity about something.

"After you enrolled at the Citadel," she said, "I thought perhaps you would make your career a military one, but then we heard that you were at Hutchinson and Company in Charleston."

"No, I never considered a career in the army," said John. "I didn't much care for such strict discipline in my younger days. I had other interests."

"What were they?" Emma inquired, looking very interested.

"What were they?" he repeated thoughtfully. "Nothing very admirable, I'm afraid–but you must allow me to plead the folly of youth on that."

"I'm sure you grew used to discipline in the army," she speculated.

"Of course! Like or not, one grows up very quickly under such circumstances. I assure you, all folly has been duly whipped out of me."

"All folly?" she echoed, amused again.

Her smile and her look, which he imagined was at least one of fondness if nothing more, filled him with happiness.

"Except for a sense of humor, I hope," he said, returning her smile. "Miss DuBose, please believe me, I am a thoroughly disciplined individual now, except perhaps for...a susceptibility or two."

"I shan't inquire about those," she replied–almost playfully, he thought.

John was about to say, in the same tone, "I wish you would," when Mrs. Screven addressed a question to him, and his precious few moments of private conversation with Emma were brought to an end for the moment.

Later, during a pause in the general conversation that had resumed, he asked Emma to read aloud to him. The others stopped to listen, too, as she began to read in English, but Mrs. Screven was soon showing signs of distaste for the subject matter. She commenced another dialogue with her brother, leaving John as Emma's only audience. As he listened, he spread out to a reclining position, propping himself up on one elbow, and tried not to fix his eyes on her too often or too long.

After a while, he casually interrupted Emma to ask a question about a passage she had just read, and when she finished answering him, he asked her another in a more earnest tone, and a lower voice, changing the subject entirely.

"Won't you come and visit Elias? It would do him good, I think."

She seemed not to mind the change of subject, but looked a little puzzled.

"You said he wasn't receiving any visitors–that he didn't

want any."

"I think he's feeling better now. It's been two weeks since he came home, and I think he is looking stronger. I believe I could persuade Elias to be a little more sociable. Will you come and see him?"

"If he's agreeable to it, I should be happy to see him."

"I could drive over and fetch you in the carriage."

Emma cut a glance toward her aunt without actually looking at her, pondering the possibility of her approval. John knew why she hesitated to answer.

"I'll bring my cousin Laura with us, too. I think Elias will allow that now. You ladies can enjoy each other's company on the way to Belle Ville."

"When?"

"Tomorrow?"

"I'll see if I may."

There had been another lull in the conversation on the other side of the garden, and when Emma and John looked up from this exchange, they saw that both her aunt and uncle were watching them with openly curious expressions.

"What is it you are plotting, Emma?" Mr. DuBose asked facetiously. "I can always tell when you are plotting something. You have no guile."

"Captain Hutchinson wishes me to visit his brother Elias at Belle Ville," she told him.

"I think that's an excellent idea," he said enthusiastically.

Mrs. Screven immediately looked dubious, and Emma hastened to explain that Miss Laura Townsend would accompany them. Mr. DuBose was less strict about such matters than his sister, and since he had the final say, permission was granted.

The next morning, John drove up to the house in an open carriage with his cousin Laura. Emma was waiting expectantly, watching from the parlor window, and when she saw them she rushed to pick up her hat and put it on. Her aunt and uncle walked out with her, and John introduced Mr. DuBose to his cousin.

Laura was wearing the gift she had been given for her birthday, a pretty new day dress of light blue figured calico. Emma, attired in black, greeted her with a kiss. Though they were not intimate friends, the two young women had spent many hours together in the work of the Ladies' Aid Society, and were fond of each other.

After a brief conversation with John and his cousin, Mr. Dubose and his sister watched the carriage drive off.

"Miss Townsend is a lovely girl," said the old gentleman, as he waved to her and Emma.

Mrs. Screven seemed to agree with a brief "hmm." She sighed and watched the carriage until it was out of sight, then finally remarked, a little peevishly, "I wonder that Captain Hutchinson did not invite us to Belle Ville."

Her brother looked at her in surprise.

"Good heavens, Adele!" he said irritably. "I'm sure we'll be invited to Belle Ville by and by. Let the young people have a little time to themselves!"

When the carriage arrived at Belle Ville, John helped the ladies down and escorted them into the house. He asked them to wait in the hallway for a moment so that he could make sure that his brother was ready to receive them. Stepping into the library, John saw that Elias was awake, and that there had been at least a slight improvement in his condition and his appearance. His face was freshly shaved, his hair neatly combed, and his thin body was wrapped in a handsome dressing robe.

"Elias, I've brought visitors for you today–two pretty young ladies," John announced.

"I'm sure I'm very poor company, but since you have insisted..."

His tone was indifferent, almost irritable, but he couldn't hide a flash of nervousness and eagerness in his eyes.

John showed the ladies in and first reacquainted Emma and Elias.

"I remember you, Miss DuBose, of course," he said politely. "How nice to see you again."

Concealing the shock she felt at seeing Elias, Laura approached him and placed a cousinly kiss on his forehead. John was sure he saw a slight blush on his brother's face afterwards; Elias certainly brightened, and quickly drew himself up to a more upright sitting position as he greeted his guests.

"John said two pretty young ladies wished to visit me. He should have said, two beauties–one dark and the other fair. Quite a feast for the eyes!"

The two young women softly laughed and shook their heads at his gallantry.

"You're not such poor company after all, Elias," John observed humorously, pleased to see his brother showing an interest in something at last.

"Poor company? You never were such a thing, Elias," Laura agreed brightly, though her heart was aching for him.

Israel came into the room with a tray and served them cool drinks.

"Cherry shrub!" said Elias, holding up his glass tumbler to admire the bright red color of the beverage. "We have such luxuries here."

He took a sip with delectation, his eyes fixed on Laura,

drinking in the sight of her with the same pleasure.

John informed his brother that their cousin had been "telling on him" on the drive to Belle Ville, and briefly reminded him of several incidents of their childhood together.

"Now Miss DuBose will think badly of me," Elias protested, though he was half-smiling. "I suppose I must confess to you, Miss Emma, we were perfect little devils, and our little cousin was an angel. We treated her very poorly."

"Oh, it wasn't so bad," Laura dissented with a smile. "Some of your pranks were very amusing."

"I thought so, too, even if you didn't at the time," Elias admitted, looking as boyish as his remark.

Laura turned to Emma.

"With these two, and my brothers, the joke was always on me," she sighed. "I wasn't clever enough to retaliate, and I'm afraid I was something of a crybaby."

"You were, a bit," Elias conceded.

"I shall give you another example of their mischief, Miss DuBose," said Laura. "Although I believe this particular little caper was instigated by my brother Tom. One day the boys told me that the pretty pink blossoms on the mimosa tree were really fairies, and that if I pulled on a broken limb that was hanging down from a bigger limb, it would wake the fairies, and they would fly about for me to see. I was only about seven years old, and of course I was foolish enough to believe them. Now, it had rained earlier that day, so it happened that when I gave the broken limb a good tug, I received a drenching shower of rain water from the leaves, just as the pranksters planned. They laughed, and I cried."

Emma had to laugh a little herself at the picture which had been created in her mind.

"Then you ran and told your father," Elias reminded her.

"He gave Tom a good whipping, and John and I thought that was very funny, until we got home and were sent to bed without supper. It was very bad of us to tease and fool a little girl so much, but you were so gullible, it was too tempting."

Elias and his cousin smiled at each other affectionately.

"You will forgive me for all that, won't you, Laura?" he asked wistfully.

"Of course, Elias."

"I won't believe you unless you hold my hand," he cajoled her.

"See, Miss DuBose," said Laura, looking at her with a delighted smile, "he is still mischievous."

John moved Laura's chair closer to Elias so that they could easily reach each other. Elias took the young woman's soft hand and pressed it against his gaunt cheek, closing his eyes a little while. Laura also closed her eyes momentarily, obviously suppressing tears, but quickly composed herself.

"Did you receive all my letters?" Elias asked her. "I know I wrote to you at least once a week, sometimes more."

"I believe I have almost all that you sent me, though perhaps a few were lost. The mails were so unreliable at times."

"Yes, they were. It was very good of you to write to me so regularly. Sometimes, letters from home were my only pleasures."

"I looked forward to your letters, too, Elias, very much," said Laura.

For this he kissed her hand gratefully, and then turned a sly look on John and Emma.

"Now Miss Emma," he said, "you ought to let my brother hold your hand, so that both gentlemen here can be equally blissful."

"Elias!" Laura scolded him. "You will make Miss DuBose

blush."

"John's the one who's turning red!" he laughed, pointing at him.

John had in fact colored a little, and looked away from Emma to hide it, but he couldn't help smiling. It did his heart good to see his brother so animated and cheerful. Emma betrayed some slight embarrassment, but nothing else she might have been thinking.

Elias's laughter suddenly ended in fitful coughing. He asked for a glass of water, which John immediately brought him from a nearby table.

"Ah," he complained, "that has set my head to aching."

He pressed his fingers between his eyes, and Laura gently stroked his hair and the side of his face. As he closed his eyes, Laura looked at John with concern.

After a few moments Elias sighed, "That's better," but when his eyes opened, they were weary and heavy with pain.

"Perhaps you should rest now, Elias dear," Laura suggested.

"I think I should," he said reluctantly. "Forgive me, ladies. I enjoyed your visit very much. Please come and see me again soon."

When Elias took his cousin's hand to kiss it again, his own hands were trembling, and his grasp was weaker.

"Goodbye, Miss DuBose," he said, reaching out to her. She gave him her hand for a moment.

"Don't let my bad manners keep you away. I'll be sure to mend them if you will promise to come and see me again, and tell me all about yourself."

"I promise," she answered warmly.

John escorted the ladies out of the room and asked Israel to sit with Elias for a while. They walked into the drawing room where Laura sat down on a chair and covered her face.

"Will you allow me a few moments to myself?" she asked in a shaky voice, on the verge of tears.

John offered Emma his arm and asked her if she would care to walk out with him to the garden. They went out through the front door and walked around the house toward a lovely spot that Elias could view from his window. It was a formal garden, bordered and given symmetry by rows of dark green shrubs.

John and Emma strolled along a graveled pathway which was, like the rest of the garden, partly overtaken by weeds and untended plants. In one quarter, some of the shrubbery had been shaped in various geometric specimens of topiary, but they had long since outgrown their original designs, and were irregular, misshapen monstrosities of their former selves. Rose bushes drooped off broken stakes, many of their leaves brown with a blight, but various species of other flowers were still blooming among the weeds, not completely choked out by them yet.

"I remember this place," Emma remarked. "It was so beautiful. It still is."

They passed under a tall arched trellis. Tendrils of star jasmine had clustered so thickly on the wooden structure supporting them that it was almost invisible now. John breathed in their fragrance, and as Emma turned her face up to his, the look in her eyes seemed to penetrate his soul with the same sweetness.

"My father planted this garden for my mother," he said. "It was neglected for a long while after she died. When he could no longer bear to see it in decay, he restored it, and kept up the place as she had. Since the war, though, it has suffered again, as you can see."

"Like our garden," said Emma.

She glanced around and saw a large, spreading mimosa tree at the end of a hedge.

"Is that the tree where you played your prank on your cousin Laura?" she asked.

"No, it was a tree at the Townsend's house, near the village."

"Ah, yes."

"Elias and I used to climb this one. We would sit up in the biggest limbs and toss the pebbles of gravel at the house, mainly to pester Israel. We broke a window once doing that and both received a well-deserved switching for it."

"How full of mischief you were!"

"I'm afraid we were."

John almost asked Emma about her brothers, if they had been such trouble, but thought better of it before the question left his lips. They walked past a row of crape myrtles which were covered with new green leaves but not yet in bloom.

"You say you remember this place, Miss DuBose," he remarked. "Your father must have brought you here when you were very young."

"He did, a few times. I was very proud to ride my pony to Belle Ville. I used to play with your younger sister, but I don't remember seeing much of you and Elias."

"That's probably just as well," said John. "You might have suffered the same fate as our little cousin Laura."

She smiled, and they walked on without talking for a few minutes. In this beautiful place, John felt an impulse to make his feelings known to Emma. He searched for words to express his growing affection, to broach the subject with some finesse and delicacy, but just as he was about to speak, they heard a door open, and Laura came out of the house to join them.

Her eyes were a little swollen from crying, but she was calm and composed now. She took John's other arm, and the three strolled and talked for a few minutes before heading back to the carriage.

Inside, Elias had been drowsing, but he happened to open his eyes as they walked past his window. When he saw Laura again he turned away and hid his face in his pillows.

In the afternoon, back at home, after her brief and welcome respite from the usual daily drudgery, Emma went about her household chores and work in the gardens like an automaton. Her mind was miles away at Belle Ville.

She relived the morning's events and conversations over and over again, smiling over some things, then feeling pangs of compassion for Elias, who looked so piteous that she had found it hard not to weep when she first saw him again. He had reminded her of her own brother Theo, who had looked much the same before he died of his wounds. But she wanted to be hopeful about Elias, for his sake, and for John's, and immediately dismissed such dark thoughts.

After a while, all the other memories of the day receded into the background, and her thoughts were only of one subject. Despite the fearful little voice inside her head that had often warned her not to think of John Hutchinson, Emma had fallen in love with him. She had been forced to admit this truth to herself the Sunday after Elias came home to Belle Ville. When John failed to show up at the DuBose place that afternoon, her disappointment had been so keen, so painful, that she could no longer deny her feelings.

She asked herself, did John love her? Emma thought she had seen the answer in his eyes that morning. But what if she was wrong? She remembered his many visits and kindnesses–and yet he had not declared himself. She grew a little fearful, telling herself that she should have perhaps heeded that voice of warning–but it was far too late for that.

CHAPTER EIGHT

WHEN JOHN RETURNED EMMA from her visit to Belle Ville, Mrs. Screven detained him for a moment while Laura waited in the carriage. She told him that she had a favor to ask of him. An old friend of the family, an elderly lady who had resided on a plantation not far from the village, had just passed away. She wondered if John would lend them the use of his carriage and do them the kindness of carrying the family to the funeral the next day. Always eager to be of service to Emma or her family, he readily consented.

"Of course, Mrs. Screven," he said. "What time shall I call for you?"

She named the time–ten o'clock–and thanked him profusely. He drove away with his cousin, secretly rejoicing that he would see Emma again so soon.

The following morning, about ten minutes before the hour of ten, John arrived, pulled up the carriage in the drive, and jumped down to adjust the horse's harness. It was a sunny, cloudless day and, like the day before, unusually warm for May.

For the funeral of this beloved old friend, Emma had again put on her one piece of clothing that was not patched or threadbare–the black mourning dress she had worn for too many such sad occasions in the past four years. She came out of the house first and waited on the porch. Seeing that John was occupied with something, she turned her attention to the untangling of a knot in the ribbons of a hat she was holding. John was standing behind the horse, and had just finished with the harnesses when he caught sight of her.

Taking advantage of his partial concealment to observe her unawares, he paused in admiration, noting as he had before how the lines of the simple but dignified black dress revealed the beauty of her figure, and at that moment, how the sunlight made her hair glow like gold. As usual, she wore it parted in the middle and gathered in the back, with a few loose curls at her temples.

Mrs. Screven came bustling out the door and stopped in her tracks, staring at John, who was staring at her niece. Her look of displeasure and, he imagined, affront, immediately caused him to turn away. He went red in the face and moved behind the horse's neck, needlessly fiddling with the harness straps a little longer. When the ladies approached the wagon he greeted them and helped them up, avoiding Mrs. Screven's eyes, and then took his place as the driver.

"Where is Mr. DuBose?" he asked.

"My uncle isn't feeling well," Emma answered. "Much against our wishes, he worked in the field yesterday–"

"And he's suffering for it today!" Mrs. Screven interrupted testily. "Theo doesn't tolerate the heat very well, you know. He is really a most vexing old fellow."

John realized now that the irritated look Mrs. Screven had sent his way had nothing to do with him. She was upset about her brother.

"Would you like me to send Dr. Townsend to see him?" he

offered, snapping the reins to start the horse.

"He detests doctors!" Mrs. Screven complained. "There was never a more obstinate old fellow in the world. He brings these things on himself, and then grumbles and groans. Now he wants to take us to Flat Rock, where the weather is better."

"Flat Rock?" John repeated dully. "In North Carolina?"

His back was to the ladies as he drove the carriage; they did not see the troubled expression that his face suddenly assumed. Emma explained that her uncle owned property in Flat Rock, and had lived on it many years, but had gone to stay with his son in Greenville in the last year of the war.

"My brother says he is quite fed up with the farm and has no hope for it," said Mrs. Screven. "He still has his house and land in North Carolina, and wishes us to come and live with him there."

"Is he serious?" asked John.

"Well, he does go on sometimes when he's not feeling well, but that's what he said."

Mrs. Screven sighed and brooded over her irritation for a while, but then began talking with Emma about their old friend who was being buried that morning.

They drove to an old family cemetery where John accompanied the ladies to the grave side service. The rector of the parish church, Mr. Shubrick, was still convalescing from an illness, and a feeble old deacon officiated, holding a handkerchief and wiping away perspiration from his face in the warm morning sun. As soon as the service was over, John retreated to the shady spot on the edge of a grove where he had left the carriage, while Emma and her aunt conversed with some friends they had not seen in a long while.

He was still stunned by the idea that Mr. DuBose was contemplating moving his family away to North Carolina. The news had struck him as forcefully as a physical blow, and he had been brooding over it ever since Mrs. Screven mentioned the possibility, finding it hard to think of anything else, though, out of respect, he tried to pay attention to the deacon's words and prayers. He had been hoping that Emma was at least beginning to care for him, but if she went away...

John heaved a sigh of frustration and climbed back up to his seat on the carriage. For a long while he stared off into the trees but did not see them. He was projecting himself into a future without her, a future in which he saw nothing but a bleak emptiness and a loneliness that he was tasting even now. He knew he had been falling in love with Emma, but was only realizing at that moment how securely and irrevocably his heart strings were already attached, and how much he needed her.

While her aunt paused for a final word with a friend who had walked with them part of the way, Emma returned to the carriage. John had heard Emma saying her goodbyes, and knew the footsteps approaching were hers. She could see him sitting on the carriage seat with his back to her, his head and shoulders sunk somewhat low. He was trying to recover from the thoughts which had been absorbing him, but for a moment, looking around, and without meaning to do so, he turned such a piercing, hungering look on her that she was shaken to the core when their eyes met.

"Oh, don't look at me like that!" she thought, disturbed.

She quickly turned her back to him with a racing heart and waited for her aunt, who was not long in arriving at the carriage. On the drive home, both Emma and John were unusually quiet, but Mrs. Screven was in a talkative mood, and hardly noticed, going on and on about scraps of news, mostly bad, concerning friends and family she had picked up during conversations with others at the burial service.

When they reached the farm Mr. DuBose was sitting out on the porch fanning himself. He smiled and waved, indicating that John should come and visit with him. John helped the ladies down and drove the carriage a little farther on, leaving it under the shade of some trees.

As he walked up to the house he could hear Mrs. Screven remonstrating with Emma's uncle, who was supposed to have remained in bed. Mr. DuBose cut her short with an impatient gesture and waved more emphatically to John, hoping to be rescued by his presence. Mrs. Screven huffed at her brother and went inside, while Emma hesitated between staying with her uncle and following her aunt into the house. When John asked Mr. DuBose if he could speak with him privately about something, she stepped inside and closed the door behind her.

"Too hot and stifling in my room today," the old gentleman remarked, fanning his face briskly.

"Are you feeling better now?" John asked, taking a seat near him.

"Yes, a good bit. I suppose you have heard all about my trespasses from the ladies."

"They said you don't tolerate the heat well, and that you wish to go back to your home in North Carolina."

"Yes, I was saying that last night. I am considering it. I am of little use here, and I don't think we'll be able to sustain ourselves on this place, even with Mr. Drawdy's help—and his son's. The poor fellow is working himself to death. I have a comfortable house and some land in Flat Rock–are you familiar with the place?"

"Yes, a cousin has a house there, and I've been his guest several times."

"Well, I have some properties in the area that I could sell. If I got a fair price for them, it would allow me to take care of my niece and sister for a good while. I was thinking that Emma could perhaps start a school there, or perhaps in Greenville, if I cannot convince the ladies to come with me to Flat Rock. My niece is very well educated, and would make an excellent teacher, I believe."

At the mention of Emma's name, John pulled his chair a little closer and glanced through the window into the parlor with a serious, preoccupied air.

"I'm sure the ladies have gone upstairs to change their clothes," said Mr. DuBose, suppressing a smile, and looking very interested. "What was it you wished to talk with me about, Captain Hutchinson?"

"Miss DuBose."

"Ah!"

Mr. DuBose's eyes sparkled, and he could no longer suppress his smile.

"I wish to ask her to marry me, with your consent," John said breathlessly.

"You love her?"

"Very much."

Mr. DuBose nodded slowly and deliberately, and adjusted his lips to a more appropriately serious expression. He had been expecting this conversation for some time now.

"That you love my niece so much is proof of your excellent judgment and sense. As her uncle, I am partial, of course, but even so, it cannot be denied that Emma is a very fine young woman. I daresay you appreciate that."

"I could not hold her in such high regard for her if I did not, Mr. DuBose. I should consider myself a very fortunate man to have her love and respect."

There was a kind of question mark in John's voice and look which Mr. DuBose understood. He smiled and said softly, "Emma is a thoughtful girl of deep affections. If I am not mistaken, I believe I have detected a good portion of those thoughts and affections being sent your way, Captain Hutchinson."

John's expression grew ecstatic when he heard this.

"I hope you're not mistaken," he said. "Nothing would make me happier."

"Well, then, I am pleased, very pleased."

"Thank you, sir!"

"Yes, I am pleased, but not very surprised, you know."

"Were my feelings so obvious?" John asked.

"They were to me," Mr. DuBose chuckled. "My sister, on the other hand, is such a creature of convention and custom that I am sure she has had little or no suspicion of your intentions, since they were not formally declared. Have you made your feelings known to Emma?"

"No, not directly...the time we have spent in each other's company–"

"Has been in the company of others," Mr. DuBose finished for him. "I understand your difficulty, young man. I tell you what, come and visit us for Sunday dinner, and if the weather is tolerable, we shall all of us go for a walk together. Emma likes to stroll down to the creek and sit by it. I'll see that Mrs. Screven and I wander by ourselves for a while to give you a little privacy. How does that strike you, young man?"

"I shall pray for good weather," John replied, smiling broadly.

Emma and her aunt finished changing their clothes and came downstairs. John had just left, and Mr. DuBose was coming back inside the house. Seeing him, Mrs. Screven was unable to restrain her curiosity.

"What was it you and Captain Hutchinson were conferring

about?" she asked.

Mr. DuBose pretended he had not heard her correctly.

"Yes, Captain Hutchinson has gone," he said.

Mrs. Screven rolled her eyes and repeated the question more loudly.

"Ah! We were talking of Flat Rock. Captain Hutchinson is exceedingly fond of the place. His cousin has a house there."

"Oh," muttered his sister. "Well, I don't know a soul there!"

"I invited him to dine with us Sunday. Let's have a nice little cold luncheon, eh? Can we manage that?"

"I don't see why not," said Mrs. Screven, and as soon as she spoke her mind was instantly occupied with the planning of a meal.

Emma walked outside alone and picked up a bucket to draw some water from the well. She was thinking about John. The way he had looked at her earlier left her with no doubts as to his feelings for her, but there was an unexpected disquiet mixed with her excitement and joy. She had never been in love before, and the strength and nature of her feelings for him, now flowing unrestrained, almost frightened her, like his unsettling look. Feeling slightly feverish in the sun, she splashed some cool water on her face.

She carried the bucket back to the house, and though there was much work to be done, she allowed herself a few minutes of daydreaming while she was alone in the kitchen.

"John loves me," she kept thinking. "He loves me."

The idea was so beautiful to her, all other concerns began to subside in the contemplation of it, leaving only happiness.

As usual, John spent his evening with Elias. They were playing chess, and were near the end of their first game, the board resting on a low ottoman next to Elias's couch. John was not as talkative as usual, and his brother noticed that he often paused with an abstracted air and looked away from the game.

"You seem very preoccupied," Elias remarked, as he waited for John to make a move.

"I'm sorry. I'll try to pay better attention since you seem to be winning. We can't have that."

"I've only seen you like this once before," Elais observed in a significant tone, referring to John's one-time passion for Miss Mason.

"That was nothing," John replied in the same significant tone, with a look to match it.

Elias raised his eyebrows.

"If that was nothing, this must be something indeed!"

"It is," said John.

"Miss DuBose, of course."

"Yes."

"I never knew her very well, but I've only heard good of her," Elias said approvingly. "Does she return your feelings?"

"I think so."

"You don't sound very confident."

"I'm not sure, but I'm going to find out Sunday. I'm going to ask her to marry me."

Elias put out his hand, and his brother took it, laughing nervously.

"I'm happy for you, John," he said.

"I hope you can say that in a few days. It's a little premature right now."

John deliberately moved a chess piece into a position which would ensure his defeat.

"How is it you never married during the war?" Elias asked him curiously. "I was sure you would take some Richmond belle to the altar."

"Oh, no," said John, with a musing smile. "Of course most of my men were married fellows, but our Colonel was more pleased with his bachelor officers and soldiers. He said that married men's minds were too often divided by concerns for their wives and children at home. I decided he was right, that I would make a better officer if I kept my mind undivided."

"There must have been temptations," his brother speculated.

"A few, but nothing came of them, and I'm very thankful for that now! When the war began, there seemed to be a mad rush for everyone to get married or engaged, and I'm afraid I knew a man or two who lived to regret such hasty decisions."

"But I'm sure that you wrote to me about one young lady in Richmond," Elias pressed him, "and I do remember that you were very complimentary about her."

"Ah, that young lady," said John, his eyes widening a little in alarm as he recalled her. "She nursed me through my first wound. Her father was one of the men in charge of the military hospitals, and he took a few of us into his home. I was suffering with an infection and some fever and delirium, and not quite myself."

"A pretty girl?"

"Very pretty. So much so, I began to think I had fallen in love with her. I remember dictating two letters to her, one for you and one for father, but I have no idea what I must have said. What did I say?"

"I don't remember exactly, but I recall wondering if your next letter might not announce an engagement," Elias answered, amused. "What happened?"

"Well…when I was well enough to converse with her in my right mind, and found out that the young lady believed there was some sort of understanding between us, I was immediately cured, you might say. She was barely sixteen, and quite childish and romantic, I discovered. She and her family took good care of me, and I was very grateful to them, but believe me, I was very happy to leave that house."

"An awkward situation!" Elias laughed. "Still, it's very funny to think of what might have happened."

"You wouldn't wish such a fate on me, would you?"

Elias shook his head.

"No," he said. "I think Miss DuBose is a much better one."

John reached over and tousled his hair.

"We must get you on your feet soon, brother. You may have to attend a wedding before long."

Late on Sunday morning, John bathed, groomed himself carefully, and, like a courting male bird out to display his best feathers, put on what he considered his most becoming clothes. He had been wearing nothing but darker clothing as a continued token of mourning, but allowed himself to dispense with the practice just this once, just for this particular day, which he hoped would prove to be a joyous one.

After buttoning up an embroidered, saffron silk vest, he slipped on his best coat and inspected himself in a dressing mirror, eyeing the cut of his fawn-colored trousers and the sheen of his highly polished shoes with satisfaction. He wanted to present himself in the best light possible when he made his feelings known to Emma, and offered himself to her, body and soul. His soul was what it was; he would let her know that it already belonged to her. His good looks were more apparent, and therefore, he hoped, more of an advantage, especially as he was so well-groomed and well-dressed today.

Nature seemed to be cooperating with him; it turned out to be a mild, breezy, beautiful day. Wavering between an exhilarating confidence and the dread of rejection, John rode up to the farm house about noon. Mr. DuBose was waiting for him on the porch.

"Just in time, Captain Hutchinson!" he called to him. "I am famished. Shall we go in?"

John followed him into the dining room where a light meal was set out on the table. The ladies came in a moment later carrying a few last dishes and took their seats, Emma noting John's exceptionally fine appearance and attire with a slight lift of the eyebrows.

Emma's appetite had been languishing for the past week; during the meal, she put very little on her plate and took tiny nibbles to give the appearance of eating. John had little interest in food, either, but he forced himself to eat and complimented the ladies on a fine meal. When they were all finished, Mr. DuBose suggested a walk. After the ladies cleared the table, they went upstairs to get their best bonnets. Emma came down holding her hat and a book, something she was seldom without on a Sunday.

It was very warm in the sun as the four walked towards the woods, but in the shade of the trees, the breezes were cooler, and the air more comfortable. Mr. DuBose said he wished to walk to the creek to see the little falls there, so they strolled in that direction. He and Mrs. Screven walked side by side just ahead of John and Emma.

Thinking of waterfalls, Emma asked John if he had ever been to North Carolina, but as soon as she did, realized it was a foolish question and apologized.

"I forgot, my uncle said you were very fond of Flat Rock."

"I'm sure I never mentioned it to you," he reassured her, noticing a little nervousness on her part, which he hoped boded well for him. "I remember our trips into the mountains, and how many grand waterfalls we saw there."

He went into some detail, and his descriptions of North Carolina conjured up her own memories of similar landscapes.

"Sometimes," she said, "when I was a girl, we would summer in Flat Rock at my uncle's house, and take trips to the mountains nearby. There were several lovely waterfalls I remember. It was all so beautiful! I should like to go back there someday. In the evenings, we would run about on the grassy hills trying to catch the lightning bugs, my brothers and I..."

As soon as Emma mentioned her brothers, a sad, pained look came over her face. Seeing this, John quickly changed the subject to draw her thoughts back to the present moment, and to him.

"What are you reading today?" he asked, looking down at the slim volume she had brought along with her.

"A book of English poetry."

"Perhaps you would read some for me," he suggested.

She inclined her head a little in tentative assent.

They walked along a well-worn path, and the woods soon thinned out as a broad part of the creek came into sight. They could faintly hear the falls now, and the gurgling of the little eddies around the rocks in the water. The falls were created by an irregular terrace of rock that projected out of the creek bed, and were no more than two feet high in most places, but they made a pleasing sound and appearance.

They paused at a shady, grassy area which sloped down into the flowing waters.

"This is where Emma likes to sit and read," said Mr. DuBose.

He turned to her.

"I'm sure you and Captain Hutchinson can make yourselves

comfortable here. Perhaps you can read to him, Emma. Come, Adele. I have been told that there is a lovely spring which feeds into the creek a little farther along. Its waters are supposed to have medicinal properties. Let's walk there and get ourselves a drink, shall we? Perhaps it will be good for my rheumatism."

Before Mrs. Screven could answer yes or no, with her arm bound tightly in his, Mr. DuBose blithely led his sister off.

John briefly held Emma's elbow as she sat down, and when she was settled and comfortable, he seated himself beside her on the grass.

"Our little falls are rather paltry in comparison to those in the mountains," she remarked, tucking her skirts more neatly around her.

"Better than none at all, though," John replied, "and perhaps even better than the grander ones."

She turned her eyes on him with keen interest and asked, "Oh, how so?"

The reason for his observation went out of his head the moment she questioned him, and it took him a few moments to recall it and put it into words. He explained that a thing in miniature could sometimes be more delightful than the same thing on a larger scale.

"That's true," Emma agreed reflectively. "Like miniature portraits. I do so marvel at them sometimes."

Happy that he had been able to offer an intelligent answer, John took a deep breath to quell his nervousness, tilting his head sideways to read the title of the little volume she was holding in her lap.

"Now Miss DuBose," he said, "let me hear a poem you like."

Prompted by this command, Emma automatically opened the book, but then paused and looked up at him with a whimsical expression.

"Why Captain Hutchinson, I have read to you so many times, I think you ought to read to me."

"That's fair," he consented, but took the book from her with some concern, wondering whether the subject matter was suitable to his purposes, or if he might make himself sound foolish.

John leafed through several pages and saw nothing but what seemed to be religious verse. It was not quite the mood he had hoped to set. He turned to another part of the volume and found a few titles that suggested love poems, something more fitting to his romantic aims. His eyes fell on the first two verses of a poem, and he hastily decided that it looked apt and promising. He briefly cleared his throat and began to read aloud.

> *"Sweet day, so cool, so calm, so bright,*
> *"The bridal of the earth and sky—"*

He looked up at Emma meaningfully, and read on.

> *"The dew shall weep thy fall tonight;*
> *"For thou must die."*

He stopped, now disappointed in his selection

"That's not a pleasant thought," he complained. "Let me find another one to read."

"Oh, no! Please go on," Emma urged him. "You've chosen one I like very much. It is a very brief poem."

Reluctantly, he continued.

> *"Sweet spring, full of sweet days and roses,*
> *"A box where sweets compacted lie,*

"My music shows ye have your closes,
"And all must die.

"Sweet rose, whose hue, angry and brave,
"Bids the rash gazer wipe his eye,
"Thy root is ever in its grave,
"And thou must die.

"Only a sweet and virtuous soul,
"Like seasoned timber, never gives,
"But though the whole world turn to coal,
"Then chiefly lives."

He pondered over the last verses, impressed with their meaning, but more relieved that the poem had ended on what was at least a hopeful note.

Emma thanked him and complimented him by saying, "You read that very well, Captain Hutchinson."

John handed the book back to her quickly before she could ask him to read more. Emma smiled as she took it, but did not read aloud. She closed the book, set it down in the grass, and turned to gaze off at the waterfalls. As John studied her profile, it seemed to him that the moment was ripe, and that he ought to speak up.

"I think you are very sweet, Miss DuBose," he said.

His voice came to her ears in a tender, amorous tone she had never heard from him before. Outwardly, she seemed to freeze in place, but inside, her heart throbbed instantly to a rapid beat, and her thoughts began swirling in a dizzying way. It had happened at last–he was wooing her–and though she had been half-expecting it, she was still startled.

Emma's eyes slowly closed and reopened as she tried to

clear her head. John shifted himself a little closer to her. Then, for some reason, she looked down at the creek's edge and noticed that her little book of poetry had somehow slid down the grassy slope, nearly to the edge of the water, and was in danger of falling in. John saw the book, too, and reached down to draw it back. Emma suddenly made a movement to rise, and he followed her lead, helping her to her feet.

"Have I offended you?" he asked uneasily.

"No, I–I don't know what to say," she stammered, avoiding his eyes.

"Say what you feel."

But she still couldn't think what to say.

"Miss DuBose...," he began.

Emma raised her eyes, and they were caught by his with such intensity and magnetism that she could not look away.

"I love you," he said. "Surely you know that."

She hesitated, but then admitted that she did know it.

"Perhaps," he went on, stepping closer to her, "perhaps I presume too much, but I think you care for me, too."

Emma dropped her eyes momentarily, but had to speak the truth when she looked up again. He could plainly see the answer in her eyes; she hardly needed to say it.

"I do care for you," she almost whispered, finding it a little difficult to catch her breath.

Without smiling, his whole face took on a look of rapture. He grasped both her hands and held them firmly.

"Miss DuBose–Miss Emma, will you marry me?" he asked.

"I will," she answered, without hesitation.

With a sigh of relief, John brought her hands to his mouth and kissed them.

"You've made me very happy," he said, pressing her fingers

to his face.

Emma fairly glowed with happiness, too, but there was also a shyness about her now that John had never seen before; she spoke with effort, and frequently lowered her eyes. This new reserve was unexpected, but he found it charming.

"I must tell you, Miss Emma," he said, smiling, "it was with much fear and trembling that I came to see you today. I said that I thought you cared for me, but I wasn't certain of it."

"You may be certain of it now," she forced herself to say.

"I'm glad we're done with all that!" he laughed. "I've been suffering quite an ordeal, especially since this talk of you and your family going away."

As he was saying this, they heard her uncle's voice, and Mr. DuBose and Mrs. Screven were soon in sight again. Emma turned to glance at them, but John was unable to take his eyes from her.

"Shall we tell them?" she asked, turning to face him again with a radiant smile.

Mrs. Screven was hobbling a little as she held on to her brother's arm. She had struck her foot against a stone and was complaining of some pain. Mr. DuBose was not sympathetic, displeased that she had insisted on returning to this spot so soon to sit with her and Captain Hutchinson.

"Captain Hutchinson has asked me to marry him," Emma announced happily.

Mrs. Screven staggered slightly in surprise.

"You have consented?" she asked.

"Yes!"

"Oh, my darling, I am so happy for you!" she cried, and completely forgot about her aching foot as she rushed over to embrace Emma.

Mr. DuBose shook John's hand vigorously as he

congratulated him.

"This is a fine thing," said the old gentleman joyfully, "a very fine match."

At the house, Mr. DuBose again took a firm hold on Mrs. Screven's arm and led her up the steps and through the door, leaving Emma and John alone in the yard just at the foot of the front steps. Emma watched them disappear with an amused expression, then, still smiling, looked to John.

"Your uncle has been my ally for the day," he confessed.

"I suspected that," she said knowingly. "He isn't very subtle. When did you speak with him?"

"On Tuesday."

"When you two were supposedly talking about Flat Rock?"

"Yes," he laughed. "The place was actually mentioned."

"I see."

"You didn't wish to go there, did you, Miss Emma?"

"No!"

John glanced over at the windows to see if perhaps Mrs. Screven might be looking out on them. When he saw that they were not being observed, he took Emma's hands again and stepped closer to her.

"May I kiss you?" he asked.

She smiled shyly and allowed a brief kiss.

"May I call you Emma when we are speaking privately?"

"You may."

"And will you call me by my name, instead of Captain Hutchinson?"

"Yes, I will do that."

"Emma, I love you!" he sighed, impulsively leaning closer and putting his face next to hers to say those words into her ear.

He drew back when they were not echoed back to him and looked at her with a quizzical smile.

"Won't you say, John, I love you?" he coaxed her.

She drew in a deep breath.

"I love you, John," she murmured, though she found it hard to look into his eyes when she did.

"That's better!" he exulted.

John remembered what Mr. DuBose had said of Emma, that she was a girl of deep affections. Now those affections were his, and he saw that they did flow deep, so much so that she could hardly bear to express them by words or looks, and at that moment he also realized, with joy and a little fear, that he was as essential to her as she was to him.

"It is difficult for you to say these things to me?" he asked softly.

"It is," she admitted, her eyes downcast.

"You don't mind if I am more demonstrative, I hope."

"No, I...I am glad for it."

She looked up at him and received another kiss.

"I am engaged to you, my dear Emma, and that makes me very happy," he said, releasing her. "Will you allow me to enjoy the happiness of your company a little while longer before I have to go?"

They walked up to the porch to two chairs placed in front of the open parlor window, and sat down to talk for hours. As evening fell, they were still talking. Mr. DuBose was just inside with Mrs. Screven, who was unusually quiet at her sewing. Emma's uncle had just put on his spectacles and was settling down to read a book.

"I think they're trying to ignore us," John said, looking pleased.

"Isn't that nice," Emma responded.

They were talking in lowered voices, and had been since the afternoon, hoping not to be overheard too much in their conversation.

John got up from his wooden chair and sat down on the floor of the porch, stretching out his legs on the first step. This took him a little farther from Emma, but out of view of the parlor. He leaned his head back against the post, looking up at her, and mouthed the words distinctly without making a sound, "*I love you.*"

It was growing dark, and his face was partially hidden in shadows, as Emma felt hers was, and for that reason it was easier for her to respond freely to such endearments. He sensed that she was less shy under this veil provided by the darkness. She noiselessly repeated the words back to him in the same way, mouthing, "*I love you.*"

"Tell me a secret," he said, breaking into a wide grin.

"What do you mean?" she laughed.

"Tell me things you've been keeping from me. When did you begin to care for me?"

Emma lifted her eyebrows.

"I'm sorry," said John. "That was an impertinent question, wasn't it?"

"It was a bit."

He was still grinning, and with her answer, laughed out loud. He felt invigorated and lighthearted, and it had been a very long time since he had experienced anything like the feeling of happiness and well-being that was overflowing in him now.

Emma was thinking seriously about what he had said in jest, and after a pause remarked quietly and significantly, "There is a secret I should tell you."

"Tell me, then."

"Actually, it's not a secret, but something I think you must have forgotten."

"Yes?" He sat up more attentively. "What is it?"

She told him how she had seen him riding in a tournament at Pineville, when he was the champion of the day, and described his embarrassing toss from a horse, and their accidental encounter because of it.

"That was you?" he said, bewildered. "I had completely forgotten that."

"There's no reason you should have remembered, I suppose."

"You were just a little girl, weren't you?"

"I was fifteen."

John was shaking his head slowly, trying to recall more details of that day. Things gradually came back to him as he searched his memory. He remembered his success that day, and his embarrassment, and now distinctly recalled, too, how he had thanked his lucky stars that it had only been a skinny little girl he had accidentally assaulted, and not the beautiful Miss Mason. He reminisced with Emma, but kept this particular detail to himself.

"I do recall our collision now, entirely my fault, of course. I hope I was properly apologetic."

"You were very chivalrous."

"It must have been very embarrassing for you," he suggested.

"I think I was more mortified for your sake."

"Oh, it did me no harm. On the contrary, I was quite pleased because the incident amused my friends so much," John laughed, then added more seriously, "Of course there would have been nothing amusing in it if I had actually done you any harm."

"You did do me a little harm," she said.

"What do you mean?"

She hesitated about her confession for a moment, but went on with it.

"I became quite infatuated with you that day, and I'm afraid I was a bit jealous of Miss Mason. I never saw you again, but I was sure you would marry her. I was surprised when you did not."

"Miss Mason was wise enough not to have me then, and I'm very glad she didn't. Sometime I shall tell you why, Emma, but not tonight. I'm too happy tonight," he said, with a smile and a doting look so charming to Emma that she easily forgot about Miss Mason.

They talked about setting a date for the wedding. They were both concerned about Elias, and wanted to wait until he was better, but wondered if that was best in view of Mr. DuBose's desire to return home to North Carolina. John was adamant that Emma could not stay on at their place without her uncle's protection.

"Do you think your uncle is serious about leaving?" he asked. "Perhaps he will change his mind now that we are engaged."

"I hope he will change his mind."

"I think he will, for you, Emma. When we are married, though, I imagine he'll want to go back home."

"Yes, I'm sure he will."

"What about the farm?" John wondered.

"I don't know. We shall have to sell it, I suppose, or lease it. When my uncle finished with the settlement of my father's estate, this land and house were really all that was left after all the debts were settled. I do wish that Mr. Drawdy could take the place."

"I'll talk with your uncle about these things. If he's willing to wait and accept some help from me, all of you can live here until the wedding."

Emma began thinking about the particulars of that event.

"I hope Mr. Shubrick will be well enough to marry us," she said.

"I'll go and see him. I received a letter from him just yesterday asking about Elias."

"Your brother was always a great favorite of his, you know."

"I know."

John happened to glance inside the house and caught a glimpse of Mrs. Screven putting food on the table.

"You're probably hungry, Emma, I've kept you out here so long," he said apologetically.

She had forgotten about food altogether, but when he mentioned it, realized that she was a little hungry. They went inside and joined her uncle and aunt, who were snacking on leftovers from their midday meal.

"I was just about to come out and invite you two in to dine with us," said Mrs. Screven, as they walked in.

She was almost giddy in her happiness for her niece, but tried to keep herself calm. Already picturing Emma as a bride, she was constantly suppressing tears that wanted to rise up in her. Mr. DuBose thought Emma looked especially radiant and lovely that evening in the candlelight, and could tell that John felt the same.

Mrs. Screven asked Emma if they had talked of a date for the wedding.

"We did, but I suppose we never quite fixed one," she replied.

Her aunt thought it proper for her to wait until a customary period of mourning had been observed for her brother. Emma agreed, and after some consultation with John, who gladly went along with anything she said, she announced a tentative date of October.

"What day in October, dear?" asked Mrs. Screven. "My birthday is the third, you know. What a joy, what a gift it would be to see you wedded on that day!"

"We hesitate to set a fixed day just now," Emma explained, "because of Elias."

"I see. Oh, yes, I understand," Mrs. Screven said feelingly. "The dear boy! I pray for him every day."

After the meal, John and Emma went out to the porch again and resumed their seats. It was dark now, and he knew he would have to leave soon, but each attempt they made at parting words somehow evolved into further conversation. This went on until Mrs. Screven spoke to Emma through the window, suggesting that the cool night air was not doing her any good.

"I shall be in presently," she told her aunt.

"The air really isn't cool at all," John said to Emma.

"It's really quite perfect, very comfortable," she agreed.

They sat in silence for a little while. Thinking of his brother again, John began to feel uneasy that he had left him alone for so long today, and reluctantly told Emma he ought to be getting back home. This time he added action to his words by rising to his feet, and she followed him to the steps.

"It's very hard to leave you, Emma, but I suppose I must," he said to her with a rueful smile.

"You will call on us again soon, won't you?" she asked.

Though John was still standing before her, she was already feeling the pain of separation, and it showed in her expression.

"You may depend on it," he assured her. "Tomorrow evening, if I may."

"Yes, do call tomorrow. I shall miss you until then."

He kissed her hand, and they said their final goodbyes for the night.

John rode home in a blissful daze, remembering every moment of the day with such relish that he hardly realized the passing of time. He was surprised when he reached Belle Ville in what seemed to be only a matter of a few minutes.

Alone in her room that evening, Emma found it difficult to sleep. The night was quiet except for a faint, steady roar of light winds that had begun sweeping over the area. It was a lonesome sound, and made Emma feel her solitude and separation even more acutely. She longed to be with John again, but knowing that was not possible for now, consoled herself by thinking of him, projecting herself back into his presence, hearing his voice saying that he loved her, and feeling the sensation of his kiss on her lips.

CHAPTER NINE

AFTER THEIR ENGAGEMENT, it seemed to John that it became nearly as necessary for him to see Emma for at least a little while each day as it was to eat and breathe. Except for a few times when evening thunderstorms prevented him, no matter how tired he was at the end of each day, he made the ride to her house, and was always quickened by the sight and sound of her. On Sundays, his visits lasted several hours—in the afternoons when Elias was usually sleeping.

He often brought Emma bouquets of flowers from the gardens at Belle Ville, or wild flowers that he found along the way, and when he learned that the DuBose household was lacking any necessities that were difficult to obtain, he usually managed to supply those, too, at least to some small extent. For her twentieth birthday in early May, he had only given Emma a small gift of more tea. This was before their engagement, when a gift of anything more extravagant would have been considered improper. Now that she was his fiancee, he wanted very much to give her some little finery or luxury that she had been doing without. He had been trying to find cloth for dresses, but with the exception of a few poor specimens of homespun, it seemed there was none to be had in

Amelia or the immediate vicinity. He decided that such a purchase would have to wait until he made a trip to Charleston, where he hoped to obtain something better for her.

One morning, while riding out of the village after a visit to the Townsends, John heard someone calling out his name. He turned and saw a lady waving to him from the front door of her house, and recognized Mrs. Reid, an old family friend. Once comfortable and well cared for in a fine home, she was now destitute and widowed, and was bartering and selling off many of her possessions in order to obtain food and fuel. John tied his horse at her gate, and she invited him inside the house. She explained her predicament and tried to interest him in some furniture and carpets she was willing to part with. It pained him to see this delicate, older lady so humbled and desperate, and he promised to send her a supply of corn, flour, molasses, and meat, refusing to take anything in exchange.

As they talked, he noticed a beautiful ivory lace shawl draped over one of the chairs she was trying to sell, and the thought came into his mind that it was something Emma would like. Mrs. Reid noticed John eyeing it and insisted that he take it as a token of her gratitude.

"You are engaged to Miss DuBose, are you not? It would make a lovely gift for her," she urged him, grateful for his help.

Sorely as he was tempted, he was not able to bring himself to accept the shawl, knowing that it was an item of value which Mrs. Reid could sell or barter for other things she needed, but he thought he might come back another day with money and purchase the shawl from her.

That evening, when John went to see Emma, she greeted him with a mysterious, intriguing look and smile.

"I received a gift today," she said. "Would you like to see

it?"

He waited in his usual place on the porch, and she brought it out to him. She was holding Mrs. Reid's beautiful shawl in one hand, and a note in the other. The lady had sent them to her in the afternoon through a friend who happened to be traveling in her direction. Emma gave the note to John for him to read. In it Mrs. Reid expressed her gratitude for the help he had given her, and added, "Allow me to retain a little pride by accepting this token as a wedding gift. May God grant you happiness in this world, my dear Emma. For the one to come I believe you already have every assurance."

"Are you pleased with your gift?" he asked her.

"It's beautiful!" she said, holding up the shawl to admire it.

But John could tell by the way she looked at him that she was more pleased with what he had done for Mrs. Reid. Emma knew that this lady was not the first person for whom he had provided assistance out of the bounty of his plantation.

"Did I do wrong not to accept it from her?" he wondered.

"I don't think you offended Mrs. Reid," said Emma. "But please don't think of offering her payment for it."

She held up the shawl again, fingering the scalloped edges and remarking on the fineness and intricacy of the work. John asked her to put it on for him. She wrapped it around her shoulders and crossed it over her dress, hiding the faded, worn fabric of her bodice with a perfect pattern of lovely ivory lace.

"It's very pretty on you," he said. "I can imagine you in a new dress when you wear that. I've tried to find some cloth for you, for new dresses, but it seems there's none to be had around here. I'll get some for you when I go down to Charleston."

"That would be wonderful!" Emma exclaimed, thrilled with the idea of wearing nice clothes again, but she quickly looked doubtful.

"John," she began hesitantly, "do you have–I mean, do you think you ought to spend money on such things?"

He told her about the cache of valuables and money which had been preserved at Belle Ville, and his inheritance from his father, including the plantation itself. The rest of the estate, or what was left of it, had been divided between himself and Elias, with the exception of a small settlement on their sister Isabella.

"Still...," Emma said uneasily. "Perhaps I can find some homespun hereabouts. It would be less costly."

John looked away, displeased.

"I am not so destitute that I can't provide a decent dress or two for my wife," he said glumly.

Seeing that it was a point of pride with him, Emma did not press her objections any further, but the next moment, regretful, he apologized, and encouraged her, in a gentler, more pleasant tone, to find some acceptable homespun if she could.

"Do what you judge is best about that," he told her, closing the subject.

They sat down on the front stairs. Emma was seated on the topmost step, and John placed himself two or three steps lower down, resting an elbow on one, and smiling up at her with an affectionate, somewhat contrite look.

He reached up and took her hand to hold. Emma was a little ashamed of the roughened skin of her fingers and palm, and her equally roughened fingernails. Her hands were those of a poor farmer's wife, not a young lady, but John seemed not to notice; nor did he seem to care that her complexion was no longer milky white. Despite the sun bonnets and wide-brimmed straw hats she wore, Emma's face and neck had a noticeable tan, and her nose was sometimes pink with sunburn. John's complexion had also been darkened by the sun, and his hands had become more calloused and rough from his daily work at Belle Ville.

Emma asked John when he meant to make a trip to Charleston. Today was the first time she had heard him mention it.

"Soon," he said. "I meant to tell you right away about the letters I received yesterday. One was from my sister Isabella. Next week she and her family will be coming to stay at Belle Ville for a while. Once they arrive I'll be able to go to the city, and I won't feel so uneasy about leaving Elias for so long with him in her care. The other letter was from my uncle's physician. Uncle John suffered a slight stroke a few days ago. The doctor expects him to recover, but I feel I must go and see him as soon as possible. It was necessary for me to go down to Charleston anyway to see about my father's estate."

"How long will you be gone?" she asked.

"A few days at most."

"Well, I suppose I can part with you for that long, if I must."

"I'm sure it won't be a pleasant journey, but the worst part of it will be being away from you for three or four days, Emma. You will miss me?"

"Terribly," she said.

He smiled and kissed her hand for that.

"My cousin Tom has been wishing to see you since I told him of our engagement. Would you like to pay him a visit on Sunday?"

"Oh, yes! Is Dr. Townsend feeling better?"

"Much better. In fact, I think he will be up and about in no time."

On Sunday afternoon John showed up in his carriage and took Emma into the village to see his cousins. Dr. Townsend was finally getting well again, though still confined to his house. He had known Emma's brothers and father well, but had not seen her in years.

The four sat in the parlor and chatted for a long while. Though Tom was polite and friendly, he was not very talkative, and constantly fingered a handkerchief which he raised to his mouth to cover and muffle his occasional coughing. The doctor laughed and joked a few times, but Emma noticed that he seemed preoccupied, and that he would often frown when he looked at John. She had the impression that Dr. Townsend was keeping something unpleasant to himself, and wondered if it had something to do with Elias.

When it was time for the visitors to leave, Laura asked for a private word with John. She wanted to speak with him about Elias. Emma kept her chair in the parlor beside Tom while John and his cousin talked in another room, and the doctor's mood seemed to brighten a little after they left.

"Miss Emma," he said, gazing at her admiringly, "I think my cousin is a very fortunate man."

She thanked him for the compliment.

He grinned and joked, "I suppose I could create all sorts of mischief for John, tell you all his youthful misdeeds, but then, he would tell you mine, so I won't do it."

"I suppose that is wise."

"Since you two became engaged, I can tell that he thinks of little else but you, you know. He says you are the finest girl in the world, and of course I don't dispute it. He tells me he is hardly worthy of you, but I'm sure you would dispute that."

"I would," she said.

"I haven't seen him this enamored in many years, since–"

The doctor paused, biting his lip.

"Miss Mason?" Emma suggested.

"He's told you about her?"

"Not very much," she admitted. "I gather she refused him."

"Yes, John courted Miss Mason for quite a while, but nothing ever came of it. I understand she finally judged him a bit too worldly. I believe she married a clergyman."

"Worldly?" Emma echoed quietly.

"Well, like many young gentlemen, John liked his spirits and cards, the races, the social life of the town—that sort of thing. I suppose it wasn't what the young lady was looking for. Evidently they weren't suitable for each other."

She made no response to all this, and her pensive expression made Dr. Townsend wonder if he had said something he should not have.

"Perhaps I am wrong about that," he went on quickly, hastening to repair any damage he might have done. "I don't know the whole story. I do know that John loves you very much, Miss Emma. And from what he has told me of you, I think that the two of you are eminently suitable for each other."

Emma looked pleased to hear John's cousin say this.

After a brief coughing spell, Tom continued, "While I was serving in the army as a surgeon, in the latter part of the war, our paths crossed once or twice. I must say I found John a changed man, very serious-minded, and utterly dedicated to the cause, and to the men he led. We had both lost many friends and relatives by that time, and towards the end he was discouraged of course, like some of us, and with good reason as it turned out. But you can be very proud of his service. He was a fine officer, and was noted for conspicuous gallantry by his commanders several times. John was offered promotion twice that I know of, but declined. He told me that he wished to stay with his men. I was a little surprised to find that he had the instincts of a mother hen, but there you are. He's a good man, Miss Emma."

"I know that," she answered softly.

Tom studied her with a smile.

"I'm very happy that the two of you found each other. It was very fortuitous. A lovely young lady of Carolina must have been a most welcome and refreshing sight for a tired, homesick soldier's eyes. John told me a bit about the afternoon he showed up at your place. The way he described himself, I imagine he must have looked something like a sand hill cracker."

Emma laughed at Tom's description of John, remembering that day.

"The last time I saw him in Virginia," the doctor went on, "he was looking pretty rough. What a sight he must have been by the time he got home!"

"I doubt his own father would have known him at first," she agreed.

Tom's smile crumbled when she mentioned Mr. Hutchinson.

"I'm sorry," Emma quickly apologized. "That was thoughtless of me."

He began a reply, but was interrupted as John and Laura returned to the room. Abruptly rising from his chair, but holding on to it with one hand for some support, the doctor laughed nervously and said to John, "We've been talking about you."

Pretending alarm, John drew close to Emma and warned her, "Don't believe a word he says."

"But Dr. Townsend was very complimentary," she protested, smiling and taking his arm.

A thunderstorm prevented John from visiting Emma the following evening, but the next day, he rode over to see her at the usual hour bringing a gift of flowers. After they talked of other things for a while, she brought up her conversation with Dr. Townsend, and asked John to tell her more about Miss Mason.

He looked reluctant and a little uneasy.

"Tom told me that he spoke with you about her," he said.

"Yes, and you–"

John went on hastily before she could finish, "All that is dead to me, Emma. Miss Mason meant something to me then, but not now. I was in love with her, or at least infatuated, but I really didn't know or understand her. I suppose I was too young and selfish to even try."

"That is why she broke with you?"

"Her father became very ill during the time I knew her, and when he died, it affected her profoundly, religiously. She changed. I did not. It was as simple as that. It was all for the best, though, for both of us. I was neither fit nor ready for marriage, though I thought I was at the time."

"And you are now?" she asked.

"I am!" he insisted. "And I can't imagine loving anyone but you now, Emma. There is no one like you."

"I only asked because I wished to understand, John," she explained, "and to know you better–to know everything about you."

"Now that you know, let's not speak of her anymore."

Emma promised not to bring up the subject again, but curiosity prompted her to ask John if there had been any other lady in his heart after Miss Mason.

"No one, Emma," he assured her. "Only you."

But to amuse her, he told her the story of the romantic girl who had nursed him in Richmond, embellishing it with some exaggerations to make her laugh. She did laugh, but also expressed sympathy for the young lady. John then turned the attention on

Emma's past, and asked about her former suitors. Emma was surprised to learn that he knew about the cousin from Georgia who had sought her in marriage.

"Your aunt told me about him," said John.

"Oh."

"I've forgotten his name. What was it?"

"Gilbert Habersham."

"You didn't love him?"

"Not in the way I thought I should."

"I am thankful for that!"

Emma told him how the young man had courted her through letters, and eventually married someone else.

"It was foolish of Mr. Habersham to give up so easily," said John, "but I'm very glad he did."

The next time John saw Emma, he was in a particularly lighthearted, affectionate mood. He was happier than usual, looking forward to seeing his sister and her family again in a day or two, and especially pleased that Elias had eaten well and even walked around a little that morning with the help of a crutch. He held her hand, which he caressed frequently between endearments, becoming extravagant in his praises of her. He told her, only half-jokingly, that he thought she was perfect, that he found no fault in her; but instead of being pleased, Emma looked troubled.

"I'd rather that you see me as I am, John, rather than what you wish me to be," she said seriously.

"But I do see you as you are, Emma," he protested.

"Not if you think I'm faultless!"

"All right, I'll admit you have your faults, but I don't know what they are," he shrugged, laughing. "Perhaps I am blinded by love."

"I'm afraid I shall disappoint you if you have such high expectations of me," she went on uneasily, frowning.

"I don't have any expectations. I just love you, so in my eyes you are perfect."

He was still smiling, and this irritated her.

"If you keep insisting that I have no faults, you shall see one become evident, for I shall lose my temper!" she complained, her cheeks flushing hotly.

John could not help but laugh again, but when he saw that Emma was really upset with him, he quickly sobered himself and took on a penitent look.

"Forgive my foolishness," he begged her. "I ought not to put such a burden on you. Perfection is a rather hard thing to live up to."

After this apology her irritation faded, but she still looked serious and thoughtful, even sad.

"Is something troubling you, Emma?" he asked. "I hope you will confide in me."

"Shall I confess my faults to you?" she asked tentatively.

"If you wish to."

Emma hesitated, as if she had already thought better of the idea, but John saw that it was something important to her, something which must have been on her mind a great deal, and he waited patiently.

"Tell me, Emma," he encouraged her.

She turned away from him as she began to speak, slowly and deliberately.

"I believe you must think me stronger and wiser than you in some ways, John, or at least in one way—my religion."

"Yes, that is true," he admitted.

"Perhaps I am a little stronger in that way—only a little—but I don't wish you to think me better than I am. I am far from perfect. It troubles me that I have been so weak and faithless at times, and so fearful. I have always been willing to accept good things from God, but the trials he has sent me in these past few years, I have not borne well."

"I think you have," he objected mildly.

She shook her head.

"No, I have not. Not long ago, I am ashamed to say...the thought came into my head that I had been given more than I could bear. The pain was so great, I was tempted to believe that, to doubt God...and to despair. But that all ended when you came to us. I began to love you, and to see that God had sent you to me."

"You believe that?" John asked.

Emma turned to him and smiled.

"I do...but we've grown too serious, John," she said with a little laugh. "Let's not talk of serious things anymore tonight."

"What shall we talk about?"

"You decide."

"Well, let me see," he said. "I have wondered, how is it that we both lived in the same neighborhood and yet saw so little of each other? I regret we didn't meet again after you were grown up."

"I don't know," said Emma. "I do remember seeing you with your family at church when I was a little girl."

"Did you ever visit Belle Ville back when you were older, during the war?"

"Only once. I had just come home from school for a while, and your father invited my family to Sunday dinner."

"After I left for Virginia?"

"Yes, I believe it was just a few days afterwards. I remember that Mr. Hutchinson talked of nothing but you."

John made a whistling sound of frustration.

"I wish I had been home," he lamented. "Emma, I'm sure if I had met you again that day, I could not have parted with you."

She laughed.

"But you were still in love with Miss Mason, weren't you?"

"We were long parted by then, and I'm certain I would have forgotten her completely after a few moments in your company."

"I think not," she demurred.

"Oh, yes! I made up my mind not to marry while I was in the army, but for you, that resolution would have been broken for fear you might marry someone else."

Emma smiled at all these pleasant speculations of what might have been.

"I suppose I ought to tell you, John," she said, "your father suggested that I write to you."

"Did he!" he responded, surprised. "I wish you had. Why didn't you?"

"Good heavens, for one thing, you would have thought me very forward."

"No! Well, perhaps I might have. Now that you mention it, I remember that my father spoke of you a few times in his letters."

"It must have made very little impression upon you."

"Emma, I suppose I still thought of you as a little girl. You should have written to me, to correct my foolish notions. Did you even consider it?"

"I'm afraid not," she admitted.

John tried to remember what his father had written to him about Emma, but could only recall his mention of her in relation to the afflictions of her family–the sad news of the death of her parents, and younger brother.

"Well, I wish you had taken my father's suggestion to write to me. Ah, what might have been!" he sighed, with real but humorously exaggerated regret. "I used to envy my friends in the army who anxiously awaited letters from their wives and sweethearts, and were so happy to receive them. You and I could have been such correspondents."

"Compose a letter for me now," she prompted him playfully.

He smiled and attempted to comply.

"Dearest Emma," he began, but faltered in embarrassed laughter. "I can't."

"I was only teasing you," she told him.

"I hope you did not keep Mr. Habersham's love letters," John said after a pause.

"Oh, no! When he married someone else, I destroyed them. I saw no good purpose in keeping them. I don't think Mrs. Habersham would have wished me to do so."

"Mrs. Habersham!" John repeated with a comical shudder. "When I think that might have been your name!"

"I like the name Hutchinson much better," said Emma.

"That's good. It will be yours soon."

When John came to see Emma the following evening, he handed her a letter, one small folded piece of paper without an envelope or postmarks. Not recognizing the handwriting on the outside, she began to open it out of sheer curiosity.

"I'd prefer that you read it later," John said to her with a meaning smile.

It's from you, her eyes asked? He nodded.

Emma put the letter away, and after he was gone, she took it up to her room to read in privacy.

Belle Ville, June 21st 1865

Dearest Miss Emma,

Though we see each other often, I did not think it right to deprive you of a letter, which is your due from a devoted lover. I do not know why I could not <u>say</u> to you last evening what I wished to <u>write,</u> except that I thought such an expression deserved more careful and deliberate consideration.

I only wish I had the poetic powers to convey to you my darling, how much you are loved. You are a refuge of peace and joy in a world that is otherwise desolate for me—a reminder and a remnant of all that is precious and good, and I promise you, when we are married, my happiness will be to make you happy. You are a great help and blessing to me, and I earnestly desire to be the same for you. Knowing that you will be at my side, I already feel stronger and better able to meet with all the uncertainties of the future.

You know my faults, past and present, and yet care for me in spite of them. I have such love for you, and believe we understand each other so well, that I feel we are one even now, as much as if we had already spoken those vows which will bind us together as husband and wife. I thank God for you, and have no doubt that I will never cease doing so.

Though we cannot now foresee what trials or hardships may lie ahead of us, you may always be assured of my love. It is something settled and fixed forever, so always believe me to be

Yours most devotedly,
John Hutchinson

Please excuse this poor little scrap of paper; it was all I could find. I have been writing quite a few letters lately and must have used all the other paper in the house. Though Dear you are now less reserved in your expressions of affection than at first, I shall understand if you do not wish to put them in writing.

Despite the postscript excusing her from a reply, Emma immediately sat down at her writing table and penned an answer to John's letter.

June 22nd 1865

My Dearest Friend,

The unexpected letter from you was so welcome and loving, I felt had to write to you in return. Though it is true I sometimes find it difficult to express my feelings freely, it is not because they are any less than yours. They are as strong, if not stronger, and give me such happiness as I have never known.

The Proverbs say, guard your heart with all diligence. I guarded mine where you were concerned at first, I must confess—but after a time, there began to flow out of it such issues of love that I could no longer offer any resistance. After putting up such a poor fight, I found myself in the dangerous situation of loving you without knowing if you returned my feelings. Yet, by that time, I knew somehow that God had brought us together, and I had an unaccountable assurance in my heart that all would be well.

Sure enough, it was.

You say you hope to be a help to me, but you already are. We are not yet married, and I already depend on you for much. I have need of your strong heart to comfort me. You have told me that you can hardly bear to pass a day without seeing me. It would distress me, too, not to see you every day now that we are engaged, though I know there have been, and will be, times when this may not be possible. I love to talk with you each evening; you are so tender and indulgent, I am sorry when you must leave. But I soothe myself with the thought that the day will soon come when we need not be saying any more good-byes.

I do love you! It is easier for me to say in a letter, but I am learning to be less reserved about such things in your presence, as you have remarked. It won't do for your wife to be anything less than lavish in her affection and admiration for you.

Now we are correspondents. (My letter paper is only a little better than yours; I have no stationery, and have taken a page from a ledger as you can see.) It is pleasant to pour out my heart to you in this way, but I much prefer to see you in person. Until this evening then, I am

Yours most affectionately,
Emma DuBose

CHAPTER TEN

JOHN'S SISTER ISABELLA and her family arrived at Belle Ville on a Wednesday, late in the afternoon as a slow, drizzling rain that had lasted several hours was finally ending. Their journey from the upstate in an old, patched-up carriage had not been a pleasant one because of bad weather, bad roads, and the generally depressing and frequently shocking aspect of some of the towns and countryside through which they had to pass. John was the first to see their carriage pull up in front of the house, and he rushed out to meet them just as the as the setting sun was peeking through the thinning clouds.

Dressed in mourning black for her father, Isabella Stewart was a tall, dark-haired woman–handsome like all the Hutchinsons, but looking a little more plump and matronly than the last time John had seen her some three years ago. When John first embraced her, he thought she had been crying, and perhaps not from joy to see her family or her home again. Her eyes were heavy with a haggard look that he had never seen before. He soon learned that she was deeply concerned again about her baby, who had been improving in Anderson, but seemed to suffer a setback on the journey to Belle Ville.

After Isabella greeted John and Uncle Israel she immediately went in to see Elias. Her husband Edmund waited in the hall with their children, two eight year-old twin girls, Louisa and Julia, his son Edmund, Jr., a boy of six, and the baby, Elias, who was asleep in his father's arms. Little Edmund and the girls only vaguely remembered their uncle John, but dutifully and shyly offered him kisses and hugs as Matthew began bringing in their baggage.

Though Isabella was somewhat tall for a woman, her husband was a full head taller. The two had always resembled each other so closely in their mannerisms and looks that people often took them for siblings or close cousins, though they were not related. John thought that his brother-in-law looked much older and stouter now, like his wife, and when Edmund removed his hat, he saw that his thick, dark hair had thinned and receded deeply, leaving a prominent widow's peak tapering down the middle of his forehead. An older man in his forties, Edmund had not been accepted into the army because of old injuries, but during the war, he had served in various capacities in the state government, having been forced to flee his home on the South Carolina coast when Federal forces captured and occupied that area in 1861. Since then he and his family had lived with relatives in Columbia and Anderson.

John gently moved aside a fold of the little blanket in which the baby was wrapped to see his face.

"Another beautiful child," he said in a hushed voice, smiling at Edmund, who smiled very weakly in reply. "Would you like to take him upstairs to his cradle? I found one in the attic and put in your bedroom."

"Yes, thank you, John."

Edmund looked at his other children and made a slight shushing sound as they began to giggle and scamper around a little.

They stayed quiet until their father disappeared up the stairs, then the little girls wandered into the drawing room to look around. Little Edmund approached John with a shy expression and took his hand.

"This is a nice house," he said. "Are we going to live here?"

"Yes, for as long as you like, if your mother and father wish it," John replied, stroking the boy's dark, curly hair.

"Will you teach me how to ride a horse, Uncle John? I want to be in the cavalry, too."

"Your father and I can certainly teach you. I'll see if I can find a pony of proper size for you."

The boy began to jump up and down at the mention of a pony, and as his mother emerged from the library, closing the door behind her, he ran over and excitedly announced the news to her.

"Yes, my boy shall learn to ride," she answered quickly, with a catch in her throat, leaning down to him.

Isabella kissed her son, and he skipped away to find his sisters.

"Elias is somewhat overcome now...both of us are," she said to John wearily, wiping tears from her eyes. "I shall take the children into him later, after he is rested. Where is Edmund?"

"He took the baby upstairs. I put a cradle in your room," John explained.

"Ah, good. I hope Elias, I mean the baby, will sleep a good long while now. He was so miserable and irritable on the journey. It was very distressing."

"You look tired, Belle. You must be exhausted. Why don't you rest now while the baby is asleep? Shall I send for Tom?"

"Yes, please, but tomorrow. I should like to see Laura, too. Is she well?"

"She is well, and Tom is doing much better. He has just

begun to see a few patients again."

"I am glad to hear it," said Isabella. "Now I think I shall do as you suggested and rest awhile upstairs. Will you mind the children for me, John?"

"I'll try to entertain them. Are they hungry, do you think?"

"Most likely. I imagine Edmund is, too."

"Send him down. We'll all dine together directly."

Isabella put her arms around her brother's neck and held him tightly for a moment.

"Thank you, John," she whispered.

Late the next morning, John took the carriage into Amelia to fetch the doctor and Laura to Belle Ville. Tom offered to take his own carriage to the plantation so that John would not have to drive them home, but then remembered that his cousin was leaving for Charleston early the next day, and realized he would want to come back in the general direction of the village to see Emma before he left.

At the house, after a brief reunion with his cousins, Dr. Townsend went upstairs with Isabella to examine the baby. The infant was still losing weight, and was even more colicky than the day before, but he could find nothing seriously wrong with the child, though Isabella told the doctor that he had been very sick in Anderson, so much so that they had feared for his life. The baby had just recently begun to take certain solid foods, as recommended by another physician, but Dr. Townsend speculated that something he was eating perhaps disagreed with his system. He made a few suggestions about the child's diet, and Isabella promised to follow them.

After administering a little oil of fennel to the tiny patient, Tom left him with his mother. She nursed her son a while, and when he fell asleep, and she joined the rest of the family downstairs for a meal.

Elias had declined to be brought to the table. Laura, seated between Isabella's daughters, only pretended to eat, and shared most of her food with the twins. She frequently gazed off in the direction of the library. As soon as the meal was over everyone went into that room and visited with Elias for an hour or so, until he began to look tired. He was then left alone with the doctor.

"You are looking better since I saw you last, Elias," Tom said cheerfully, taking his patient's wrist to feel the pulse.

"If you say so," was the indifferent reply. "You are certainly looking better, Tom."

"Well, I am not nearly at full strength, but I get closer each day, as you do, I see."

Elias gave the doctor an incredulous look he did not notice. When Tom was finished with his examination, he stepped out to find his sister Laura waiting just behind the door in the hall.

"May I see him alone a little while?" she asked her brother in a whisper.

He nodded reluctantly, opened the door for her, and left it partly open as she went inside. Elias raised his head above the back of the sofa when he heard the rustling of her dress.

"Laura!" he said, looking pleased.

She swept around, placed the customary kiss on his forehead, and sat down in the chair closest to him.

"You are looking better today, Elias," she said, after studying him for a few moments.

"That's what Tom said–but I'm sure he always says that to his patients. It's his duty as a doctor, I suppose. But from you, I take it as a sincere observation."

"Are you feeling better, dear?" she asked.

"If to be in less pain than usual is to be better, then I suppose I am today."

"I'm so glad!"

Noticing a little cushioned footstool near one of the other chairs, Laura fetched it and drew it up beside the daybed. She seated herself to face Elias, and seated so low, she was now at eye level with him. He smiled and settled back on his pillows, enjoying her beauty and nearness.

"It's very nice to have you to myself, Laura," he said. "If the others come in, tell them to go away."

"I shall," she laughed softly.

Laura pulled a small parcel of papers which had been tucked away under a sash of her dress.

"These are some of the letters you wrote to me, Elias. I should like to read them with you. May we?"

"But I don't have your letters, Laura. They were all lost," he said, eyeing the papers hesitantly. "Yours were always much better."

"You don't wish me to read my favorites to you?"

"No."

He looked away, frowning.

"I'm sorry, Elias," she murmured, drooping a little with disappointment.

"I'm very dull, I know," he said, slowly turning back to her. "But I don't like to think about those days, or anything I wrote about them."

"Not even your last letter?" she asked, her eyes full of secret meaning.

"My last letter..."

"Don't you remember it?"

"I remember...I...never received a reply."

"I wrote to you in reply the day I received it–just before you were wounded, I think. Do you remember what you wrote to me, Elias?"

"Not exactly. But I do think I'd like to remember that particular letter exactly. You may read that one to me if you have it."

"I should like for you to read it to me," Laura urged him. "It would be so nice to hear it from you, in your voice."

He assented reluctantly. She removed the letter from its little cover, unfolded it, and handed it to him to read aloud.

Elias read silently for a few moments, skipping over the greeting and a few opening lines, then began: "After a hard march to this place, we have enjoyed a day's rest since. I have found pen and paper and time today to write to you and others dear to me. I have thought about our conversation during my last furlough, and all the things I wished to say to you, but did not. I am not fearful in battle, trusting God–"

Elias stopped, glowering, and thrust the letter back into Laura's hand.

"Take it. I can't read this," he said.

"Shall I?" she asked.

"If you wish."

Laura found the spot where he had left off and continued: "...trusting God to do with me as He sees fit, but in your presence, Laura, I turn coward. Even if they were not spoken, you must have read something of my feelings in my eyes. You looked expectant and then, when we parted, a little disappointed (or so I imagined).

"What I should have said to you in person is easier to write, though it is not really easy, since I do not know for certain how you will receive it. Nevertheless, I don't see why I ought not to tell you the truth, even if it is not received favorably. I believe I know you well enough to guess what my chances may be, unless I am so blind as to have mistaken the nature of your affection (and that may well be!). The truth is, I love you, and long to hear you say those very words to me.

"Now I am at a loss, wondering what you might think as you read what I have just written. Whatever you wish to write to me, please do so quickly and relieve my suspense. If you feel as I do, please send me also a likeness of your sweet self. I make this letter brief, as the mail must go out now or not at all today. This is not a long letter, but I have labored over it with great care and many loving thoughts of you. If your reply is favorable I shall thank God for it more than any other blessing, and begin another letter to you which will contain a question you might easily guess.

"Yours most affectionately and hopefully, Elias Hutchinson."

"And what did you reply, Laura?" he asked after a silence.

"I don't remember exactly," she said, "but the essence of my reply was, that I loved you, and had always loved you, and that your letter made me very happy."

"You love me?"

"I do."

"I want to kiss you," he said sadly.

"Then kiss me, Elias."

"I'm so wretched-looking, you don't want that."

"But I do."

She raised herself up and put her face close to his invitingly. His eyes suddenly alive with ecstatic emotion, he leaned forward, put his hand behind her head, and gently brought her lips to his.

"This," he whispered, still holding her close, "is an intoxicating medicine."

Laura slipped her arms around his neck and nestled her head against his chest.

"I love you, Elias. I want you to be well again. I want to be with you always."

"With you in my arms, I almost believe that is possible," he said.

"It is possible! Your doctor and your nurse have said so, so you must believe it."

"I much prefer my nurse."

He pressed his face against the softness of her hair, which smelled of rose water, and asked for another kiss. She was lifting her head to offer her lips a second time when they heard voices in the hall, just outside the door. They released each other, and she sank down to her seat on the footstool again.

John and the doctor entered the library.

"Elias says you must go away," Laura promptly informed them.

The two men paused and exchanged a surprised, quizzical look.

"He must tell us that himself," John replied.

"Go away!" they heard an irritable voice say from the couch.

"We are reading his letters together," Laura told her brother, holding up one for him and John to see.

"We must be leaving soon, Laura," Tom said regretfully. "I need to rest."

"Just a few more minutes?" she begged. "Just fifteen minutes, Tom."

"Oh, very well."

Dr. Townsend and John went out, but left the door wide open behind them. During this interruption, Elias had been watching Laura intently, and after studying her fervent, hopeful expression a few moments, he suddenly grew remorseful. When they were alone again, a look of suffering came over him as she took his hand, kissed it, and held it against her face.

She looked up at him.

"Elias! Are you in pain?"

"It isn't right," he said, turning his face away to hide it. "It's wrong of me."

"To kiss me?"

"To give you any hope. To deceive myself that there is any hope."

"But there is hope!" she insisted.

Elias pulled his hand from hers, sank down in his bed, and wearily and clumsily drew the covers up to his neck.

"I'm very tired now," he sighed. "I have no more strength. Your brother is waiting for you." Laura reluctantly rose to her feet and looked down at him with a confused, tearful expression.

"Your brother is waiting for you, Laura," Elias repeated, closing his eyes.

"I am going," she said sadly, but then, brightening, added, "Oh, Elias, I see. I have expected too much from you, too soon. We have tired you out today. You'll feel better when you are rested, dear. We'll talk again soon, just you and I."

She quickly kissed his face a last time, and left him without another word.

John returned to Belle Ville after dark, later than he had planned. He had meant to stay at the DuBose farm only an hour or so, to say his goodbyes to Emma and her family before leaving for Charleston, but found it difficult to tear himself away from her.

When he got back to the house he went into the library and looked in, and finding that Israel was with Elias, who was asleep, he returned to the drawing room where he had seen his sister sitting alone. Isabella patted the cushion of the sofa, inviting him to come and sit with her. She had been waiting to have a private talk with her brother.

"The house is so quiet now," John remarked, taking a seat next to her.

"Edmund is upstairs putting the children to bed."

"So early?"

"He is going to read to them. They find him very entertaining when he reads stories to them. He does much better than I do."

"Is the baby better today?" John asked.

"A little. I think he is slowly improving, thank God."

"Tom is very confident about him."

Isabella smiled and gazed at her brother affectionately.

"You look well, John," she said. "Much better than I could have expected. I have been so distracted about the baby, I have neglected to tell you such things, and how good it is to be here with you and Elias again. He and I were talking of you yesterday. He was the first to tell me how, in this wreck of a world, you have fallen in love."

She congratulated him on his engagement to Miss Emma DuBose.

"I remember her," Isabella mused. "Father wrote to me about the death of her parents and her brother Richard."

"Her brother Theodore also died," John added.

His sister sighed and shook her head with sorrow and sympathy.

"She is all alone, then?"

"An uncle and aunt are with her."

"And Providence has promised her a husband, hm? A very fine husband," she said, patting his handsome face fondly.

John smiled, remembering how his older sister had so often

assumed this motherly tone and manner with him.

"Father always had such love and esteem for that family, especially Dr. DuBose," she went on. "He would be so pleased that you are marrying his daughter. She is the very person Father would have chosen for you, I believe. I recall that Miss Emma had fair hair, did she not? And she was rather slender."

"You haven't seen her in many years, Belle. Emma is much changed."

"I'm told she is very lovely, and I am very happy for you, John. Elias says you adore the young lady."

"I do."

"I am so happy for you, brother," Isabella said feelingly, but her smile faded, and during a brief silence she grew meditative, almost melancholy.

"What of Elias, John?" she said. "What do you think?"

"Tom says there is hope."

Isabella averted her eyes so that he would not see the skepticism and fear in them.

"Elias is changed. Don't you find him changed?" she asked.

"Wounds like his can make a man–"

"I don't speak of his physical condition," she interrupted. "Elias is so moody, so changeable! He was very happy to see us at first, and so affectionate to me and the children, but the next time I spoke with him, he was cold and aloof and gloomy. Is he like that with you, John?"

"Sometimes."

"Yesterday, he was fine at first. I brought the baby to him, and he wanted to hold him. When I asked Elias to pray for him, he shocked me with such an angry look, and said that he didn't pray anymore."

"He said that?" John asked, troubled.

"Yes!"

"I didn't know about that, Belle. I have seen bitterness in him, but not that. I was hoping that his spirits would improve as his body grew stronger."

"I think he must be hiding something of himself from you. Elias always looked up to you so much, it must be that he does not want you to think badly of him. He does not care so much what I think of him, though I know he loves me. It seems to me that he is as sick at heart as he is in his body. He is not himself. He asked my forgiveness for his coldness later, but refused to talk with me about what was troubling him. Perhaps he would talk with you, John."

"When I come back from Charleston, I shall try to speak with him," he promised.

"We must pray for him," she said anxiously.

"I do, Belle."

"Has he seen Reverend Shubrick since he came home?"

"Mr. Shubrick is recovering from a long illness. He has asked about Elias many times, though, and even sent him a letter. His wife told me that he would soon be well enough to visit Belle Ville."

"I wish him to come here as soon as possible. I shall write to him."

There was a lull in the conversation as they both became absorbed in private thoughts about their brother for a few moments. Isabella then straightened up her drooping posture and attempted a smile.

"How nice that Mr. Shubrick is getting well now," she said more brightly. "He can perform your marriage ceremony. Have you set the date?"

"Not really, though we hope to marry in October. We thought it best to wait."

"Because of Elias..."

He nodded, and Isabella answered with an understanding nod of her own, and asked, "Pardon my inquisitiveness, dear, but does Emma have a wedding dress, or any prospect of one?"

"I don't know. We haven't talked of such things yet."

"Is she tall?"

"Not quite as tall as you."

"Well, if she is in need of one, I have a lovely white gown that would do. I should like to offer it to her. With some mending and a few alterations, I think it would do nicely for a wedding dress."

"I shall tell Miss Emma about it. I doubt she has such a dress, or any prospect of one. Her clothes–well, you know how it is."

"It is so with nearly everyone," said Isabella. "But how nice it will be to have a sister. I should like to see her soon. A wedding is such a happy occasion. We have need of a happy occasion to look forward to these days. Edmund and I will help you both in any way we can."

"Thank you, Belle."

The next morning, John rode into the village. He left his horse with Dr. Townsend and walked to the recently rebuilt depot, where he caught a train for Charleston.

A busy Saturday passed at Belle Ville, followed by a quiet Sunday. Isabella spent much of the morning with Elias, hoping to cheer him, or to at least elicit some interest from him with conversation, but he was not very talkative, and asked to see the children. They came to visit him, and he seemed to enjoy watching little Edmund and the twins play with their little wooden animals and Noah's ark. When it was time for them to eat their midday meal, the children left, but Isabella stayed with Elias. He had a slight fever and refused food, protesting that he had no appetite.

In the late afternoon Isabella was expecting another visit from Dr. Townsend. He drove up in his buggy after dinner bringing a note for her from Mr. Shubrick. The clergyman wanted to see Elias, and asked for a convenient time later in the week. Isabella told Tom that she would write a reply for him to deliver to the priest when he when he returned to Amelia. She also informed the doctor that Elias was feverish and had eaten nothing all day.

She brought the doctor into the library and resumed her seat there next to Elias. Just before Tom's arrival they had been talking about little Elias, his namesake, and the general consensus in the family that he looked much more like his mother than his father.

"Just like you, Elias," Isabella had told her brother. "You always resembled Mama much more than Papa. You have her dark hair and gray eyes."

Elias had asked to see a photograph of their mother, and was still holding it and looking at the little portrait when his sister walked in with the doctor. He handed it back to Isabella after she sat down again.

"I miss her," he said quietly. "I miss them both."

Dr. Townsend greeted his patient and also took a seat. Elias noticed that his sister was holding a letter in her hand, and asked about it.

"It's from Mr. Shubrick," she said.

Elias frowned.

"He wishes to see you. May I bring him here?"

"No!" he answered emphatically.

"Why not, Elias?"

"I don't wish to see any priests or chaplains or–"

He put his hands to his forehead, which had begun to ache.

"Don't bring him here," he finished, closing his eyes.

"Mr. Shubrick asked me if you still intend to study for the ministry and take holy orders," said Dr. Townsend. "Do you?"

"You can tell him no," Elias replied, glaring at his cousin and sister reproachfully. "I'm finished with all that. There's no need for him to come and see me."

Isabella was close to tears.

"Let me examine him now, Belle," the doctor said to her gently. "Do you mind?"

She rose and left the room. Tom lifted his cousin's arm, and as he took his pulse, which was abnormal, he inadvertently let a sigh of discouragement escape him. Elias seemed untroubled by it, and even made a facetious remark.

"I thought you men of science were to be always dispassionate."

The doctor stared at him with a look verging on anger.

"It's not so easy when it comes to one's own flesh and blood," he answered, then asked, with unconcealed exasperation, "Why, Elias? Why have you not eaten anything today?"

"What does it matter?"

"What does it matter! Cousin, you have a chance to recover and live, but not unless you fight for it. You're not fighting."

Elias feebly waved his hand in a dismissive gesture.

"I'm done with fighting," he said sullenly. "And what is there to live for?"

"Those who love you."

"Those who love me will be better off without me. I shall never be a well man again."

"You don't know that!" the doctor protested.

"Better for me–better for everyone–when I am gone."

Elias was now speaking in a matter-of-fact tone that angered

Tom all the more, but he restrained himself, smothering his feelings, and quietly went on with the examination. When the doctor was finished he asked, "May I sit with you a little while?"

His patient gave a slight shrug of the shoulders, and Dr. Townsend took the seat nearest his couch.

"Elias," he said in a gentle, pleading tone, "please tell me something. Why don't you wish to live?"

Elias looked into his cousin's eyes intently.

"What does it matter? I believe I shall die, whether I resist or not. I begin to feel it now. You can see it, too."

Tom denied that he saw anything of the sort. He crossed his arms and stared at his cousin expectantly, waiting for an answer. Looking harassed, Elias turned away, but after a few moments he turned back to Dr. Townsend and spoke, in a hesitant, resentful tone.

"When things began to go badly for us, I prayed to God, don't let me outlive my country. If we're to perish, I prayed, let me die first. I wish I had."

"But there must be something in you that wants to live, cousin, or else you wouldn't have survived your wounds," the doctor argued.

"I was wounded before I heard of our defeat. After you operated on me, I was better, but I wasn't sure if I would live, and I wanted to come home very much, to be here, and to see you all once more, whether I lived or died."

Elias suddenly covered his eyes with trembling hands to conceal his emotion.

. "When I learned that the end had come for us, I wanted to curse God and die. I almost did–I came very close!"

His whole body was shaking now, but he was so weak, he could hardly produce a sob. Little groans escaped him in shallow, shuddering breaths. Dr. Townsend was not a particularly religious man, but for some reason it disturbed him deeply to see one who had been so devout now so embittered and shaken in his faith.

"You're angry with God?" he asked.

Elias sank down and turned his head away again, nestling it deeper into the pillows to hide his face.

"What if I am," he muttered listlessly.

"You think he's forsaken you, Elias?"

"Yes!" he gasped, and abruptly drew himself up, staring straight ahead, his jaw convulsively clenching with anger. "Me, and my country!"

"I don't think God had anything to do with our losing the war," Tom responded, trying to remain, outwardly at least, cool and composed.

Earlier, when Isabella had said something to him about Elias being sick at heart, the doctor had dismissed the idea; now he began to see that she was right–but he kept on trying to reason with him.

"I think it was only in the natural order of things," he went on calmly. "We made our mistakes, of course, but the enemy had more money, more men, more munitions...and more ruthlessness."

But Elias seemed not to hear him; his staring eyes were fixed and burning with his own feverish, embittered thoughts.

"We thought he was with us, and for us," he said hoarsely, quivering with emotion.

He drew in a deep breath and continued fiercely, "We should have fought the devil with fire! We should have marched on Washington when we had the chance, and burned it to the ground, just as they burned our cities. And then set up gallows for every damned Republican! The tallest for the tyrant who led them, though hanging would have been too good for a wretch who made war on Americans. He made war on Americans!"

With this last, frenzied exclamation, his voice broke, and he crumbled down into his bed, exhausted with impotent fury.

The doctor suddenly felt completely helpless and bewildered in the face of such violent passion and despair, and could think of nothing to say. He regarded himself as a poor comforter, like one of Job's friends.

"I'm in pain," Elias moaned. "Give me something for it."

CHAPTER ELEVEN

JOHN'S TRAIN ARRIVED IN AMELIA around four o'clock in the afternoon. After fetching his horse at the Townsend's, he paid a visit to the DuBose farm and enjoyed a brief reunion with Emma.

She was sitting on the porch with her aunt and uncle in the late afternoon as he rode up, and could barely restrain herself from running and throwing herself into his arms when she saw him again. John wanted very much to embrace and kiss her repeatedly, but in the presence of her family contented himself with a kiss to her cheek. He was carrying a parcel wrapped in paper and tied with a ribbon. It was a gift he had brought from Charleston for Emma. She opened it immediately at his urging, and gasped to see a quantity of beautiful light blue muslin.

"Oh, Captain Hutchinson!" Mrs. Screven exclaimed admiringly. "How lovely!"

"It is the very color of Emma's eyes," Mr. DuBose remarked.

"It is, isn't it?" said John, looking into those eyes tenderly. "I remembered how you admired Miss Townsend's dress of the same color, Miss Emma. I hope you like it."

"I do!" she cried.

"There are nine yards. I was told that is enough for a dress."

"It is more than enough," Mrs. Screven assured him.

Later, when Emma and John were alone at their usual places on the porch, she asked him about his uncle.

"He is much better, I think," said John.

"I'm so glad. Your company must have done him good."

"He said it did, and it did me good to see him again. Seeing Charleston again, well, that is another matter. I hope you are not vexed with me for buying you a gift there."

"Oh, no, John."

"Good. I hoped it would not be the cause of our first quarrel."

"Why should I quarrel about that?" she protested.

"Well, if not this, I'm sure I shall do something to displease you sooner or later," he laughed. "I might wish to buy you more nice things like the muslin, and you'll refuse to let me do so, and then we'll be put out with each other until one of us gives in."

"Hm," she said with a musing smile, "and who will be the first to do that?"

"We shall see," he said, taking her hand to kiss it again. "I missed you very much, Emma. Did you miss me terribly as you said you would?"

"I did! I'm so glad you're home."

The mention of that word made John think of Elias, and he suddenly felt anxious to see him again. He had been more troubled than usual about his brother since his conversation with Isabella about him. Though he would have liked to stay longer with Emma that afternoon, he began to feel the fatigue of his long journey, and reluctantly confessed this to her.

"You must go home and rest, then, John," she insisted. "Shall I see you tomorrow?"

"You may depend upon it."

At the house the first person John encountered was Israel,

who was just coming out of the library, closing its door very slowly and carefully as John was closing the front door behind him.

"How is Elias, Israel?" he asked.

The old man hung his head, unable to look John in the eye and answer truthfully. Israel had nursed many sick children and adults in his lifetime, and had seen a number of them pass away. He had been hoping against hope for Elias, but it was his judgment now that the young man was dying.

"He's havin' a bad day today," Israel finally answered. "Some days is better than others."

John could see that he was being evasive.

"Do you think he'll recover?" he pressed.

Israel kept his head down.

"Only the Lord knows that," he mumbled.

John took this as a "no." He moved toward the door, but Israel put out an arm to stop him.

"He's sleepin' now. He needs his rest. Miss Belle, she's in there with him."

"Has Dr. Tom been here today?"

"He just left, just a little while ago."

In the late evening, after the children had been put to bed, Edmund took a turn sitting with Elias. Dr. Townsend had given him a pain killer which kept him asleep. John was waiting to speak with his sister as she emerged from the room, looking weary.

"Has there been any improvement in Elias?" he asked anxiously after he greeted her with a kiss.

"There has been a change in him for the worse. He seems feverish all the time now, and at times, I think he is nearly delirious."

"What did Tom say?"

"He said that Elias could still recover, and that we ought not to despair."

John scrutinized his sister's face intently, looking for any sign of deception. She did not want to believe that Elias was dying any more than he did, and only told him what the doctor had told her, which was ambiguous enough to keep some hope alive for both of them.

They went into the drawing room and sat down to talk. John asked about the baby, and was happy to hear that the little one was doing much better. Isabella asked him about their uncle and his trip to Charleston. He told her that their Uncle John was improving and in good spirits, unlike the old city, which he seemed reluctant to discuss.

When John asked Isabella how things had been at Belle Ville in his absence, she began to rattle off all that she and Edmund had been doing for the past few days. They had both been working hard, and her description of some of the more menial labors they had taken on jarred him a little. It was strange for him to imagine this elegant couple engaged in some of the work servants had always done before. They seemed willing enough to submit to their lot, and to be dependent on the help of other family members, but John wondered how long this state of things would endure. Isabella's nature was one that yielded to fate with religious submission, but Edmund was not so passive; he had his pride, after all. John had heard him speak enviously of some relatives who had fled the country rather than live under Yankee domination, and speculate on places abroad that he might take his own family, if the money could be found to do so.

As Isabella talked, John thought of her as she had been in her younger days. He had seen his sister only once or twice a year since her marriage, and only a few times during the war. He tended to remember her as she had been before that event–a somewhat languid, refined beauty who had been sought by the best beaux in the parish, and admired by young gentlemen of the first families of Charleston, where she had attended school. It was there that she had caught the eye of Edmund Stewart, and married him within six months of their first meeting. Though delicately nurtured as any young lady of her class, Isabella had as a young bride immediately taken on numerous and demanding responsibilities as the mistress and household manager of her husband's plantation, following her mother's example, and doing so very competently. John was filled with admiration at the way she had begun to take on the same responsibilities, and even more, at Belle Ville.

Isabella's husband, he could tell, depended on her a great deal. John remembered Edmund as a strong-minded man, always composed and self-assured, but he had marked a change in his brother-in-law since their last meeting during the war, sensing an understandable bewilderment in him now, and sometimes, even fear. A few days after Edmund Stewart arrived at Belle Ville with his family, the two men had become reacquainted and more comfortable with each other, and Edmund confessed to John how anxious he was for the welfare of his family. When John assured him that they were all welcome to live at Belle Ville for as long as they wished, his brother-in-law thanked him with fervent gratitude, and said that he no longer felt himself a homeless wanderer. Later, when it was evident that his infant child was out of danger and destined for a full recovery, John noticed that Edmund brightened a little and seemed more like his old self at times. Though still very worried about her sick brother, Isabella also became more enlivened when she saw her little son growing healthy again. One grief, at least, was past.

"I think it is good for you to be home, Belle," John remarked when she had finished her recital of the day's activities. "You are good for Belle Ville, and it is good for you."

She smiled in agreement, but then had to conceal a yawn.

"I think I have done enough good here today," she sighed. "And now it is time for rest."

John kissed his sister good-night, and before going upstairs, he looked in on his brother. Elias seemed to be sleeping peacefully. Edmund was reading by candlelight, and put a finger to his lips to keep things quiet as John approached.

"Shall I stay with him now?" he asked in a whisper.

"No, no, you rest," Edmund answered in the same way. "I'm going to sleep in here tonight."

John thanked him and went up to bed.

The next afternoon, Dr. Townsend paid another call. Elias was awake, and Tom went straight in to see him. When he had finished examining Elias, Belle went in to sit with him, and the doctor came out and sat down with John in the drawing room. The doctor looked depressed, and John took this as a bad sign concerning his brother's condition.

"What's wrong?" he asked anxiously. "Is Elias worse?"

"Not much worse that I can tell, but no better."

Tom ran his hands over his eyes and forehead as if trying to massage away a headache.

"Are you sure you're well enough to be out again so much, Tom?"

"I'm well enough," he sighed.

He lifted his eyes to John's with a strange look of dread and sadness. John could see that there was something very important on his mind; with an unpleasant sense of foreboding, he waited for the doctor to speak.

"John," he began quietly, "there's something I've been

meaning to tell you since I got back. I've put it off for your sake, and mine. Being so sick I didn't feel up to it, and I thought you needed time to absorb the blow of seeing Elias so–reduced."

Dr. Townsend paused, and John waited for him to continue. Before he did, he craned his neck and looked around the room and the adjoining rooms in every direction.

"Do we have privacy here?" he asked.

"For now," said John. "Everyone is out of doors for the moment, except for Israel and Belle, in the library."

"It's not about Elias," Tom reassured him again, seeing his worried look.

John felt a momentary relief, until he looked into his cousin's somber eyes again.

Tom took a deep breath and began, "You recall my letter in February, the one I wrote to you from here while I was home on furlough for illness...it contained the sad news of your father's death."

"Yes, of course I remember it," replied John.

"I told you that he had been ill with the influenza, but I think you should know that he did not die of it. When I wrote to you to inform you of his death, I supposed you would assume that he had–that his death was a natural one. At the time I couldn't bring myself to tell you the truth. I thought it would be too heavy a burden for you to bear while we were still at war, so I decided to wait."

"How did he die, Tom?" John asked, outwardly calm, but sickening inside.

It took a moment for Dr. Townsend to force out the answer.

"It is very hard to tell you, John," he said in a choking voice, then went on more quickly, "The soldiers who came in February...after the larger group of about thirty left, three of them returned two or three hours later. I'm not sure of the time. They apparently tried to make your father tell them where he had hidden valuables. They...they took him upstairs to his bed and hung him by the neck from the top frame..."

Tom lowered his eyes. His nostrils widened; his lips compressed; and his jaw worked with emotion.

"He wouldn't tell them, John. The thieves were only a few feet away from what they wanted, but he wouldn't tell them, so they killed him."

Sitting motionless and mute, John suddenly covered his face. With increasing agitation, the doctor went on in more detail.

"One of the first group of soldiers had already tried to make Israel talk, and when he protested, he was knocked unconscious. Fortunately Israel was still unconscious when these other soldiers came back, or they would probably have strung him up, too, thinking that he might know the whereabouts of the gold. When Israel woke up later and found your father's body, he was alone in the house. Apparently, the Yankees had taken Amos and hung him from a tree to make him talk, and when the other servants saw this, they ran off and hid themselves in the woods and swamps. Israel found Amos outside, revived him, and sent him to fetch me. He didn't know what else to do. Most of the village had been burned, and most everyone had fled from the area. The Yankees had even burned down the court house. There was no court, no law to apply to, and the enemy had moved on to Columbia. There was nothing I could do. Nothing!"

Dr. Townsend broke down on this last word, heaving and shuddering with tearless sobs. John tried to speak but couldn't at first; he had to clear his swollen throat to produce a husky semblance of his voice.

"I'm sure you did all you could, Tom."

When John finally uncovered his face, it was lifeless-looking and set like a stone. The doctor looked up at him sorrowfully, but with a sense of relief that he had finally unburdened himself of the secret he had been keeping so long.

"I wrote down everything Israel told me," said Tom, pulling out several folded sheets of paper from his coat pocket. "I also recorded what I found when I came to Belle Ville. I made two copies. Israel has the other. I gave it to him in case something happened to me."

The doctor placed the papers on a table beside John's chair.

"We musn't tell Elias," he added. "Not now, not for a long time. Israel and I have agreed on this, and I'm sure you understand that it's necessary. No one knows about all this except myself and Israel. I'll leave it up to you whether you wish to tell Isabella now, but I don't think I would do that."

John automatically and slowly nodded his assent. It was taking a while for him to realize the full import of what he had just been told. He had been listening in a daze, and was only now beginning to feel the blow fully. Not clearly hearing or understanding what the doctor was saying to him at that moment, he reached over to the table and took hold of the papers, but when he tried to read, his eyes would not focus properly, and the words seemed to swim in front of them in a blur. He asked his cousin to read it to him.

"I hope it is coherent," the doctor said a little apologetically. "I was very distressed and shaken when I took down what Israel told me. I tried to put most of what he said into my own words. I meant to rewrite it, but never got around to it."

Tom began reading aloud the old butler's account of what had happened, sometimes quoting Israel verbatim as he had dictated it to him:

One of the 'bluecoats' demanded to know 'where all the silver and such been hid.' Israel replied he did not know, and was stuck in the head by the soldier's gun and fell down unconscious. When he woke up, he could hear the soldiers in another room, and dragged himself to the door to see what was going on. Mr. Hutchinson had just come down the stairs with a sword in his hand, wearing 'his grand-daddy's coat from the old war.' He seemed to be a little out of his head with fever, and talked of his grandfather, but clearly demanded that the soldiers leave his house. They threatened him with their bayonets and made their own demands for his valuables, but Mr. Hutchinson refused to divulge anything, saying, shall I leave my family destitute? No, I die first. We'll hang you from a tree, old man, said the officer in charge, then you'll talk. Mr. Hutchinson tried to raise his sword in self-defense, but was so weak he could barely keep his grip on the hilt. Then he fainted to the floor. The officer, whom they called lieutenant, cursed and kicked him. Where's the old house servant? he asked his men. When Israel heard him say this, he crawled back to the spot where he had been knocked down and pretended to be unconscious. The man who had struck him walked in with the officer. Israel heard the officer cursing the soldier that struck him in the head. This man most likely knows, he says, and now you've knocked him senseless, you fool. The officer told the soldier to take one of the other house servants out and hang him up to get him to talk. They seized Amos, who begged for his life and swore that he knew nothing, but the soldiers hauled him outside and put a noose around his neck. Then another bluecoat rode up to the house and reported rebel cavalry not

far down the road, and the officer immediately gave orders
for his men to leave. He left with Mr. Hutchinson's sword
and other things stolen from the house. Israel managed to get
to his feet, but before he could make it to the drawing room,
where Mr. Hutchinson lay, he lost consciousness again.
Some two or three hours later, when he woke up, he went
upstairs to find him murdered. Israel–

John stopped the doctor there. "I can't hear anymore," he
said.

When Tom paused in his reading of Israel's statement, he
looked up and saw the old man standing in the doorway. John
turned to him.

"Is this true, Israel?" he asked. "Is this what happened?"

"Yes, sir," he said mournfully. "That's the gospel truth."

Israel was holding an empty decanter. He had been on his
way to fill it when he overheard his own words about Mr.
Hutchinson. He waited to see if anything else was required of him,
but John turned his eyes down to the floor and leaned over, holding
his head in his hands, unable, or unwilling, to speak. Israel and the
doctor exchanged a glance, and the old man moved on to get water
for Elias.

Dr. Townsend remained in his chair, waiting. The relief he
had experienced with his unburdening had faded, and was now
replaced by a sickly feeling deep in the pit of his stomach. He
imagined that John must be feeling something similar, but
multiplied many times over.

Several minutes passed in silence until John finally looked
up and asked, "What's to be done, Tom? I can't seem to think
clearly."

"I don't know that anything can be done, John," Dr.

Townsend answered somberly. "But there is something else you ought to know. It happened about a week after your father was killed—something extraordinary."

"Tell me about it then," John urged him.

"Are you sure you wish to hear about it now?"

"Go ahead...I ought to know what happened, as you say."

The doctor took a deep breath and began to tell John what happened at Belle Ville after the murder of Mr. Hutchinson.

Though still recovering from a serious illness, Dr. Townsend was well enough to tend to some of his patients, and he rode over to Belle Ville one morning to see Mr. Childress, who was bedridden with influenza. After a visit with the overseer, he walked up to the house and found Israel on the portico, and as they began to converse, Amos came running up looking extremely agitated.

"What's wrong?" asked the doctor.

"They's a stranger out to the gin house. Sick or drunk, I think. Maybe a Yankee."

Tom immediately went to his horse and took a pistol out of a saddlebag, and Amos hurried on ahead to the gin house, opening the door for Dr. Townsend and Israel when they got there.

"Over in the corner," he whispered, pointing to that spot.

Tom gestured to Amos and Israel to stay put as he walked inside. He heard a rustling sound, and a low, deep groan, followed by faint, unintelligible mumblings, and then saw a human figure in the darkened corner Amos had pointed out. A man in long, dark greatcoat was sitting on the floor with his back to the wall, fumbling with the cap of a canteen, trying to either remove or replace it. The coat was partly open at the waist, and a gun belt was visible there.

As Tom drew closer, he could hear that the man was speaking a foreign language, which he soon discerned was German.

A knapsack was propped against the wall near his feet.

In one swift move, Tom kicked the knapsack away and stood over the soldier with his pistol pointed at his chest.

"Give up your arms," he demanded.

The stranger's head wobbled upward, and he stared at Tom in open-mouthed stupefaction. He was a heavyset man close to middle age, with thick black hair and a bushy beard that framed the sallow, sagging flesh of his face. He wiped his bleary eyes with his sleeve and squinted as he kept looking up to perceive who was speaking to him.

The doctor repeated his demand. The soldier seemed to understand this time, and flopped an arm over to his holster. He sighed as if overtaxed by the effort as he leaned forward and handed it up, grip first, to Dr. Townsend.

"Why are you here?" he asked the stranger.

"I don't mean no harm," said the man, in a thick German accent. "I just needed a place to rest. I am very sick. I am looking for a priest."

"A priest! Are you a soldier, a deserter?"

"Yes," he admitted, hanging his head, which bobbed up and down a little with his continued sighs and groans.

Tom heard the voice of Israel close by. He had stepped inside, and was peering toward the corner where the doctor stood with evident curiosity. As Israel spoke, the soldier suddenly looked up with a strangely confused, wondering expression, as though he recognized the voice, but could not place it. Noticing this, Tom asked Israel to come closer.

The old butler approached gingerly and stood beside him.

"Have you seen this man before?" Tom asked him.

Israel studied the soldier, but even in the dim light, recognized him as one of the Yankees who had raided Belle Ville the week before, and denounced him as such. Tom handed the soldier's knapsack to Israel and knelt down beside the man, eyeing him with anger and contempt.

"You've been here before, soldier. Do you remember?"

"Yes, I–I thought it looked familiar," the man answered warily.

"This is Belle Ville. The master of this place, Mr. Hutchinson, do you remember him?"

"The old man? Oh..."

The soldier shrank back with a skulking, apprehensive look.

"He was my uncle."

"Was that your uncle? Oh," he said, suddenly looking more frightened.

"Tell me what happened the day you came here."

"I didn't do nothing to him, I swear! I tried to stop them. He was just a feeble old man, after all," the German panted.

"Who did it? Who killed my uncle?"

The soldier knit his brows in an exaggerated expression of puzzlement and looked away momentarily.

"Someone killed him?" he mumbled.

"He was murdered that day."

"I didn't have nothing to do with that! When I saw him, he was alive!"

"What did you see?"

The sick man sighed, coughed, and took a deep breath before he spoke.

"I will tell you, yes, I will tell you. You see, that day, we are in the nice parlor, and your father, he comes down the stairs with a fine old blue coat on, dragging a sword. I was surprised, and I says out loud, I never saw a rebel uniform like that before. This made our lieutenant very angry, and he says to me, you stupid Dutchman, that is from the Revolution! Oh! says I, *them* rebels! Which makes him so angry he strikes me. The lieutenant asks your father his name, and pretends not to know who he is. Your father says, surely then, you have heard of my grandfather–the hero of the battle of– something, I don't remember–and the lieutenant laughs at him. Your father tells us to leave, and tries to raise the sword he is holding, but he is too weak. When the others go to string him up, he faints, so they take one of the darkies out to hang him and make him talk, but then a scout comes and tells us rebel cavalry are coming, and we leave."

"Who came back to the house after you all left?" Tom asked.

"Who came back? Oh, yes, I remember...everyone was talking about the fine sword, and saying that such a fine house must have much more treasures, and they were angry we went away so soon, especially when it was only a false alarm about the rebels. The lieutenant said we had to move on, but he permitted some men to go back to make the old man talk, and bring back whatever they could get."

"Who were these men?"

"I don't know! I didn't see. I just heard of all this. I didn't have no part in it, I swear!"

"I doubt that," the doctor said fiercely. He had the distinct, unshakeable impression that the man was lying.

"I tell you the truth! Black deeds I have done but not this one. That's why I got to find a priest. Like I said, I am very sick, and liable to die any day, and I don't want to go to hell!"

The man looked genuinely terrified, but John still found it hard to believe he had played no part in his uncle's death. The soldier reached out timidly as if to take hold of his hand or sleeve, but then drew back.

"Why are you here? You say you are looking for a priest?"

Tom asked him.

"I—I have not been well for a while, and after we left this place, I got very sick, and the doctor tells me he can't do nothing for me. I felt so bad, I wanted to shoot myself, but one night, my mother, you see, she comes to me in a dream. She says to me, 'My son, you are dying now. You are an evildoer whom justice will not suffer to live. Forget this world, and think of your immortal soul. Before it is too late, seek forgiveness.' And then she reaches out to me, and touches my face. I swear, I swear! I felt that touch, for it wakened me! When I ask the doctor, he tells me I am surely going to die, so I run away to look for a priest. I can't find no Catholic church, and I am so sick and confused, I don't know where I'm going. Ain't there no priests in this country?"

Raising his voice as he asked this question, the soldier wearily wagged his head in exasperation.

"It's the whiskey!" the deserter declared with sudden vehemence, bringing himself bolt-upright. "I tell you, the drink, it makes me a madman! The devil gets in me, and I do terrible things!"

"What have you done? No doubt you're a thief."

"Yes, but the officers, they tell us to do these things. Forage liberally, they say! And they wink at us, so we take everything we can, and burn or break the rest. Some of the officers, they take so much, they will be rich men after the war."

"What else have you done?" Tom asked him with a simmering look.

"I shot a reb prisoner–I shouldn't have done that. That was murder. And me and others, we take the darkey women, and do what we want with them," the soldier muttered.

"But I don't touch no white women!" he quickly added, with several rapid blinks, seeing the other's mounting disgust and infuriation.

Tom seized the man's collar, fighting an urge to wring his neck.

"I don't believe you!" he exclaimed savagely. "I ought to kill you now and send you to hell where you belong!"

"Please don't!" the German wailed abjectly, breaking into sobs. "I got to find a priest!"

"What was your officer's name?" Tom demanded. "You didn't mention it. Who is this lieutenant?"

"I won't tell you his name if you mean to kill me!"

Trembling with anger and physical weakness, Dr. Townsend let go of the man's collar and staggered to his feet. He tried to clear his mind to think what he ought to do next, and then suddenly remembered one of his other patients, a refugee from Charleston. The man was a Catholic priest who had been staying with his brother just outside Amelia, and though he was very old and ill, Dr. Townsend thought he might be well enough to see this man. He knelt down again, and with great effort, quelled his rage.

"Perhaps you can do some penance before you die," he suggested.

"What do you mean?" the German sniveled, wiping his face with the backs of his rough, pulpy hands.

"Can you write in English?"

"Yes, pretty good, but I don't spell so good."

"You write down what you have told me, about what happened at this place last week, and sign it, and swear it is a true account. I want the name of your officer."

"I will do this," the soldier promised, "if you will find me a priest."

Amos was asked to bring a wagon around to the gin house, and Israel held a gun on the soldier as Dr. Townsend pulled him up to his feet. When the German noticed that his own pistol was pointed at him, he gave a sputtering, mirthless laugh.

"You don't need no gun for me," he sighed.

The wagon pulled up, and Tom helped the soldier into the back of it. The soldier asked for some water, and Amos jumped down and went back inside the gin house for the canteen he had left there. Finding it empty, he filled it at the well and returned it to him. Tom had already taken the reins and was waiting impatiently for him.

They set off for the village. The soldier kept himself hidden, reclining in the bed of the wagon under an old piece of burlap. On the way, to distract himself from his troubles, he uncovered his head and began talking to Dr. Townsend of his life in the army, of other soldiers and officers he liked or disliked, and places in Georgia and South Carolina he had helped to burn and plunder, sometimes lapsing into mutterings in German as though conversing with himself.

The soldier laughed when he spoke of his experiences with his army in the village of Amelia.

"Our bummers, they went in ahead of us and began to set fire to the town before the rest of us came. When we got there, the general told a newspaper man with us that a bad Jew of the town had started the fire, and the newspaper man reported it so. Uncle Billy, he is such a liar! It was very funny!"

The doctor turned a withering look on him, and the soldier, seeing that his companion was far from amused, shut his mouth and kept quiet for the rest of the ride. They drove on another mile or so and pulled up at the residence of Mr. Connor, a small cottage that looked to be in need of much repair. An elderly gentleman was working in a vegetable garden in the yard, and looked up as Tom jumped down from the wagon seat.

"Doctor Townsend," he said, with a slight Irish brogue.

"May I have a word with your brother?"

"For what purpose? You said before there was little you could do for him."

"There is a sick soldier who believes himself to be dying. He is Catholic, and has asked for a priest."

Mr. Connor glanced over at the wagon.

"You brought him here?" he asked, looking a little disturbed.

"Yes."

"I will ask my brother if he is willing to see the man. He is not well, as you know."

"I understand, but if you will please ask him, I should be most grateful, sir."

The gentleman went into the house and in a few minutes returned to the door, gesturing for Tom to come in.

"Is the soldier able to walk?" he asked.

"Yes, but if you please, I should like a word with Father Connor first."

"Very well."

Mr. Connor pointed toward a door that led into a small bedroom, and Dr. Townsend knocked there and entered. Inside, a thin, elderly man who had just risen from his bed was buttoning up a faded black frock coat.

The priest had a sickly color to his complexion, and he trembled all over with a slight palsy. Only a few strands of white hair were left on his head, and his cheeks were sunken from too many missing teeth. He seemed frail and ancient, but his pale blue eyes radiated kindliness and intelligence.

"A soldier is asking for last rites, is he?" the old man queried.

His broken, quavering voice was more distinctly Irish than his brother's, as were his turns of speech.

"Perhaps in time," said Tom, "but I think he is more anxious now for confession."

"Is he, now? Well, I will hear his confession. Is he indeed dying?"

"He says he is very ill. A doctor has told him he will die soon."

"Oh, 'tis a shame. Is he an Irish lad? One of our Irish volunteers?"

"No, he's German."

"Ah!"

The doctor paused uncomfortably.

"Father Connor," he said, "I must explain something. This man is not a Confederate soldier. He is a deserter from the Union army."

The old man's eyes grew larger.

"He is a criminal," Tom went on. "I brought him here because he promised me that if I found him a priest, he would sign a document attesting that some of his fellow soldiers were responsible for the murder of my uncle at Belle Ville. I do not care about this man. I only want my uncle's murderers brought to justice."

The priest shuddered and backed up against the bed, putting his hand down on it to support himself.

"I am sorry to distress you, Father. I know you are not well, but if you will hear this man's confession, it would do me a great service, and even though he is a criminal, and a Yankee, I suppose you might wish to be of service to him, too."

"What crimes has he committed?"

John told the priest what the German had already confessed

to him in the vaguest terms possible. The old man's kindly face turned hard, but he consented to see the soldier. Tom brought him to Father Connor and left the two alone.

He waited in Mr. Connor's small parlor. About a half hour passed, and the German soldier finally emerged from the other room, wiping his eyes with his sleeve. He stumbled past Tom and went out the front door. As the doctor rose to follow him, the priest came out and approached him. The old man was trembling violently, but not with palsy now. His yellowish complexion was splotched with red patches of choler, and his thin, sunken lips were pressed together in anger. He opened his mouth to say something, and then looked away as if he had thought better of it, but was so distraught that he tottered and almost fell to the floor. Tom moved quickly to catch him and help into a chair.

"Thank you," the old man whispered breathlessly.

"I'm sorry I had to bring him here," Tom apologized. "There was no other way..."

Father Connor weakly grasped his hand and patted it.

"I understand," he said, calming.

He suddenly took hold of Tom's hand again and gazed into his eyes sorrowfully. Again he looked as though he wished to say something, but once more he hesitated and remained silent.

Tom waited, and the old man let go of him and lowered his head.

"I shall pray that justice is done for your family," he said.

The soldier was waiting at the wagon as Mr. Connor, resting from his labors in the garden for the moment, eyed him with fear and hostility; the German's coat did not completely hide his blue uniform. Tom nodded his thanks to the gentleman as he returned to the wagon, and there helped the soldier climb back into it. They drove to his house in the village where his sister Laura immediately came out to meet him, puzzled to see her brother returning in a wagon.

"Go to your room, Laura," he told her. "I have a sick prisoner here. He is an enemy soldier, a deserter. I found him at Belle Ville."

Her eyes were full of questions, but she had no wish to see another Yankee soldier, and obeyed her brother.

Dr. Townsend led the soldier inside to the parlor and sat him down at a writing table. The man asked for some food, and when he had finished with a small meal of cornbread, he began to write out his testimony. The soldier leaned closely over his work with a dull, dogged expression, writing steadily, and pausing now and then to look up and ask about the spelling of a word as Tom watched him impatiently.

The German seemed to take an interminable time at his writing, but finally concluded the document, and signed his name at the bottom of the second page. The doctor briefly scanned his shaky scrawl to make sure he had included the name of the officer, which was Potter.

The soldier groaned and laid his head down on the table.

"Eh, I am having such pains again! Do you have any whiskey?" he asked.

Tom answered an emphatic "no" and, as the soldier raised his head, and for the first time, the doctor took a critical look at the man to assess his physical condition, concluding that he was in the last stages of liver disease.

"Now that I have what I want from you, soldier," said Tom, "I don't know what I shall do with you."

The soldier laid his head down again, and his broad back began to shake with soundless laughter.

"Well now," he said, "I have what I want, too, so if you want to shoot me, it's just as well now. Yes, I think I would rather have it over with quickly."

"Why should I shoot you? You say you are dying."

"Have a little pity on me, then. Let me die here in peace. I have nowhere else to go. Give me a bed somewhere…and there is something else I will tell you."

"What do you mean?"

"Something important. Something you will wish to know, I promise you, but let me die in peace here."

There was a small wooden outbuilding near the house, little more than a woodshed, but it was the only place Dr. Townsend could think of to put the man. He went into another room and gathered up some blankets and pillows, but, stricken in conscience, he soon changed his mind.

"Come with me," he said to the soldier.

The German rose from his chair and followed Tom into a small room off the parlor. There the doctor made a bed for him on the carpeted floor.

"It's too cold at night to put you outside," he said. "I'll find a cot for you, but tonight, this is all I can offer you."

The soldier thanked him and sought a chair in the corner of the room, collapsing in it as if exhausted.

"Now tell me about that important matter," said Tom.

"I will, I will. Let me breathe a little."

The soldier took in several deep breaths and sighed. He closed his eyes a few moments, but then opened them and went on haltingly, frequently gasping for breath, "Your uncle–the killing–I confess, I had a part in it."

The soldier faltered, grimacing with shame. When Tom recovered from his surprise, he said angrily, "So you were lying to me before!"

"I was afraid to tell you," answered the soldier. "I thought you might kill me before I could find a priest!"

"You killed Mr. Hutchinson?"

"I—I was drinking, you see. That day we found some whiskey in the town, and when the three of us go back to the plantation, we find the old man, and two of us hang him from his bed. He wouldn't talk, so we hanged him up again. The next thing we know, he is dead."

"Who were the others with you?"

"Eh, I wrote it down for you."

Tom had been standing in the doorway while the man spoke, and now leaned against it for support, feeling weak and overcome with emotion. He made a movement to turn away, but the soldier rose from this chair and came to him, falling on his knees and catching at the hem of his coat.

"*Bitte!*" he implored in his own language. He frowned mournfully, and tears came into his bleary, sunken eyes. He tried to speak, but his voice failed him at that moment.

Tom detached the man's fingers from his coat. The soldier tried to seize his hand, but it was withdrawn too quickly.

"Please!" the soldier pleaded, shaking and wincing with strange, low, staccato sobs. "I want to ask your forgiveness. For what I did, I ask your forgiveness. Will you–?"

"Don't ask *me* for forgiveness," the doctor replied wrathfully, as he turned his back on the man and walked away.

For the next several days, the soldier kept to his bed, growing weaker and refusing most food and drink, but accepting medicine for pain. Finally, he lapsed into unconsciousness, and a few days later, Dr. Townsend went into his room one morning to find him dead.

CHAPTER TWELVE

THE DOCTOR PAUSED AND WAITED for some reaction from John, but there was only silence again, and reaching into his coat and pulling out more papers, he concluded his story.

"I left here the day after we buried the German. I had recovered, and had to get back to my regiment. On my way north I met with a soldier returning from North Carolina. He said he had been furloughed for wounds, but he was heading for Columbia, and I think he had simply left to see about his family. At any rate, he told me my regiment was in North Carolina, and when I rejoined them, I found that Elias's regiment was also there. Not long after that, he was wounded at Bentonville."

Tom opened the folded papers and held them out to John.

"This is the soldier's confession," he said. "I didn't read it very carefully at the time, I'm afraid. I was most interested in the name of the officer in charge of the men who came here the day of the murder, thinking that there might be some hope of getting justice if we knew that. When I read it again this morning, I found that the soldier had left out the name of one of his comrades—the one who waited downstairs and stood guard—and the name of the other man is such a scrawl, and so blotted with ink, that I couldn't make it out."

John looked up from the writing and asked in a bewildered voice, "Is there any hope of justice?"

"I don't know," said the doctor. "I do know that your father wasn't the only one to suffer in this way. I have since found out that this happened to others. While General Sherman's army occupied Amelia, some of his soldiers did the same thing to old Mr. Winthrop in much the same way. They hung him from his own bed, but he gave in and told them what they wanted to know before they killed him. Later, he considered reporting this crime, but he was advised by everyone he consulted that it would be useless, even dangerous to pursue the matter, and so he did nothing. I've heard of other cases, too. It seems to have been a common mode of operation with these–I almost said men, but they could scarcely be called that."

The strain of his emotions began to take an effect on the doctor. He broke down into a coughing fit, and suddenly looked weakened and pale.

"You should rest," John told him.

"Just let me sit here for a while," Tom said breathlessly.

Israel was just returning with the water for Elias, and heard the sound of coughing from the drawing room. The butler stepped in with a tray and offered Dr. Townsend a small glass of water. He drank it and closed his eyes for a few moments. John took the pieces of paper containing Israel's account and the soldier' confession, folded them, and put them in his pocket.

He thought of Isabella. Imagining the horror with which she would receive the revelation of their father's murder, he decided that Tom was right. She should not be told, at least for the present. So then, among the murdered man's children, at least for now, the burden of this knowledge was his alone to bear. John asked the doctor to convey a message to Emma on his way home, to tell her he could not see her that evening.

After Tom left, John went outside and made his way to the family cemetery. It was late afternoon, and the setting sun was casting elongated gray shadows of the trees and headstones. He stood in front of his father's grave until the shadows disappeared, and as the gloom of twilight replaced them, he slowly walked back to the house.

That night John avoided supper with his family and kept to his room. There at his writing desk, he read over the two papers Dr. Townsend had written, and forced himself to begin copying the soldier's statement on sheets of paper he had torn out of an old ledger. Later that night, while he took his turn sitting with Elias, sleep eluded him. His thoughts obsessively returned to all he had been told that afternoon. The whole scenario played out in his mind over and over again, maddeningly so for hours, and with every return, the thought of what these murderers had done to his father, and the idea that most of them would be free to live their lives and go unpunished, seared his soul like the touch of white hot metal.

When Elias woke up shortly after dawn, John was glad for the distraction. He busied himself attending to his brother's needs. He tried to conceal his wretchedness, but Elias, even through the fog still in his brain from medicines, could see that something was wrong.

"You don't look well, John," he said.

"I didn't sleep well."

"Because of me?"

"No," was the answer, with no further explanation.

Around eight o'clock Israel brought in breakfast, and John left Elias in his care. An hour or so later, Isabella asked to speak with John. Edmund was now with Elias, and Israel was standing beside her. She was worried because Israel had informed her that their brother was not eating. The three went into the drawing room to talk, and had just sat down there, when they were interrupted by a knock at the door. Israel answered it and soon came back to announce that a Yankee officer was asking to speak with the owner of the plantation. Isabella shuddered in aversion and immediately left the room.

"Show him in," said John.

The butler brought the officer into the drawing room, and he introduced himself as Captain Edwards. A short, beardless young man who carried himself with a businesslike air, he had been unfavorably impressed with the somewhat faded grandeur of the house when he first saw it on his approach, and now, as he glanced around its interior on his way in, exhibited the same air of disapproval. He bowed very slightly as he greeted John, who only rose to his feet but offered no other courtesies.

They sat down, and Captain Edwards explained the reason for his call. He drew out a small sheet of paper from a coat pocket, and elaborated on his mission by reading off the entire text of certain printed general orders pertaining to the freedmen and land owners. He then asked that all the workers be assembled so that he could speak to them and have them sign or make their mark on a contract he had prepared.

"I'll have my manager Mr. Childress do that for you," John said to him curtly.

They walked out of the house and happened to find Mr. Childress right away. He had been on his way to the house to see John about some livestock he had discovered to be missing, most likely stolen during the night. Captain Edwards let both men read over the sharecropping agreement, the terms of which were less generous than the ones Mr. Childress had already settled on with the field workers.

About an hour and a half later, the young officer returned to the house and asked to see John again. Captain Edwards found him in the same chair in the drawing room, and sat down in the same seat he had occupied earlier, mopping perspiration from his brow with a handkerchief. He paused, hoping to be offered a glass of water or something else to drink, but seeing that no such kindness was forthcoming, he asked to meet with the house servants.

"How many are there?" the captain asked, unfolding some sheets of paper he held in his hands.

"Not many," John answered.

He went to find Israel, and in a few minutes, walked back into the drawing room with him and Sibley the cook. She was a plump, very dark, round-faced woman who faintly and pleasantly smelled of the biscuits she had been preparing in the kitchen. Keeping her big brown eyes cast down, she wiped some flour from her fingers with her apron and shyly sat down opposite the young officer at his urging. A moment later, two other women, a maid and a laundress, also came in and took a seat.

"This is all?" said the young man.

John made no response, and Israel explained in a low voice that some of the house servants had "run off."

The captain asked a few more questions of John, wrote out four simple contracts detailing their obligations and wages, and then read each aloud to the respective parties. Israel and the three women listened attentively, and when the officer was finished, they looked over at John questioningly, wondering if all this met with his approval.

"If you're satisfied with these terms," John said to them, "it is up to you to sign them as the officer has asked."

Captain Edwards held his pen over one of the contracts and

asked the butler his name. He wrote it out and had Israel make his mark beside it. Sibley and the other two women did the same on their agreements.

"That's all then," said the captain. "Thank you."

The servants left to go back to their work, and Captain Edwards pulled out the other contract for the field workers, to which he had made some alterations. He read it aloud again for John, who listened, or rather seemed to listen, as he stared at the officer with a brooding expression. He was not listening, but thinking of his father again. When the captain finished reading he asked for John's signature, and, looking up at him and holding out the papers, he was met with such a look of sheer hatred that he drew in an audible breath of astonishment and was left speechless for few moments.

He took this hostility as an expression of Mr. Hutchinson's resentment against the imposition of government authority in his affairs

"Some of the planters are not treating their former servants as well as you do, sir," he said somewhat indignantly, by way of justifying his presence.

"Almost all of the planters are now as poor as their former servants, sir," John replied sharply.

When the young man finally left the house, John went to the window and looked out, glad to be rid of him. The captain had tied his horse under the shade of a tree, and he stopped to take a long drink from a canteen before mounting and riding away. A moment later, Mr. Childress came walking up the steps, and John went to the door to let him in.

"You missed quite a speech, Captain Hutchinson," he remarked.

"What did he say?"

"Well, he said to them, in so many words, that they must work or starve. He was not as blunt as that, but that was his point. I suppose he did give them some good advice, to work hard, be civil, and stay put, but most of them did not seem altogether pleased with him, especially after he read them the agreement. I suggested some changes, which were accepted. A few hands asked if they would be given any land, and the captain told them no, that they were asking for too much. So many rumors and lies are circulating still, I suppose they've kept up some hopes, but I think they have already begun to discover that the Yankees are a rather treacherous reed to lean on."

John waved his hand contemptuously to dismiss the subject of Captain Edwards, and Mr. Childress began to tell him about the missing livestock. The two men were just finishing up their conversation as Isabella appeared. Her worried expression reminded John of their earlier concern. Mr. Childress went back to his work, and Isabella and her brother returned to the drawing room to talk about Elias. She wanted John to speak with him, to convince him to eat; she had already tried, with no success.

"I'll do whatever I can, Belle," he assured her.

She thanked him, but his weary, gloomy look, which she imagined had to do only with Elias, distressed her. Isabella had held out little hope for him all along, and now was becoming utterly discouraged. She brought up Reverend Shubrick again, but John felt sure Elias would not change his mind and allow the clergyman to visit him.

They heard the sound of Dr. Townsend's buggy pulling up in front of the house, and Isabella rushed out to see him in private. John could hear the low murmur of their conversation on the portico. It did not last long. Tom walked in, acknowledged John, and went straight into the library.

At dusk John rode over to visit with Emma. She was very happy to see him, but knew at once that he was troubled about something. His smile was weak, the look in his eyes dull without the usual ardor and happiness she saw in them when he was in her presence.

"How is Elias?" she asked.

"He's growing weaker. He's not eating."

"Oh, John!" she said feelingly.

Emma pressed his hand, and as he looked into her eyes, he could see that she was suffering for him. Elias was only part of the reason for his suffering, but he let her think otherwise, undecided as to whether and when he would tell her about his father.

"I am sorry I could not see you yesterday," he apologized.

"You mustn't worry about that, John. If you cannot come here to see me, I shall understand."

They sat down on the steps of the porch, and he asked her to tell him about her day. The sound of her voice and the sight of her was a welcome distraction from his troubles and at least a little comfort to him. Towards the end of his visit, Emma's aunt and uncle came out to spend a little time with John. Mrs. Screven mentioned that Reverend Shubrick was finally feeling well enough to hold services at the church in Amelia again. Her eyes, and Emma's, traveled to John with the expectation of an offer of his carriage for Sunday. Knowing that Emma was longing to go, he did not disappoint them.

The next day, on a warm, cloudy morning, John arrived with his carriage and drove Emma and her family into the village. She breathed a sigh of relief and gratitude when she saw that the building, a beautiful stone structure of Gothic style, was still standing and intact, though she was distressed to see the condition of its interior. The church had been used as a stable by the invading army, and all the handsome old oak pews had been removed and broken up for firewood and burned along with the prayer books. The altar and some of the stained glass windows had been damaged, and the silver communion service was gone; like everything else of value, it had been stolen. One of the vestrymen had made a number of rough wooden benches for seating, a temporary measure until it was possible to provide the church with something better.

Most everyone knew John, or knew who he was, and seemed glad to see him. He saw many women who were now widows or bereaved mothers, and missed the faces of the men and boys who had once been at their side. Much of Mr. Shubrick's flock had been scattered or lost; the seats were barely half filled, and no more than twenty-five persons made up the congregation that morning.

During the service, John observed Emma's earnest, attentive expression as she drank in the beauty and spiritual nourishment of the liturgy, something for which she had long been starved. He was happy for her, but did not find himself much soothed by it, nor by the priest's sermon urging resignation to the will of God. At the end of the service, when it was time for communion, Emma rose to follow her aunt and uncle, but John stood up and turned in the opposite direction as he entered the aisle. Pausing, she touched his arm and looked at him with an expression of concern and inquiry.

"I'll wait for you outside," he said to her quietly, and walked out of the church, keenly conscious of his conspicuousness as the only member of the congregation not taking the sacrament.

As the people left the chapel, no one made any remark on his behavior, at least in his hearing, and the priest, who had known him most of his life, spoke to him and embraced him as warmly as ever. Later, when John was able to have a few moments of private conversation with Emma, she asked him, very hesitantly and gently, about what had happened at church. There was such bitterness and hatred in his heart, it had not seemed right to him to take communion, but he could hardly tell her this without explaining why, and he had not yet made up his mind to do that.

"You must be patient with me, Emma," he said, almost in a whisper.

The wounded look in his eyes made her feel regretful for having questioned him.

"I will," she promised.

CHAPTER THIRTEEN

RETURNING HOME ON SUNDAY AFTERNOON, John caught sight of Dr. Townsend's buggy in front of the house at Belle Ville, and pulled his own carriage up behind it. As he walked inside, he happened to see Israel coming out of the library. The old man was hanging his head, and his shoulders were slumped in an attitude of discouragement.

They said nothing to each other as John passed by him and opened the library door. The doctor was standing over Elias. He had just given his patient a strong painkiller, and was watching him drift into unconsciousness. John went around the couch to see his brother. In his drug induced repose he appeared serene, but he was looking more shockingly fragile and skeletal than ever.

He looked to Tom with a terrible question in his eyes.

"A few days at most," said the doctor.

"Have you told Isabella?"

"I shall tell her before I go."

Feeling weak and unsteady, John sat down in a chair opposite Elias's couch. He resisted the thought that his brother was dying, but could no longer deny it now. The fact slowly worked itself into his consciousness, and with its painful realization a thousand memories of their childhood together crowded into his mind all at once. But even in the face of this equally painful loss, eventually, all John's thoughts seemed to lead back to his father.

In the early evening he went upstairs to his father's room, which was now his, and sat down at the large secretary desk there. Except for a few documents concerning the estate he had removed to send to his attorney in Charleston, he had left these papers undisturbed until now. He looked through the drawers and compartments for Mr. Hutchinson's correspondence with the vague hope of finding a letter or two his father might have begun for himself or Elias that was never sent, hoping that he might hear from him one last time in that way. John found two stacks of letters tied with white string, his own, and those from Elias, written during the war, but there were no unfinished letters. It appeared that Mr. Hutchinson had saved them all, and two in John's handwriting were separated from the others and tied together with a piece of red string, as though they were of some special significance.

John untied the red string and opened the first letter. It was dated January 23, 1865, and had been written in response to the first news of his father's illness.

Dear Father,

I am sorry to learn of your indisposition, and hope to hear of an improvement very soon in this new year. Hale and hearty as you have always been, I am not much worried. Your next letter, I trust, unlike your last brief one, will contain all the news of things at home. I like to hear of the usual goings-on and imagine myself among them again. Does that surprise you? I am proof, I suppose that 'absence makes the heart grow fonder.' Absence from home has indeed done that for me, along with other things I have been called upon to endure, and more often than not I see many things in a much different light than I used to.

Some years ago I did not relish the thought of following you in what you have always wished for me. Now, however, the peaceful pursuits of country life begin to appear to me more and more as a vision of Elysium, despite all the attendant difficulties and responsibilities, large and small, that used to repel me. Perhaps it is only homesickness bending my inclinations, but I sometimes think now that I could not wish better for myself than the honorable and useful life you have led. I do not say these things merely to cheer you—these thoughts have been brewing in me for a long time— but who knows what will come of them? When this terrible war is over, there may be nothing left to return to.

You must pardon my gloominess, but we have all been heartsick lately since we heard of the fall of Savannah. Such news does little good for men who are barely subsisting on very meager rations indeed, and doing without sufficient clothing and protection from the cold weather. I have been waiting for the box you spoke of in your last letter. It is taking a long time to get here, but if it reaches me at all, no matter how late, I shall be grateful.

Reuben has constructed another enviable winter quarters for us, not as good as some we have had in the past, but better than most. The poor fellow is as homesick as I; I caught him unawares in his private lamentations only last night. Billy went lame for a while but is now recovered.

Any news of Elias? I have not heard from him lately. I have had some dreams about him, and cannot say they are pleasant ones, but I think they are only the worries and fears

I banish in my waking hours coming to assail me in my sleep. For all I know he may be more comfortably situated than I am. I hope so. I was sorry to hear that Theo DuBose was wounded. I hope he will recover now he is home. That family has suffered very severely indeed.

Yesterday I received a letter from Belle in Anderson. The family seems to be comfortable there. The town, she says, has been kind and hospitable to refugees. She is feeling a little better now, and talks of coming to see you as soon as she is well enough.

Yours respectfully,
John Hutchinson

John remembered that about a month and a half after this letter was written, he had received one from Tom Townsend, and was surprised to see that it had been sent from Amelia. At the time he had not known that the doctor was home on furlough, recovering from an infection he had suffered from an accidental cut by a bone saw. Though softened and framed with expressions of sorrow and condolence, the doctor's letter was brief and to the point: Mr. Hutchinson was dead. John knew that his father had been suffering with what Israel had diagnosed as influenza, and, though he was shocked it had struck down such a strong, vital man—with no other explanation offered, John naturally assumed at the time that Mr. Hutchinson had succumbed to his illness.

He refolded the letter and picked up the second which had been set aside with it. It was a short note which had preceded the other, dated a few weeks after he had received his second serious wound in battle in Virginia, and hastily penned in reply to several letters his father had written to him expressing a concern for his spiritual welfare.

Near Petersburg
Dec. 5th 1864

Elias has written me another letter in the same strain of your last one, dear Father. His concern is very gratifying, although my own wickedness is not a topic I would select for correspondence. You both seem to fear that I shall die on the field of battle, unconverted, and be lost to the family forever. My brother's apprehensions, and yours, I know are sincere and deep, but I must tell you that I do not think it right or true that those who love me will suffer torture because I am not in heaven or worthy of it. If, as you say, all things are in God's hands, then so is my fate, and whatever that may be, I submit that you and the future parson ought to be stronger in your resignation to the divine will, and have confidence that you will be given the strength to bear whatever burdens may come. If it is my fate to perish in this war, I hope that my family will at least find consolation in the knowledge that I died in the highest earthly service–the defense of my country. But I intend to try to come back to you alive.

I am sitting in a tent with four or five men talking, sometimes to me, and hardly know what I have written with such distractions. I cannot reply to all your questions, Father, or put your mind at ease, but I will tell you that I have begun to think more seriously and more often of spiritual things. You will be pleased to know that our brigade is fortunate in having an impressive chaplain, Mr. Girard of Charleston, a Presbyterian, who combines strong emotion with a strong intellect. He always draws a large crowd and is far and away the best preacher I have ever heard, unsurpassed, I should think—and I am not one who enjoys being preached to, as you know. I still cannot say it is something I greatly enjoy, but Mr. Girard is an arresting speaker and, if nothing else, gives me food for thought.

Reuben is well and says howdy to all at home. I enclose a note listing my requests. Please do not fail to send the items as soon as possible. My sword belt is about to go to pieces, and I must have a new bridle, or money to buy one. Remember me to all inquiring relations and neighbors.

Your affectionate son,
John Hutchinson

It was easy for him to see why these two letters had been set aside from the rest. They must have given his father a measure of hope concerning his most fervent prayers for his eldest son. John had written so many letters during the war, he could hardly remember writing these, but now, as he read this last one, memories of Mr. Girard came back to him strongly.

The pieces of memory which had taken the longest to return after his head wound were those of the hours and days immediately preceding his last injury. All of his memories had long since been restored to him, but they had come back to him in a disconnected and vague way at first, and had been overshadowed during and after his return home by matters of sheer survival, his concerns for Elias, and his feelings for Emma. John now recalled his conversation with the chaplain and the events of that day more vividly, and the ominous feelings haunting him a number of days beforehand.

The day that conversation took place, his brigade was encamped on a farm which had been the scene of a bloody battle the year before. The open field beyond them still bore vestiges of that contest in the form of some scattered bones of men and horses. John had set up his tent at a choice, level and sunny spot at the edge of his company's camp, near that of an infantry regiment which was part of his brigade. In the late afternoon, just before dusk, he was sitting outside the tent cleaning his pistol.

As he reassembled his weapon, John noticed a tall, lanky young infantry soldier walking around with a trudging gait. He was shouting out a general question to all his fellow soldiers in the immediate area.

"Anyone got a coffee mill?" he kept asking.

Most heads were shaking "No," but one private called back, "We ain't got no coffee, so what's the use of a mill? Where'd you get coffee round here?"

"Traded with a Yank for it a while back! Can't stand it no more–got to have some," the lanky soldier answered, his voice fading to a mutter. He walked around aimlessly for a while mumbling some more complaints, then disappeared from view. After a few minutes he came back to the place where he had put down his gear, a spot near the campfire, and sat down on the ground with a bulging haversack.

As John happened to glance in that direction again, he saw the young man removing part of a bleached human skull and a sturdy lower leg bone from his bag. The skull had been cracked open to form a bowl. The soldier took coffee beans out his pouch, poured them into the upturned skull, and then using the leg bone as a pestle, began pounding and grinding them.

John paused and watched the man with only the mildest sense of revulsion, being largely inured to such horrors by now. Reuben, who was seated beside him cleaning his rifle, had been observing the soldier with a look of amazement and disgust.

"I wouldn't drink that coffee, would you, Cap'n?" he asked John.

"No, I don't think I would."

Another soldier sitting behind John and Reuben, a grizzled old veteran who had overheard their exchange, leaned back to them to say, "I wouldn't drink it neither! What if it ain't a Confederate noggin? Might git poisoned by Yankee brains."

Despite his repugnance, Reuben could not resist a good joke, and doubled over, wheezing with laughter. Everyone around wanted to know what was so amusing, and the old soldier merrily repeated his jest for the entertainment of his comrades. It was considered fairly good, and made the rounds of much of the infantrymen's camp in slightly varied forms, causing eruptions of laughter with every repetition, until it finally reached the soldier with the coffee, who only scowled.

John was in a gloomy, irritable mood, and the continuing sounds of laughter and conversation began to grate on his nerves. He suddenly felt suffocated by the multitudes all around him, and when he finished cleaning his gun he went inside his small tent to seek what seclusion could be found there.

For about a week he had been oppressed with a heavy sense of foreboding. Throughout this time he knew that a battle was ahead which promised to be a fierce and desperate one, and now that it was only a day or so away, he was feeling even more acutely what he believed to be a premonition of his own death. He had known a few other men who had experienced such presentiments, and each one of them had perished soon afterwards.

As darkness fell, John tried to clean himself up a little. In recent months he had begun to grow a beard, finding one less troublesome than daily shaving, but had not done much in the way of grooming it lately. His beard and hair, like his overall appearance, had grown quite shabby. He knew he would see some of his superior officers at the religious service scheduled for that evening, and there was even a rumor that General Lee might show up, so he did all he could to make himself more presentable.

That evening the crowd which assembled in a large open area illuminated by several campfires was much larger than usual. The soldiers knew they would be going into battle the next day or so, and many had come to hear Mr. Girard's preaching for that reason. Others were there to catch a glimpse of the revered general. John, who was not immune to the prevalent idolatry, circled the crowd looking and listening for signs of General Lee's presence, but as the music of a hymn began, it became apparent that the great man was not in attendance, though there were many other high officers there that night including the commanding general of the brigade.

After an opening prayer, Mr. Girard began to preach. His text was taken from the words of Jesus in the eighth chapter of the Gospel of John, "Ye are from beneath; I am from above; ye are of this world; I am not of this world. I said therefore unto you, that ye shall die in your sins; for if you believe not that I am he, ye shall die in your sins."

It was not unusual for Mr. Girard to speak on the subject of death and perdition, especially in anticipation of a bloody battle, but haunted as he was by forebodings of his own death, John was beginning to feel that on this night, the clergyman had been given a message meant particularly for *him*. For this reason he listened with intense but uncomfortable attention. His discomfort increased to the point that he wanted to leave, but he was hemmed in on all sides by other soldiers, and could not easily move away. He tried to think of other things, to let his mind wander, but his attention was always drawn back to the chaplain whose words, in time, began to penetrate him like a sharp sword.

After the service, he sought out Mr. Girard for a private conversation. He had to wait his turn, as more than a dozen other soldiers and officers were at the clergyman's tent to speak with him. Rather than wait in their company, John returned to his own tent for a while, and when he came back, the last of the men who had been there before him was emerging. He was a colonel, an older man whom John knew only slightly. He had been weeping, and turned his face away as he passed, looking ashamed of his emotion as though it were something unmanly. The chaplain saw John and beckoned him inside.

Mr. Girard had been praying fervently with the colonel, and was recovering from his own emotions as John sat down in a chair opposite his.

"What is your name, Captain?" he asked gently, wiping his eyes with a handkerchief.

John told him.

"My name is John," Mr. Girard said, smiling. "You are from South Carolina?"

"Yes."

"Ah, so am I–from James Island. Where is your home?"

They talked of their respective homes a while. When the conversation turned to the reason for his visit, John paused uneasily, not knowing where to begin. The chaplain asked him if he was a member of a church, and learned that he had been raised in the Episcopal faith. Unused to speaking of such intimate, uncomfortable matters, it was only with great difficulty that John could disclose his mind and heart to the clergyman, but Mr. Girard was patient, knowing men of his proud class well.

"I have not lived as I should," he finally confessed. "I have not lived as a Christian. For the past several years, I have devoted all my energies to the service of my country, and I am willing to give my life for it, but lately...lately it has become clear to me that I must be personally prepared for death."

After waiting for him to say more, Mr. Girard responded quietly, "As must we all."

"I was deeply impressed...by your words tonight," John went on haltingly. "I see now... there is no other hope for me...I think I may die soon."

The chaplain gave a solemn nod.

"God is merciful," he said, studying John compassionately.

There were no others waiting to speak with the chaplain by this time, and after they prayed together, Mr. Girard talked with the young captain further. Nearly two hours had passed when John finally left him, and that night in his tent, for the first time in many nights, he slept peacefully.

A day later on the battlefield, he received the wound which finally brought an end to his military service, but not his life.

As John put away the letters he had written to his father, he thought again of the desperate prayer he had uttered as he fell in battle. That prayer had been answered, yes; he had been allowed to go on living, but in living, forced to drink from very bitter cups indeed—defeat, a dying brother, and a murdered father—all of which, in sum, so hard to bear, that if were not for his love for Emma and his family, he might have wished that last wound to have been a mortal one.

He thought about Mr. Shubrick's sermon that morning about submission to the will of God, then remembered what Emma had said of herself, that the trials she had been sent she had not borne well. He knew that he was not submitting as he perhaps should, or bearing his own trials very well, and that in his bitterness, he had been shunning rather than seeking God—but how, he asked himself—how much was a man expected to accept without question or complaint?

John gathered up all the letters and put them away in a drawer. Without undressing, he fell into his bed, and was so tired after his restless night that he fell asleep within a few minutes. His sleep was deep and dreamless, but lasted only a few hours. He woke up in a moonlit room, and his first thoughts—of Elias—were very painful ones. He remembered now how he had promised Isabella that he would speak with him, to find out what was troubling him so much, and that he had never done so. Wondering if his brother was awake and in need of anything, he lit a candle and went downstairs to check on him.

As he opened the door of the library, the light of the little flame he held added to the dim illumination of a guttering candle next to Edmund's chair. He had taken a turn staying with Elias through the night, and was sound asleep in an armchair opposite the couch. John heard his brother's voice.

"Who is there?" Elias asked weakly.

John walked in and set down the candle in its holder on a table.

"Is there anything I can do for you, Elias?"

"No. I've been awake for a little while. I think a dream woke me. I don't remember it, but it disturbed me."

John crumbled to his knees beside the couch and put his face down against the cushion.

"Brother," he groaned, "I am grieving for you."

Elias stretched out a shaky hand and put it on his head. "I'm sorry, John...I'm sorry that I'm causing everyone so much pain," he whispered. "But you mustn't let it drag you down and pull you under as it has me. There are others who are depending on you, you know."

Elias felt John nodding, and heard a strangled, "I know."

His hand slipped off his brother's head, and he feebly drew it back across his chest.

"I wish I could be of help," Elias went on, slowly and quietly, "but it's no use. I shall be gone soon."

John wanted to protest, to contradict, but kept quiet in order not to interrupt. He waited, and it seemed a long time before his brother spoke again.

"I must make my peace," he finally sighed.

After another long silence, John prompted him with his last word, hoping he would say more.

"Peace?" he echoed questioningly.

John waited again, and when there was no answer, he lifted his head and saw that Elias had gone back to sleep.

"Sleep, then," he whispered, "find your peace."

As he rose to his feet he cupped a hand on one side of his brother's face and kissed the other, then made his way to another armchair next to Edmund and sank down in it heavily. At dawn, Isabella came in to find the three of them asleep in the library.

CHAPTER FOURTEEN

ELIAS WAS IN GREAT PAIN late on Monday morning, to the point of groaning and crying out loudly, something he had never done before. John dispatched Matthew on a fast horse to summon the doctor to Belle Ville. Tom came as quickly as he could and administered an opiate. While they waited for the drug to take effect, John and Isabella watched their brother writhe and moan, their souls in equal agony.

"He'll sleep now," said Tom, looking down at his patient with an anguished expression.

They all sat with Elias for a while, watching and waiting, but when it was clear that he was merely resting peacefully, Dr. Townsend asked to have a private word with John. The two men left the library and walked out to the portico together.

"How is Belle holding up?" the doctor asked him.

"She's holding her own, I suppose. She spends every moment she can with him, except to nurse the baby. Mrs. McColl is keeping the children."

"That's a help."

"She's been very helpful."

"And how are you?"

John had no answer for this question, and ignored it. He asked the doctor if he needed any more money to buy medicines for Elias.

"You've given me plenty, John, and I made sure to purchase as much as I could. Easing his pain is really all I can do for him now."

"How is Laura?"

"Not well, I'm afraid. She seems unable to accept the fact that Elias is dying. She is a little...irrational to tell you the truth. I have never seen her like this before. She begs me to bring her here to see him."

"Perhaps you ought to," John suggested.

"No, I don't think so, not until she can acknowledge the truth."

Changing the subject, John mentioned that he had made a copy of the soldier's confession.

"I have made a decision to do something about this," he told the doctor. "I can't just let it go. I have to see if there is any hope of justice. It may be there is no hope of that, but I intend to report this crime so that there is at least some record of it."

"What are you going to do?" asked the doctor.

"I'm going to take the papers over to the district headquarters in Blackwood today."

"You're going into the lion's den. Be careful, John."

"I will."

Matthew walked up to the portico leading a saddled horse, and as John took the reins from him to mount, he said to the doctor, "If Isabella asks about my absence, tell her I've gone to Blackwood on some business. That's all you need say."

Tom watched him riding off with a feeling of hopelessness he had not let John see, wondering at the futility of it all. When he obtained the soldier's confession, he had felt a rush of hope, but now it seemed to him that there was very little basis for it, after all. Any possibility of justice appeared remote.

On the way to his destination, John passed through Amelia, and as always, was disheartened by the spectacle of the large striped flag flying over what was left of the village in the square where the courthouse had once stood. As he was riding along the main street, another unpleasant sight met his eyes as he passed by some of the black soldiers who had been stationed here since the end of the war. It was humiliating to have United States Colored Troops as part of the garrison occupying the town–even so, despite their occasional demonstrations of insolence or menace, he regarded them as pawns rather than real enemies, and they were far less abhorrent to him than the crowds of white Yankee soldiers he saw some two hours later when he arrived in Blackwood, the headquarters of their military district.

John saw that the enemy had done its work in this place, too. Much of this formerly prosperous town had been burned, the rest left in shambles, and its railroad and everything connected with it had been completely destroyed. The Yankees had taken over one of the commercial buildings to use for their offices. John tied his horse in front of a laundry next door, and an old Chinese man leaning in the doorway of the establishment eyed him gloomily as he walked past.

He made inquiries and found out that a general named Wallis was in charge. A young clerk, a lieutenant in rank, showed John to his office on the second floor.

The general was a short, stout, clean-shaven man of middle age neatly dressed in a fine new uniform. His high, deeply lined forehead was topped with thinning brown hair that was carefully arranged and heavily pomaded. He did not rise from his chair behind a large desk when John was escorted into his office and introduced by the clerk.

"Have a seat, Mr. Hutchinson," he said, pointing to a chair directly in front of him. He nodded to the lieutenant, who closed the office door behind him, leaving the two men alone together.

"Well," began the general, "you look like a sensible man, so I am sure we can dispense with the pleasantries. They are few and far between these days among the likes of us, eh?"

He smiled and seemed amused with his own observation, but eliciting no such response from his visitor he promptly went on more seriously, "You will forgive me for being direct, Mr. Hutchinson, but I am a very busy man. What is your business here today?"

"Since you wish it, I shall be direct with you, General Wallis," said John. "It has come to my knowledge lately that a very serious crime was committed by some of your soldiers during the last months of the war."

"What crime, Mr. Hutchinson?"

"The murder of my father."

The general slowly laced his fingers together on the desk and leaned forward with a grave expression.

"When and where did this happen?" he asked.

"In February, at Belle Ville Plantation near Amelia."

"That is indeed a very serious charge."

"I have proof. I have statements as to the facts."

The general raised his brows in surprise, creating broken rows of wrinkles that went all the way up to his hair line. He asked for the details of the alleged murder, and John related the whole story, as Israel had told it to Dr. Townsend.

"Israel is willing to testify to it," he added in conclusion.

General Wallis sniffed and made a dismissive gesture.

Honor in the Dust

"You may bring in this man to so attest, but I tell you quite frankly, none of my men would convict a fellow soldier on negro testimony."

"And yet I hear that you accept their testimony readily enough when it is offered against ex-Confederates."

"You mustn't believe everything you hear, Mr. Hutchinson," the general answered, smiling blandly. "Have you any other proof of this crime?"

"I have a written statement from one of Lieutenant Potter's soldiers."

John pulled out several folded sheets and handed them to General Wallis.

"Papers," the general muttered and sighed under his breath as he took them. "I am eternally beset with papers."

He read over the first two sheets briefly and set them down on his desk. After a few moments of reflection, he leaned over the statements again, turning to the second page of the soldier's confession to note the name of the writer.

"Klaus Beerschnieder," he sneered. "What a ridiculous name! Where is this man?"

"He is dead. He was a deserter. He made his way back to Amelia trying to find a priest he said, and he died there after making this confession."

"If you will excuse me for a few moments, Mr. Hutchinson, I shall make some inquiries about this matter."

He rose and left John alone for about a quarter of an hour, during which time, judging from his reception so far, he reflected doubtfully on the possibility of receiving any satisfaction from the military authorities. When the general came back he returned to his desk with a drawn-out sigh. He shrugged, held up his hands helplessly, and let them fall on the desk with a thud. Looking down at the statement of the German soldier, he shook his head.

"As for this," he said, "I'm afraid the testimony of a deserter will not carry much weight. News of his absence came to us in a report a month or two ago, and I am informed that this Dutchman was a very untrustworthy sort, a man of very bad reputation, and a drunkard."

He shrugged again and looked down at the papers on his desk, his eyes avoiding those of John, which were fixed on him in anger.

"A physician, Dr. Townsend, found my father hung from his own bed," John said slowly and deliberately, trying to remain calm. "He did not witness the murder, but he can attest that there was one."

"Have him do so, then."

"I have, sir. His statement is attached to the others before you."

The general resumed his seat, picked up the papers again, and read over Dr. Townsend's statement. When he had finished he put his hand to his mouth and rocked back and forth in his chair as if deep in thought, assuming an air of sympathy and mild indignation.

"I shall, of course, submit a report detailing your charges, Mr. Hutchinson. If any of our soldiers committed such a crime, they shall be punished for it accordingly. The difficulty is, identifying these other two men who were with the Dutchman after so long. We must find Lieutenant Potter, and then it is not certain he will remember who they were. And even we do identify these soldiers, proving them guilty–well, you understand that is another matter."

"I only ask for justice," John replied.

"Did anyone actually witness the soldiers committing murder?" asked the general.

"No."

"Ah, well..."

General Wallis gave John a long, doubtful look meant to intimate the hopelessness of his cause, but went on, "As I said, sir, I shall submit a report. That is all I can do until we are able to obtain more information. The circumstances are unusual, as you are bringing these charges so long after the fact."

"I understand."

"Do I understand that you also hold Lieutenant Potter culpable in the death of your father, Mr. Hutchinson?"

"I imagine there is no legal case against him, but I don't think he is to be held faultless. He sent those men back to Belle Ville. He must have known what sort of men they were."

General Wallis frowned, rather affronted that an officer of his army should be implicated in such criminality with any proof.

"Well," he said somewhat irritably, "it would be difficult to prove that Potter sent them back with the intention to commit murder, and if he did, I don't suppose he would confess to it."

"No, I don't suppose he would."

John's sardonic, resentful tone displeased General Wallis, who eyed him sternly and said, with a note of warning in his voice, "You were well advised to bring your complaint here to the proper authorities, Mr. Hutchinson. Some of your people are out for rather indiscriminate revenge, and an outlaw in this district has killed one of my men. I understand that such hotheads are more accustomed to your Code Duello for getting their justice, but–"

"This is a criminal charge we speak of," John interrupted brusquely. "Not an affair of personal honor. And even if it were, such a matter would be settled in that way only by gentlemen."

By this last statement, the general understood John to mean that Lieutenant Potter was doubtless his social inferior, with whom he would not condescend to engage in a duel. The son of a shopkeeper, General Wallis felt the insult to some degree as if it had been directed at himself. Fancying that there had been an insolent, derisive gleam in John's eyes, he was reminded how much he detested these haughty Southern aristocrats, haughty even in their ruin.

He pushed back his chair and rose to his feet with an air of finality.

"I don't think I can be of any further service to you today, Mr. Hutchinson," he said drily. "I shall do as I have said, and if there are any significant developments, you will be notified."

John rose, thanked the general in an uncivil tone, and left without further conversation. Frustrated and furious, tasting only gall and abhorrence in his soul, he had to pass through a kind of gauntlet of Federal soldiers on his way out, and could not get to his horse fast enough.

As John was riding out of the village of Blackwood, he noticed a young man slowly shuffling along, his head hung low. His clothes were a poor and clownish combination of mismatched, ill-fitting garments, but he wore a battered Confederate cap. He looked ill and disoriented, and walked in a precarious, lurching way, as if he might fall forward on his face at any moment. John rode over to the young man and spoke to him.

"What is your name?"

The young man paused and looked up at him unsteadily. He was little more than a boy, thin, homely, and hollow-eyed, and he looked familiar. His eyes were half-closed with faintness or fatigue.

"Nathaniel Drawdy," he answered.

John immediately recognized Jeb Drawdy's older son. The family had not heard from him in months, and had all but given him up for dead.

"I'm John Hutchinson. I know your father. I'll take you to him."

"You'll take me to Pa?" the boy asked incredulously, as though he thought he might be dreaming.

"Think you can get up on this horse, Nat?"

John put out a hand for him, but the boy was as limp as a rag doll, and his grasp too weak. John jumped down, picked him up, and helped him up to the horse's back behind the saddle.

"Put your arms around me," he said as he remounted. "Hold on to me so you don't fall off, son."

He rode to Jeb Drawdy's house at a walk, afraid Nathaniel might not be able to hang on at a faster gait. He tried to talk with him, but the boy seemed confused, possibly delirious, and after a while, when John felt his head pressed against his back, he knew that he had succumbed to sleep. John took hold of his bony hands and held them tightly against his middle.

When they reached the Drawdy farm, no one was in sight. John woke the boy and helped him dismount. Someone opened the door of the house and peered out. It was Henry Drawdy who, seeing Nathaniel, rushed out to seize hold of him.

"We thought you was dead! We thought you was dead!" he sobbed, encircling and clasping his brother with his long, wiry arms like a vise.

Both men helped him inside to a bed.

"Henry, am I home?" the boy moaned.

"You're home, Nat."

"I'll send word to Dr. Townsend to stop by here," John said to the younger brother.

"We got no money to pay a doctor," he replied uneasily.

"Don't worry about that, Henry. Don't I owe your father a

debt for all he has done for the DuBose family? I'll get Dr. Townsend here as soon as possible."

John rode to the DuBose farm and found Nat's father working in the corn field.

"Mr. Drawdy," he called to him, "I have good news for you."

The farmer looked up from his work with a casual air, as if he were in no expectation of hearing anything momentous. He walked to the edge of the field where John was waiting.

"I found your son Nathaniel in Blackwood and brought him to your house. Henry is there with him now."

"He- he's alive? Nat?" the boy's father stammered in disbelief.

"He's exhausted and ill, but he's alive. I'll send Dr. Townsend to him directly."

Mr. Drawdy threw down his hoe, and trembling with excitement, took off for his house at a run, not slowing down as he shouted back his thanks to John.

Emma was in one of her gardens and heard his voice. She walked within view of the corn field and saw Mr. Drawdy running away toward the road while John sat on his horse and watched him.

"John!" she called to him. "Is something wrong?"

He dismounted and walked toward her, leading his horse.

"Mr. Drawdy has gone to see his son Nathaniel."

He told her how he happened to find the boy in Blackwood and brought him home.

"How good of you! I'm so glad the boy is alive after all! Is he all right?"

"I think so. I hope so. I was going to find Tom to see to him, but not before I spoke to you, Emma."

He smiled faintly, but she could see that John was troubled

about something, and instantly thought of his brother.

"It must have made you think of Elias when you brought the boy home to his family. Is he no better?"

Elias was doing worse lately, and John told her this, but he made no mention of what was torturing him besides.

"I'm so sorry, dear," she said gently. "We pray for him, all of us, every day."

"I know you do, and I'm grateful. I ought not to give up all hope where he is concerned."

Despite the slight smile he maintained, she had never seen John looking so dejected.

"I wish Mr. Shubrick could go and see Elias. He–"

"Elias won't see him," he cut her short.

Emma was surprised.

"Why not?"

"I can't talk about that now, Emma. Forgive me, but I should go and look for Tom."

"Yes, of course," she said.

"I'm sorry, Emma."

She took off one of her soiled gloves, put her hand around his neck, and kissed him on the cheek. He smiled and thanked her for it, but did not return the kiss. As she watched him ride away, she wondered why.

On his way to Amelia, John happened to ride up behind Tom's carriage. He was on his way home, but immediately turned around and followed John back to the Drawdy farm. John waited outside with Mr. Drawdy and Henry while the doctor examined Nathaniel.

The father was choking back tears. He was relieved and happy to have his son home, but horrified at his condition. Nathaniel had been held for many months as a prisoner of war in

Illinois.

"I can't hardly believe what he's told us, Captain Hutchinson. He walked home all the way from Chicago, 'cept for ride he hitched on a wagon for a hundred miles or so!" Mr. Drawdy lamented, shaking his head in disbelief. "Chicago! And him sick as a dog!"

The farmer took a deep, shuddering breath and went on mournfully, "Said he near froze to death this winter in that place, and they was treatin' our boys real cruel."

"Nat told me he'd be dead by now for sure if a doctor hadn't kept him in the hospital," added Henry. "Said they had it a little better there."

A look of anger and indignation flared in John's eyes as he heard these things, but quickly faded; he was too swallowed up in his own troubles to take on those of others.

"Dr. Townsend will take good care of him," he assured the Drawdys somberly.

John began the ride home, but after a few minutes, turned his horse back in the direction of the DuBose farm. He was thinking about Emma, and remembered how he had left her looking rather bewildered earlier. He had not been able to hide his anguish from her, and considered that he ought to let her know the cause of it, but as he rode on, he vacillated, wondering if he should burden her with this terrible revelation after all. He resolved not to tell her. Then again, he thought, Emma knew and read him so well, it was doubtful that he could continue to hide it from her much longer. When he made up his mind once and for all to tell her, he spurred his horse from a walk to a canter, anxious to see her again and find some consolation in her presence.

It was late afternoon, and Mr. DuBose was sitting alone on

the porch. He heard the brisk, heavy thudding of hooves on the road, and when the horse came into view, he was a little surprised to see that John was the rider. The young man had always approached the house at a more leisurely gait before.

The horse was sweaty and puffing as he was slowed down to a walk near the house. John jumped down and greeted Mr. DuBose, but did not walk up the steps.

"I wonder if you would allow me to have a private word with Emma, sir," he said, with an uneasy, agitated air. "There's something very important I must discuss with her."

Though somewhat startled, Mr. DuBose did not question him.

"I shall tell her you're here," he said, getting up from his chair.

Mrs. Screven had heard John's voice from inside the house. She was heading for the door as her brother entered, but he blocked her way and asked where Emma was.

"Upstairs, I believe," she answered, perplexed. "What is wrong? You look so serious."

"Please do not go out, Adele. Captain Hutchinson wishes to speak to Emma alone."

"Whatever about?" she asked anxiously, following him as he walked toward the stairway.

"I don't know," he said irritably. "For heaven's sake, Adele, they are engaged to be married! Don't be so meddlesome!"

And with this rebuke, he left her standing at the foot of the stairs. Emma was just coming out of her room as Mr. DuBose reached the second floor.

"Captain Hutchinson is here to see you," he told her.

"I thought I heard someone riding up," she said.

"Emma, dear, he wishes to speak with you alone."

His statement gave her pause, and she looked at her uncle inquiringly.

"You must ask him what it's about. He didn't confide in me," he said mildly, patting her cheek. She followed her uncle downstairs, and he accompanied her as far as the porch.

John looked calmer now, and managed something of a smile when he saw her.

"I wonder if you would care to walk with me a little while, Miss Emma," he said.

She looked to her uncle, who gestured his permission. John's hands were clasped behind his back, and he kept them that way as she came to his side. Mr. DuBose resumed his seat and watched the young couple walk across the yard towards the woods.

"You're very mysterious today," Emma remarked after they had strolled a while in silence.

"I don't mean to seem mysterious, but I wished to speak with you in private."

There was something strained in his voice, and she tried to look into his eyes, but he was staring straight ahead as they walked.

"What is it, John?"

"Let's walk down to the creek," he suggested. "We can talk there."

Emma was very curious about this matter he wanted to discuss. She would have enjoyed the rare experience of being completely alone with him, if she had not been so concerned, and even a little afraid now.

They sat down in the same spot where he had proposed to her, on the grassy slope by the water. John watched the waters of the creek and was quiet for a few moments. Emma waited. When he finally turned and faced her, she saw only misery and turmoil in his eyes.

"What is it, John? Is it Elias?" she asked anxiously.

He gazed off toward the waterfalls again, and realized that the time had come to be truthful about Elias with her—and with himself.

"He's dying, Emma," he answered quietly. "There's no doubt of it now."

She let her face fall against his shoulder.

"I'm so sorry, John. Your heart must be breaking."

He breathed in a deep, long breath and let it escape as slowly.

"I don't know that I had much hope to begin with, but I wanted to believe he had a chance."

She turned her face up to his, and as they looked at each other, Emma saw very soon in the way his eyes began to wander with his thoughts—that Elias was only one of his woes.

She slipped her arm around his and put her cheek against his sleeve.

"Is that what you wished to tell me, John?" she asked.

"There is something else..."

She had never heard such a heavy, disheartened tone in his voice; her hand involuntarily tightened its grip around his arm.

"I found out something about my father...about his death," he went on. "He was murdered, Emma."

"Oh, John, how horrible!"

"Yankee soldiers hung him with a rope from his own bed, to make him tell where he'd hidden valuables, but he wouldn't. Tom was here when it happened. He told me several days ago."

"That's why you went to Blackwood, then," she said, "to their headquarters."

John nodded and told her about the deserter who had later showed up at Belle Ville.

"Before he died, this man gave Tom the name of the officer in charge. With that, it may be possible to find out who the other murderers were," he continued with a tense, wrathful expression. "I intend to find out...if it can be done."

"But what can you do?" she asked apprehensively.

Suddenly overwhelmed with anger and bitterness, he burst out, "I'd kill them if I could!"

She buried her face in his sleeve, weeping.

"John! They would hang you!" she sobbed.

"Emma!"

He put an arm around her, instantly reviling himself for his loss of self-control.

"Emma, please listen to me. I spoke in anger. I can't go after these men myself–it's likely they will never be found."

She raised her face and looked at him with a stricken and bewildered expression, shuddering with convulsive breaths.

"Forgive me, Emma," he pleaded. "I've made you distraught. It was wrong of me. I only sought justice. I've done all I can. I've made charges and given the military authorities the evidence. The rest is in their hands–unless they're all murderers as well as vandals and thieves."

"Will they go after these men?" she asked.

"I don't know. I hope so. I can only hope," he said, though, since his interview with General Wallis, he had begun to share Dr. Townsend's view of the matter—that it was folly, a waste of time and effort, and that these men would never be brought to justice.

John wiped the tears from Emma's face with his fingertips. She closed her eyes at his touch, and he leaned close and gently kissed her eyelids.

"I didn't mean to hurt you, Emma," he said. "I would never do that."

She threw her arms around him.

"Oh, John!" she said tearfully. "You came to share your sorrows with me, and I only brought you more! Please forgive me. You are my dearest friend. You are my life!"

He pulled her to him tightly, pressing his face against her hair.

"I will be stronger, I promise, but I couldn't bear the thought of losing you, John. I could bear anything but that."

"That won't happen, Emma," he reassured her. "You won't lose me."

"Oh, how can you love me?" she cried. "I am so weak and worthless!"

"Weak? Emma!" he said reprovingly. "No one who is weak could have borne all that you have. You may be worn down by all that, but you're not weak. And so far from being worthless–you must never say such a thing–except for my family, you're the only good thing left to me in this world."

"I love you," she whispered fervently, burying her face in his coat. "I love you!"

Her shoulders rose and fell with deep breaths, and they sat holding each other until she grew calm again. John finally broke the silence.

"We should go back now, Emma. We'll talk on the way."

He helped her to her feet, and she held on to his arm as they walked through the woods. He told her more details of what he had learned concerning his father's death, this time speaking calmly and quietly, showing no signs of the anger and menace which had alarmed her. Emerging from the trees, they paused in the shade at the edge of a field. From here the house was in view; Emma's uncle, still on the porch, saw them leaning against a wooden fence while their conversation continued.

Once she regained her composure, Emma tried to find comforting things to say to John, but he told her that it was merely being near her that helped him the most. They talked of Elias again. She wanted to go and see him, and John promised to take her to Belle Ville very soon.

"My uncle and aunt will be very sorry to hear about your brother," she said, then looked up at John questioningly.

"Don't say anything to them about my father," he responded. "I haven't told Elias or Isabella about it. I don't know that I shall ever tell them."

CHAPTER FIFTEEN

A DISTURBING NOISE ROUSED Mrs. Screven from her sleep that night. Emma was crying out. She sat up in her bed, electrified by the sound. She had not heard it in so long that she thought she might have been dreaming, until she heard another, fainter cry. She threw on a robe and rushed to her niece's bedroom.

Emma woke up when she heard the door open, and sat up, breathing hard.

"Emma, dear," her aunt said solicitously. "The nightmare again?"

She hung her head and nodded. Mrs. Screven came and sat down beside her at the edge of the bed.

"I had hoped you were finished with all those bad dreams. You've been so happy lately, my darling, I thought they might never return."

"I hoped that, too."

Mrs. Screven took her niece's hand and squeezed it. They sat in silence for a while, until the older woman spoke up again in a low, confidential tone.

"You have never told me so, Emma, but I know what you are dreaming about when you are so troubled like this. It was that terrible day your brother died."

"Yes," she admitted.

"What John told you today about his brother must have made you think of it."

"That's true."

"Have you told John about it?"

"No! And please, don't you tell him. I'm not going to speak of it, not now. John has too many burdens to bear right now, and I won't add another one to them. Perhaps I shall tell him someday, but not now."

"I promise I won't mention it, Emma," her aunt assured her. "As for myself, I try not to think of it, ever. It was the worst day of my life!"

Mrs. Screven cringed as some of the memories of that day came back into her mind. But with great effort, she banished these thoughts, and tried to console her niece as best she could. After they had talked for a while, Emma began looking sleepy again, and Mrs. Screven went back to her own bed.

Alone in their rooms, both women began drifting off into sleep, but soon opened their eyes again in the darkness as that awful day began to replay in their minds again against their will.

"Henry, tell us, what did you see?"

Their neighbor described, "Yankees, all over the place! They come in hollerin' like demons."

He was panting out the words, still out of breath from having run nearly two miles as fast as he could. Henry reported that he had watched the enemy soldiers for a few minutes from his hiding place at home. They were killing or carrying off all the livestock, he said, stealing everything of value from the house and barns, and then setting fire to the buildings and whatever was growing in the fields and gardens.

"When Pa saw 'em coming down the road, he sent me out to the woods. Said they might think I was a soldier, and would take me prisoner or kill me, so I come here to warn you fore I hid myself. They'll be here soon, I'm sorry to say."

Henry had found Mrs. Screven downstairs at the DuBose house when he arrived breathlessly at the door, and she had immediately brought him up to a bedroom on the second floor where Emma was taking care of her brother Theodore, who was so ill from an infection in his wounded leg that they feared he was dying. When they all heard what Henry had to say, the women covered their faces in horror, and Emma's brother rolled his eyes with excitement and outrage. He pushed back the covers and made a movement to get up from his bed, but was so weak he that fell back with exhaustion at the effort.

"Theo, please calm yourself," Emma begged him, coming to his side.

"We must hide the valuables," he gasped.

"I don't think there's time," said Henry.

"Quickly, Emma!" Theo implored, seizing her wrist. "Do as I say! Hide the silver and–and we have some gold money–but where to hide it?"

"Let me do it," Henry offered.

Theo nodded gratefully.

"The gold is in that purse," he said, indicating a leather pouch on top of a bureau. Henry stuffed it into his pocket. Thinking of all the valuables in the house, Emma now regretted that she and her aunt had not taken the precautions so many others in the area had of hiding things from the expected invaders, but they had been so concerned about Theo's health, and so preoccupied with his care, that it was something that had gone neglected.

Emma refused to leave her brother's room, and Mrs. Screven quickly went downstairs to show their neighbor where the family's silverware was stored. Emma walked to the window, and from there soon caught sight of Henry running toward the woods to the east with a bundle in his arms. A moment later, she let out a cry of terror. Dozens of blue-coated soldiers were pouring out of the western woods near the road letting out loud hurrahs, whoops, and yells. Henry disappeared behind the trees just as the soldiers reached the first outbuildings.

A few men on horseback approached at a walk as the mass of soldiers swarmed over the farm. This group rode up to the house. One who was obviously the commanding officer paused and looked over the place with narrowed eyes, his long, sandy mustaches twitching with nervous excitement, while his men followed their orders, beginning a frenzy of pillage and destruction which they and the rest of their army had repeated hundreds and hundreds of times over on farms, towns, and plantations throughout the parish lands, from the Georgia border into the heart of South Carolina.

Emma watched from the window of her brother's bedroom. After a while, she could hear the footsteps and voices of the soldiers inside the house. She expected to be burst in upon at any moment, but still could not take her eyes off the scenes outside. Tears streamed down her face as she witnessed the ruination of her homestead in disbelief and anguish. What the soldiers could not take for themselves in the way of corn, oats, and other foodstuffs, they were burning or otherwise ruining. Wagons belonging to the farm were loaded up with these looted supplies, and the valuables being stolen from the house. Bales of hay from the barn were piled in the yard and lighted with a torch to make a great bonfire. The soldiers threw tools, the pieces of the farming implements they had smashed, and anything else they could find to feed its flames. At the same time, the torch was being applied to all the outbuildings of the farm.

The worst of it to her, however, was the fate of the animals.

The slaughter started with the dogs, all of which had been barking madly since the arrival of the raiders. Those who were not in their kennels were confined in a pen, powerless to escape, and the soldiers bayoneted or shot them like fish in a barrel–even Dr. DuBose's prize female spaniel and her pups. Their frenzied, terrified bays, yelps, and howls diminished with the continued sounds of gunfire until they were all silent. Emma could not bring herself to look at her brother, who loved these dogs. Even if he could not see, he could surely hear what was going on.

In the pastures the soldiers were herding the cattle together, driving them into a paddock with the horses. The soldiers led off a few of the finer steers and many of the horses, and then shot the rest. Scores of the animals fell to the ground and writhed for many long minutes in their death throes. A small herd of sheep scattered in terror but were soon cut down, making horrible screams and bellows Emma had never heard from them before. All the swine were bayoneted, and of those already being butchered for meat, a few were still living as their hams were being cut from their quivering bodies. She watched the soldiers chasing down the chickens and geese and wringing their necks. Of these the men took as many as they wished for their own consumption; the rest they tossed away to rot. Other bluecoats were making a game of squeezing or stomping some little bantam hens to death. One soldier caught a young tom turkey and laughingly held it up by its feet, and even after all she had witnessed, what he did next made Emma recoil in sickened revulsion.

"He is plucking the bird alive!" she cried out involuntarily.

With this exclamation she looked over to her brother, who

had been peculiarly silent. His eyes were shut tight, his mouth was wide open, and his head was thrown to the side stiffly in a strange, contorted way.

"Theo!" she screamed, rushing to his side.

He was dead. Emma fell against the bed and wept.

Mrs. Screven was downstairs watching from another window as the officers on horseback approached the house. The soldiers were already swarming across the yard, getting very close, and she saw they meant to enter the house. Though she was trembling with fear, she went out the front door, closed it behind her, and stood against it, barring the way, and trying to put on a brave face. The commanding officer made a motion for his men to wait. They crowded around the porch, but did not set foot on it.

"You must step aside, Madam," said the officer in command, a captain. "We mean to search this house for arms."

"We have no weapons here except for a few hunting rifles, which I will give to you," Mrs. Screven replied hoarsely. Her mouth and throat had gone dry.

"We shall see for ourselves," he replied.

"My nephew is very ill upstairs. Please do not disturb him. He is in such a state, the sight of you might be the death of him."

"We won't disturb your nephew," the officer assured her. "Who else is in the house?"

"My niece, and a servant."

"Your names?"

She told him the names of all those in the house.

"Our cook Hannah is in the kitchen house. She's very old– she's harmless!"

"Step aside, please, Mrs. Screven," the captain repeated, coldly polite.

"Give us a guard, I beg of you," she pleaded, raising clasped hands.

"Of course. You shall have a guard."

He nodded toward one of his soldiers nearby, a stocky sergeant with a heavy, graying mustache and beard, who shouldered his rifle and promptly went up the steps.

"What room is it, ma'am?" the sergeant asked.

"At the top of the stairs–the door is closed. Please do not disturb him."

The man touched his hat with a slight bow of the head, and she moved out of his way to let him inside.

"Now, Madam," said the officer. "I advise you to remain where you are. Do not try to interfere with my men's duties."

Still trembling, Mrs. Screven experienced a wave of faintness and made her way to a chair on the porch. From here she watched the soldiers piling into the house, and could hear the tramp of their heavy footsteps inside, their voices and laughter, the clatter and noise of their movements, and the clinking of ceramic and metal things. She realized they were not only searching the house but also looting it. On both floors they were busily rummaging in closets, trunks, bureaus, presses, wardrobes–everywhere. Mrs. Screven had heard of the Yankee armies doing the same in their march through Georgia, and had not been expecting any better treatment at their hands, yet she was stunned and disbelieving when it actually began to happen in her own home. She nearly jumped from her seat when a deafening crash came to her ears from inside, accompanied by laughter and a strange, resonant twanging sound. Looking in a window, she saw that the piano was being chopped into pieces with axes. Other pieces of furniture were also being demolished or carried off.

Mrs. Screven wrung her hands in anxiety over her nephew, praying that the guard would keep the others out of his room. After a while, a soldier emerged from the house triumphantly waving two large candlesticks in the air, the only large pieces of silver left behind by Henry. The man's haversack was bulging with other goods, and he had draped two costly lace shawls around his neck. He showed the candlesticks to the commanding officer, who nodded his approval, and indicated that these items were to be added to his own private share of the takings.

When the soldiers had finished ransacking the house, the officers dismounted and went inside. Mrs. Screven followed them in. The few pieces of furniture left were in disarray, mostly broken or overturned on the floor except for a heavy sofa, and many fine things which had graced the rooms were gone, including family photographs and portraits, and much of Dr. DuBose's library. All that remained were several scattered volumes which lay on the floor, torn and trampled.

The officers, three in number, strolled around the first floor of the house in a group as if taking a tour. Mrs. Screven stayed in the parlor where a private was still going through a desk. He was opening each drawer and emptying the contents on the floor. A photograph of Emma fell at his feet. He picked it up and asked who she was.

"My niece," said Mrs. Screven, automatically reaching for the picture, which the soldier immediately pocketed.

"Good looking," he remarked.

"Why are you doing this to us?" she cried. "Didn't your mother teach you that it is wrong to steal?"

"Soldiers don't steal!" he laughed. "We confiscate."

The private turned back to the desk and continued to go through its contents. Letters and papers were mostly all he found, but one drawer held, along with letters to the family from Emma's brother Richard, a lock of his blonde hair enclosed in a tiny envelope. Emma had hoped someday to have it braided and set with his small daguerreotype portrait in a case. The little envelope was not sealed, and a portion of the hair spilled out when it fell to the floor. The soldier stared at it for a moment, leaned down to pick it up, but then hesitated.

"Whose yellow hair is this?" he asked. "Your niece's?"

"Please leave it be," Mrs. Screven pleaded. "It is my nephew's hair."

"Is he a reb soldier?"

"He is dead!"

"Good!" said the man, putting his foot down on the envelope and hair and grinding them to pieces with the sole of his boot. "One less for us to kill."

The soldier eyed Mrs. Screven's hands.

"I'll take that ring you're wearing," he said.

"But this is my wedding ring!" she protested.

"Give it to me, or I'll take from you, damn you!" he threatened.

She removed the ring and handed it to him.

"What else have you got?" he demanded.

"Nothing!" she cried, but her hand involuntarily went to her throat, where a little gold chain was partially visible.

The soldier reached out for her neck, but drew back his hand when he heard footsteps behind him. The officers were returning to the parlor.

"Give me back my ring!" she cried.

The soldier only laughed and walked away, and the officers ignored her complaints. Mrs. Screven went to the foot of the stairs, looked up, and saw that the guard was standing at his post in front of her nephew's room.

The captain in command glanced at her with a lift of the

eyebrows as if to say, "You see? I am a man of my word."

Mrs. Screven saw that one of his officers, a young lieutenant, was chewing on a piece of corn bread he had taken from one of the soldiers who had raided the kitchen. Despite her terror, she approached him and burst out angrily, "If you take all our food, and deprive us of all our means of subsistence, we shall starve!"

"You are suffering for what you have done," the lieutenant answered her coolly. "This is the penalty of rebellion."

The captain made an impatient gesture.

"Where is this niece of yours?" he asked Mrs. Screven. "We have not seen her."

"She is with my nephew."

"Upstairs, gentlemen," he said.

The scabbards of their swords slapped and scraped against the rails, and their spurs jingled, as the three men ascended the stairway. At the top step, the guard saluted the captain. Emma's grieving was interrupted when he entered her brother's room with the other officers. He comprehended the scene immediately.

"My sympathies, Miss DuBose," he said, though his tone of voice was as devoid of sympathy as his eyes. He was a hardened soldier, with dirty work to do, and could allow himself no tenderness of heart. He had also found his dirty work quite profitable.

"You will tell us where the valuables of the house have been hidden," he said, dropping the pretense that his men were merely searching the place for arms.

"We've hidden nothing. There was no time," Emma answered, surprised that a lie had come so instantly and unthinkingly to her lips.

"Come now, miss. There must be more than what we have found," he insisted.

"There is nothing!"

Emma was not a skillful liar, and the officer studied her doubtfully. His soldiers had found and taken the remains of the family silverware, some jewelry, a few gold coins, and Confederate paper money and bonds, but he knew all the tricks of the enemy by now, and was certain there must be more valuables hidden away somewhere. While she talked with the captain, one of the other officers was searching through a wardrobe and a bureau. Another went down on his knees on the other side of the bed to inspect under it, and then probed beneath the mattress for hidden treasures. Emma watched them; the captain ignored their activities and her indignant looks.

From the yard below, the captain heard a sudden eruption of shouting and laughter and went to the window to see what the commotion was about. Two of his soldiers who had gone out into the woods to look for buried treasures had found and seized Henry Drawdy before he could hide the DuBose family belongings. They had taken the purse of gold and the sack of silverware from him and were now punishing him for his offenses with kicks and blows. The officer beckoned Emma to the window.

"Who is this man?" he asked her.

"Our neighbor. Oh, please stop your men!" she begged him. "He is just a boy! He was only trying to help us!"

"They won't kill him," the officer replied casually.

He paused and gazed at Emma's hair and face with obvious admiration for a moment, then turned to the other officers.

"I think we are done here, gentlemen," he said, and they all left without another word.

Mrs. Screven rushed up the stairs as they left the house.

"Emma, darling! Are you all right?" she cried.

Emma had sunk to her knees beside the bed, holding her

brother's lifeless hand.

"He is dead," she whispered.

"Did they–?"

She shook her head. Mrs. Screven approached the bed and tearfully took her nephew's other hand. Then Emma remembered their neighbor.

"Poor Henry! They were beating him half to death!"

Emma went to the window and saw that the soldiers were falling into a line of march behind their wagon train. She caught sight of Henry lying on the ground near the roaring bonfire. When the soldiers were almost out of sight, Emma and her aunt rushed downstairs and out into the yard. The young man was groaning and trying to raise himself up, and they helped him to his feet. He was cursing the Yankees, but stopped as they took hold of him. He begged the ladies' pardon for his strong language.

"Them devils was callin' me trash," he fumed. "Said they'd love to kill all the secesh trash in this state."

"Are you seriously hurt?" Emma asked him.

"I am beat to a pulp, but I think nothing's broken but my nose."

One of his eyes was swelling shut, and a stream of bright red blood was trickling down from each of his nostrils. He wiped them with his sleeve, grunting with pain.

"Thank God they did not take you prisoner!" Mrs. Screven exclaimed.

"One of 'em said he wouldn't be bothered with no prisoners," said Henry. "He'd a killed me, but I swore I weren't no soldier, and the others stopped him. I ain't no soldier yet, but I'm sure as hell gonna join up now, and Pa can't stop me!"

"Henry!" Mrs. Screven scolded him. "You've just turned sixteen! You musn't think of going into the army. Your folks need you more than ever now."

"The army needs me more. I'm joinin' up now, sure as hell! Beg your pardon, ladies."

"Can you walk, Henry?" Emma asked.

"Yes'm. Just let me rest a little while."

They let him lean on their shoulders, and walked him over to the house, where he sat down on the lowest front step. Emma found a cracked china cup which had been left behind by the soldiers and brought him some water from the well in it.

"Thank you, thank you," he sighed. "Can anything be saved?"

He was looking toward the barn which was closest to the house. It was only partially engulfed in flames, and two elderly servant women were already trying to douse it, carrying water as best they could in broken buckets and tubs. Emma and her aunt hurried out to help them, and within a few minutes they had rescued the one building from complete destruction. By the time Henry was able to walk again his assistance in that task was no longer needed. He and Mrs. Screven followed Emma as she walked around to survey the scene of burning buildings and fields, shattered fences, trampled and turned up gardens, and the bloody carcasses of animals.

No species had escaped the depredations of the enemy. Leaving the porch, Emma had even caught sight of the motionless tail and hind legs of their old pet cat Aaron protruding from under the house, where he had obviously been trying to flee to safety. His ginger fur was parted in a gaping bayonet wound which had nearly cut the animal in half.

"Oh, Lord help us!" Mrs. Screven wailed, looking around in all directions. "Emma, what shall we do?"

"We must salvage any meat we can," she said. "It will keep

for a while if the weather stays cold enough. We must do that first, then see what can be saved from the ground."

Mrs. Screven began weeping.

"Oh, what wretches! What fiends!" she sobbed.

Though shaken herself, Emma begged her aunt to compose herself. Henry asked Emma about her brother, and when he learned that he was dead, he left for his place to check on his parents and make a coffin. The two women went back into the house to prepare the body for burial. Nothing had been taken from this room, and Emma and her aunt found a good suit of her brother's clothes and dressed him in them. When they were finished, Emma went downstairs to wait for Henry.

Sitting down on a couch in the parlor, she felt numb and exhausted now, after all the grief and horror she had experienced that day. She looked around the room in its disorder, noticing the absence of countless cherished possessions, and something in particular alarmed her. Where were her pictures of her mother, brothers, and father? She made a move to get up and search for them, but fell back on the sofa in despair. What was the use? Except for the larger pieces of furniture, the soldiers had stolen nearly everything that could be carried off. The table which had held all her family photographs and albums was empty. They had even stolen her memories!

Emma felt like weeping again, but there were no tears left in her. Her limbs felt heavy, almost paralyzed. She stared at the floor with a blank mind, without feeling. Then she noticed the bare wooden floor at her feet, where there had once been a rug. The raiders had taken an old, worn, nearly worthless oriental carpet from the room. It was almost funny.

A moment later, Emma looked up when she heard the sound of a horse's hooves in the yard. Suddenly energized again with fear, she ran to a window. A lone cavalryman was dismounting from his horse. His uniform was Confederate. He drew a revolver from its holster and cautiously looked around.

He was a very young looking man with a reddish moustache and a short goatee. His clothes were faded and somewhat tattered, and his horse was not a prime specimen, but he was well armed. Two carbine rifles flanked his saddle along with a sword in its scabbard, and around his waist he wore a belt which held a gun holster and a large Bowie knife in an iron sheath. His collar indicated the rank of lieutenant.

He saw Emma in the window, put away his gun, and raised his hands in a gesture to indicate his harmlessness. She went out to meet him warily; refugees who had come through the area recently had told of Federal soldiers masquerading as Confederates and up to no good as such. She introduced herself, and though the young man would not reveal his name, his accent and manner seemed genuine. He told her that a large enemy force was advancing on Amelia, but did not explain his presence in the area except to refer to himself as a scout. Emma had heard that a small band of Confederate soldiers were in the area to defend the village, and wondered if he was one of them. If so, he was one among only a few hundred trying to hold off an army of tens of thousands from what he described. He asked her if he could water and feed his horse at her place.

"You are welcome to the water, sir, but I doubt there is anything left to feed your horse," she answered.

"I see you have had visitors," he remarked, glancing toward the bonfire still raging near the barn. "We had best put that out, miss. The sparks might carry to your house. I am surprised to see it still standing. "

The servants who remained, all women except for a little

boy named Rufus, were still gathering what few containers they could find and filling them at the well. Emma and the soldier assisted them. The metal pots were dented and cracked, and the buckets had to be plugged to hold water.

A younger, attractive slave woman who had hidden herself in the woods during the raid was inspecting her cabin, which had not been spared in the general pillage. She was weeping in her apron, bewailing the food and other belongings robbed from her house, having discovered that even her humble cooking utensils had been stolen. Her little son Rufus, who been in charge of feeding and caring for the dogs, was holding a dead puppy and squalling over it and its slaughtered siblings. Emma noticed that the boy was shivering as he wept. She began shivering herself, and only at that moment realized just how cold a day it was; in all the tumult and emotion of the morning she had hardly been conscious of the weather.

When all the fires were extinguished, Emma headed back to the house. The Confederate officer was washing the soot from his hands at the well. He watched her as she was about to round the corner of the house, where she suddenly stopped, bringing her hands to her mouth. She turned and ran back in his direction, but he was already running to his horse.

"Yankees!" she announced breathlessly. "Two on horseback!"

"Just two? Are you sure?"

"Yes!"

"Go inside, Miss Dubose. I must hide my horse."

She hurried into the house through a back entrance, told Mrs. Screven and Hannah about the approaching danger, and instructed them to remain upstairs with her dead brother. Emma went back downstairs and peered around the edge of an open window. She saw the two Yankee soldiers slowing to a stop at the front steps, and caught a few words of their conversation as they were dismounting and tying up their horses. One of them was riding a mule, and she recognized him as her guard. The other soldier was a younger, clean-shaven man with pale skin and jet black hair.

"Remember them silver spoons that was in the hollow tree, McCarty?" the older man was saying. "I went back and caught an old reb fetchin' 'em after we left the place."

"Old devil thought he was in the clear! Didn't reckon on you, did he?" the other answered, and both laughed.

Emma shrank away from the window and moved to the front door. When she opened it, the two soldiers were already walking up the steps. Her guard grinned broadly and tipped his hat to her.

"Why have you come back?" she demanded angrily, fearful, but steeled by the presence of a protector.

"We are to search again, to find those things you've hidden," replied the older man, still smiling offensively.

"I told your commander, we've hidden nothing. We had no time," she said indignantly, not having the presence of mind to remember that she had already been caught in this lie.

"Well, he don't believe you. Step aside, miss, we are coming in."

Emma backed into the house.

"Private McCarty, you go in that dining room and check them floorboards, and mind you watch my back."

"I'll do that, Sergeant Swain," the younger soldier answered.

The sergeant kept his eyes fixed on Emma as the other man walked off and left them alone together. He drew closer to her, and she moved into the parlor. Swain followed her in and set his rifle down against a table.

"Now I'll take that brooch you're wearing," he said, reaching toward her neck.

"Don't touch me!" she gasped, shrinking back.

He laughed.

"You reb women are pretty damn clever at hiding things in your clothes. Just yesterday we found a purse full of gold sewed into an old lady's petticoat! Little as we found in this house, I know you got more gold and jewelry tucked away somewhere. You give it up now, or you'll have cause to regret it."

"Leave me alone!" she cried. "I have no gold or jewelry besides this!"

Terrified, Emma backed away from him and placed herself behind the sofa. Her hands were trembling as she removed the brooch pinned to her dress, and she tossed it in the soldier's direction, declaring again that it was all the jewelry she had left. He picked up the little cameo at his feet, inspected it briefly, and put it in his pocket. She heard a noise from the dining room, and her eyes momentarily darted in that direction. Swain paid no attention to it, assuming it was merely McCarty doing his work. He approached Emma, but she kept him away by circling the couch.

"Now pretty miss, be still. I'll get ye ere long, anyway," he chuckled. "Want me to call in my friend McCarty, too? You don't want that now, do you?"

"Leave me alone!" she shrieked.

The sergeant's expression turned angry.

"I've a mind to burn this house down if you don't do as I say," he threatened. "I have my Lucifers with me, see? They never fail!"

As he spoke, he pulled out a box of matches from a pocket, struck and lit one, and set fire to the torn upholstery of an overturned chair with it.

"Care to change your mind now, miss?" asked the sergeant.

Emma only answered with a glare. The next moment, she caught sight of the Confederate officer in the dining room doorway. He was silently sheathing a bloodied Bowie knife and drawing his revolver. She averted her eyes from him instantly. All the while, the Yankee sergeant had his back to the doorway as he continued to alternately coax and threaten her. Then suddenly, tired of delays, he lunged across the sofa and grabbed Emma's arm. The other man was on him in a flash, removing a pistol he wore at his side. As soon as he was disarmed, the officer let him go and stepped back a few paces.

Swain faced the Confederate soldier and immediately went to his knees to beg for his life.

"Don't shoot! I surrender! I surrender!"

The officer gestured to Emma, directing her to his side of the room. She moved behind him, her face white as wax. She was shaking so much that she had to steady herself on an armchair beside him. He ordered the sergeant to put out the fire he had started, and Swain immediately beat out and smothered the flames with his hat.

"You are surrendering to me," the officer said calmly.

"Yes! Yes!"

"You wish me to follow the rules of war, then, I suppose."

"Rules of war, yes! I am surrendering to you. I am unarmed!"

"Have you no rules against thievery in your army?"

Sergeant Swain had broken into a cold sweat and was quaking more violently than the young woman he had just attacked. His ashen face grimaced and twitched with terror.

"Have you burned houses?" asked the Confederate.

"No!"

"Who burned all the farms and houses I rode past today?"

"It wasn't me!"

"You're lying," said the officer, nodding toward the smoldering chair.

Swain cut a glance at Emma. The Confederate glanced at her, too, and advised her to leave the room. Emma turned aside, but she was too weak in the knees to walk; they almost gave way when she tried.

"For God's sakes, man, I surrender!" the sergeant wailed, with a gesture of supplication.

Emma made another attempt to leave, but suddenly felt faint and stumbled. As the lieutenant caught her arm, Swain took advantage of the momentary distraction to reach into his partly open coat. He pulled out a small pepper-box revolver, but before he could get off a shot, the other man had put a bullet into his gut. The sergeant fell forward, writhing and groaning in agony. The lieutenant stepped closer to him and looked down.

"I'm sorry," he said, with a strange, sardonic lightness in his voice, "but we're playing by Yankee rules now."

He finished off the wounded man with a bullet to the head, and Emma, who had covered her eyes, involuntarily screamed at the deafening sound and concussion of this second blast. The lieutenant stared down at the lifeless body of the sergeant for several long moments with a look of grim satisfaction, and then turned to her.

"I'm sorry you had to witness that, Miss Dubose," he said.

Emma felt faint again, and slid into the armchair which had been supporting her. She looked up at the young man with a horrified, uncomprehending expression, and he frowned.

"You think me heartless?" he asked her sharply. "You

haven't seen what I've seen. We have orders to shoot house burners."

"Do not apologize, sir," she said, heaving with deep breaths. "I am very grateful for your protection."

The sound of gunfire had sent Mrs. Screven flying downstairs, crying out for Emma. She saw the bloody corpse of the soldier on the floor and staggered in the doorway.

"I am all right, Aunt!" said Emma. "This officer has protected us."

"Where is the other one?" asked the lady, starting with a sudden fright.

"He's dead," replied the young man.

She groaned in relief, but then her eyes widened at the thought that the horde of Yankee soldiers might return to take revenge.

"What if the others come back?"

"No doubt they are moving on, ma'am, but I shall bury these men in the woods, and their gear. Bring me sheets or carpets to cover them. We must clean or burn what has been bloodied in here."

The two women did as he directed, and burned bloody rags and upholstery behind the house. In less than an hour, the Confederate officer returned from the woods carrying a small shovel that was part of his equipment. A few minutes later, he came into the house with a full haversack. He had gone through the soldiers' pockets and saddlebags and recovered a trove of mostly stolen goods which he presented to the ladies. He gave them sacks of meal, flour, coffee, and sugar, silver spoons, greenbacks and coins, a gold watch, and pieces of jewelry, keeping only some hardtack and a little coffee for himself. Emma was grateful for these things, especially when she found her brooch among them, but disappointed not to find any of her family portraits among the items, except for one, a small daguerreotype of her favorite cousin, Gabriel DuBose. The last she had heard of him, he was a prisoner of war in the North.

The mule belonging to one of the dead Yankee soldiers did not bear an army brand, so the nameless officer left it for Emma. She insisted that he take the other soldier's horse to replace the decrepit mare he rode. He gladly accepted the trade.

"My Rosinante may be of some use to you after some rest and pasture," he said. "If not, there may be a little meat on her bones for food, though I should regret such a fate for the old girl. She has served me well. I have taken the Yankees' weapons, and I will leave you my own pistol for your protection. It is a bit battered but serviceable."

Turning down an invitation to share in what little food they might prepare for a meal, the lieutenant transferred his saddle and gear to his new horse and went on his way.

CHAPTER SIXTEEN

JOHN WAITED IN THE DRAWING ROOM while the doctor was administering more medicine to Elias, whose fever had worsened. Nearly an hour passed before he heard the library door open and close again. Dr. Townsend emerged in discouragement, with a look verging on tears, but squared his shoulders and tried to compose himself as he walked into the other room.

"Any change?" John asked faintly.

"I'm sorry, John," he said. "It won't be long now...a day or so...maybe hours."

"Will you stay?"

The doctor nodded.

"On my way in, Mrs. McColl asked me if would see about one of her little girls. It doesn't sound serious, but I should walk over there. I'll be back shortly."

After Tom left the house John went back into the library, and was soon joined by his sister, who had just put the baby down for a nap in her room. It was mid-morning now. Israel had been sitting with Elias since dawn, and went to get himself some breakfast. About an hour after he left, Isabella heard her baby crying and had to go back upstairs.

Elias was asleep, but his breathing seemed unusually rapid.

It was a hot day, and already uncomfortably warm inside the house. Dr. Townsend had removed all the covers from Elias except for a light sheet across his lower legs. John saw his brother make a writhing movement with his shoulders, and as he turned his face toward him, noticed perspiration on his forehead. John picked up a cloth to dampen, but found that the decanter of water on the table was nearly empty. He left the room to fill it.

He was absent from the room little more than three minutes, but when he walked back in, he experienced a momentary sensation of foreboding.

As he approached the couch, he was struck with his brother's strange look of immobility. A feeling of horror came over him, but faded as he convinced himself that Elias was only sleeping as usual. Then, as he came closer and had a better view, he could see the absolute stillness of his limbs and chest, and that his lips were parted in a ghastly grimace, his eyes half-open.

He was gone.

John had seen many dead men on the battlefield, some of them his friends and relatives, but he could hardly bear to look at his brother's lifeless body, especially his face. His body—without his soul, without himself—was too awful to contemplate. Putting down the decanter, John lifted Elias's limp arm and felt for a pulse to make sure he was not mistaken, and then quickly hurried out of the library. In the hall he closed the door behind him and leaned against it, gasping for breath.

Why, he wondered, why did people say that the dead look peaceful? Perhaps some do before they die, while there is still a self to feel or foresee something, but not afterward, certainly not afterward, he thought. He had just seen that with his own eyes. At that moment he felt he had never seen anything more horrible.

After the first shock of grief had passed, John felt paralyzed, numb and inert. There were practical things to be done, other people to be told, but he could not think what should be done first. He kept leaning against the door of the library, and might have remained there in his stupor indefinitely, but a knock at the front door roused him. He opened it in automatic, unthinking response.

Mr. Childress had come to see him, but was too startled by John's expression to speak at first. Dr. Townsend was walking up the front steps at the same moment. When he saw John's face, he knew instantly that Elias was dead. The three men went into the library.

"Where is Isabella?" the doctor asked tearfully, when he saw that no one was with the body.

"I must tell her," said John. "I just found him—just now."

Mr. Childress sadly offered his condolences. John knew his brother-in-law was out looking over the cotton fields, and asked his manager to tell Mr. Stewart to come to the house immediately.

"I'll do that, sir," he said. "I'll go right away."

John went upstairs to find his sister. He met Isabella as she was closing the door of her room behind her.

"Belle," he said quietly. "Elias..."

"No!" she cried, and rushed past him to go down to her dead brother.

John slowly followed Isabella down the stairs. In the library, she had knelt by the daybed to embrace Elias, and Tom was kneeling beside her with his arm around her. The doctor had closed the young man's mouth and eyes. Elias looked asleep now, and John no longer felt the horror he had experienced earlier.

"I was with him since you left us, Belle," he said. "He was asleep, and I left the room for just a few moments to get some water. When I came back, he was gone."

"He died alone!" she sobbed.

John gasped in pain.

"Forgive me!" she said, immediately lifting her stricken face to look up at her brother. "I didn't mean it as a reproach. You couldn't have known. I only wish I could have spoken with him just once more, to say goodbye. I should have stayed with him. Oh, I should have stayed with him!"

"Even if one of us had been with him," the doctor said gently, "he would probably not have been aware of it."

John went to his knees beside his sister. She kissed him and begged his forgiveness again, and he put his arm around her.

Dr. Townsend was on his way to the village to meet with the priest and make arrangements for the funeral. After comforting his wife, Edmund left the house in search of Reuben to tell him that a coffin was needed. John and Isabella stayed in the library, sitting with Elias for a long time without speaking. She was calm now, and kept her eyes closed in prayer. Israel had gone off to grieve in private, but soon returned to the room with a stoical demeanor.

In the late afternoon, John rode over to the DuBose place to break the news of his brother's death. On his way home, he stopped at Dr. Townsend's house where Rev. Shubrick had just left. The funeral, a grave side service, was set for the following afternoon.

The day of the funeral was very warm, the sky overcast and gloomy, and threatening to rain soon. The grave had been dug in the family cemetery that morning, and the open coffin rested on a wooden platform next to it.

Laura had been so distraught the previous day that her brother had decided not to allow her to see Elias until just before the funeral began. Holding on tightly to Tom's arm, she looked down into the open coffin, but almost immediately looked away, and broke down into tears again. Isabella embraced her young cousin, whispering in her ear, and after a while Laura grew calmer.

Rev. Shubrick leaned on his son's arm as they walked from the house to the cemetery. A slight, scholarly looking man of more than sixty years, he had not fully recovered his strength after his long illness, but his beautiful voice was nearly as strong and clear as ever, and the words that he uttered gave John unexpected comfort. The priest had known Elias well, and despite what he had heard of the young man's angry, bitter spirit at the end, he added some consoling words at the conclusion of the formal burial service, assuring the mourners that Elias was now finally at peace, in a place where he had his victory after all. Rev. Shubrick spoke of him hopefully and confidently, quoting a promise from the Scriptures.

"If we believe not, yet He abideth faithful; He cannot deny himself."

Emma stood by John's side, and his sister was next to her on her husband's arm. Though there were a number of tearful faces around her, Isabella did not cry. Her eyes were solemnly fixed on the ground at her feet, and never seemed to leave it. All the freedmen had been invited to the funeral, and almost all of them attended, surrounding the small gathering of family and friends who stood closest to the grave. Israel, Amos, and Matthew stood with the inner circle of mourners.

After the service, Emma wanted to stay at Belle Ville a little while longer, and her aunt and uncle went out to the garden to take a walk while she waited for John to return to the house. He and Isabella were saying their goodbyes to Rev. Shubrick and a few of their guests. When these had all gone, John and his sister walked inside and parted ways in the hall. She went upstairs to rest, and John soon found Emma in the drawing room.

She was seated in an armchair which faced the empty fireplace, and he walked over to her wordlessly and dropped to his knees on the floor to sit at her feet. Facing the hearth, he rested his head against her skirts and reached up, seeking her hand, which he kissed and then held on to against his shoulder.

"I wish," Emma said quietly, "I wish I had been given more time with Elias. I wish I could have known him better...before he was taken from us."

"He would have loved you, as I do," said John, kissing her hand again. "Someday I'll tell you more about him, but not now. It's too difficult...now."

"I know."

They sat in silence for a while. Gradually, John emerged from the numbed daze of shock and grief that had rendered him unable to think of anything but his brother, and his thoughts began to drift toward the future. Except for Emma, it seemed bleak. The four walls that surrounded him, and all they contained, his very home, depressed him with all its reminders of his most recent losses, his father and brother, as well as other family members long gone. He wished that he were elsewhere, anywhere else, that he could escape to some other place where there was nothing to make him think of them at every turn. He began to contemplate some means of escape, and without thinking the matter through clearly, wondered something aloud.

"Emma, if I asked it of you, would marry me sooner than we planned, and leave South Carolina with me? I mean leave forever."

The question surprised and troubled her, but she answered calmly, "If it were necessary, I would go anywhere with you, John."

"Others are leaving. I know of quite a few who have already moved away or are planning to do so. I have heard that the Whittmores are going to California, but I should want to go farther away than that."

"Where?"

"I don't know. To England, perhaps. We would be welcome there. I've heard that some have also gone to Brazil and Canada."

Brazil and Canada struck Emma as strange, wild places, whereas England presented a more pleasant prospect, but she immediately shook off the distracting thought of travel to faraway countries.

"But what about our families?" she asked.

John had no answer to this question. Releasing her hand, he drew in a deep breath, and his shoulders drooped low with its exhalation. Emma gently stroked his hair. He closed his eyes, and with her touch, felt his sudden, anxious impulses dissipate. He let his head sink down on the cushion of the chair, but soon bent it back to look up at her.

"Forget all I just said, Emma. I really didn't mean it."

He sought her hand again and held it tightly.

"This is all I shall ever want," he said. "This is all I shall ever ask of life, that you not be taken from me."

A few minutes later, the front door opened, and Emma's aunt and uncle walked in. She and her family returned to the carriage waiting for them in the front yard, and John drove them back to their place.

Everyone was unusually quiet on the way home, and in his private thoughts, John once more began pondering the future. By the time they reached the farm, his mood had grown gloomy again, like the dark sky overhead readying itself to rain. He walked Emma to the door, but declined her request to stay awhile.

"I am not good company right now," he told her.

"I don't care about that," she answered. "We needn't talk. Won't you stay?"

"I ought to go home," he responded, but as soon as he spoke, the thought of walking back through the door of his own house depressed him so completely that he changed his mind.

After John unharnessed his horse and stabled her in the barn, he and Emma sat out on the porch and watched the rain storm which soon began. The sky put on quite a show for them, booming with thunderclaps, flashing with lightning, and bending and tossing trees with furious gusts of wind. Emma said that she enjoyed such spectacles of nature, but the lightning became so alarming that John took her inside. They returned to the porch when the worst of the storm had passed.

He stayed for supper, but ate little. He left just after the meal in order to get home before dark. At Belle Ville, he saw Dr. Townsend's buggy in the driveway. Isabella had invited her cousin Laura to spend a few days with her, and Tom had just brought her back with some clothes and a few effects.

John met the doctor on the portico just as he was leaving to go back to the village, and drew him aside there for a private conversation.

"How is Laura?" he asked.

"Rather fragile," Tom replied. "Belle saw that, too. I'm grateful she invited her here. I think Laura needs the company of another woman, and Belle has always been like an older sister to her. I think they will be a comfort for each other."

"I'm glad to hear it."

John heard voices nearby from inside the house. Thinking they might be overheard, he asked the doctor to walk with him to his carriage. There, he told Tom about his visit to Blackville and his conversation with General Wallis.

"The general told me he would submit a report," John concluded, "but I have my doubts that anything will come of it, even if he does."

"That seems likely to me," the doctor replied. "I doubt the

military authorities will take any further action on your behalf."

"We shall see. I don't know, but perhaps you're right. Perhaps there's nothing more to be done."

"It seems to me...," Tom ventured hesitantly. "It seems to me justice has been done, at least in part. Don't you think so?"

"I don't know what to think," John answered. "I haven't been able to think clearly at all these last few days. I don't understand–why."

Tom sighed wearily and put his arm around his cousin's shoulder.

"Well, John," he said, "they say that time heals. Perhaps someday, it might also bring a little illumination."

Deep in the night, in silence and complete, moonless darkness, John awakened from a dream.

In it he had seen Elias walking across the fields of Belle Ville in bright sunlight. Radiantly healthy and strong, he was moving through the middle of a glowing field of ripe grain, and reached out and pulled off one golden head of wheat, which he put to his mouth. John called out to him from a distance, and the next moment, in the strange way of dreams, they were both standing in the family cemetery.

Elias was standing beside his own grave, and over it he held out his hand and crumbled the little ear of wheat, letting its seeds fall to the ground and scatter on the bare brown soil. Before he vanished, he smiled at John, who was weeping, and embraced him and spoke.

"Don't worry about me," he said. "Don't worry about me, brother. All is well."

As John opened his eyes, he could still feel his brother's body in his arms.

CHAPTER SEVENTEEN

ELIAS WAS GONE, but the house at Belle Ville stirred with life as before with the presence of John's sister and her family. Her twin daughters, who celebrated their birthday a few days after the funeral, liked to play now in the sunny room where Elias died, knowing nothing of his sufferings there. Isabella had been tutoring the girls herself, but finding that this was a little more than she could handle in addition to her other responsibilities and work, she had put their education aside for a while, hoping that a lady who once ran a school for girls in the village would eventually resume her teaching there. The little boy, too young for schooling, often followed his father and uncle around the house and in their work on the plantation.

One evening, about a week after the funeral, another heavy thunderstorm kept John from riding over to visit Emma. The day after that, he was determined to go and see her, rain or shine. In the late afternoon, the skies were clouding up again, but he reckoned he could make it to the DuBose farm before the storm broke. As he was saddling his horse, he heard Isabella calling to him from the portico. A letter had arrived for him from their uncle in Charleston. He and his sister had received notes of condolence from Mr. Hutchinson two days earlier, so he was a little surprised to receive another communication from him so soon. John took it with him to read on the way.

Once on the road, he pulled out the letter and opened it.

Charleston July 9th 1865

My Dear Nephew,

I hesitate to write of business so soon after our family's grievous loss, which has affected me even more than the passing of my beloved brother, but I thought by doing so I might offer you all some measure of hope, which is a form of comfort, in a proposal which may benefit you and your sister's family.

Before the war you told me it was your wish to remain in Charleston and pursue an occupation in a commercial house here, namely mine, and it delighted me to offer you employment and prospects for a future partnership. During the time you were with us I believe you gained sufficient experience and insight into the business to be of great use to me now. Since my affliction I have not recovered enough strength to visit the office more than twice a week. The health of my chief partner Mr. Gordon has become so poor of late that he has been confined to an invalid's bed, and I am working with only one clerk, Mr. Hopkins. I have need of you, nephew, if you will consider returning to Charleston and to your former occupation.

You have visited the city recently, and have seen for yourself the decay and inactivity of the waterfront. In these dark and uncertain days, I hardly know what to expect for the future. Sometimes I am despondent for my city and my state now that the Republic is in its grave. I can offer you no guarantees of great prosperity, but I think it reasonable to assume that in time, this firm must return to something of its former standing. The business is a wreck at present, but there is much to be salvaged, and much to be restored if possible. We must first concentrate our efforts on selling or shipping the extensive property of our European correspondents and friends purchased here during the war, and fortunately not all lost. With so much of the railroads destroyed and yet to be rebuilt, it will be difficult to transport cotton from the interior to our port, and I have no doubt there will be interference from the military authorities in these endeavors, but we must try, and hope that some success attends us.

As for Belle Ville, I know there is much uncertainty concerning labor, but if anyone can make any success of it, or at least earn a living from it, it is your sister's husband. It seems to me you would do well to turn the place over to Edmund, who knows only planting, and has need of such an opportunity and a home for his family. It would relieve Isabella's mind, I am sure, to be settled again, especially in a place which holds so many fond memories for her. I can offer you and your bride a home in my house, where your presence would be most welcome and, I assure you, a pleasure and a comfort to me.

Think on what I have written, John, and let me know if you will consider my proposal. I think it may be the best arrangement for all concerned. May God bless and comfort you all.

> Your affectionate uncle,
> Jno. Hutchinson

It took John a few moments to absorb the full import of his uncle's proposal, and as he read over the letter a second time, he experienced a feeling close to exhilaration, even joy, at the thought of returning to Charleston.

When he arrived at the farm it was almost dusk. Emma was sitting out on the porch waiting for him. She had already put away her sewing in the fading light, and rose from her chair as he walked up, receiving him in a wordless embrace.

As the two released each other, they heard Mrs. Screven inquiring through the open window.

"Yes, John is here," Emma told her. "He'll come in and see you in a little while."

"Very good," they heard her say from inside.

John took his usual place at the top of the steps. Emma decided to sit in the same spot, facing him and leaning against the opposite post.

"I had hoped to come and see you yesterday," he said quietly, "but the weather prevented me."

"I don't expect you in such weather, John."

Emma studied him and reached out to push back a stray lock of hair which had just fallen across his face.

"You look a little thinner," she observed with concern. "Have you been unwell?"

"No, I mean, I haven't been physically ill. I suppose my appetite hasn't been what it should be for a while, but that all started with you. I suppose it's continued for other reasons."

"You must eat, dear," she urged him gently.

"I will, Emma. I promise. I don't want you to be anxious about me."

"You'll stay for supper with us, then."

"I'm sure I'm not expected."

"I'm sure you are. My aunt is no doubt setting a place for you right now. Now, you'll dine with us, won't you? I wish to see you eat a good meal."

Emma led him inside, and as she had predicted, the table was set for four. Her uncle was already seated, and beckoned John to join him. Emma disappeared for a few minutes and returned with serving dishes of food, followed by her aunt carrying the same. Mrs. Screven gave John an especially tender smile when she greeted him.

John fulfilled his promise, eating until he felt that Emma was contented with him. He even enjoyed the food a little more than he had expected. After the meal they returned to the porch and looked out on the rain shower which had just begun. What little thunder they heard was far in the distance, and the sky only occasionally brightened in some quarter with far-off lightning. He asked her about her day, but she had nothing remarkable to report except a letter from a cousin. He responded by mentioning the letter he had just received from his uncle.

"I'd like for you to read it, Emma. I think you will find it very interesting, but before you do, let me ask you a question. What would you think of living in Charleston after we are married?"

She answered this question with one of her own.

"What about Belle Ville?"

The place had for so long been identified with the Hutchinson family, she found it hard to disassociate the two. In answer, John pulled the letter out of a coat pocket and gave it to her to read. When Emma finished and looked up at him, there was a smile on his face, the first real one she had seen in a long time.

"What do you think, Emma?" he asked.

"It is very interesting, as you say."

"I really think Edmund can do better with Belle Ville than I could. I have no wish for it to go out of the family, but I...I see no future for us here. The city has changed, of course, for the worse, but it's a place I love, and I think I could provide better for you there."

Emma listened with an abstracted, neutral expression.

"I don't know what I think of living in Charleston," she said, peering far off beyond him as if trying to envision the city. "The idea has never crossed my mind. But if you think it best, John, I have no objection."

She looked at him and added softly, "Wherever you are is my home."

He gave a slight sigh of relief.

"I love Belle Ville, Emma, but there are too many ghosts haunting me there, and for now at least, I find them too oppressing. Can you understand that?"

"Yes, I do understand."

"Would it grieve you to leave this parish?"

"I should miss some friends, but there is little else left for me here. My aunt and uncle talk of returning to Greenville after we marry."

"Then I think the change will do us both good," he said, taking her hand in his own. "The only unfortunate thing about it is I think my uncle will wish me to come to Charleston very soon."

"When would you go?" she asked in a falling voice, as she suddenly realized that a separation was imminent.

"Perhaps next week."

"Oh."

"I don't wish to be parted from you, Emma, but if we must wait until October to marry, it will be necessary. I think it is best for us to wait anyway. Judging from what I saw when I was in Charleston and from what my uncle has written about what is going on there, it is not a fit place to bring you to just yet."

"You would come back to Belle Ville occasionally, wouldn't you?"

"Of course! How else could I bear three months apart from you?"

"Three months," she echoed a little sadly. "You must write to me as often as you can, John."

"I'll do that, and look for your replies. I wish I had a likeness of you to take with me, but I know you don't have one."

He leaned closer and touched her hair.

"Perhaps you might spare me a few strands of this beautiful stuff," he suggested.

"I shall make a little keepsake for you," she said.

"Thank you, Emma."

John was more animated and talkative than she had seen him in a long while, and he began to tell her about his early days at Hutchinson & Company, and the interesting and colorful characters he had encountered on the busy wharves of Charleston before the war. The life of a clerk, he informed her, was not as dull as one might imagine, and had led him into some adventures and, at least on one occasion, serious hazard, when he was called upon in the middle of the night to charter a boat and take a pilot out to a French vessel in distress off the bar. The seas were rough and the winds violent that night, and he nearly drowned in his attempt to board the ship by a rope thrown down to him, but he had been successful in the end, and helped to bring the crippled steamer into port, a recovery that resulted in a handsome profit for the company.

Emma listened, smiling, happy to see him showing signs of hopefulness about the future once again as he talked about the past.

When John returned to Belle Ville, he showed his uncle's

letter to his sister and brother-in-law. Edmund read it first, then Isabella, and they both looked up at John inquiringly as she finished.

"What do you think?" he asked them.

"Belle Ville is yours, John," his sister answered hesitantly.

"I agree with what our uncle has written," said John. "Do you, Belle?"

Edmund and Isabella looked at each other, conferring with their eyes, and a hint of a smile showed on their faces as they turned back to him.

"I should like for you to have Belle Ville," John urged her. "I should like for you to have a home here again."

"It's very generous of you, John, and our uncle is right–it would be a great joy to us to have a place of our own. Edmund, dear, what do you think?"

He looked at John and said, "I'd very much like to have a place to call my home, too, but I wouldn't wish you to give up the place just for our sake."

"It's not just for your sake," John assured him. "I told you I agreed with Uncle John. I think his proposal is the best course for all of us. To be honest with you, Edmund, I think you have a much better chance of success here than I do, and I believe my chances would be better in Charleston."

"Have you spoken with Emma about it?" Isabella asked.

"Yes, she is agreeable to it."

"I think it only fair that you should retain some interest in the property and the crops," she said.

"If that's what you wish, Belle. We'll work out any terms you like."

Edmund's face broke out into the first full smile he had shown since his arrival, and he shook John's hand vigorously.

Isabella embraced her brother with a kiss. Relief and gratitude were in her eyes, as if a great burden had been lifted from her shoulders.

The baby woke up from a nap and began to cry, and his mother went to tend to him. John and Edmund sat in the drawing room talking about planting, the local soils, and differences between the Sea Island cotton to which Edmund was accustomed and the upland variety grown in the interior of the state, like that at Belle Ville. Isabella soon returned with the baby and sat down with them. Little Elias was in a good mood now, and was laughing in his mother's lap as she played a game of hide and seek with him by covering and uncovering her eyes and making little sounds of surprise.

Edmund paused for a moment to watch his wife and child, but then turned back to John to continue the thread of their conversation.

"I know it isn't going to be easy, John," he said. "Everything's going to be much more difficult for planters now. Belle Ville has fared better than most places, at least for this season. What will happen next year is anyone's guess, but I'd like to be hopeful. This year I think we'll have a fairly good crop to send to Hutchinson and Company."

"It certainly looks that way," John agreed.

"Yes, thank God," Edmund murmured, sending another glance in the direction of his wife and son.

John rose to his feet and asked his brother-in-law if he would come upstairs with him.

"There's something you should see," he said.

When they were halfway up the stairs, Edmund began expressing his gratitude again to John for his generosity. John waited until they were well out of Isabella's hearing before he answered.

"Don't think me more generous than I am, Edmund," he said. "I've told you that this arrangement is not just for your sake, so my reasons are not entirely unselfish. I must confess the place is more of a burden to me than a blessing, especially now, and I'm very glad to turn it over to you. Everything in this house and everything around it reminds me of Father and Elias, and at present I find that rather hard to bear."

"Yes, I can see that, John, and a change of place can be very healthful, I'm sure. I don't blame you."

John showed Edmund the secret place in his father's bedroom where the family's valuables had been hidden. His brother-in-law helped him move the massive bed aside, and John pulled away the panel to reveal the little attic room. The air in this unventilated space was heated like an oven, and John decided that it would be best to remove anything that might be damaged by it now. He and Edmund pulled out nearly everything and placed the boxes and the silverware on the bed. The last items to be removed were two fine paintings, portraits of John's mother and father in gilded frames.

Edmund paused to admire the portrait of Mrs. Hutchinson.

"How beautiful she was," he said. "Belle is much like her, don't you think?"

"Very much like her," John agreed.

His eyes lingered on that face a while. His memories of his mother had grown somewhat dim, and he drank in the sight of her to refresh them. He was holding the painting of his father, but could not bear to look at it. He gently placed it face down on the bed.

One of the boxes in the hidden cache of valuables contained the papers documenting the chain of title to the family property of Belle Ville. John opened it to show them to Edmund. An old, sturdy piece of parchment unfolded to a reveal a large manuscript filled with neat, straight lines of a quaint antique handwriting in faded brown ink. This was a royal grant of five hundred acres authorized by King George III and signed by the colonial governor of South Carolina. The original survey of the land was attached to it, a beautifully inked and colored plat, along with an ornate wax seal the size of a man's palm. A half-dozen or so old deeds, some larger in size, some smaller, attested to the successive purchases of neighboring properties by John's grandfather and great-grandfather. One small addition of land dated to his father's tenure, and with it was another handsome plat showing the boundaries of Belle Ville in their present completeness, and the locations of buildings, roads, fields, groves, swampy areas, and woodlands.

"I pass these on to you for safe-keeping," John told his brother-in-law.

"I'll take good care of them," he promised.

John picked up a small rosewood box and handed it to Edmund.

"These are my mother's jewels," he said. "They were left to Isabella."

Edmund opened the lid, peered inside, and moved around the pieces of jewelry as if looking for something in particular.

"Ah," he said disappointedly, "if there were only a wedding ring in here, you could give it to Miss Emma."

"I hadn't thought of that," John confessed.

"You must take something for your bride," Edmund insisted. "She must have some adornment for the wedding."

He held up a beautiful, delicate strand of pearls and dangled them in front of John's eyes.

"Emma would like those, I think," he said, as the necklace was placed in his hand.

After he removed the pearls Edmund noticed something

tucked away in the corner of the box. He reached in with one finger and pulled out a ring, a delicate floral filigree band of gold.

"Here we are!"

"I remember this ring," said John, carefully taking the little band between his finger and thumb. "Mother wore it often."

"It's beautiful. Miss Emma will be very pleased."

"I'll ask Belle. These belong to her now, after all."

"Oh, Belle will be happy for Miss Emma to have these things. She was wondering the other day about her mother's jewelry, and wanted very much to provide a ring for you."

"Then I shall accept it. We'll just borrow the pearls for the wedding then."

That evening John sat down with his sister and her husband to discuss the settlement of their father's estate. Mr. Simmons had sent him a copy of the will, which apportioned very little to Isabella. At the time it was written, she was thought to be well provided for by her husband's wealth and a small inheritance she had received from her mother. But almost all of that wealth had been wiped out, and John felt it was only fair to offer her half the gold money their father had left behind.

Tears came into her eyes.

"No, John," she said, shaking her head emphatically. "You are too generous. Father bequeathed it to you. You will have a wife to support, and a family soon, no doubt."

John tried to talk her into taking half the money, then a third when she refused that amount. Edmund remained silent, and even got up and sat down farther away from the two as they argued. He had once been traumatized by a nasty squabble in his own family over an inheritance, and though the dispute going on between John and Isabella was of a very different nature, the subject of inheritance brought back such bad memories that he wanted nothing to do with it. He found one of the last cigars in the house and began smoking it for nervous relief.

When John finally made his sister understand that he would have some income from the estate, she agreed to take a third of the money.

"But no more," she said. "You don't know what may happen with those investments abroad. Who knows but that the government may seize them, as they did Edmund's property."

"I don't see how," said John.

"We saw in an Augusta paper not so long ago that the administration in Washington designed vengeance upon those who had supplied the wants of our army and people through the blockade. Uncle John was running the blockade, you know."

"I know, Belle, but these are father's holdings."

"Yes, but you will be Uncle John's partner—oh, I don't know," she sighed. "We don't know what will happen. They can do what they like with us now, and our property."

When Mr. Childress learned that Edmund Stewart would be taking over at Belle Ville, he decided that it was time for him to move on, and came to the house late one afternoon to speak to John about the matter.

"My brother has written to me again," he said, "and wishes me to come and help him as soon as possible. I think his request is more out of brotherly concern than necessity, but I'd like to go back home and live where I have my family around me."

"I understand," said John. "You've been a great help here."

"I wonder if I might have those testimonial letters I mentioned to you before, Captain Hutchinson."

"Of course."

Mr. Childress shrugged doubtfully with his armless

shoulder and explained, "It isn't likely, but I was thinking that those papers might be of use to me in some other endeavor sometime, you see. I had hoped one day to sit under my own vine and fig tree again, so to speak, but I don't know that I shall ever be able to work a farm of my own. Even so, I was thinking I might earn a little money as a manager on someone else's for a while at least."

"I'll look for them."

"I am much obliged," said Mr. Childress. "And if you please, sir, I wanted to let you know I'll be coming back for Leila, I mean, Mrs. McColl. Yesterday I asked her to marry me, and she has consented to do so in due time."

"Well, I am happy for you both," said John, looking surprised.

"Captain Hutchinson," he went on hastily, "I hope you'll not think badly of either of us. I know that Mrs. McColl is not long widowed, and believe me, sir, when I addressed her, there was never such an awkward, roundabout proposal made by a man in the world, for I did not wish her to think me unseemly in any way, but I wished her to know my feelings for her before I left, and...and she was not offended. We don't wish to call ourselves engaged, but she has promised we may do so next spring. That makes us both more hopeful, you see."

"Yes, I can see that."

"When I find her a place to live until we marry, I'll be back for her and the little ones. She hopes some of her kinfolk will be able to take them in."

"I'm sure Mrs. McColl will be happier among her own folks."

"She's a good little woman, Captain, and she is always telling me how grateful she is to you for all you have done for her."

"Apparently I've done more than I ever expected," John

replied with a smile, patting Mr. Childress on the back.

John wrote a letter to his uncle accepting his offer, and the same afternoon, he rode to the DuBose farm to see Emma and to tell her that everything was settled. She greeted him at the front steps, and though she tried not to show it, he could tell that she was upset about something the moment he saw her.

"What's wrong, Emma?" he asked.

"My uncle wishes to return to Greenville, and to take us with him," she answered.

"Greenville! Has something happened?"

"Yesterday he received a letter from his son, my cousin Peter. He is ill, and needs his father's help."

The idea of Emma moving so far away came as an unpleasant surprise to John. Amelia was less than eighty miles from Charleston, and the railroad between the two places had recently been restored; Greenville, on the other hand, lay in the upstate some two hundred miles from Charleston, and as far as he knew, the railway connections to it had yet to be repaired.

"Have you told him that I'm going to Charleston?" he asked.

"I told him it was likely. You have made up your mind, then?"

"Yes, it's all arranged, Emma. You and I agreed that it was for the best."

"I know," she murmured. "But I suppose I shall see you much less often if I must go to Greenville, and perhaps not at all, until we are married."

Such a depressing thought silenced John for a moment as they looked into each other's eyes sadly.

"Your uncle is determined to do this?" he finally asked.

"I'm afraid he is set on it, and he refuses to leave me and my aunt here alone again."

"He is right about that. You can't be left alone."

John sank down on the first step, and Emma sat down beside him. He looked off across the yard with a thoughtful, troubled expression, but an idea soon came to him that made him brighten a little.

"Emma," he began, turning to her, "what would you think of living at Belle Ville until we're married? I'll not be there. I'll be in Charleston. Do you think your uncle would allow it?"

A smile slowly spread across her face.

"I think he might," she said, then added hesitantly, "But if you should come to visit–"

"You think your aunt will consider it improper? You could stay with Mrs. McColl, or even live at her place. It's a very comfortable house, and it's less crowded than the big house with only Mrs. McColl and her children there."

"Yes, I think that would be best," Emma mused.

"Let me talk with your uncle about it," said John, getting to his feet. He put out a hand and helped Emma up, and they went inside the house.

Mr. DuBose was reading in the parlor. He looked up over his spectacles at the young couple as they approached him, and could see at once that something significant was in the air.

"Ah, Emma has told you," he said to John.

"She has, sir. May I have a word with you?"

Mr. DuBose put down his book and offered John a chair beside him. Emma left the room. John searched for the right words to say, but before he could speak, Mr. DuBose began to explain his position.

"My son Peter has asked me to return to Greenville. He is ill, and needs my help. I know my son, and he would not ask this of me if there were not a matter of necessity. I have obligations to him, and to my niece and sister, and I cannot leave them here unprotected, so I must take them with me. I know Emma doesn't wish to go off so far from you, John, but it's only for a few months."

"I understand, sir."

"What was it you wished to speak to me about?"

John bowed his head and began hesitantly, "I wonder–"

He paused, and Mr. DuBose waited for him to go on.

"I wonder," he resumed, "if you would allow your niece to stay at Belle Ville. My sister's family is there, as you know, and Emma could live with Mrs. McColl in her house until we're married. I know this is an extraordinary request, sir, but then, these are...peculiar times, and circumstances."

Mr. DuBose sorrowfully agreed that they were.

"Mrs. Screven could even stay with Emma, if you like," John added, as an afterthought.

"No, no, my sister is indispensable in this case. She's a very good nurse, although a rather exacting one, and she is very anxious to be of help to Frederick and his family."

Mr. DuBose sighed, but then smiled and chuckled softly to himself.

"It appears you two are not well resigned to this separation," he said.

"Three months seems a painfully long time not to see Emma. I had hoped to come back home to visit with her and my family at least a few times during those months."

Still smiling, Mr. DuBose gazed at the young man, and, remembering his own youth, and what it was like to be in love, he mulled over John's request and decided that he could see nothing harmful in it. He acquiesced.

As the two men talked further of the family's plans for the

immediate future, John wondered what would become of the farm.

"I have discussed that with Emma," said Mr. DuBose. "Mr. Drawdy has expressed a desire to purchase the place, but of course has no funds. I advised my niece to lease the farm to him for the rest of the season for a modest share of the proceeds from the crops. He has certainly earned the rest for himself by all his work here, but if he has no better prospects by the end of the season, and there are no other interested parties, I suppose I shall have to advertise it for sale in the newspapers. I don't know what else to do."

"Is Emma agreeable to that?"

"Yes. It saddens her, of course, to part with her family's home, but in these times, we are left with little choice."

"That is true. Do you think you will decide to remain in Greenville with your son?"

"It is a possibility. My sister has no desire to live in Flat Rock, and I am getting a little old to live alone, so we shall see, we shall see."

Emma came back into the room while Mr. DuBose was speaking. Seeing the smile that widened on John's face when she appeared, she knew that her uncle had agreed to let her stay at Belle Ville, and rushed over to the old gentleman to thank him with a kiss.

CHAPTER EIGHTEEN

THE DAY BEFORE JOHN WAS TO LEAVE for Charleston, he brought Emma and her aunt to Belle Ville for a farewell supper. Mr. DuBose had stayed at home. He was uneasy about leaving the farm unoccupied, and felt a little unwell besides.

Isabella greeted Emma with an embrace and began talking about the dress she had mentioned to John. Emma glanced at him with slight puzzlement.

"I clean forgot to tell you, Emma," he said, looking apologetic.

"I told John some time ago that I had a white dress I should very much like you to have," Isabella explained. "I think it would make a lovely wedding dress. You are more slender, but then so was I when I had the dress made for me, and I see that we are close in height. I think it would do very nicely for you."

Emma thanked her with obvious pleasure and excitement. Unsuccessful in a search for anything better, she had already resigned herself to the fate of wearing a plain blue muslin dress which was to be made from the fabric John had brought her from Charleston. Though she was grateful at least that it would be a new dress, and not something faded and patched, she had hoped to wear white.

As they all walked into the drawing room, Emma noticed a beautiful piano in a corner and remarked on it.

"Do you play?" Isabella asked her.

"Yes, but it's been quite a while since I had the opportunity to do so."

"And do you sing?"

"I do, a little."

"Wonderful! It will be good to have music in the house again. I am not musical at all, but Edmund sings beautifully. You must favor us with a song sometime."

"If you wish."

John smiled at Emma, looking pleasantly surprised.

"You never told me you had these talents, Emma," he said.

"We never talked of music, did we?"

"Well, now he knows," Isabella laughed. "You will be a revelation for us all."

At dinner Mrs. Screven was her usual talkative self. Her late husband having had some relatives named Stewart, she plied Edmund with questions on his family connections until she determined that they were related by marriage through a distant cousin. She doted on the twins who were seated at the table with the adults, and asked after the other two children. Edmund the younger had been banished to the kitchen during the meal for bad behavior, and the baby was sleeping. After dessert, the boy made his appearance. He hid shyly in his mother's skirts at first, then, after some wooing from the guests, began finding various ways of showing off for his new admirers. When Isabella brought the baby downstairs, Mrs. Screven promptly requested to hold him.

"What a fine little fellow," she cooed, wagging her head and making faces that soon elicited a toothless smile from the infant.

Reluctantly, she gave him up so that everyone could have a turn at holding him, but managed to get the baby back in her arms before long. Little Edmund grew jealous and began some noisy antics to draw attention to himself. His mother gave him a severe look and seized his arm.

"You will come upstairs with Mama," she said.

He protested, but she kept a firm grip on him, and asked Emma if she would like to come up to her room to see the dress they had spoken of. On the stairs the boy did his best to break free but was unsuccessful. His mother put him in a bedroom and told him not to come out until he was prepared to behave himself, but as soon as the ladies entered Isabella's room they heard him scuffling down the steps.

"Edmund will deal with him," said his mother, rolling her eyes upward for a moment. "Our son has been quite difficult lately. I fear he was somewhat neglected for a while because of the baby's illness, but we are trying to make it up to him now, and hope to see his behavior improve."

Emma was extremely pleased with the dress. Isabella carefully folded it and wrapped it a sheet so that she could take it home to make the alterations.

Downstairs, Edmund Jr. was seeking the attention of his uncle. John was standing beside the chair of Mrs. Screven, who still had possession of the baby, as well as the company of the twins at her feet. The little boy took hold of John's leg and tugged on his coat.

"Pick me up! Pick me up, Uncle John!" he begged.

"He wants to be held like a baby," one of his sisters teased him.

"I'm not a baby!" he yelled indignantly, and so loudly that it made his baby brother whimper and cry a little.

His father glared at him, displeased with the noise. John looked down at his nephew with a pretense of sternness.

"What do you want, boy?" he asked.

"Hold me upside down like you did before!"

"You mustn't be so noisy and make your brother cry."

"I'll be quiet!"

Little Edmund climbed up on a chair and put out his feet. As John took hold of the boy's ankles and raised him up in the air, Isabella and Emma came back into the room.

"Mama, I'm a possum!" he giggled.

"You're a monkey," she said, taking advantage of his helplessness and some exposed belly to tickle him.

"No!" cried the child, laughing.

John swung him around a few times and gently put him down on a large ottoman. The child immediately scrambled to his feet and threw his arms around his uncle's neck.

"Do it again, Uncle John!"

"Not tonight. Tomorrow, I promise."

"But you leave tomorrow."

"I'll see you before I leave. If you behave yourself, I shall bring you a present from Charleston when I come home for a visit."

"I'll behave!"

John squeezed his nephew until the boy squealed gleefully.

"There, you be a good boy now," he said, releasing him with a kiss.

Remembering what his mother had called him, the boy began talking about monkeys, and made this his theme for the rest of his visit with the adults. When it was time for the children to be put to bed, Edmund took charge of his son, and Isabella, carrying the baby, instructed the twins to say goodnight to Uncle John and their guests and follow her upstairs. Mrs. Screven had been telling them a story, and the girls begged her to come up to their room and finish it for them.

"Do you mind, Captain Hutchinson?" she asked. "I shan't be long."

"There's no hurry," he said.

After they were left alone, John sat down on the sofa beside Emma. She had placed the dress Isabella had given her on the cushion on the other side, and was smoothing out the wrinkles in the sheet with a caressing movement of her fingers and a thoughtful expression.

"This is a luxury," he said to her softly.

"I hardly expected to have such a lovely dress," she agreed.

"No, I mean being alone with you."

He took her hand, entwining his fingers in hers.

"It's a luxury I look forward to enjoying every day, sometime not too far in the future."

"So do I," she replied, smiling a little as she looked down at their interlaced hands.

"Emma," he said, "I'm sorry I forgot to tell you about the dress. I'm sure it is something very important to you. If you don't like it, I'll see to it that we find you another one, a better one."

"I do like the dress, John, very much. It's beautiful. I have no need of anything better."

"I hear Mrs. McColl is a good seamstress. She can alter it for you if that's necessary. If you have need of anything else for the wedding, write to me, and I'll see if I can get it for you in Charleston. I hope you will write to me often, Emma."

She promised that she would.

"I shall bring a very special gift for you on my first visit home," John announced mysteriously.

"Oh?" she said, intrigued. "What is it?"

"A surprise. Something you will like very much, I believe."

"Tell me," she coaxed him, leaning closer to look deep into his eyes, but he refused to divulge the secret. John kissed the hand he had been holding and fondling and returned it to her.

"This is too tantalizing," he complained. "Being so near you. I think I shall have to remove myself."

He sank down in an armchair near the fireplace, stretched out his legs, and picked up some letters. On the first envelope he recognized the handwriting of a cousin and opened it with interest.

"George Taylor," he murmured.

Emma asked who this was.

"My cousin in Charleston–another relative who wasn't sure if I was alive or dead for a while."

"What does he say?"

"Well, for one thing, he's glad to know that I'm alive," said John, smiling, but as he read on his smile faded.

"Bad news?" Emma asked, watching him.

"The rest of his note is condolence. He heard about Elias from Uncle John."

John folded up the letter to its former compact size, but still held it, absently fingering the edges as he thought about his cousin.

"Was he a good friend of yours?" Emma wondered.

"I suppose we should have been better friends than we were. He's one of the finest men I ever knew. I'm afraid I used to begrudge him that, unjustly of course...but my father would sometimes hold him up as an example to which I should aspire, which made me a bit resentful, I suppose. Anyway, I'm glad he's alive. George was engaged before the war. I wonder if he ever married? He doesn't say."

"You must introduce me to him."

"Yes, I'd like for you to meet him."

John thumbed through some other letters, old communications already opened and read, looking for a particular one from his uncle in Charleston. He found it and smiled.

"Did I tell you what my Uncle John wrote about our engagement?" he asked Emma.

"I don't think so."

"Let me read that part of the letter to you. I think you'll like it. I wrote to him and told him all about you when we first became engaged. He was very pleased to learn that I am marrying a DuBose."

"Really?"

John scanned the letter and found the passage he wanted her to hear. As he read, he deepened his voice and added a bit of pomposity in facetious imitation of his uncle.

"The DuBose family is of an old and very highly esteemed lineage. Obviously you have found a woman who is much too good for you, and this is what you need."

Emma was laughing.

"Ah, you laugh because it's true," said John.

"No!" she protested, still mirthful. "It's the way you read it."

"My uncle is a very wise man."

"I hope to meet him soon."

"He is anxious to meet you, Emma."

The next day, John was very tired when he reached his uncle's house in Charleston in the late afternoon. He had been able to spend only a few minutes at Emma's house for a parting visit with her, and with her aunt and uncle, who were to leave for Greenville the following day. Then he had ridden into Amelia, said his goodbyes to his cousins the Townsends, and soon afterward boarded the train for Charleston for a journey of five hours or so in a hot, crowded car. When John reached the city, he expected to find a carriage waiting for him at the depot, but found there was no one there to meet him. He waited a while, and then set out for a long walk to Tradd Street carrying a full valise and a heavy portmanteau.

Mr. Hutchinson was sitting on the piazza as John approached the house. He had fallen asleep while waiting for his nephew, and his head was slowly sinking lower on his chest. Observing him in repose, John thought the old gentleman looked older and frailer, and even a little thinner, though his figure was certainly not a thin one. He had always been a strong, active man, but recent years of poor health had rendered him much less so, and as a consequence he had grown quite portly. His once handsome face had broadened and fattened like the rest of him, and his dimpled chin rested on several folds of flesh between drooping jowls partly hidden by gray whiskers.

John called out to Mr. Hutchinson, and he woke with a start, and greeted him with a smile and a wave. He embraced his nephew when he reached the piazza and set down his bags.

"You must be quite fatigued from your journey today in this heat, John," he said.

"I am, but it is good to be with you again."

"I am very glad to have you back, nephew. It will be very nice to have family in the house once more. I have had some supper prepared for you. Come inside!"

John looked around for a servant to carry his bags.

"Where is Caesar?" he asked.

"He left me. They have all left me, but it's just as well. I wouldn't have them back if I could," Mr. Hutchinson muttered, frowning, but added with a fleeting look of pain, "except perhaps for Caesar."

Now John understood why no one had met him at the

depot.

"We'll manage," he said, patting his uncle on the shoulder.

"I have an Irish lady to cook for me, a widow, Mrs. Kiley. Her daughter is here during the day to help her clean and do the washing."

John picked up his bags and, following his uncle inside, took them upstairs, where he washed the dust off his face and hands and put on a clean shirt. When he came back down, Mr. Hutchinson was waiting for him in the dining room where two places were set at the table. He indicated a chair, and John gladly took it. There was a delicious aroma in the air traceable to the steam rising up from a covered soup tureen.

Mr. Hutchinson saw John looking at the tureen and apologized.

"The weather is so warm, I am sorry now I did not ask for a cold meal for you, nephew."

"Oh, hot or cold, I don't mind. I'm so hungry I'll gladly eat anything you put in front of me."

"How is everyone at Belle Ville?" asked Mr. Hutchinson.

"They are well."

"I was so worried about Isabella's baby. Is he doing well now?"

"He is much better. He's getting quite fat again."

"They must come and visit me sometime. I haven't seen her little ones since–since–"

Mr. Hutchinson looked puzzled and tried to remember the last time he had seen his niece's family.

"Oh, well," he went on, making a gesture of dismissal, "Belle must bring them to see me. She is always reluctant to do that, for she says I am a spoiler of children."

"You are! She has enough trouble with little Edmund as it

is."

"Is he a scamp?"

"I'm afraid so."

"Then he takes after his uncle John," said Mr. Hutchinson.

"Which one?" the younger retorted.

They laughed, and Mrs. Kiley came into the room to serve the food. She was a tall, plump, middle-aged woman with graying hair and a florid complexion. Mr. Hutchinson introduced her to John, and she acknowledged him with a quaint curtsey.

"I hope you like Irish stew," said Mr. Hutchinson. "It's the best thing Mrs. Kiley makes, and she's a very good cook."

The lady suppressed a big smile of pleasure down into a crooked little smirk as she ladled out the stew into his bowl.

"Only a little for me, Mrs. Kiley. I'm not very hungry."

John took a taste of his stew and complimented Mrs. Kiley on it. Her red complexion grew even redder, and she thanked him and left them with another curtsey.

Mr. Hutchinson asked John about his "bride-to-be."

"She is well," he said, pausing over his food with a momentarily wistful expression.

"You miss her already, don't you?"

"Yes," he admitted, "it isn't pleasant to be separated from her."

"Three months isn't so long a time to wait, is it?"

"Ah, there you're wrong, uncle."

"No, no. We'll keep you busy here, young man, and the time will pass quickly, you'll see."

"I hope so."

"My clerk Mr. Hopkins has been eagerly anticipating your arrival, and is very anxious for your help. I thought of inviting him here this evening, but then I realized you might be too tired to talk of business. I have had some offers of co-partnership from Europe I wish to discuss with you, but we'll speak of that tomorrow."

"I'm not too tired, uncle," said John. "This good food has revived me."

He asked his uncle about the blockade running his ships had done during the war, and related Isabella's concerns about the matter. Mr. Hutchinson did not seem very worried about it, and reminded John that he had been running the blockade for the first two years of the war as a private enterprise, and that although his exports and imports had indirectly benefitted the cause, he had not been officially connected with the Confederate government.

They sat at the table for over an hour discussing the affairs of Hutchinson and Company, and moved into the drawing room to continue the conversation until well after dark. Finally, an irrepressible yawn rose up in John, as he suddenly felt his fatigue.

"Take any room you like upstairs," said his uncle. "The stairs are too much for me now, and I have a bedroom down here. The room I used to occupy is the largest and best."

"My old room is fine for now, uncle."

"But you must take the better one when you are married."

"If you insist."

"I do!" Mr. Hutchinson laughed. "I must tell you, nephew, I intend to be very indulgent with your bride. I am determined that she shall be happy here."

"So am I."

Covering another yawn, John got up from his chair.

"I should like to make an early start tomorrow. What time is Mr. Hopkins usually at the office?"

"Oh, don't concern yourself that you will arrive earlier than Mr. Hopkins. The counting house has become the home he prefers."

"Why is that?" John asked.

"Several years ago," said Mr. Hutchinson, "for reasons I have never quite understood, he married a lady who has since made his life a misery."

"Poor man!"

"One must be careful to marry wisely. Be thankful that you have chosen well, nephew."

"I am thankful."

"Mr. Hopkins has no religion, and apparently no sense when it comes to women, but he is honest, and wise and knowledgeable in business, and has managed our affairs wonderfully despite many difficulties. I daresay you can learn much from him."

"I shall do my best, uncle."

After a little more conversation, mostly about Emma, John escorted his uncle to his room and then wearily climbed the steps to his own upstairs. He remembered that he had made Emma a promise to write at the first opportunity, and sat down at his old desk where he found pen and paper.

Charleston, 12th July 1865

My Dearest Miss Emma,

I arrived here safely this afternoon and fulfill my promise to by writing to you tonight. The ride on the cars was long and unpleasant, and I am very tired, but it is sweet to spend a little time with you at least in imagination before I go to bed. I am in my old room, in which nothing has been changed since I left it four years ago. A few of my clothes are still here, and one of my old uniforms.

My uncle appears a little frail but seems to be in good spirits. He looks forward to having you here, and is very anxious to please you so that you are satisfied with your new home. He is an inveterate spoiler of children and now, it seems, brides, but he is certainly not more anxious than I am to please. I think you will like this house very much. It has some of the most extensive grounds in this part of the city, and a fine garden surrounded by a high wall. I think I must have described it to you before, as I remember now how your eyes grew large at the mention of a garden. I'm sure you may garden here to your heart's delight. The grounds have been somewhat neglected for several years, so there will be much to do if you wish to take it on. I am willing to help you if you like. This is a most comfortable house. Off the room which is to be yours (ours) there is a dressing room with a good bath in it with hot and cold water, and washing stands with marble tops.

It is very warm here, but I am so tired I don't think any discomfort will keep me from sleep tonight. I miss you very much already, my darling, but my uncle promises me that he will keep me very busy, and that the time will go by quickly. I know that you will keep yourself busy—you always do. My eyelids are growing heavy. I keep them open with difficulty now, so I must bring this letter to a close and go to sleep. If I am fortunate, I shall dream of you.

Yours with much love,
John Hutchinson

A few days later, he wrote to her again.

Charleston, 15th July 1865

My dear Miss Emma,

I have your little keepsake before me. It occupies a place of honor in my desk now, and I contemplate it as I think of you and write. I have made a good beginning at Hutchinson & Company, I believe. Bleak as things are, I am not discouraged, and I am determined to work my hardest. If we fail, it will certainly not be from lack of effort on my part. My uncle was right that the time would pass quickly while I am busy—the days have flown by.

I can scarcely describe for you how difficult things are here in Charleston. Many former residents have been returning to the city to find themselves destitute, their houses confiscated. When their homes are returned to them, as many are, they are usually emptied of most valuables and furnishings, although I understand some belongings have been reclaimed.

An old friend came to my office yesterday looking for employment. The government is demanding taxes on his house which he cannot pay. His wife is ill, and he has no means to afford a physician nor sufficient food for his children. They are forced to occupy the second floor of their own house, the first floor having as its resident the wife of a Union officer, who says she will be leaving soon. My friend was once a respected and reasonably wealthy man of this city, and was of high rank in the Confederate Army, but his health has been impaired from wounds, and he can do no arduous labor of any sort. He sought a clerical position with us, but I have no such thing at present. When I gave him *what money I could spare, he could hardly keep from weeping before me. I almost wept myself, to see such a man so humiliated and broken. He is a distant cousin. I shall try to do more for him.*

So far several others have come to me seeking employment, but I have none to offer. It is very painful to turn them away, especially old friends. There is little work to be had in the city, and far too many in need of it. It seems that distress, poverty, and humiliation are universal these days.

It is well that we put off our wedding for a few months. I would not have you here as things are now in Charleston. The conditions are not good, to say the least. There is much lawlessness. The last military orders have disarmed all the citizens, and all must be shut up in their houses by eight o'clock p.m. (I do not go out after dark in any case.) I understand that the reason for the latter restriction is the frequent brawling between the white and black troops occupying the city. These fights are reported to have resulted in shootings, and at least one killing I have heard of.

Our neighbor just down the street complains bitterly of the house next door to his. It is full of soldiers who make the night hideous with their noisy revelries, often into the early morning hours. I can sometimes hear them through my window. If this state of affairs continues, I will not bring you here, even if we must wait longer to marry.

It is raining now, a heavy, steady rain, and that sound is all I hear tonight. I am glad for the quiet that it brings. In such moments of peace and solitude, I think of you, and try to remember all our conversations. Any further conversations are limited to letters for a while, so I anxiously await one from you. One is on its way and shall reach me soon, I trust.

Give my love to all at home. I shall write to Belle tomorrow. Tell her that Uncle John has just sent off a letter to her today. I shall be seeing my cousins George and Albert Taylor tomorrow, and will tell you about them when I write again. It will not be so long before we see each other, dear Emma. In the meantime, believe me ever to be

Yours devotedly,
John Hutchinson

Three weeks later, John sent off a letter to Belle Ville announcing his imminent arrival there. On the day he was expected home, Emma spent much of the afternoon in the garden, listening for the sound of a horse or carriage in the drive.

She had insisted on making herself useful in the household, and had taken on the responsibility of tutoring Isabella's daughters as well as the McColl girls. Today, despite the heat, Emma brought them outside, and the children took their lessons in the shade of the trees. Towards mid-afternoon, she let them all run off to play a little earlier than usual. She waited by herself for another hour, and as the shadows began to grow longer, walked out to the front lawn.

A man on horseback was just turning into the cedar-shaded drive, and she knew immediately that it was John. He had borrowed a horse from Dr. Townsend in the village. He quickened his gait when he saw her, and was soon jumping down from his saddle.

"Emma! What a welcome sight!" he said.

As they rushed together, he put his hands to her waist and picked her up off her feet several inches. When her feet touched the ground again she threw her arms around his neck.

"I've missed you, John! But everything is better now. You are home."

"It's very good to be home, especially when I'm greeted like this."

"How is your uncle?" she asked.

"Very well, in fact much improved lately. Now, darling, while I have you to myself–"

He released her and reached into a coat pocket.

"The gift I promised you, Emma," he said, pulling out a diminutive box covered in dark green satin.

She opened the box and found a beautiful gold ring inside.

"It was my mother's," he said. "Do you like it?"

"Oh, John," she sighed. "It's lovely."

"I had to have it made smaller for you, your fingers are so slender. Your aunt gave me the measurement. She said you wore the same size. Will you try it on for me?"

Emma slipped the ring on the proper finger, and it fit perfectly.

"I wanted to surprise you."

"I am surprised!"

"Then my sister can keep a secret after all," he laughed. "I was sure she wouldn't be able to do that."

"No one breathed a word about a ring," she said, holding up her hand to admire her gift.

"You didn't think I would let you go without one, did you?"

Emma slid her arm through his and they walked close together and talked as he led his horse down the drive. Children soon came spilling out of the house looking for the gifts John had promised them, and he stopped to open a saddlebag containing a small package of candies and paper kites he had purchased in Charleston.

"Gimme! Gimme!" they all laughed, jumping up and down in excitement.

He began to open the package, but hesitated, drawing it up out of their reach.

"Perhaps I ought to ask your parents first if you have all been behaving while I was gone," he teased them.

"We've been good! We've been good!" they insisted repeatedly.

John eyed little Edmund doubtfully, but smiled and handed out their rewards. Before running off with Julia, John's niece Louisa told him that she and her sister had a gift for him, but would only giggle when he asked what it was. After the children had scattered with their presents, Emma informed him that the twins were going to honor him with a musical performance after supper. As they walked on, John found out that in addition to schooling Isabella's daughters, Emma had also begun teaching them how to play the piano. Their mother had given them lessons before, but after a long interruption with no instruction, the girls had forgotten much of what they had already been taught.

John wondered that they could learn enough in only three weeks to give a performance.

"Oh, it's just a few simple tunes," said Emma, "but they have worked very hard just to please you and their mother and father. They are going to sing for all of you, too."

He promised to be duly appreciative.

That evening, after the twins played their tunes with only a few mistakes, they were warmly applauded, and then sang a duet with two weak, sweet little voices and Emma's accompaniment on the piano. Their performance was followed by another duet sang by

Edmund and Emma, and John heard her lovely singing voice for the first time.

Later, as he walked her back to Mrs. McColl's house, he complimented Emma again on her singing and playing. They strolled along slowly in the moonlight, reluctant to part for the evening. Mrs. McColl was just taking her girls inside to put them to bed as they arrived at the house. The young widow bid John good night and went inside, but Emma lingered on the porch with him a while.

A bright full moon had just risen above the treetops; Emma and John could see each other clearly in its silvery, ghostly light. They sat on the steps, and he wanted to know all she had done and thought about while they were apart. She asked him the same, and they talked for two hours.

John had been acting a little more cheerful ever since receiving the letter which offered him a new beginning in Charleston, but tonight, Emma noticed that he was a becoming even more like himself again, like the man she remembered in the early days of their romance. A glimmer of life and love had returned to his eyes, and he seemed more absorbed in her than his own troubles.

He told Emma that he had another gift for her, and she smiled expectantly as he reached into one of his coat pockets and pulled out an envelope.

"Perhaps you will not be so surprised by this one," he said. "You requested it in one of your letters."

"John, you have had your likeness made for me!"

"As you wished."

Emma opened the envelope which enclosed a small photograph. She carefully removed the little portrait from the cover and held it up to admire, but could not make out the details to her satisfaction.

"Let me take it inside, to the lamp," she said, getting to her feet.

John automatically rose when she did, but remained on the steps. Emma soon came back, and they sat down again together.

"Oh, thank you, John," she said, slipping the photograph back into its envelope and pressing it against her heart. "It is a very good likeness."

"Do you think so? I thought I was perhaps too–frowning."

"No, I don't think so. Your eyes...look a little sad, but that is just your natural expression. I like the photograph very much. Perhaps it will make me less lonely for you."

John asked her how she liked being a teacher and about her pupils. He wanted to know if they were bright.

"Oh, yes, very bright. They are really quite eager to learn," said Emma. "The McColl girls are rather restless sometimes, but then they are younger than your nieces."

"I'm sure you are a very good teacher. Your uncle told me once that he thought you might perhaps teach a school in Flat Rock or Greenville."

"He had some such scheme, I believe. You know, I don't think I ever told you, but my uncle tried to convince me to come and live with him and his family in Greenville after my father passed away."

"And did you consider doing that?" John asked, surprised.

"Yes, very seriously. There was only myself and my aunt for a while, and we were afraid sometimes. We were just on the point of accepting his offer when my brother was wounded and came home."

"I'm so glad you did not go to Greenville," said John, with a look of profound relief. "If you had, we might never have met again."

"It was very painful and difficult for us those last months of the war, but it all turned out for the best–at least for me," she said, smiling at him fondly.

When it was time for John to return to his house, he walked her to the front door, and they paused to say goodnight there. She watched him go down the steps and walk away, but he had not gone far before he turned around and came back to her. Emma stood facing him with her back to the door as he drew close. He placed his hands against the door frame, one on each side of her, and put his face down to hers.

"I wonder, Miss Emma," he murmured, "if I might have one of those rare, highly prized kisses of yours. I've been living on one or two from long ago, and my food of love is almost gone. You wouldn't have me starve, would you?"

His face took on a pathetic look, partly real, partly affected, which made her smile.

"I thought music was the food of love," she protested playfully.

"Only yours," he replied. "But even that only whets the appetite."

She laughed, but her eyes gave consent, slowly closing, as John pressed a lingering kiss to her lips.

"There," he whispered. "I shall live on that for a while. Goodnight, Emma."

"Good night," she said, and watched him walk away again, lit by moonlight, until he disappeared into the deep shadows cast by the trees.

In September preparations for the wedding began in earnest. Isabella had become impatient to see how the dress she had given

Emma would look, and after Mrs. McColl spent a few hours on its alterations one morning, she brought over one of her crinolines to the house and insisted that Emma wear it so that the skirt of the dress would fall properly when she tried it on.

During the final fitting, Isabella waited in the parlor. When Emma emerged from another room in her bridal attire, she seemed very pleased.

"Emma, it's just as I envisioned it. You look so lovely."

The bride-to-be stood still, and Isabella circled her and looked her up and down to inspect the cut of the dress. Mrs. McColl stood by proudly and confidently, fearing no criticism of her skills as a seamstress.

"Perfect," Isabella declared. "The fit is perfect. Mrs. McColl, you are a wonder."

"Thank you, Mrs. Stewart. Isn't she beautiful?"

Though Emma was a little embarrassed by all the attention and admiration, she admitted that she loved the dress, and thanked Isabella for it repeatedly in her enthusiasm.

"It's been so long since I wore anything so nice," she said.

"Will you allow me to arrange your hair?" Isabella asked her. "Let me arrange it in a style you may wish to wear for the wedding."

These preparations, though a little premature, were such a pleasant distraction that Emma consented to let Isabella do as she pleased with her. She sat down at the dressing table in her room, and Mrs. McColl placed a towel around her shoulders to protect her dress. The twins and the McColl girls came in to watch the combing, curling, and arranging, but were sent out when they became too restless and noisy.

When Isabella was finished with Emma's hair, she stepped back to admire her work. She had styled two braided tresses on each side which made a loop and swept back into a high chignon, revealing the graceful curve of the neck. In the front, loose, small curls framed Emma's face down to the chin.

"Your hair is so fine and soft, and such a lovely color," Isabella complimented her.

She removed the towel and maneuvered Emma in front of a long mirror to see the complete picture of the dress and hairstyle.

"It's very pretty," said Emma, touching the curls. "I've never worn it quite like this before."

"This is the way you must wear your hair for the wedding, don't you think? I shall arrange it for you again just so for the occasion."

Emma smiled at herself in the mirror, anticipating that day. But the dress of black that hung from a hook on the door reminded her that the time was still several weeks in the future, and Mrs. McColl helped her out of the wedding gown, which was put away, not to be worn again until October.

Isabella's husband had ridden into the village that day, and returned to Belle Ville with some correspondence. One of the letters was for Emma. It was from John, and she saved it to read later in the evening in the privacy of her own room.

Charleston, Sept. 7th 1865

My dearest Miss Emma,

Do you realize that little more than a month remains until our wedding? As the time draws nearer, my sleep at night grows more restless, and my appetite begins to dwindle just as it did when I first fell in love with you. But I wonder why I should be lovesick now? I don't understand it.

Perhaps it is from missing you so much, and the anticipation of the happiness that is so near.

It is a chilly, rainy night here which makes me lonelier for you than ever. To comfort myself, I picture the two of us at Belle Ville tonight sitting side by side in front of a great roaring fire. Today the weather began to turn unusually cool in the afternoon, and I was too lazy to build a fire in my room, so I am partly under the covers as I write in my bed. I have written many letters today, but this is the only one that gives me pleasure since it allows me to turn my thoughts to my favorite subject.

You asked about Mr. Hopkins in your last letter. He is as doleful as ever. He would live at the offices if he could, to escape his family. He is always there when I arrive in the morning and still present when I leave in the evening. He often invites me to a restaurant to take supper with him, and sometimes I do. I feel rather sorry for him. I don't remember if I told you before, but during the war he married a widow with two children, and has lived to regret it. Before he met this lady, he had considered himself confirmed in bachelorhood, and now wishes he had stayed that way. Bachelorhood is a sad fate, but sadder still may be a bad marriage. Poor man! I feel my blessings and good fortune very keenly when I contemplate his situation.

There is some news in the household. Caesar has returned from his foray into the cruel new world—disillusioned but philosophical, and quite unrepentant. Uncle John is glad to have him back, but won't show it. One is as obstinate as the other. Obstinacy is a family trait found frequently among the Hutchinsons, so you must prepare yourself for it. I'm afraid I have even been accused of it from time to time. Now that I recall, your own uncle is a rather obstinate gentleman, so I suppose you are already accustomed to it.

I go about my daily duties here wearing something of a blinder, trying not to see what I do not wish to see. I find I must focus my energies very narrowly on business and little else. All the pleasures of society seem to be gone, at least for me, except for the company of my uncle and my cousins the Taylors. Conversations with other old friends and acquaintances whom I encounter almost invariably turn depressing. More ladies have been returning to the city, and almost all I see are dressed in black. One hardly sees a dress of another color. I know it is the same at home, but there are so many more of them here. Though I try to be hopeful, to be truthful I cannot help but feel, as I have since the war ended, that we are in for much worse than we have already experienced.

I know you have wished it, but I have not gone to church here yet. I shall wait until you can attend with me. I wish to please you in that, and shall try to be the man you wish me to be, and conquer this bitterness. Emma, I am trying to understand all that has happened. No, not so. I think I shall never do that, not in this world. But I am not so blind that I do not see how all these afflictions have been tempered with mercies—you foremost among them.

Kiss my nephew and nieces for me, and tell them again that if I hear they are behaving themselves I shall bring some treat from Charleston for them (and for Mrs. McColl's little girls, also). I am glad to hear that the littlest one there is thriving—kiss him for me, too. I take the cars to Amelia on Friday next, and I am looking forward to my last visit to you all as a single man. The next time I make the journey, I shall arrive as a groom, and bring home a bride with me. This house will be a much brighter and happier place when you are here, my darling.

Yours with much love,
John Hutchinson

CHAPTER NINETEEN

EARLY ONE MORNING IN OCTOBER, there was a wedding at the little Episcopal church in the village of Amelia. It was a small, private gathering. Besides a few friends which included Mrs. Reid and Mrs. Shubrick, the Townsends attended, along with Isabella and Edmund and their daughters. Representing the bride's family, Mrs. Screven and Mr. DuBose had come down from Greenville accompanied by two female cousins (one married, the other single) who were Emma's closest friends. Other cousins and relatives of the bride and groom living elsewhere had been unable to attend for various reasons. Some were still scattered abroad as refugees of war, or had been left with no means to travel; others were still afraid to leave their homes.

The day was sunny but mild, and inside the church there was a faint coolness in the air emanating from the thick stone walls and floor. Though still supplied with crude, temporary benches in place of pews, the interior of the building had been restored to some extent and decorated with flowers and greenery for the ceremony. Emma's unmarried cousin Clelia served as her bridesmaid, and the other supplied the music on an old organ which had recently been repaired for services. Mrs. Screven thought that Rev. Shubrick was looking well again as he entered the sanctuary and took his place before the assembled guests.

Standing with the priest, John faced the door of the church, and when Emma appeared there, his heart began to race wildly. He had seen her earlier, when he helped her out the carriage in which she had arrived with her family, but now that she was about to approach him as his bride, he had to fight back the tears of emotion that were welling up in his eyes.

Just before Emma started down the aisle, as she paused in the doorway on the arm of her uncle, she looked up at him. He was so much like her father that when she gazed into his eyes, they seemed to be her father's eyes, and for a few moments, despite her happiness, she felt the absence of her parents and brothers so keenly that she began to cry. Guessing her thoughts, Mr. DuBose pulled out a handkerchief and touched it to her cheeks.

"No tears now, my dear," he whispered, encouraging her with a smile.

She took a deep breath, composed herself, and in a few moments was at John's side, standing before Rev. Shubrick, who smiled on them both briefly and then began the familiar ceremony with a solemn expression and tone of voice.

"Dearly beloved," he began.

When John took Emma's hand to give his troth, he was trembling a little, but spoke the words perfectly, and she repeated the same words softly before the ring was slipped on her finger. The minister prayed, then joined the hands of the bride and groom together and said, "Those whom God hath joined together, let no man put asunder."

Finally, he pronounced them man and wife, and added a blessing.

"God the Father, God the Son, God the Holy Ghost, bless,

preserve, and keep you. The Lord mercifully with his favor look upon you, and fill you with all spiritual benediction and grace; that ye may so live together in this life, that in the world to come ye may have life everlasting. Amen."

After the ceremony, Emma and John went to the Townsend's house to prepare for the journey to Charleston on the morning train. Isabella and Edmund accompanied them, and in the carriage, they laughed about Tom and Emma's pretty cousin Clelia. Everyone had noticed his attentions to her the evening before. During the wedding supper Isabella had hosted at Belle Ville, the doctor had monopolized the young lady's company much of the time. John had overheard a few words of a whispered conversation between Emma and Clelia, and wanted to know what she had said.

"Now that I am your husband, your friends can't expect you to keep any secrets from me," he argued humorously.

"Or from your sister," said Isabella, leaning over to touch Emma's hand.

"Well, I suppose it really isn't a secret," she said, though with some misgivings. "Clelia told me that Tom asked if he might write to her. She gave him her permission, but afterwards felt anxious about it. She asked me about his character. He was so greedy of her company last night, I think she became a little afraid of him."

"Afraid of Tom!" John laughed. "He is quite harmless. Do you think they would be a good match for each other?"

"I don't know," Emma replied. "I shall leave that to the two of them."

"That's very wise," Isabella agreed.

John had never seen Tom so attentive to a young lady before, and wondered if his bachelor days were numbered. He also wondered about his cousin Laura, who was herself, that same evening, the object of the attentions of Rev. Shubrick's oldest son, a handsome young man who was soon to be ordained as a priest.

At the house, Isabella accompanied Emma upstairs to Laura's room to help her change clothes for the trip to Charleston. The bride put on her light blue dress, the only new one she owned besides her wedding gown, and a short, wine-colored jacket her sister-in-law had given her. Isabella had also supplied her with a small brimmed hat of matching color. After a few attempts to place it at the most becoming tilt, she secured it to Emma's hair with a pin, careful not to disturb any of the curls and coils she had worked so hard to perfect earlier that morning.

"There," she said, making a final adjustment. "It sits very prettily on you with your hair gathered up high in the back."

There was a knock at the door. Isabella opened it.

"Are you ladies ready now?" John asked, peering in a little sheepishly. "We must leave to catch the train very soon."

"I am ready," Emma replied.

Isabella left the room to fetch her shawl and hat, and John stepped in to pick up his wife's valise and trunk. As he passed behind her to get them, Emma bent her head forward and looked down to check the bow fastening the top of her jacket. Seeing the nape of her neck so temptingly exposed, he could not resist placing a kiss on it as he passed behind her again carrying the baggage. She gave a little laugh and shiver, but any further kisses were prevented for a while by a long bluish lace veil she draped over her hat.

Edmund and Isabella drove to the depot with the newlyweds to see them off. There were many other passengers at the depot when they arrived, and it looked as though the waiting train would be somewhat crowded. The floorboards of the low, newly rebuilt platform creaked under their feet as they stepped out of the small station building with their baggage, and John and Emma lingered there in conversation with Isabella and Edmund until the conductor called out "All aboard!"

After an exchange of embraces and kisses, they said their final farewells. A porter they had engaged picked up Emma's valise and trunk, and as the crowds pressed forward on the platform, John followed the man and held her arm protectively. Keeping very close to her husband, she smiled up at him through the gauzy veil covering her down to her shoulders.

Isabella and Edmund watched them board the train and remained on the platform until it was out of sight.

When Mr. and Mrs. Hutchinson arrived in Charleston they found Caesar waiting for them at the depot. John spotted him immediately leaning against a post with his arms crossed, his eyes cast upward in boredom. Of towering height, and sporting a distinctive, lopsided hairstyle with an emphatic part on one side, he was hard to miss.

It was about four o'clock in the afternoon when their carriage pulled up to the house of the elder Mr. Hutchinson on Tradd Street. The newlyweds walked arm in arm up the brick steps to the small front porch, and John felt a great sense of relief and contentment as they approached the familiar entrance–relief not just that their day's journey was over, but that a new phase of life so long awaited and longed for, had finally begun. His uncle had been on the lookout for a while by then, and opened the door for them himself. Setting his cane aside temporarily, he embraced his nephew first, and then stepped back to be introduced to Emma as she raised her veil to greet him.

Mr. Hutchinson took hold of Emma's hands and looked her over approvingly.

"You have given me such glowing accounts of this young

lady," he said to John with mock indignation, "How is it you failed to mention she is beautiful?"

"I reckoned you could easily see that for yourself," he replied humorously.

Mr. Hutchinson laughed and asked permission to kiss the bride. Emma leaned forward and received a kiss on the cheek.

"You are very welcome here, my dear."

She thanked him, and Mr. Hutchinson insisted that she address him as "Uncle."

"Perhaps you'd like to wash up a little before we dine," John said to his wife, noticing that she was brushing dust off her gloves and sleeves.

"Yes, if I may."

"I'll show you to our room, Emma."

"I should be happy to do that for you, my dear," Mr. Hutchinson explained apologetically, "but as John may have told you, I haven't been able to climb those stairs in months."

Caesar was already on his way upstairs with Emma's baggage. They followed him up the steps and a short distance down a hallway to their bedroom, and he glided out as they walked in.

"The dressing room is this way," said John, guiding Emma through the large bedroom to a smaller adjoining chamber.

"What luxury!" she marveled.

This room, which he had described for her in one of his letters, contained a handsome dressing table, two wash stands with marble tops, all of mahogany, and a large bathtub. Emma quickly washed her face and hands and stepped back into the bedroom to admire its elegant furnishings. John was placing her valise and suitcase on the bed for her to unpack. She sat down in a dainty chair upholstered in white and gold and looked around her with an incredulous smile.

"How do you like it?" he asked, though he already knew the answer from her expression.

"It's such a lovely room, and house, I can hardly believe it, that this is to be our home."

"This is the largest bedroom. My old room is down the hall."

"Will you show it to me?"

"Of course, I'll do that after you put away your things, or did you wish to rest a while? Perhaps you are tired."

"I'm not tired at all," she said.

Emma unpinned and removed her hat as she got up from the chair. John sat down in another and talked with her while she unpacked her clothes and other personal belongings she had brought with her. He was a little dismayed to see her pulling out some of her old dresses, which looked all the more forlorn and shabby in their new setting, but said nothing about them. He had been in Charleston long enough now to know that all the other ladies would be similarly dressed for the foreseeable future, and he knew that Emma would not wish to do any differently.

There was a knock at the open door of their room. John conversed with Caesar there a few moments and came back in to announce that supper would be served shortly. At the mention of food, Emma suddenly realized how hungry she was. Downstairs, they found Mr. Hutchinson waiting for them by a side door. He wanted to show Emma the gardens before it was dark.

From the end of the piazza, Mr. Hutchinson pointed out the gardens, most of which lay behind the house, separated from the carriage house and other outbuildings by a low stone fence. In the fading light of dusk, she looked out over a large expanse enclosed by high, heavy brick walls partially covered by ivy, and in the shadiest places, moss. It was a garden of formal design, with many low boxwood-bordered flower beds in the shapes of diamonds, circles, ovals, and squares, the paths threading among them covered with pounded oyster shell. Some of the beds were bordered by stones, and in the center of it all there was a little wooden summer house, somewhat Gothic in style, with a green pointed roof. Growing in the far corners, and scattered at various spots, were shrubs and ornamental trees which would bloom in the spring and summer. A few white marble garden seats were placed in front of arched niches in the brick wall, and one sat next to the little house facing the rear of the yard.

"This is so lovely," Emma complimented her uncle, although she was really seeing the place as it once must have been, and might be again, rather than what it was. It was all really in a sad state of neglect, said Mr. Hutchinson, and he lamented that the gardens had not been taken care of as they should have been for a long while.

"This used to be my place of refuge from the troubles and tedium of business," he reminisced. "I could walk among these flowers and trees and feel myself refreshed and comforted. My dear wife was so fond of her flowers, especially the tulips. Every spring, when they bloom, I remember how she tended and took such pride in them. Our old gardener passed away five years ago. He was so knowledgeable and skillful, I scarcely knew how to replace him, and when the war began, I'm afraid I neglected the place in favor of more pressing concerns."

"Emma is quite the gardener," John told his uncle. "I'm sure she could have this place blooming and thriving in no time."

"Ah, yes. I remember that you told me so. Well, you may certainly do anything you like with it, my dear Emma, but only if it pleases you."

"I should like it very much," she said, still gazing out at the scene before her with a thoughtful expression. In the back of her mind she was already contemplating one of the first changes she hoped to make–a very practical one, that of planting a winter and summer kitchen garden.

After the meal, John's uncle took Emma on tour of the first floor of the house. It was not an old home, as she had expected, but a dwelling of relatively recent construction dating from the previous decade with some modern conveniences and innovations she was glad to see.

Lastly, Mr. Hutchinson showed John and Emma his room. Since his illness he had been unable to go up and down the stairs, and had converted a study on the first floor into a bedroom.

"I'm quite comfortable here," he said, "though I do miss my old room. Ah, it's just as well."

"Emma and I will gladly give it up for another when you are able to take the stairs again," John assured him respectfully.

"That day may never come, but we shall see."

They walked back into the next room, the main drawing room, where Mr. Hutchinson pointed out a piano to Emma.

"John tells me that you play and sing," he said.

"A little."

"I know that answer is too modest, my dear. It will be good to have music in the house again. Will you favor us tonight?"

"If you wish."

Later in the evening, after the meal, Emma played several tunes on the piano and sang to one of them. As she bowed her head over the keys, the spiral curls that framed her face fell forward and hid her eyes, and John left his chair and walked over to the piano to observe her with a better view. She finished a song and looked up at him with a smile.

"Do you sing?" she asked.

"Very badly," he laughed.

Emma turned to his uncle and asked if that was true.

"I'm afraid it is," Mr. Hutchinson admitted. "Alas, my dear! You are not married one day, and have already discovered a grave deficiency in your husband!"

"It is no such thing," she protested, though she took his statement facetiously, as he had intended it.

"I used to have a right handsome singing voice myself," said the old gentleman, nodding proudly. "But no more."

Emma asked Mr. Hutchinson about the sort of music he liked, and they talked on that subject a while. During their conversation, John put his elbows down on the top of the piano and rested his chin in one hand while he listened, his eyes drawn mainly to his wife. At one point, when Emma turned back to John, such a look passed between the two that Mr. Hutchinson could see that his existence had been momentarily forgotten. He cleared his throat and made a movement to rise from his chair, but his legs and his cane wobbled, and he sat back down with a sigh of frustration.

"Will you assist me, John?" he asked.

John came to his uncle's chair and helped him to his feet.

"Despite the excellent company, I find myself growing fatigued, and I think I must retire now. You must pardon the frailty of an old man, Emma."

She rose from the piano seat and took his other arm.

"No, no, I am fine now. I walk very well, but sometimes, after they have been sitting for a while, my old legs don't wish to support me immediately."

He placed a light kiss on Emma's forehead and said good night to her and his nephew. Caesar, who had been looking in and listening to the music from the hallway, followed Mr. Hutchinson to his room to help him to bed.

"Shall we go upstairs now?" John asked.

Emma took his arm, and as they walked through the

drawing room, he picked up an oil lamp from a table to light their way. At the top of the steps, she glanced toward the room he had promised to show her.

"You wish to see my old room?"

Emma nodded, and he opened the door for her.

"There's really nothing very interesting about it," John remarked, turning up the lamp to better illuminate the place.

"It is interesting to me because it was yours," she said.

"The quarters of a poor, lonely bachelor hold no interest for me anymore," he laughed, then added more seriously, "Uncle John offered me his old room when I first returned, but I didn't take it. His was the best of the bed chambers, and I wanted it to be ours."

This bedroom was somewhat smaller, but it was just as handsomely furnished as the other. Emma noticed that the basin on the wash stand was full of water, and that its marble top was laid out with a comb, a brush, and other personal articles. A nightshirt and a handsome dressing robe were draped over a chair.

"I haven't moved my things to our room yet," John explained. "I thought I might change clothes in here tonight, to give you some privacy."

"Thank you," she murmured, and glanced at a bookcase near the bed. "I see you have a library. Tomorrow I shall see what you have in there."

Emma wandered over to a writing table next to a window.

"Is this where you wrote your letters to me?"

"Most of them," he answered, approaching the desk to stand beside her.

The little keepsake she had made for John, a lock of her braided hair encased in a little frame, occupied the central nook of the little hutch that sat on top of the table. Inside a drawer that was partly open, she saw her handwriting on an envelope.

"I have kept all your letters," he said. "I have read them all many times, especially the first."

"I kept all of yours, too, John. I have brought them with me to my new home."

"Do you remember what you wrote to me in that first letter?" he asked, putting his arm around her waist, then quoting her words, "The day will soon come when we need not be saying any more good-byes."

She looked up at him and smiled.

"I'm so glad," he murmured, "that day is finally here at last."

Mr. Hutchinson took his breakfast very early as usual, but instructed the cook to have another morning meal ready later. He heard Emma on the stairs at about nine, and she entered the drawing room and greeted him.

"Where is your husband?" he asked.

"John will be down directly," she said brightly.

"Well then, come and sit and talk with me while we wait for him, my dear."

Emma sat down on a sofa next to his chair. He asked her if her new home was to her liking.

"I never expected to have such a fine home," she replied gratefully. "It is much more than I hoped for."

"You must let me know when you are ready for me to turn over the keys to you as the lady of the house."

"Oh! I am not quite ready for that. You must give me a day or two to acquaint myself with the household."

"Of course!" said Mr. Hutchinson. "And you must let me know if you need or desire anything which is not already provided. It is many years now since a lady has been in this house, and I fear we might be lacking in something you might want."

"So far I've lacked nothing. Your home is very comfortable."

"Our home, my dear," he corrected her.

"John and I are very grateful to you for all you have done for us," she added.

"Good heavens! I am very happy to have you here. For a long while after the evacuation, living in this house alone, all my family scattered far away, it was a terrible time for me—watching the empty houses of my neighbors being plundered by Yankee soldiers—"

"You did not evacuate?"

"I was too ill, but fortunately Caesar stayed with me through the worst of it. He protected the house as well as he could, but still, it was an awful, difficult time. Believe me, I was very glad that my nephew came back to me this summer. I consider myself very fortunate indeed to have some family left to me, and here with me. John has been working very hard these past few months to salvage what is left of the company and to revive it. I have never seen him so industrious, and I am sure, my dear Emma, that you are the principal reason for it."

John heard his name being spoken as he walked into the room.

"Good morning!" Mr. Hutchinson welcomed him. "I've been having a very pleasant time getting to know your lovely wife. Emma says she is very happy here, and has not yet confided her complaints to me."

He put an emphasis on the word *yet*.

"Oh, no?" John smiled at Emma, whose expression was a mixture of surprise, amusement, and a little embarrassment. He knew his uncle was joking, and laughed with Mr. Hutchinson as the old gentleman leaned over to pat Emma's hand apologetically.

"I'm sure I haven't given my wife any cause for complaint–yet," he said humorously, taking a seat next to her and kissing her hand. "Uncle John is only teasing you, darling. This is one of his chief delights, especially with children and young ladies."

"Let me redeem myself," chuckled Mr. Hutchinson, picking up a book which had been partially concealed by his coat on the sofa, a copy of the *Ladies' Southern Florist.* He handed it to Emma.

"A little wedding gift for you, dear."

"Oh, thank you, Uncle!"

"It was the last thing I purchased for my dear wife. It pleased her very much, but she was not able to enjoy the book before she passed away. I hope you'll enjoy it."

"I know I shall. I have long wished to read it and make use of it."

The morning air was a little chilly but comfortable after breakfast, and John took Emma out for a stroll in the garden. Mr. Hutchinson watched them from a window as they walked arm in arm.

She knew the names of many of the plants they saw and seemed knowledgeable about the particular conditions and care most of them required. They paused to admire the little summer house in the middle of the yard, then went inside. Emma thought the place was beautiful, and said she especially liked the view of the garden from the largest window. John put his arm around his wife.

"You are a garden, Emma," he whispered, pulling her aside for a kiss.

In the afternoon, after Mr. Hutchinson retired for his usual nap John brought out a photograph album he had promised to show Emma, along with a little ornate box which contained family portraits painted in miniature. They sat down with these on a sofa in the drawing room.

She examined the miniatures first, wondering at the beauty and intricacy of their art. A half-dozen gentlemen and ladies of the previous century, some with powdered hair and wigs, was the first group she asked him about.

"I know this gentleman," she said, holding up an exquisite ivory miniature of a Continental officer. "I saw his portrait at Belle Ville."

"My great-grandfather, Colonel Thomas Hutchinson," John informed her.

Emma asked which lady was the colonel's wife, and he pointed out a little painting of a pale, gracefully posed young woman with dark eyes.

John could not remember who a few of the other ancestors were; one of them wore a uniform from the War of 1812, another from the time of the Mexican War.

"My uncle would know," he said. "I believe they are his wife's family."

Emma turned her attention to another group of portraits, gentlemen in dark, high-collared coats and bristling cravats, and ladies in Empire dresses and fashions of later decades. John showed her his grandparents, and she noted a strong resemblance to him in his grandfather, who was also named John Hutchinson.

"You have the same color hair and eyes," she remarked. "It's really quite the same face. I like this one the best."

Emma set aside the box and picked up the large photograph album bound in green leather. It began with his father's generation. The first picture that met her eyes was a portrait of the Hutchinson family. John's father stood behind a chair in which his wife sat with an infant in her lap. He towered over a teenaged Isabella, a boy of twelve (John), a younger Elias, and a dark-haired little girl, Lise, whose hand held on to the train of the baby's dress.

Emma smiled to see John as a boy. She only vaguely remembered him at this age. Her smile faded as she noticed that John's were fixed on the face of his father, and she quickly passed on to the next photograph, a daguerreotype of John's uncle and his late wife.

"Aunt Harriett passed away not long after that likeness was made," he told Emma.

"They had no children?"

"Two that died in infancy."

"How sad. She has a sad expression."

"Her health was never good."

Emma turned the page and found several portraits of his uncle's wife at different ages, and after that, images of three other ladies.

"My father's sisters," said John. "The lady in the center is Aunt Sarah, Mrs. Porter. The one on her right was Aunt Catherine, Tom's mother, who passed away many years ago. The other lady, Aunt Mary, is no longer with us, either. She was George Taylor's mother."

The next page held a card-sized photograph of John in a tightly fitted cadet uniform. He was standing next to a curtain with one arm resting on a pedestal.

"At last I see you in a proper uniform!" Emma exulted. "How old were you in this one?"

"About seventeen, I suppose."

"How serious you look."

"I do look rather glum, don't I? I must have been thinking of all my demerits."

Emma laughed and turned the page to discover two more portraits of John in uniform, the first one that of the Charleston Light Dragoons. He was seated in a chair in a rigid military posture, looking dignified and only a little less stern than he had in the preceding picture.

"You look so handsome," she said, "and very soldierly."

Looking at this particular picture, he made a sound of displeasure that he did not explain. Emma's eyes lingered on it a while, then traveled to the opposite page, where she admired him in his cavalry uniform. In this photograph his posture was more relaxed, and his face had a resolute, placid expression.

"That likeness was made just after I arrived in Richmond. I never had such a fine uniform again."

"I do wish I had seen you in it," she said, with a "tsk" of disappointment and a little sigh.

"So do I, and if you had, we'd have been married long ago."

He leaned close to Emma and pressed a kiss to her cheek. She turned another page, and a portrait of Elias in military uniform met their eyes. She began to close the album, but John stopped her.

"It's all right," he said gently.

They gazed at the handsome, earnest face of the eighteen year-old boy in silence for a few moments, and read an inscription his uncle had written in the book at the time of his death:

> *May every link in the chain of love*
> *Which is broken here on earth by the hand of death,*
> *Be joined again in Heaven.*

"How beautiful," Emma said quietly.

John kept staring at the photograph intently.

"What a fine boy he was," she went on feelingly. "I am glad we have this likeness. This is how I wish to remember him"

John nodded and said quietly, "It is how I shall remember him, too, always."

On the opposite page there was a photograph of Isabella and her family, and after this, more portraits of her and her siblings at various stages of life. Several portraits of the Taylor family followed, and the Porters, along with a carte-de-visite of George Taylor in Confederate uniform.

"This is the cousin you have mentioned in your letters?" Emma asked.

"Yes, that's George."

"I see quite a family resemblance," she remarked admiringly. "He is a fine-looking man."

John smiled and agreed. There were a few more pictures of more distant relatives, and finally, after a blank page or two, Emma found some stereographs of scenes in Europe. She had never seen these double photographs before. John told her his uncle had bought them in England just before the war. As Emma looked through the stereograph cards, he pointed out some of the places he had visited once on his European tour, and mentioned that his uncle had traveled more extensively on the continent.

"*Mon oncle* is quite the world traveler, you know. He has many more of these, and many tales to tell of them," he said. "I think you will enjoy his company."

"Oh, I'm sure of it. It will be nice to travel with him, if only in imagination."

On the lower shelf of a nearby table John happened to notice the viewer for the stereographs, a wooden device which resembled a large pair of opera glasses, and brought it to her.

"Here, let's you and I take a look at them," he said. "Choose where we shall go first."

Emma selected a scene of Lake Geneva.

"Ah, good. I've been there."

He arranged the photograph in the viewer for her, and

Emma was surprised by the effect when she looked through the lenses.

"The picture has depth," she remarked. "It almost looks real."

John told her all he could remember about his experiences in the beautiful picture that was before her eyes, then chose a few more for her, the first a view of Trafalgar Square, and told her about his days in London.

"I should very much like to take you to all these places you admire," he concluded, as Emma sighed over a scene of the English lakes and mountains.

"It's something very pleasant to dream of, isn't it?" she replied wistfully.

John looked over the new shipment and order books in his office and shook his head as he reflected on the difference in these volumes and the ones he kept before the war. What a change! From figures that had numbered in the hundreds of thousands of cotton bales each year to a mere few hundred a month now, along with some modest amounts of rice and rosin shipped abroad by Hutchinson & Company. The old ledgers and other business records were only a memory now. They had been sent to the state capital for safekeeping, and had been destroyed, along with the city, when it was burned by the enemy during the war. Mr. Hutchinson had kept copies of some important documents in his home, and these had survived, but the rest, the irreplaceable records of over thirty years of business, were lost forever. John remembered them well from his days as a clerk, and how meticulously he had recorded so many transactions in those massive old volumes.

He had been away from work for several days, all he could spare for a brief sort of honeymoon at home with Emma, and in his absence a pile of correspondence had accumulated on his desk. He had just opened a letter from the company of Monsieur Dieterich in Le Havre inquiring about a shipment of cotton the previous month, and another from a merchant in Liverpool on the same subject, and was checking the index of the ledger book to find those records, when he was interrupted by the appearance of Mr. Hopkins, a balding, bespectacled gentleman of fifty, round of face and form.

"Ah, John!" he said, looking unusually cheerful, "I have received your uncle's kind invitation to dine with you all tomorrow night. At last I shall meet your bride! What is it, a week now since you were married?"

"Exactly a week today. My wife looks forward to meeting you."

"From what your uncle tells me of the lady, I shall be very glad to make her acquaintance," Mr. Hopkins replied eagerly.

John politely inquired about Mrs. Hopkins, and learned that she was away visiting a sick, elderly relation from whom, he added with a look of displeasure, "some inheritance was expected."

John smiled and nodded a little awkwardly, hoping his friend would not begin to talk of his family and unhappy home life as he sometimes did. He had much to do that day, and no desire to remain past hours to finish his work.

"I see you are busy with the correspondence," said Mr. Hopkins, noticing the letters on his desk. "I shall leave you to it. But do tell Mr. Hutchinson to expect me without fail!"

John promised that he would. When Mr. Hopkins was gone he remembered what he had been doing before, but as he tried to turn his attention to the ledger, his thoughts immediately wandered again. He had heard that morning that an old Charleston firm in the same line of business as Hutchinson & Company had closed its doors forever. The sons who were to have inherited the business had been killed in the war, and with the recent passing of their father, the business, already in bankruptcy, had also died. Hutchinson & Company might have easily met with such a fate, he reflected somberly.

Most of the old major business and banking firms of the city had been wiped out, and those few that remained seemed to leading only a very precarious existence these days. So many of them were like the pitiful veterans that were sometimes seen on the streets, the amputees and broken men, hobbling along and barely existing. Hutchinson & Company was also broken and crippled, yet it had survived. How much longer it could survive he was unable to tell, especially when everyone and everything in the state was at the mercy of a hostile government. As John's eyes took in the meager figures recorded in the shipment book, he wondered if the company would ever be prosperous again. This did not appear to be likely, yet there was nothing to do but persevere and hope for the best.

He spent the rest of the afternoon answering most of the letters on his desk, and left the office a little earlier than usual to keep an appointment with his cousin Albert Taylor, to discuss some legal affairs of the company. John walked to his office on Broad Street, and afterward, stepped into an office a little further down Broad to see Mr. Simmons, his father's attorney. He had sent a note to John that morning informing him that there were a few documents concerning the estate which required his signature.

As John walked home, his thoughts went back to his earlier worries about Hutchinson & Company, and he tried to imagine all the possible future scenarios that awaited him, good and bad, and the likelihood of each one. But things were so unsettled and uncertain now, it was difficult to see much into the future, and he realized it would probably be better not to try. What he had to deal with in the present demanded all his strength, and discouragement was not something he could afford.

Emma was outside in the yard when John reached the gate of his uncle's house. He could see her through the interstices of ornamental ironwork at the top of the wooden door, and paused to watch her. She had been looking over the various sections of the garden, and was penciling a few notes on a small tablet she held. Though not dressed for gardening, she leaned over hesitantly, and he smiled when he saw that she was unable to resist the urge to begin pulling up a few unsightly weeds at her feet.

John kept watching his wife, drawing in a deep breath, and just as his lungs filled and expanded with the air, his heart seemed to do the same with a fullness of love and gratitude for her. She seemed to be happy here, and he took this as a further proof that he had made the right decision for their future. It was pleasant to see her safe and content within these high solid walls which, to some extent, kept out the rest of world, and allowed them their own private one within.

So this was to be his life, he thought. To return to her at the end of each day, and to feel her warmth beside him every night. It was what he had wanted, and it was his. In this marriage, his strongest hopes and desires had been fulfilled. Why so many others so dear to him had been thwarted or destroyed, or why the world outside these four walls was a desolation, he did not know, and could not bring himself to fathom as yet. Right now he only knew how thankful he was for the love of this young woman.

Emma looked up when she heard the gate opening. She saw her husband, and a moment later, they were in each other's arms.

The End

About the Author

KAREN STOKES, an archivist with the South Carolina Historical Society in Charleston, S.C., is the author of *Belles, A Carolina Love Story*, a historical novel set in the Civil War South, and *The Soldier's Ghost*, a gothic novella set in the ruins of post-Civil War Charleston.

She is also the author of *South Carolina Civilians in Sherman's Path*, a non-fiction book released in June 2012 by The History Press, and is the co-editor of *Faith, Valor, and Devotion: The Civil War Letters of William Porcher DuBose*, published by the University of South Carolina Press in 2010.

Also from the Author

FICTION:

Belles: A Carolina Love Story
The Immortals: A Story of Love and War
The Soldier's Ghost: A Tale of Charleston

NON-FICTION:

A Confederate Englishman: The Civil War Letters of Henry Wemyss Feilden (Co-editor)
A Legion of Devils: Sherman in South Carolina
Carolina Love Letters
Confederate South Carolina: True Stories of Civilians, Soldiers and the War
Days of Destruction: Augustine Thomas Smythe and the Civil War Siege of Charleston
Faith, Valor, and Devotion: The Civil War Correspondence of William Porcher DuBose (Co-editor)
The Immortal 600: Surviving Civil War Charleston and Savannah
South Carolina Civilians in Sherman's Path

From Shotwell Publishing

Green Altar Books (Literary Imprint)

A New England Romance & Other SOUTHERN Stories by Randall Ivey

Tiller by James Everett Kibler

GOLD-BUG MYSTERIES (Mystery & Suspense Imprint)

Billie Jo by Michael Andrew Grissom

To Jekyll and Hide by Martin L. Wilson

Splintered: A New Orleans Tale by Brandi Perry

Non-Fiction

A Legion of Devils: Sherman in South Carolina by Karen Stokes

Annals of the Stupid Party: Republicans Before Trump by Clyde N. Wilson (The Wilson Files 2)

Carolina Love Letters by Karen Stokes

Confederaphobia: An American Epidemic by Paul C. Graham

The Devil's Town: Hot Spring During the Gangster Era by Philip Leigh

Dismantling the Republic by Jerry C. Brewer

Dixie Rising: Rules for Rebels by James R. Kennedy

Emancipation Hell: The Tragedy Wrought By Lincoln's Emancipation Proclamation by Kirkpatrick Sale

Lies My Teacher Told Me: The True History of the War for Southern Independence by Clyde N. Wilson

Maryland, My Maryland: The Cultural Cleansing of a Small Southern State by Joyce Bennett.

My Own Darling Wife: Letters From a Confederate Volunteer by John Francis Calhoun. Edited with Introduction by Andrew P. Calhoun, Jr.

Nullification: Reclaiming Consent of the Governed by Clyde N. Wilson (The Wilson Files 2)

The Old South: 50 Essential Books by Clyde N. Wilson (Southern Reader's Guide, vol. I)

Punished with Poverty: The Suffering South by James R. & Walter D. Kennedy

Segregation: Federal Policy or Racism? by John Chodes

Southern Independence. Why War? by Dr. Charles T. Pace

Southerner, Take Your Stand! by John Vinson

Washington's KKK: The Union League During Southern Reconstruction by John Chodes.

When the Yankees Come: Former South Carolina Slaves Remember Sherman's Invasion. Edited with Introduction by Paul C. Graham

The Yankee Problem: An American Dilemma by Clyde N. Wilson (The Wilson Files 1)

FREE BOOK OFFER

Sign-up for new release notification and receive a FREE DOWNLOADABLE EDITION of *Lies My Teacher Told Me: The True History of the War for Southern Independence* by Dr. Clyde N. Wilson by visiting FreeLiesBook.com or by texting the word "Dixie" to 345345. You can always unsubscribe and keep the book, so you've got nothing to lose!

Southern Without Apology.

www.ingramcontent.com/pod-product-compliance
Lightning Source LLC
Chambersburg PA
CBHW051440260626
47162CB00001B/182